Praise for CJ England's *The Mylari Chronicles: Eyes of Fire*

Rating: A Perfect 10 "...EYES OF FIRE creates a wonderful emotional rollercoaster that will have readers crying buckets for Talia, groaning at Calion, and finally smiling when the couple gets their relationship right. The suspense of secret prophecy, threat of war, and social challenges make this book a must read. I am on pins and needles until the next book in the series is available. I rate CJ England's EYES OF FIRE a Perfect 10."

~ *Mel, Romance Reviews Today*

Rating: Joyfully Recommended "...I highly recommend reading Eyes of Fire because Ms. England demonstrates through her writing that Love can bring out the best in us, it can overcome the worst in us, and yes, it can even crush the seeds of hatred. After all, there's something irresistible and heartwarming about that old saying, "Love conquers all.""

~ *Patrice, Joyfully Reviewed*

Rating: 5 Crystal Balls "I loved this story. CJ England just gets better and better. I cannot wait to read the next installment of this wonderful series. I love the way CJ England can make you hate a character one minute and love him the next. ...she pulls you into her stories so much you feel a part of them and you just cannot let go. And you do not want to and you cannot wait to see what happens next."

~ *Melanie, Enchanting Reviews*

Rating: Recommended Read "EYES OF FIRE is the most sensational book I have read this year. ...If you're looking for an action packed adventure with terrific romance and sensual scenes, EYES OF FIRE is the story for you. ...I can't wait for the next in this series!"

~ *Willow Rayne, Dark Angel Reviews*

Rating: 5 Stars "...CJ England is able to craft novels which speak to the heart. Mere words cannot express the magnitude of THE MYLARI CHRONICLES: EYES OF FIRE in terms of rousing creativity. ...Knowing this is only the first book in The Mylari Chronicles series makes me a very happy reader."

~ *Amelia, Ecataromance Sensual*

Rating: 5 Angels, Recommended Read "...CJ England is a genius in creating magical places and characters so memorable it's hard to just forget about them. ...This is one book so worth reading and I can't wait for the next one in the series."

~ *Lena, Fallen Angel Reviews*

Rating: 5 Cupids "...The Mylari Chronicles-Eyes of Fire is an epic novel. It will take you on a wild ride and you will not be able to forget this. The love scenes are scorchingly hot and it was a pleasure to read it."

~ *Blanche, Cupids Library Reviews*

Rating: 5 Hearts "...CJ England pens a believable read that makes the reader feel the excitement and the enchantment. The emotions of Talia can be felt throughout the read and has the reader feeling her sorrow, pain, and joy. This is one breathtaking read that absorbs."

~ *Linda, The Romance Studio*

Rating: 5 Klovers "...This is one of the best fantasy novels this reviewer has read in awhile. England's novel has it all- an ancient prophecy, a magical world, fully developed characters, and emotional scenes that will leave the reader reaching for the box of Kleenex!"

~ *Anne, CK2S Kwips and Kritiques*

Rating: 5 Rings "...I highly recommend this story; it's my first by this author, but I intend to look out for her other books!"

~ *Annie of Euro Reviews*

Look for these titles by *CJ England*

Now Available:

The Don't Series
Don't Spank the Vamp (Book 1)

Coming Soon:

The Loropon Lust Series
Bless the Beasts (Book 1)

The Don't Series
Don't Tempt the Phoenix (Book 2)

The Mylari Chronicles:
Eyes of Fire

CJ England

A Samhain Publishing, Ltd. publication.

Samhain Publishing, Ltd.
577 Mulberry Street, Suite 1520
Macon, GA 31201
www.samhainpublishing.com

Eyes of Fire

Print ISBN: 978-1-60504-146-9
Digital ISBN: 1-59998-932-8

Editing by Jennifer Miller
Cover by Scott Carpenter

First Samhain Publishing, Ltd. electronic publication: May 2008
First Samhain Publishing, Ltd. print publication: March 2009

Dedication

For my wonderful husband, Jonathon,
who gives me a reason to write all those love scenes.
I live to see the fire in your eyes!
I love you, K. I. S. A.

Prologue

A female's low chanting could be heard as the king made his way up the narrow, winding staircase. It was dark, dank and musty smelling in this part of the old castle. A place he hated to visit and rarely did. He wouldn't be here today if *she* hadn't sent him that frightening message.

Come to me, oh Faerie King.
I have seen the future in my visions.
Our world is to be no more.

As he puffed his way up the stairs, he worried. What could the Oracle, or *Tári* as she was known in the Elvish tongue, mean? The old female only broke her silence when a true vision occurred. Otherwise, she was content to stay here in the highest part of the castle, murmuring spells and incantations.

The king stepped up the last stair with a sigh of relief. He was growing old. His son would soon be taking the throne and he would be glad to rest. Stepping through the arched doorway, he saw her.

She was old. No one knew how many years she carried on her bent and withered form. She stood over the small altar, a thin stream of wood smoke almost obscuring her shadowed face, a face the king had never seen. A tattered black cloak covered her nakedness. Gnarled hands moved in rhythmic motions over the fire. Her aged voice muttered even older words.

When the king had caught his breath, he spoke in a sharp voice. "You sent for me?"

The old female's movements didn't change. Her voice didn't stop its chanting. The king watched for several minutes and then tried again, addressing her by name in a politer tone.

"*Tári*...please. What have you seen?"

This time the old crone went still. "I see the future, King Daralis, of the Calen'taur Elves. I see *your* future."

"Speak of what you see."

The Oracle of the elven people bent forward into the smoke and spit into the flames. The fire sizzled and changed color to a deep, dark blue. "I see the end of the world, my king. I see the end of our people."

The king staggered and put a hand to his heart. "What say you? Our race dies? How can this be?"

"I see a war. A war to end all wars. It will destroy our kind. The elven people will be no more."

"When?" the old king croaked out.

The crone shook her head. "I do not know. The time is not given in the vision. It may happen in your time or your son's. It could occur a millennium from now. Our race will end."

"Is there nothing that can be done?"

She chuckled and reaching down, pulled a knife from her cloak. "Give me your arm. If you truly wish to know the answer to your question, you must give the goddesses something in return."

"What?" the king asked warily.

"Just your blood, oh king. The blood of royalty. If you want to find a way to protect your people, I must have your blood."

The old king hesitated. It wasn't that he minded giving his blood. He'd given much of it on the battlefields. He just wasn't sure he trusted the old crone, Oracle or not.

"Decide quickly, my king. The fire burns low."

Swallowing, King Daralis lifted his arm and reached to the Oracle.

Grasping it in a surprisingly strong hand, she pushed back his sleeve. She quickly made an incision just above the vulnerable spot on his wrist. The blood began to flow in a steady stream into the fire. It sputtered and belched smoke, before finally the flame leapt up almost singeing the hairs on the back of the king's outstretched arm. He cried out and tried to jerk away, but the old female held him firmly, her skinny fingers circling his still-bleeding wrist.

The fire continued to burn, the smoke pungent and thick,

turning the color of the leaves in early spring. It filled the room.

"Your offering is accepted, oh king." She released his arm, and he stumbled back from the fire.

Sinking to his knees, he pulled a handkerchief from his pocket to bind the wound as the smoke became even thicker. He could barely make out the elderly female beyond the altar. Her mumbling and chanting grew more urgent.

Suddenly, she pushed back the hood she wore and showed her face to the king for the first time. Even though she was his elder by many centuries, her lined face still carried the beauty of the ages. He gasped when he saw her eyes were covered by a thick white film.

The Oracle was blind.

Slowly, she raised her arms over her head and began moving them in a circular motion, causing the swirling smoke to follow. Soon all the smoke in the room was spinning, as she stood in the center. The king could feel the wind as it lifted his long hair from his shoulders. He braced himself against it as the Oracle turned her sightless eyes on him.

"You ask for help, I give to thee,
a message from the goddesses three.
Spears without, a knife within,
treachery will seek to win.
Death, despair and pain will come,
all your work will be undone.
A mighty war, your people's end,
will come, on that you can depend.
Unless true passion can guide the day,
and give to you a stronger way.
A human female will be the one,
to save the kingdom, you've begun.
She will be the first of three,
to break the hold fortune has on thee.
Varol thysi...passion's force come true,
breaks through traditions old and new.
Only in acceptance can salvation be,
one of your blood holds the key.
An heir to the throne will this create,

he will win out over fate.
His father's heart, destiny will kiss,
he will carry your mark upon his wrist."

As suddenly as it began, the wind ceased and the smoke disappeared. The oracle slumped, exhausted, to the floor, while the magical fire extinguished itself in a flash of light.

The king was left with the stench of burned blood and the bitter knowledge his people's worst enemy...was their only hope.

Chapter One

The door burst open and a young woman rushed out onto the balcony. She moved to the railing and looked out over the forest bordering her parents' property. Her breasts heaved with emotion. Her eyes were blind as she stared out at the darkness. Putting her face into her hands, she shuddered with the effort it took to control her anger.

Two days...just two days was all it took before her parents started in on her. Natalia, Talia for short, had come back to her old home in southern Oregon to try to bridge the gap between them. What she wanted for her life and what they wanted were two very different things. After several days of polite conversation and strained silences, Talia had been glad when her dad brought up the subject of her future.

She sighed as she remembered the look on their faces when she'd told them she wasn't going back to college for the spring semester. If that hadn't been bad enough, when she told them she wanted to go backpacking in Europe and attend an art school in Paris, her father had blown his top.

"No daughter of mine is going to be running around in a foreign county. You'll stay in the good old U S of A where you belong. Forget it."

No amount of talking, pleading or explaining worked. Finally, Talia told them she was going anyway with money she'd saved and the legacy left to her by her grandmother. Her father ranted and raved and her mother wept, but the only thing that had come out of the evening was Talia's promise she would be out of their hair come morning.

She rubbed her eyes and bit her lip to keep from crying. Her parents never understood her. They wanted her to get a good education, find a nice man and settle down nearby so they could enjoy the grandchildren she would give them. But that wasn't what Talia wanted.

Ever since she was a child she'd had this feeling she didn't belong here. She ached for something she couldn't see, longed for something always just out of her reach. She wanted to travel, but since her parents weren't the traveling type, she'd spent her whole childhood going no further than Portland.

The first major battle with her parents occurred on the day she turned eighteen. When she informed them she was going to take a year to see the country before starting college, they went ballistic. They cajoled, then argued and then threatened, but it did no good. Talia had gone.

She took her savings, put her suitcase in her little car and headed for the east coast. She spent the whole year traveling from place to place, working when she needed to. Looking for whatever was missing in her life. She hadn't found it, but she'd had a great time trying.

So, she came back and started school. She'd known immediately living with her parents wouldn't work, so she transferred to another college and finished her first two years. Every time she came home to visit, the rift between her and her parents widened. Her mom tried setting her up on blind dates. When she refused to go, it just made her parents angrier.

It wasn't that she didn't like men. She did. And she knew they liked her. She wanted to get married...someday. None of the boys she'd met so far got her juices flowing. Not even enough to do anything more than a little kissing and petting. Talia had the feeling there was someone special waiting for her. She just knew her soulmate was out there somewhere and when the time came, she would find him.

Sighing, she left the balcony and went inside to take a shower.

She never saw the figures staring at her from the dark edge of the woods.

After her shower, dressed in a long white nightgown, she brushed her teeth and then her hair until it shone. She pulled back the covers on her bed and pulling her suitcase out, she packed up the few items she'd removed.

If she tried, she could get out of here before her parents got up in the morning. She wasn't looking forward to seeing them any more than they wanted to see her. Casting a quick look around the room, she saw it was empty of her things. She put the suitcase and her backpack next to the door.

Restless, she walked back out onto the balcony. The weather hadn't been bad, but the air was heavy, like a thunderstorm was coming. Leaning on the railing, she gazed at the forest. She loved its dark, tangled paths and moss-covered trees. She'd spent most of her childhood in those woods and knew she would miss them if she never came back again.

A movement at the edge of the tree line caught her attention. She often saw deer feed in the meadow and Talia held her breath hoping she would get a last glimpse before she went to sleep. The figures moved out into the broken moonlight and she frowned. They weren't deer. They were too big and bulky for that. They moved in a shuffling, awkward way that made her narrow her eyes. What were they?

Moving quickly now, the two dark forms came closer, becoming more distinct. She couldn't get a good look at them because the moonlight chased in and out amongst the scattered clouds. She got the impression they were men, but she wondered why they would be sneaking around the forest this time of night. Maybe they were poachers.

She bit her lip, almost calling for her father, when the two figures walked up to the edge of the building. As they reached it, the moon came out from behind a cloud and Talia gasped.

The figures below her window weren't men. In fact, they didn't look human at all. Their massive heads, twice the size of a normal man, dwarfed their huge bodies. Misshapen and hideous, their faces turned and looked up into hers.

Don't look at them! Her mind screamed it instinctively. Before she could look away, the bigger of the two met her eyes and she froze. She watched in horror as they began to climb up the side of her house. The one who'd captured her with his stare never took his eyes off her. Desperately, she tried to move, but she couldn't. She was trapped, held immobile by his gaze.

It didn't take them long to scale the wall. When they reached the balcony, the one holding her captive shifted his eyes for a moment, and she could move.

Whirling around, she ran back into her room. She opened

her mouth to scream but was grabbed from behind. A huge, scaly hand covered her mouth, the other arm wrapping around her torso.

Talia fought, her hands scratching and gouging, but it had no effect on the skin of the creature holding her. She took a deep breath and immediately wished she hadn't. Her captor stank of excrement, sweat and an odor so foul, her stomach rebelled. She bit back the urge to throw up, wriggling in disgust as the creature ran its hand down her side feeling every curve of her body. She continued struggling, her legs kicking wildly, trying to make contact with the sturdy form behind her. Who were they? What did they want?

The creature turned and Talia saw the other one lurch through the doors. In the light of her room, she could see the ugliness of the thing. Two small, pig-like eyes peered at her through masses of wrinkled fat. A snout, running with snot and dirt sat above a wide mouth with huge, blubbery lips. The stained, filthy clothes it wore were responsible for part of the stench that surrounded him.

It reached out a fat hand and poked at her breast. "I...want." The rough voice left Talia in no doubt of what it meant. "Give!"

She began to tremble uncontrollably.

The other shook its head. "No. Must give...Father. He want." It didn't stop running its hand up and down her body and her gorge rose again.

The creature in front of her actually pouted. "Want...fuck now!" It reached for Talia, but the one holding her cuffed its partner along side of the head. The blow would have felled a small tree, but the thing barely felt it.

"After...Father. Fuck after Father. He...first." Carrying her, it walked toward the balcony.

Talia intensified her struggles, writhing and clawing at any part of the disgusting body within her reach. She tried to kick backwards, hoping to connect with some soft vulnerable spot, but the creature remained unfazed, ignoring her muffled screams.

"Get bags. Make look like girl go. Push car in water. No one find."

Go? They wanted to make it look like she disappeared? No one would look for her. Where were these things taking her?

Who was this father they spoke of?

She fought harder. The fat hand on her mouth moved slightly, providing a target for her to sink her teeth into. It tasted terrible, but it seemed like the one tender place on its body, because the thing bellowed and dropped her.

Landing on her hands and knees, she was up again in a flash. Screaming, she ran towards the balcony and freedom. She got to the railing before a blow to her head made her world explode into darkness.

࿐

The wood was so silent, not even a sparrow sang. It was waiting. Several moments passed, but no animal stirred. They knew what was coming.

With a loud howl and a crash of light, the time void appeared. Leaves and small debris flew around, creating a vortex of wind and sound. The thundering of hooves could be heard and out of the mouth of the void leapt a black horse and rider. Calion Sáralondë, Prince of the Calen'taur Elves, had arrived.

On his way home to Calen'taur he'd sensed a disturbance in the faerie myst on the eastern side of the elven boundaries. It had happened before, usually when an animal blundered in. The mysts were littered with the bones of those unlucky few, but every once in a while it was cause for concern, with a human or faerie getting lost inside.

He stretched his long, lithe, muscular body. Sore from the constant riding, he looked forward to a long soak in his hot pool when he got home. Once he checked out the disturbance, he could be on his way. He knew many wouldn't bother, but Calion was more careful than most.

"Let us go, Roch'mellon." The horse snorted and sprang into an easy jog. "When we finish here, there is a nice stable full of oats and hay for you, my friend."

Since Roch'mellon always looked forward to that, he picked up his speed to the boundary.

Just a few minutes later, Calion reached the edge of the faerie myst. Surrounding the entire faerie world, it consisted of a wall that separated the faerie world from the human one.

Humans could not see the myst. Only those with faerie blood could see it and only a true faerie, properly equipped, could pass without trouble through the vapors.

Inside the myst lived the spirits of all those faerie folk who died deaths not fitting for faerie. Those who died in treachery or suicide. By execution or witchcraft. A terrifying place for a faerie, for a non-faerie it was certain death.

He slipped from his horse's back and patted Roch'mellon on the neck. "I will return shortly." The horse snorted his agreement and wandered off to a patch of grass to graze.

Walking towards the myst, Calion drew his sword from its sheath. The mystical sword *Cylys,* meaning honor in the Elvish tongue, glowed magically as it sang its name aloud. Pointing the sword at the fog, he watched as an opening appeared in the swirling haze. Shielding himself with his own magick, he stepped inside.

A long time later he stepped back out, his once smiling face now tense with worry. He whistled and when Roch'mellon ambled over, he vaulted onto his back. "Sorry, boy," he stated, his knees urging the horse into a fast gallop. "We have trouble."

Once in the myst, he had easily picked up the trail of what caused the disturbance. He became immediately more cautious when he discovered orc sign. Orcs were the elves' natural enemy in the faerie world.

While centuries ago, a truce had been declared, there was still much hatred and mistrust between the two races. The elves regularly patrolled the border between the two lands, just to make sure the orcs did not breach the elven kingdom. To find they crossed into the human world gave Calion great concern.

Using his elven senses, he followed the trail left by the two orcs. He noted the spot where they entered the human world. Without leaving the myst, he trailed along its edge until he found where the orcs reentered the faerie realm.

What disturbed him most was they hadn't returned alone. It was bad enough when a faerie traveled into the human world, but to bring one back, a female human no less. That went against everything faerie believed in.

Why had they gone against all that was written? What did they want with the human? He clucked to Roch'mellon to go faster, his trepidation increasing. He knew what they would do to a defenseless female, human or not.

༄

Talia woke slowly, wondering why her head was pounding. She had an awful taste in her mouth, as if she'd vomited and forgotten to brush her teeth. She moaned, moving her head slightly to see how badly it hurt.

A rumbling of voices stopped her dead as the memory of what happened to her raced back. Cautiously, she opened her eyes and almost recoiled, whimpering, at what she saw.

She stood in what she thought must be a dungeon. Dreary and dark, the only light came from huge, twisted candles placed all around the room. There were no decorations, no color, just weapons of all sorts hanging on the walls. She cringed when she glimpsed blood congealed on one of the axes. Turning away in disgust, she noted one barred door and the only windows were at least forty feet up the walls.

The same smell she associated with the creatures who had taken her permeated the air, making her gag. Her gaze swept the room and to her horror, she saw her two captors sitting at a large table. They sat with a third, larger creature who stuffed its ugly face with the carcass of something she didn't recognize. She saw others in the room, sitting at smaller tables with less food, but all just as hideous to look at.

Looking up, Talia realized her arms hurt because they were bound tightly over her head. She tugged, but the knots held tight. Biting her lip, she tried to beat down the fear threatening to overwhelm her. She wasn't going anywhere that way. She'd have to figure something else out.

As she took stock of herself, she noted other than a few bruises, she was unharmed. Only one strap of her long nightgown was slightly torn. Apparently, the *father* hadn't touched her yet. A sweet feeling of relief coursed through her body. She wasn't sure how much longer her luck would hold, but for now, she remained untouched.

She watched as the creatures—she wasn't sure what they were yet—argued among themselves. They had no table manners, often reaching into one another's plates to steal food. The three sitting at the head table were arguing about her. She couldn't hear all their words, nor could she understand them, but the way they kept glancing up at her made her feel like she was going to be dessert.

ᘓ

Calion followed the orc sign out of the elven forest and into the swampland orcs considered their territory. He recognized their destination now. He'd been this way before, tracking his enemy. His adrenaline pumped and his magick jumped to the surface, ready to be released.

When he came to the edge of a twisted swamp, he dismounted, leaving Roch'mellon to hide. "Be safe, my friend. I will find you when needed." When he slapped the steed on the rump to send him off, a spot on his left arm burned. He rubbed at it absently.

He crept along the tree line, keeping himself in the shadows of the contorted, deformed trees that outlined the swamp near where the orcs' castle sat. While not the smartest of creatures, what orcs lacked in brain, they made up in guile and bulk. They very rarely posted sentries, because they refused to believe anyone would dare enter their domain.

He slunk along the side of the castle. Looking up, he saw the windows high overhead. Taking his bow from his shoulders, he grasped the string with both hands. Closing his eyes, he cast a quick spell. When his eyes opened he held a length of rope, stiff at one end and long enough to reach the window.

Placing the stiff end in the bow, Calion took aim and with the skill that made him a hero in battle, the rope arrow silently sped through the open window and wrapped itself around a column just inside. Slinging his bow over his shoulders, he grabbed the rope between his hands and walked quickly up the side of the castle wall.

Climbing quietly inside the window, he hid in the shadows. Frowning, he rubbed at his smarting arm again. He must have stumbled into a toxic plant of some type. The goddesses only knew what horrible things grew in the darkness of an orcan swamp.

As his eyes adjusted to the murky darkness, he could hear the orcs eating down below. He wrinkled his nose at the disgusting smell of the beasts, but he edged out further onto the sill to look underneath.

The room was full of orcs, with Udaogong, the orcan king sitting at the head table with his sons, Braduk and Modak. It looked as if the meal was almost finished. Calion hoped they would take enough time eating so he could find and save the female. With most of the clan here, then he would be free to... A sudden movement caught his attention and he shifted to the right of the pillar. He swore silently.

There to the left of the king's table stood the human. She was tied to the wall, her hands uncomfortably stretched over her head. The human was slender, but the curves...definitely female. Her long blonde hair covered most of her face. She struggled against her bonds and he swore again under his breath. Getting to her now would be near to impossible. He looked around the room, searching for ideas.

The natives are getting restless, Talia thought as she pulled against her ropes. After watching their behavior closely, she'd determined the two beasts that had kidnapped her were males as were most of the others in the room. Now that she had observed them long enough, she recognized the male-type tunics and pants. The females, although hideous and just as disgusting, wore a single piece of material that covered their hairy bodies as they served drink and food to the males. The women creatures didn't make Talia feel any safer. All she could think about was what had been said about the *father* fucking her. This many males in a room couldn't be good news.

Under her eyelashes, she watched as the older creature at the table finished his drink and slammed the goblet down. The whole table jumped beneath the impact. He got to his feet and lumbered over to her. His stench was even more revolting than the others and she cringed in disgust. Grunting, the beast ran his leathery hand down her arm. She pulled away from him, but he laughed and grabbed her again.

"I will fuck you, human," the thing said. Drool ran down one fat cheek. The other creatures laughed and punched each other.

"Let me go," Talia cried. She twisted her body away. "Why are you doing this?"

The creature fondled himself and chortled thickly. "You are chosen. We not let happen. I fuck...not him."

She stared at him in horror. What was he talking about? Who did he mean? She thought back to the few boys she'd dated over the last months. There hadn't been one she'd let get near her panties. "Please, you've got the wrong person. Let me go!"

The monster laughed harder and pulled her closer. "Fuck you, now!"

With one hand he reached down and opened the fastening of his pants. He lifted out his swollen cock and rubbed it against her.

She screamed, trying to twist away from him. His penis was huge, over twelve inches long and as big around as her upper arms. A grayish green, it had blue veins popping out all over it and a green mushroom-shaped head. She hadn't thought anything could smell worse than his breath, but she was wrong.

He rubbed at her again and lifted the hem of the thin nightgown. He was going to rape her right here! In front of all of them!

Talia fought harder, kicking at him with her strong legs, managing to connect one dead in his groin.

The beast howled in pain and released her, backhanding her across the face. She felt the warm saltiness of blood spurt in her mouth as her vision grayed. The creature reached out his hand again to grab her body.

Swoosh! Something flew by her to bury itself in the hand of the monster. His roar almost deafened her. The creature let her go and backed away holding his wounded hand.

She stared in amazement at the arrow that protruded from it. Where had that come from? She heard the screaming of the other things as they drew their weapons and looked around them for an assailant.

Suddenly, the room filled with a thick, sweet-smelling fog. It was so dense Talia could no longer see the monster in front of her.

She was brave...for a human. Calion had been disgusted when Udaogong pressed his filthy cock against her. Instead of mewling in fear and fainting as he expected a female human to do, she fought back, giving Udaogong a good kick in the mansack and distracting the orc enough so he could act. As soon as his arrow struck, the elf shot the rope arrow into the ceiling.

He closed his eyes and muttered an incantation. Fog, smelling of the *baroli* flower, poison to the orcs, flowed into the room. When thick enough to hide his actions, Calion moved, leaping off the ledge and swinging down to where the human stood tied to the wall. He landed right in front of her.

She almost screamed when he appeared. Pressing herself back against the wall, she watched as he hooked the rope over his arm and turned to her.

He stared at the female for a long moment, shock rendering him speechless. He hadn't seen very many humans before, but even compared to an elven female, she was the most beautiful thing he had ever seen. Long blonde hair, the same color as moon mist, straggled down over her naked shoulders. She was petite, yet with a shapely body of slender hips, tiny waist and nicely rounded small breasts, easily seen in the torn and ragged gown she wore. The female had a heart shaped face with vivid green eyes and lips, that while bloody and bruised, were still full and kissable.

His body warmed in a quick rush and all the blood went straight to his groin. Just looking at her made his magick sing.

He saw her fear and he wanted to reach out and pull her against him to comfort her, but he didn't think she would accept his touch so soon after almost being raped by Udaogong. Something moved inside him when she cringed away from him, but he ignored it, and pulling out his dagger, he cut the ropes above her head.

Talia's arms fell down, the blood rushing back into them, making her eyes tear in pain. The tall man seized her arms and rubbed them, wanting to help, but then dropped them with a curse. He pushed back his sleeve to reveal an angry welt on his arm. He stared at it for a moment, before he shook his head and then began rubbing her arms again.

She could hear the choking cries of the beasts around her as the fog sent them to their knees, but the sweet smell didn't hurt her. Feeling began to return to her hands, and she bit her lip to keep back a cry of pain. As if he knew it, he raised his head and looked straight at her.

He was classically handsome, with strong features and firm sensuous lips. His coal black hair reached midway down his back, held back from his forceful face by two braids tied by a leather thong. She blinked in shock when she noticed the pointed ears and eyebrows and then swallowed hard when she met tilted, piercing sapphire blue eyes.

"Who are you?" she whispered, unable to look away from the heat she saw in his eyes.

When Calion saw her confusion, he dropped her arms and stepped back from her. He chastised himself for his thoughts. It was forbidden for an elven male to even think about a human female. He willed his body to cool down and then held out his hand.

"I am Calion, of the elves. Come with me if you wish to live."

Maybe because of the promise she saw in his face, the female didn't hesitate, but just placed her hand in his. His eyes flared hot for a moment. "Put your arms around my neck and hold on. We must go up...to get out."

Nodding, her heart in her throat, she wrapped her arms around his neck and allowed him to press her against his chest. She gasped aloud as they both flew into the air, high above the heads of the monsters beneath. She could feel the strong pull of Calion's muscles as he swung them up as far as he could and then continued the climb on a second conjured rope, hand over hand. Talia hung helplessly as the elf man did all the work, lifting them both to safety.

A muted shout came from below, and she cried out as an ax was hurled at them, barely missing Calion's shoulder. He grunted and pulled harder, his arm muscles straining with the effort.

"What can I do?" she asked breathlessly as another ax and then an arrow flew by.

"Nothing," he gritted out, his arms screaming from the exertion. Between the strain of climbing the rope, as well as having the female bumping between his legs, concentrating on anything was difficult. "Try not to move." He felt the female nod against his chest, sending another wave of longing through his body. He didn't have time for thoughts like that right now. By the goddesses, he didn't even know her name.

As they approached the window sill, his body gave a hard jerk and he grunted in pain. One armed, he swung her onto the ledge and then protecting her body with his own, swung himself up as well.

When he did so, Talia saw an arrow piercing his upper arm. "Oh my God...you're hurt."

He glanced down at the wound and then ignored it, taking the arrow rope and wrapping it around the pillar. He ducked easily when another arrow came their way. "Climb back on."

Talia stared at him. "What about the arrow?"

"No time now." He held out his arms and settled her against him once again. "The fog is confusing their senses. We must escape before it dissipates."

Climbing over the side, he started swiftly down the wall. After just a few steps they both groaned painfully.

Each step threw Talia hard against Calion's groin and then back into even harder contact with the wall of the castle. Now she fought a furious headache, and him a raging hard on.

"Stop," she pleaded. "This isn't working."

"We must continue." But he came to a stop, breathing heavily. His chin dropped to her head.

She thought quickly. "I have an idea." Without saying anything, she hitched herself up and wrapped her legs around his waist.

She felt the hardness of his body immediately and blushed like a rose, burying her face into his chest. The feeling of his erection against her set off tremors of feeling, making her insides warm. "I'm sorry," she mumbled. "I thought this might be easier."

Calion gritted his teeth, not answering her. Her softness pressed hard against his cock. Knowing it would only get worse before it got better, he continued back down the rope, hoping to make it down to the ground before he disgraced himself. Once his feet hit the dirt, she slid back down his body, making him groan out loud.

She turned worriedly to him, missing the flare of passion glowing in his azure eyes. "We have to take care of this!"

Calion nodded, thinking the pain of removing the arrow might get rid of the arousal that clogged his mind. "I have to break the tip off."

"You can't do it unless you have an extra set of arms. Let me." She stepped closer and wrapped her hands around the arrow, just behind the tip. She looked up and smiled at him hesitantly, her dimples flashing. "All right?"

At that moment, after being bathed in the warmth of the female's smile, Calion would have allowed her anything. All the pain disappeared and he nodded, not certain of his voice. What was it about this human?

Talia bit her lip as she concentrated. She heard the sound of tramping feet in the distance.

"Hurry," he urged, as he stared over her shoulder.

"Hold still." Without further ado, grunting with the effort, she snapped the shaft in two.

He didn't say a word, didn't even react to what she knew must have hurt him, but just reached up and with a hard yank pulled the shaft from his arm. A gush of blood followed his action.

Gasping, Talia bent and ripped a large strip of fabric from the hem of her nightgown and quickly wrapped it around his arm. "That will stop it for a while but it needs—"

"We are out of time. Run. Now!" Grabbing her hand, Calion raced across the meadow. He headed toward the mold-ridden trees at the edge of the swamp, pulling the female behind him. He glanced at the castle, his gaze going to the band of orcs that burst from the doorway. When the creatures caught sight of the fleeing prisoners, they let out a loud roar and came lumbering after them.

"They're coming," she cried, terrified. "What are they? Why do they want me?"

He looked at her. "I do not know why they think raping you will help them, but I can tell you what they are. They are orcs."

She looked over her shoulder, a mistake, as when she saw the number of monsters—orcs—chasing after them, she stumbled, almost going down. Only Calion's elven quickness prevented her from falling. They continued to run until they gasped for air.

"All that jogging is sure coming in handy," she panted.

"What is jogging?" Calion risked a look over his shoulder. He saw no orcs and they were almost to the edge of the wood.

"It's like slow running for exercise. You know...to keep in shape."

His eyes caressed her scantily clad form. "It is working."

She blushed and stumbled again.

"Be careful, my lady. I did not rescue you only to have you

fall on your lovely face."

A loud crashing noise behind them made them jump. He cursed in Elvish and jerked her along faster. "If we can get out of the swamp, I can draw on the wood's magick to help us."

Talia ran as fast as she could. He could draw on magic? She felt like she was stuck in a nightmare, or a rip-off of a Tolkien book. Orcs and elves? Any second she expected to see a hobbit or a wraith jump out at her.

The stitch in her side turned into a cramp and her legs were numb. She didn't say anything for a long time, not wanting to slow them down, but eventually her legs gave out and she stumbled...hard.

"I can't," she whispered raggedly. "I'm sorry. I have to stop. Go on. Save yourself."

Calion looked back at her. The female breathed shallowly, her face red and glowing with sweat. Her arms and long legs were scratched by branches and bushes. He noticed for the first time her feet were bare, and still she'd run through whatever he'd thrown at her without a whimper of complaint.

Without a word he turned and swept her up in his strong arms.

She struggled against him, terrified she would make him lose his life along with hers. She didn't know how fast an elf could run and she couldn't bear the thought of him dying.

"Put me down," she murmured. Tears of fear and pain ran down her cheeks. "If they have me, they will forget about you."

His jaw clenched as he continued the pace. In his lifetime he'd heard many stories of cowardly humans. They were not fit to be in the company of higher beings, such as elves. In just a short time, this female had taken all those stories and proved them untrue. If all humans were like her, they were a force to be reckoned with.

"No," he answered. "Where I go, you go."

Finally, they entered the elven wood. Calion felt any weakness leave him as he unconsciously drew the magick into his body. He stopped and turned around.

"Will they follow us here?"

He looked down at the female snuggled in his arms. "We will see how badly they want you." He turned and continued at a fast walk into the forest. "If they come after you, it will be the first time they have entered an elven domain since the last war."

As if in answer to her question, a group of orcs burst from the tree line at the far edge of the wood and lumbered their way. Calion shook his head in astonishment. They would break centuries of peace to come after one human? He looked down at her. What *was* so special about this female?

Turning, he ran into an overgrown area of the forest, a plan forming in his head. He ran hard for several minutes before he found what he was looking for...a large tree with roots bulging up out of the ground.

Stopping beside it, he set the female in one of the spaces between the roots. Breathing hard, he steadied her, noting she fit perfectly under his chin. He took her face in his hands and stared intently at her.

"Do you trust me?"

Chapter Two

Talia blinked at him. "Of course."

"Just like that?" He smiled. "I did not believe humans were like you." Shaking his head at himself, he pulled her over to the tree. "Then trust me now."

The elf man sat and pulled her down to him, her face pressed against his chest, her legs drawn up and underneath one of his hard thighs. He pulled his cloak out from under him and swirled it around, covering them completely.

"What—"

"Shhh..." he whispered. He bent close to her ear. "Whatever you hear, you must be absolutely silent. Do you understand?"

At her hesitant nod, he hugged her to him tightly and then pulled his sword. The sword sang its name, making her jump. "You must also promise not to move, not for any reason." His breath fluttered across her cheek and she trembled.

Again, she nodded.

"Good, now we wait."

Talia was struck by the intimacy of their pose. Pressed tight against him, every inch of her upper body was in contact with his. Her arms wrapped around his back and her legs tucked under a thigh as hard as the tree roots around them. She felt his breathing and his heart pounding against her own. She was woman enough to recognize that the hardness between Calion's legs was for her. She'd seen the heat in his gorgeous eyes.

His nearness made her body respond in kind. A trembling, melty sensation she'd never experienced before. What was happening to her? She wanted to run her hand down his chest. To touch his hard, strong body for herself. She closed her eyes and smothered a groan. In the middle of fighting for her life and thinking about sex? Now was definitely not the time.

Calion felt her soft breasts against his abdomen, how they brushed against him every time she took a breath. The fire in his loins grew in direct proportion to his erection. He knew she was aware of it, she wasn't stupid. Was she disgusted? What would she do if he pulled her head back and plundered her soft lips as he wanted? He groaned inwardly. He was crazy. Thinking about mating with a different race, the biggest *sardai*—taboo—of all. On top of that, they were in a battle for their lives. Now was definitely not the time.

They sat there, waiting. The warmth of Calion's body made Talia relax. A great weariness stole over her and she yawned. She felt like she'd been awake for days. Her eyelids drooped. It would feel so good to take a quick nap. She snuggled closer and closed her eyes.

She relaxed, her body softening against his, and Calion wished wholeheartedly he could let her sleep, but it was too dangerous. He knew the orcs were close.

"*Tia maer...*" he murmured. "I am sorry, but you must stay awake. It is too risky to rest now." Talia jerked at his voice and she immediately knew why he'd spoken. Even that tiny movement might have given them away.

"Sorry," she breathed. She felt a brush of his lips against her hair signaling the acceptance of her apology and she wondered sleepily what he'd called her.

They both stiffened as they heard the sounds of heavy feet nearby. The footsteps tramped towards them. Talia pressed her face against Calion's chest, wondering how the cloak would keep them from being seen.

The stomping feet came closer and to her horror, stopped just in front of them. She squeezed her eyes shut in terror.

Calion tightened his grip on his sword. *Cylys* pulsated with magick, ready to spring into action at its master's words.

"No find." A heavy gruff voice rang out and shocked them both.

The elf smiled when the female kept her word and didn't move. Even though he'd half expected an orc's voice, he was surprised to hear Modak, Udaogong's youngest son.

"Father...angry. Must find female. Fuck now. Fuck before...too late." Calion also recognized the gravelly voice of Braduk, the orcan heir to the throne. He frowned as he heard the desperation in the creature's tone. The female began to tremble and he held her closer to comfort her. He knew she couldn't help it, even an elven woman would shake at the thought of being raped by an orc.

"Smell them. Dirty elf...pretty human. No see," Modak whined. His brother's response was a cuff to his head.

"*Ba-gronk*," Braduk snarled, swearing in Orcan. "Find...destroy prophecy." He sniffed the air. "Must kill elf. Fuck human. Find now!"

Talia listened in fear as the two orcs discussed killing her and Calion as easily as someone would discuss what they might have for dinner. Her ears snagged on one word. Prophecy? What did that mean?

Calion also heard it. This human involved in an orcan prophecy? In what way? He frowned and held her tighter. Even more reason to keep her safely out of their hands. He knew she was terrified. She still trembled and had burrowed as close to him as she could. He hoped if the time came, she wouldn't get in the way of his sword arm.

The two orcs didn't seem to be in a hurry to leave but stood and argued over where to search next. Though anxious at their presence, he relaxed a little, knowing that his plan worked and they both were invisible to the orcs' eyes.

Suddenly, an orcan voice shouted from another part of the forest. Braduk and Modak grunted and ran heavily away. Calion listened, his elven ears following their passage as they crashed through the wood.

He felt the female relax and he bent to her, speaking quietly. "Do not move yet."

She stilled instantly and he once more was impressed with her. Humans did not have the talent for being absolutely motionless, as elves did, but even frightened she'd held her own. They waited, Calion listening hard for any sounds that told him the orcs were returning, but he heard nothing. Finally, after so much time passed he felt the stiffness right down to his bones, he used his magick to trace them. He asked the trees where the orcs were.

After several long minutes, the trees gave him his answer. They'd left the woods. Sighing in relief, he bent his head to tell the female everything was all right, but at the same time, she raised her face to better hear him and their lips met.

Fiery sensation raced through Calion's already overstimulated body. The chance meeting of their lips wiped all pain, fear and worry about touching a human out of his mind. He went on pure instinct. His body burned to make her his own. Slanting his hard mouth across hers, he devoured. Not a tentative first kiss, this, but one that instinctively knew just where and how to touch her.

His teeth nipped at her lips, demanding entrance, and when she opened to him, his tongue plunged inside seeking the warmth within. He groaned at her taste. She was sweet, but with a hint of spice that made him crave more. His tongue thrust inside her mouth in an imitation of what his body desperately wanted to do to hers.

Talia couldn't breath, couldn't think. She hadn't realized how badly she'd wanted him to kiss her until he did. His kiss was different than any she had known before. His mouth was hard and demanding and she reveled in the mastery of it. When his tongue insisted entrance, she pressed against him, holding him tighter as he plumbed the depths of her.

At her uninhibited response, Calion's control snapped. He forgot all about the orcs. He wanted to bear her to the ground and put out the fire burning inside him. He reached up to toss the cloak off and as he did so he dropped his sword. The sound of magick being lost as his sword crashed to the dirt brought him back to reality with a thud.

What had she made him do? No elf dropped his sword! It was unheard of. He pulled back from Talia and with one hand, he uncovered them. He stared down at her as he took deep, panting breaths.

Leaning against him, her eyes half closed, she too was panting for breath. Her lips were swollen by the force of his kisses. He watched as her eyes slowly opened and looking at him, she blushed like a maiden. Even in his turmoil, the sight of it charmed him. The throbbing in his cock hadn't abated, so he took a deep breath and moved her carefully away from him, picking up his sword as he did so.

Cylys sang in protest of his actions, but he carefully wiped it off and standing, sheathed the blade. The thought of his cock being sheathed by the female's warm quim made him shift in need.

Talia felt as if she were under a spell. The touch of his

mouth made all coherent thought flee. She'd responded to him as never before and she knew she wouldn't have protested him laying her on the ground and taking her, orcs or no orcs. Her body ached for his possession.

But now, even though she could still see the bulge in his pants and the need in his eyes, he pulled away from her, distancing them. The look on his face teetered between anger and desire. She suddenly felt chilled.

"Are you all right?" His harsh voice made her jump. She looked away from his angry eyes, flushing even deeper. She stiffly got to her feet, not seeing his helping hand.

"I'm fine," she answered. She worked at keeping the embarrassment from her voice but didn't quite manage it.

Calion frowned as he looked at her. She'd wrapped her arms around her body as if to protect herself from him. The thought made him angrier. She responded to him as well. It should not have happened, but he had not forced her. Without thinking he reached for her. Her gaze flew to his, filled with a wariness that smote his heart. He held her by both arms, turning her to fully face him.

"I am sorry," he said, his jaw clenched. "I should not have touched you. But you wanted me to. Do not deny it.

Her mouth dropped open. Then her eyes frosted as she understood him. "I wasn't the one who stopped, Calion. You're the one who is angry. You're the one who acts like kissing me disgusts you." She tried to jerk free, but he held her easily, glaring at her with narrowed eyes.

"I am elven, you are human. We are of different races. I should not even be touching you now."

"Then don't," she shouted, pulling away. "I wouldn't want you to dirty your hands." She stared at him, her chin lifted in pride as she wondered how something so beautiful could turn so ugly.

Calion glared at her. "Keep your voice down, human. Or would you prefer the kiss of an orc instead?" He swore as she went white, pain filling her eyes. Gathering her back into his arms, he bent his head, pressing his lips to her fragrant hair as he struggled with his temper. After a moment he calmed enough to speak.

"I am sorry."

"It was a filthy thing to say." She sniffed into his tunic.

"Yes." He did what he wanted to do earlier and ran a caressing hand up and down the back of the thin gown she wore. Her flesh was warm and soft.

He sighed as he admitted, "I do not expect to feel desire for a human. I took it out on you. For that I apologize."

Talia let him hold her for a moment. She grinned suddenly. He was confused? It seemed guys were alike, no matter what their race. None like talking about their feelings.

"I amuse you?" He pulled back to look down into her dancing eyes.

"No, not really. I'm just thinking of something."

"And what is that?"

No way was Talia going to tell him what she was thinking. She searched quickly for a distraction. "Ummm, I'm thinking I've never kissed a guy who didn't know my name."

He grinned. "We did not have time for a proper introduction." He stepped back from her and bowed low at the waist. "I am Calion Sáralondë, Prince of the Calen'taur Elves. This is my people's domain. You are welcome here."

A prince, huh? Getting into the spirit of things, she swept him a beautiful curtsy. "I am Natalia Jennings, of Rogue River, Oregon. My friends call me Talia. I thank you for making me so welcome."

He laughed at her wry comeback. "Talia. It suits you. A name as beautiful as the one who wears it." When she blushed again, he felt the now-familiar warmth begin to burn in him again. What was happening to him?

After a short silence she asked. "How did you do that thing with the cape? They were right in front of us. Why didn't they see us?

He thought a moment. The best way to tell her would be to show her. "Watch." Picking up his cloak, he winked once at her and then covered himself with it. He heard her gasp and with a silent chuckle he moved until he stood behind her. He watched as she lifted her hand and tried to find him.

"Calion?"

Even though he knew she trusted him, he could hear the fear in her voice. "Here," he said quickly, not wanting to tease her anymore. She whirled and reaching out, gently eased the cloak from his head. The feel of her hands made the passion fire up in him again. His eyes glowed.

Seeing him like that, the truth of his need written in his face made Talia go weak in the knees. She forgot all about the cloak.

"I want to kiss you."

Calion's eyes blazed. Forgetting all he'd said before, he bent and pressed his mouth to hers. Desire and need flared up and dropping the cloak, he wrapped his arms hard around her, lifting and fitting her soft body against his. He groaned as her tongue danced inside his mouth. His body was so hot, he felt like he was on fire. Only the strange burn on his arm flamed hotter.

He tore his lips from hers. "This cannot be. We must stop." Ignoring his own words, he bent back to her and kissed her until she couldn't breathe.

Talia was shocked at the impact of her thoughtlessly spoken words. She felt him fighting his feelings, his good sense battling his need for her. A part of her reveled in that, knowing how badly he wanted her. She gave herself up to the wonder of his lovemaking.

When Calion knew he was losing control again, he buried his face in her neck and held her. He couldn't believe he was shaking in his boots. Wrong time, wrong place and definitely the wrong female, he thought to himself.

He waited until he could control himself enough to release her. He bent and picked up the cloak from the ground and then took her by the hand. "It is time to go. We must find a safe place to rest and recover, and you need those scratches taken care of."

"You're wounded too." Her voice was thin, as if she were having trouble speaking.

He looked at her, saw the bewilderment in her expressive eyes and frowned. Could it be, she too didn't understand what was happening between them? Perhaps she was as surprised as he.

Wanting to comfort somehow he gently kissed her dirty forehead. "My wound as well. Come...let us find a *Malesia* tree."

They walked in silence, each lost in their own thoughts. After a while she asked, "How is it we understand each other? You've said your tongue is Elvish."

"We are speaking in what is known in this world as Common. It is the tongue different races speak when they get together." He helped her over a fallen log. "It is very similar to your human tongue."

"So all the people of this world speak Common?"

"Most do. Some, like the rock trolls of the high North, choose to speak only their own language. They do not mix with other races."

She chewed on that for a while. "That thing you did with the cape. Did it make us invisible?"

Calion started. He hadn't been thinking about the cape, but of the unwelcome differences between the race of man and the race of elves. He struggled to bring his thoughts back in line. "It does make us invisible, but only by taking on the attributes of what is around it."

"It's like camouflage?"

"I do not know this word."

She wrinkled her nose. "Ummm...like a bug can take on the color of the leaf he is on."

"Yes, that is what the cloak does. The orcs thought we were part of the tree."

They were both silent for a while, before she asked. "What's a malaria tree?"

Calion wasn't surprised at the question. He was learning to expect it. She was curious, for a human. "The term is *Malesia*. It means *Sanctuary* in the Elvish tongue."

"It's a beautiful name, but what good will a tree do us?"

"You will see when we get there. A *Malesia* tree is very special."

"Do you know where one is?"

He smiled at her. "Oh yes. These are my woods. I know them very well. I just did not expect to need a *Malesia* this day."

"It wasn't part of your day to rescue me." She looked up at him in admiration. "But I'm glad you did. You were wonderful."

Calion swelled at her praise like a youngling. This was getting ridiculous. "Thank you. Any plan that works is a good plan, but I did have something else in mind."

"What?"

"My plan was to spirit you away quietly. I did not know they would be so interested in you, they would keep you with them." When he saw her shudder, he went on quickly. "I would have taken you to where my horse Roch'mellon hid and then galloped away to safety."

She stopped dead in her tracks, and he looked at her in surprise. "You have a horse? Where is he? Is he safe?" The worried questions spilled from her, and Calion's chest tightened at her obvious concern for an animal she didn't even know.

"Shhh, *Tia maer...* Roch'mellon is fine. He knows to hide himself from danger until I find him." He pulled her to him. She opened her mouth to protest and without thinking, he kissed her lightly. The arguing stopped immediately and Calion thought of how pleasant preventing quarrels with this female might be.

Remembering who he was kissing, he frowned as he forced himself to continue walking. "I will call him to us when we reach the *Malesia* tree. I want to get you to safety first."

Another comfortable silence ensued. "What did you call me?" Talia finally asked curiously. "I heard you say it once before."

Calion blinked as he replayed their conversation in his mind. "Ahhh... *Tia maer...*"

"What does it mean?"

He shrugged uncomfortably. He didn't usually use endearments, but this one popped out naturally. "It is not important."

Talia slanted him a look. "When you say that it makes me think you called me something bad, like garbage breath, or knothead."

The human idioms made Calion laugh. "Those are still better than what Braduk called his brother."

"Braduk?"

"He is the heir to Udaogong, the king of the orcan people. His brother is Modak. They stood before us in the forest."

"They're the ones who kidnapped me," she said thoughtfully. "I recognized their voices." Then she frowned. "What did he call him?"

"There is no word that exactly matches it in your tongue. The closest is..." He thought for a moment. "Dung pit."

She burst into laughter, making him grin. "Oh, that's perfect. That's just what they smell like."

He nodded his agreement. "Tell me about what happened to you."

"Not so fast. I want to know what *you* called *me.*" She blinked as a rush of ruddy color flooded Calion's neck and cheeks.

After a long moment, he shrugged. "It means in your tongue...sweet. My sweet."

"Ohhh." She was moved by the endearment as well as the elf's embarrassment. "That is very...sweet," she finished lamely.

He muttered under his breath and kicked at a small stone in their path. "Now you will tell me what happened to you."

Talia stifled a giggle at his obvious discomfiture. Smiling, she relayed her story to him as they walked.

He listened in silence. When she finished, he stayed quiet for a long time before he spoke. "Do you think they came after you specifically? Would any human female do?"

"I...don't know." The hesitation in her voice was apparent. "I just know they wanted *me.* They even put all my things in my car and pushed it in the lake so it would look as if I left."

"Hmmm, that shows forethought. Something not often seen in an orc. I wonder how they knew you would be there."

"Oh, didn't I tell you? I grew up in the house just outside of the woods. I used to play in them as a child. I've always loved the forest."

Calion stopped and stared at her as memory flooded back. He'd often watched the forest, when he became curious about the human world. He'd seen a child playing unafraid in the wood. She was that child? The connection made him even more confused.

"What is it?" She'd noticed his distraction. "Is someone coming?

He blinked and focused on her again. "No, not at all. I remembered something I had forgotten."

He looked around him and realized with a start, they were close to the *Malesia* tree. He started forward quickly, her hand firmly in his. They went around a corner and there it was, in the clearing. "We are here."

Talia looked around her. She saw a small meadow, but at the center was the most perfect tree ever seen. At least five feet in diameter, it grew high into the air. Its branches were ideal for climbing. If she hadn't been so tired, she would have been tempted to climb up into the clouds. "It's beautiful."

He stepped up close to the tree. “Yes, it is.”

“How does it work?”

“You tell me.”

She considered that. “Well, since it is called ‘Sanctuary’, it must be a place that is safe. And if you have brought us here to rest and heal, it must be some type of a treehouse.”

He raised an eyebrow. “Go on.”

She chewed on her lip, making Calion want to groan. “I don’t see any structure up in the branches, so my guess is it’s some type of magic tree. One you can transform in some way.”

He gave her his devastating smile in reward, a little shocked at how accurate her guess was. “Very good...for a human.”

Talia wrinkled her nose at him. “It feels like magic.” Bending, she touched a flower, smoothing its petals with her fingers. She missed the startled look on his face.

“You can feel the magick?” Calion knew his voice sounded strained, but he couldn’t help it.

She frowned at his expression. “Can’t you?”

He started to snap back at her with an explanation about the differences between humans and elves, but shut his mouth quickly. It would do no good. She didn’t understand she’d said anything extraordinary. Still holding her hand in his, he pulled her forward and placed his hand on the base of the tree.

“*Malesia...Ai shael Malesia.*”

They felt a tingle, as if an electric shock laced through their palms. Talia gave a gasp and then stared when the leaves began to shudder, as if the big tree was waking up.

Calion stepped backward, pulling her with him. They watched as the tree began to reshape itself. It heaved and moved and finally, a wooden door appeared in the trunk.

“After you, my lady.” He grinned as he watched her stare in awe at the door. He reached over and pushed the door open.

Talia stepped inside expecting to see the hollowed out trunk of the tree, but what she did see was an old fashioned cottage. “Oh wow.”

It boasted a bunk bed on one side, with a woodstove and small icebox on the wall to the right of them. The opposite wall to the beds had a framed window, with a shelved bookcase and sink underneath. In the center of the room were a small table and two chairs. Everything was as neat and tidy as a pin.

"It's perfect," she sighed, remembering all the times she'd built her own little playhouses in the woods. If she could have imagined them real, they would have looked just like this.

Calion groaned silently, caught between watching the enjoyment on her face and the need he felt for her when he saw the bed. Thank the goddesses the trees didn't come with bigger mattresses.

She turned to him. "What about the orcs? Won't they look for us here?"

"Orcs cannot see *Malesia* trees. They can only be found by elven folk."

"They can see the door in the trunk. Even they're not that blind."

He chuckled. "Go outside and shut the door. I will let you back in."

"I don't understand."

"Just do it," he said patiently.

Talia went out the door and pulled it shut behind her. To her absolute shock, the door vanished right before her eyes. The tree once again looked like any other tree in the forest. A moment later, he opened the door, making it reappear in front of her unbelieving eyes.

"Oh," she breathed, as she touched the tree with reverent fingers. "That is so cool."

Calion grinned. He found it very enjoyable to see his world through Talia's eyes. It made everything fresh and new.

"Come inside and get comfortable. "I will go see if I can find anything for us to eat."

She stumbled as she walked back in. "Go see?"

Smiling, he ran a comforting finger down her cheek. "There is no food here. I for one am very hungry, and I want to see if I can find my horse."

The look in her eyes as he touched her made him move back, his body jumping at the desire he thought he saw in the green depths. He needed to get out of there. "I promise you. No one can get into a *Malesia* tree without permission. We have been given sanctuary here. No one else may enter."

"Promise?"

He knew she didn't mean to doubt his word. "I swear this

to you." At her hesitant nod, he turned and left, shutting the door behind him. It vanished without a trace.

Talia moved to the window and watched as he jogged into the trees. A moment later she was all alone. Panic seized her, but she fought it down.

"I've made it through being kidnapped by orcs, flying though the air on a rope, being kissed witless by a very handsome elf and watching a living tree grow a door. I think I can manage being alone for a little while."

She stared out the window, noting the exact place her rescuer entered the forest. As she turned, she saw Calion's cloak sitting outside the treehouse in plain view of whoever might happen by.

Knowing the cloak could signal their location to any marauding orcs, she opened the door and ran to get it. She made sure she left the door open, but when she turned around with the cloak in her hands, the portal had vanished, leaving her standing outside, terrified and trembling.

She whimpered in fear and ran back to where she remembered the door being. There was nothing but rough bark beneath her questing hands.

"The door..." she breathed. "Where is the door?" She searched for several tense moments before accepting the fact that without a warm body inside to keep the door open, the tree closed back down. Talia bit her lip, drawing blood. The pain cleared her mind. Somehow she needed to get back inside.

Swallowing, she placed her palm against the tree as Calion had done. Wetting her lips, she tried to remember the words. "Ummm...*Malesia...Ai shael Malesia.*" She felt the same tingle in her hand, but nothing.

"Come on," she begged. "Remember me?" She tossed the cape over her shoulder and put both hands on the tree. "Again... Please! *Malesia...Ai shael Malesia.*"

She stumbled back as the tree heaved and then the door popped into view. "I did it!" Talia did a little jig, clapping her hands in joy.

Her jubilation was cut short as a hand spun her around and then grasped her arms in a bruising hold. She cried out in relief when she saw Calion, but went still when she saw he was in a towering rage.

"What did you do?" he shouted at her, shaking her like a

rag doll. "Tell me immediately!"

He'd been half a mile into the forest when he remembered his cloak. When he stepped back into the meadow, the first thing he saw was Talia opening the *Malesia* tree, something that should have been impossible. Fears, doubt and confusion rushed into him all at once. Something was going on and by the goddesses, he would find out what.

"Stop it! Calion, you're hurting me." She tried to wriggle away from him without success.

He gave her another hard shake. "I asked you a question. What is happening here? How did you open the *Malesia* tree?"

Fear and pain colored her eyes a dark emerald. "I saw the cloak. I knew it wasn't safe to leave it outside, so I came to get it. I didn't mean to get locked out! It just happened. I'm sorry."

All at once, Calion realized he was hurting her and his hands immediately gentled. "What about the tree, Talia. How did you open it?"

"I remembered the words. I'm sorry. I was a-afraid and I wanted to be inside. I just s-said the words and the door came back."

He only stared. She'd just turned his world upside down. Only an elf could open a *Malesia* tree. He knew that as well as he knew his own name, and no matter how much he may want her to be, Talia was no elf.

When he released her, she stumbled away from him, running through the open door. Lost in thought, he rubbed the fire that burned hotter above his wrist. He stepped inside to see Talia against the far wall looking at him with wary eyes.

"*Kydaer ol ei plyi,*" he swore roundly, making her flinch. He'd hurt her and now she feared him. The thought stabbed at his heart. Ignoring her fear, he went to her and took her in his arms. She didn't fight him, but held herself stiffly, her face turned away. With a gentle finger, he turned her face back to him.

"*Tia maer...* Forgive me. Again I spit angry words at you. I am sorry." When she just looked at him, he placed a gentle kiss on her lips and felt them tremble. "You frighten me."

When she jerked in astonishment, he smiled. "You are a human, Talia. Yet you are in my world and are doing things you should not be able to do. It is unnerving."

"I don't understand," she said softly.

He bowed his head until his forehead touched hers. "You are connected to this place in a way no human has been before. First, you tell me you sense magick and now you can open a *Malesia* tree. It is impossible."

"I just did what you showed me," she objected. "I spoke the words, felt the tingle and then it opened. Although, I did have to say it twice."

"Felt the...tingle?"

"Yes." Talia nodded. "I felt it the first time when you opened the tree. We were holding hands, remember?"

"And you felt it again, when you did it on your own?" She nodded again slowly and he sighed. "You must have absorbed something when we opened it the first time together, but that is not supposed to happen. You are human!"

"You keep saying that! Like it's a disease or something." She tried to pull away, but Calion held her tight.

"Not a disease, but it is something!" The elf felt frustrated with all the unknowns. Plus, there was the pain in his arm and wound, as well as the need that slammed into him each time he touched her.

He knew the stories about elves who wanted to mate with humans. Tall tales that young males tried to scare each other with. Legends of your cock turning green if you let a human female hold it, or even worse, it falling off if you actually mated with one. But now, with the reality staring him in the face, he didn't know how to feel. Everything in him wanted to mate with this female, no matter how strongly his mind warned against it.

With another oath, he pushed her back against the wall with his body, letting her feel his arousal. He crushed her mouth with his, taking her head and holding it so he could slant his lips over hers. His tongue probed her soft lips, demanding she open to him. When she did, melting against him, he groaned and devoured her.

The change came so suddenly Talia didn't know how to deal with it. First angry, then gentle and now angry again. But as his lips mastered hers, she realized she just didn't care. She knew he was angry for wanting her because she was human, but she didn't care about that either. He'd rescued her when he didn't have to, and he made her want to totally surrender to a man for the first time in her life.

He'd protected her and then infuriated her and then kissed

her so beautifully, she wanted to die from his caresses. She didn't care he was an elf. When he touched her like this, all she cared about were the feelings that sprang up between them.

Calion groaned when he felt Talia's arms wrap around his waist. Passion flared as her peaked nipples brushed against him. Wanting, desperately needing, he dropped a hand from her face and took one of the sweet mounds into his hand and squeezed. She arched against him, crying out his name, and her knees buckled. His mouth continued to ravage hers as he held her against the wall. He brushed a thumb over her nipple, bringing it to an even harder point. He shifted, treating the other side to the same mind-numbing pleasure. She writhed against him, moaning into his mouth and he could feel her nails digging into his back. She was so responsive it drove him crazy.

His cock was so hard he hurt, and he wanted to drive himself into her, over and over again. He was blind to everything except his own passion. As he began to unfasten his pants, he heard the faint nicker of a horse. He stopped for a moment, shaking his head, but Talia moved against him and, lost, he covered her mouth with his one more time.

He pushed himself against her, his cock throbbing, already wetting his pants with pre-come. He began to lift the flimsy gown and take her against the wall, when the nicker came again, this time more insistently, and they both froze.

Calion swallowed. He wasn't sure whether to curse or thank Roch'mellon for his sudden appearance. All he knew was he was in an agony of mating need, something he'd never felt before in all his years of life, and for this woman. This...human.

That thought was like a cold shower, and he carefully stepped back from Talia, holding her until she got her legs working. He didn't look at her as he answered gruffly. "It is my horse. I should go see to him."

Talia could see him withdrawing from her again, so she lowered her hands and clasped them in front of her, wondering how he could distance himself emotionally, so quickly.

"All right. I'll wait here." She was proud her voice came out so steady.

"I will find him and then go to hunt. I will return as soon as I can."

She nodded soberly. "I'll be fine."

"Do not leave."

Talia had to smile. "I won't. I'll be right here when you get back."

"That is what I am afraid of," Calion said under his breath as he dropped his hands to his side. He saw she'd heard him by the way her chin came up.

Knowing he needed to get out of there, he turned and left, slamming the door behind him.

This time Talia didn't watch him go.

Chapter Three

Calion came out of the *Malesia* tree at a run, hoping exercise would burn out the lust throbbing in his body. He knew the approximate direction of Roch'mellon and as soon as he hit the forest, he sent out a mind-call. The horse answered with a joyful scream and within minutes, they found each other. He threw his arms around his steed's neck, burying his sweaty face in his mane. "It is good to see you, my friend."

Roch'mellon shoved at him with his big head, just as happy to see his prince. Snuffling noisily, his flaring nostrils took in all the odors on his master. The animal gave a snort when he smelled the scent of a human female, as well as the pungent smell of arousal.

"Yes, I found her. But she is not what I expected. She is not like any female I have ever been with."

Roch'mellon gave another wry snort and Calion laughed dryly in response. "You are correct as usual. She is a female I wish to be with longer. And therein lies the problem."

He swung himself up and with a gentle press of his knees, he sent the horse plunging forward. They raced through the trees to a hunting area near a large river where the animals came to drink.

Sending Roch'mellon off to feed, Calion knelt near the river. He offered a swift prayer of thanks and sent a mind-call out to those who might be prey. As he waited for his dinner to arrive, he grimaced as the pain in his shoulder reminded him of his arrow wound. He rotated it slowly, knowing he would need to take care of it soon, before it sickened. When he felt the stinging above his wrist again, he pushed up his tunic sleeve and stared at the angry burn, wondering where it came from.

Suddenly he frowned.

The burn wasn't a burn at all, but a scar. An old scar. He trailed a finger over it, flinching as he did. It was inflamed and swollen. The scar had been with him since infancy, before then, if you believed the midwife. Supposedly, he'd been born with it. But it never gave him trouble before. Just another odd happening that had occurred since Talia appeared in his world.

A movement to his right caught his attention and he turned to see two long-eared *vardors*, half hopping, half dragging themselves to him. He rose and crossed to them, sensing the injuries that already pushed them near death. He petted them, thanking them for the gift of their lives. Quickly and painlessly, he broke their necks.

As he dressed and cleaned the *vardors*, he considered what to do with Talia. It was the first time he'd been clear of her disturbing presence and could think about what happened.

His first instinct was to take her to the myst and send her back to the human world where she belonged. No human should see the faerie world. He remembered the things she could do, as well as how she made him feel, and he didn't want to send her away. His body rebelled at the thought. But they didn't have a future together. It was best for both of them to stop things from going any further.

Then the orcan prophecy came to his mind and he frowned. If he sent her back to her world, would that keep them from taking her again? The thought of her in the hands of Udaogong and his sons made Calion's protective instincts rush to the fore. For the first time in his life, he wanted to guard and defend a female. It unsettled him all over again.

He went to the river to wash his hands of blood and viscera and called to Roch'mellon. Suddenly he needed to be with Talia.

For a long time, Talia stayed where he left her. Closing her eyes, she thought of how he made her feel. One minute she was furious with him and the next, she wanted to eat him up like a chocolate ice cream cone. She felt safe with him, even though he infuriated her half the time. Just something about being in his presence made her feel things she hadn't before. And when he touched her, she knew in her heart she wouldn't have prevented him from doing whatever he wanted with her.

He was the one who'd been strong enough to stop. She'd

been a puddle of desire when the horse had neighed. When he pushed away from her, everything in her screamed to pull him back and finish what they started, but pride came to the rescue. It would be hard enough to forget him when she went home, let alone how she would feel if he made love to her.

Oh please. I'll never be able to forget him. She snorted and then turned and stared at herself in the mirror. Groaning at what she saw, she examined the bruised and dirty face that looked back at her. No wonder he stopped.

"I wish I could take a bath," she murmured. She rested her forehead against the cold glass of the mirror. "A hot one with lots of bubbles and perfume. I feel so dirty."

The words had barely left her mouth when the sweet scent of flowers tickled her nostrils. Turning, she stared in astonishment. Where the table had been now stood a huge bathtub filled to the brim with fragrant, soapy bubbles. A fluffy bath towel lay on the lower bunk for her to use afterwards.

"Where did you come from?" she wondered aloud. Grinning, Talia realized she wasn't as shocked as she should be. She must be getting used to the elven magic around her.

Pulling off her torn and stained nightgown, she left it lying where it fell. She never wanted to see it again. Sliding carefully into the tub, she couldn't help moaning in pleasure. "This feels wonderful. Thank you, *Malesia* tree."

It took her three scrubbings before she felt clean again. The magic water never got dirty and never went cold, so she knew she could stay and soak forever. She rested her head back against the rim and with a deep sigh, fell asleep.

Calion found her that way, lying back in a tub, her face peaceful. He stopped dead in the doorway, staring as his gaze swept hungrily over her. She was so beautiful, by far the loveliest thing he'd ever seen. His body stirred and he found himself envying the bubbles that clung to her breasts.

Pulling the door shut quietly, he went over to the tub. He could just make out the shape of her body under the water. He stifled the urge to climb in with her and contented himself with running a curious finger down her cheek.

Slowly, her eyes opened. She blinked a couple of times and then smiled sleepily at him. "Hi."

He cleared his throat of the lump that formed there. Her sexy smile was free of fear for the first time. She looked at him like he was the only male in her world. An elf would give much to have his lady look at him that way.

"Enjoying yourself?" he asked, struggling with his thoughts. He smiled, amused, as she finally woke up. She gasped and crossed her arms in front of her chest. The momentum almost sent her head under the water and she struggled to sit up without showing him her breasts.

"I'm sorry," she gasped as she spit water out of her mouth. "I didn't hear you come in."

Calion didn't speak. Again, she had done it without even understanding. "Talia, where did you get the tub?"

She swallowed. "I just wished for it and it came." Her eyes filled when she saw the same look of frustration appear on his handsome face. "I'm sorry. I did something wrong again, didn't I?"

He shook his head in weary acceptance. She couldn't help doing what she did. He touched her cheek again. "No, *Tia maer*... I am beginning to see there is much about you I do not understand. Again, you called the magick."

"I just wished."

"Perhaps for you, that is all it takes." He grinned. "You could have asked for a bathing chamber. Then, I would not have been able to walk in on you."

Her brow furrowed as she tried to understand. "I could have called a whole other room?"

"Watch."

Talia saw Calion close his eyes and concentrate. A moment later a door appeared on the wall next to the mirror. He opened it and she saw another tub, steam rising from it."

"I will bathe also," he said, beginning to unlace his tunic. "When I am done, I will cook our dinner. Afterwards, I will need you to look at the arrow wound. It pains me."

She wanted to jump up and look right now, but her embarrassment at being naked made her slide back under the water. "All right," she murmured quietly.

His gaze caressed her face one more time before he entered the other chamber and shut the door.

As fast as she could manage, she climbed out of the tub

and wrapped herself in the soft towel. As she dried her long hair, she heard him call her from the other room.

"What?" she shouted back.

Calion realized she wasn't going to come anywhere near him while he was bathing. Her modesty amused and charmed him. To melt in his arms as she did and then be embarrassed with him later...he shook his head in wonderment.

"I have asked for clothes for you," he called. "I did not think you wanted to wear the gown any longer."

Talia stared at the closed door. Her emotions were so jumbled, his thoughtfulness made her want to weep. "Thank you," she managed. Sitting on the bunk, she wished the tub away. She still jumped when it vanished and the table and chairs reappeared in its place.

A beautiful green gown lay over one of the chairs. The dress had an embroidered square neckline and a high waistline which flowed into a long, elegant skirt. The sleeves were of pale green silk. A green ribbon for her hair and a pair of emerald slippers finished the outfit.

She finished drying her hair and after finger combing it the best she could, she tied it back in the green ribbon. She tried the slippers, but her feet were too sore to wear them.

Dropping the towel, she slipped quickly into the dress. It fit as if made for her, the soft fabric hugging her body. The neckline came low, showing a generous amount of cleavage, but after no amount of tugging would make it higher, Talia gave up. She struggled with the back fastenings, her fingers unaccustomed to elven fashions.

Strong hands pushed hers aside and she went still as he brushed his fingers across her shoulders and moving gently down her back, closed the fastenings of her dress. Her pulse quickened and she thanked him breathlessly as he turned her to him.

The impact of her beauty staggered him. The green dress matched her eyes perfectly, just as he'd asked. She looked fresh and young and other than the bruise at the corner of her eye, she looked as if she had never been kidnapped or fought for her life.

His eyes traveled downward and widened at the nearly naked breasts which pushed upward out of the plunging neckline. "That is quite a dress."

"Is it okay?" She tried to tug on the bodice again, to no avail. "This seems so low. It's not what I normally wear. I'm a T-shirt and jeans sort of girl."

He had no idea what those things were and honestly didn't care. He was more interested in what he saw in front of him. "It is fine. I asked for a female's dress. Since the tree knows me, it gave me one for..." He hesitated, realizing too late because the *Malesia* tree knew him, it knew the only woman that would stay with him in this way would be his *torear*, or mistress. But he couldn't very well tell her that.

"For what?"

"My sister," he finished, squirming a little.

Talia frowned at that but quit worrying about her dress. She lifted her face and found herself looking at Calion's chest. His presence already warmed her body, but when she really looked at him, her mouth went dry.

"Oh wow," she whispered, not even knowing she spoke aloud.

He'd left his tunic off and was naked from the waist up. His stomach was flat, with hard muscle and not an ounce of spare flesh. The only hair on his body was a thin black line tracing its way from his navel to below the line of his pants.

Heat began to pool between her legs and she hurriedly moved her gaze from that area of his body. His trim waist made way to a muscular chest with broad shoulders. His arms, Talia could see, rippled with muscle. Now she knew how he'd pulled them to safety. He was the strongest man she'd ever seen.

Calion groaned. Didn't she know how he would react if she looked at him that way? She stared at him like a *tar* who'd stumbled into a dish of fine cream. He held himself fiercely in check, his body aching already, hoping she wouldn't touch him, yet praying that she would. She licked her lips and his jaw begin to tic in the effort of holding back. She was driving him mad.

Finally, she raised her eyes to his, obviously flustered. "I...I should clean and bind...the wound. While you...ummm...have your shirt off."

She looked away, and he sat, carefully adjusting his ever-present erection. He tried to control himself enough to speak. "The bath cleaned it. There are medicine and bandages in my pouch." He watched as she got the supplies and sitting next to him, gently began to smooth the cream on the wound. It was torture.

"You have good hands," he said hoarsely. He groaned when he realized he had a perfect view of her beautiful breasts.

Talia thought she'd hurt him. "I'm so sorry," she apologized. She started to move away, but he grabbed her hand.

"No, I am fine. Please finish."

She watched him with wary eyes as she carefully wrapped Calion's upper arm. He was acting very strange, all tense and jumpy. When she was done, without thinking, she pressed her lips against the bandage.

"There," she said brightly. "In my world a kiss will make it all better."

Calion hissed at the feel of her lips against his body. Any more of this and he would have her on the table, her breasts spilling out of her bodice and her skirts up over her head.

He got up quickly, and going to the other room, grabbed a black tunic and put it on. The effort made his wound sing, but he stubbornly ignored it. When he came back into the main area, the door and the bathing chamber disappeared.

"Relax," he growled, not meeting her eyes. "Dinner will be ready soon."

Talia stepped back, flinching at the pain in her feet. They'd stiffened as she cared for Calion's wound. "Can I do anything?"

"*No.*"

She sat at the table and watched him. He moved with no hesitation. He knew what to do in a kitchen, but she could see his anger. Once, he turned and caught her staring at him, and he glowered at her before turning back to his chores. Not wanting to make him angrier, she rose and made her way painfully to the window.

It was nighttime and there was a full moon out. She could see a horse she thought must be Calion's grazing at the far end of the meadow. The view was as beautiful by night as it was by day. Stars filled the sky, but she saw they were different than the stars back home.

She sighed deeply, thinking of his anger. Maybe things weren't so different. No matter where she wound up, people got mad at her. She fought back the tears of loneliness that suddenly formed.

Calion heard the sigh and looked over at her. She stood by the window staring outside. The way she held herself let him know she was upset. He finished seasoning the *vardors*, knowing it was his temper that bothered her, but he couldn't seem to help it around her. She must know what she did to him.

He set the pan on a magical flame that didn't burn, but cooked more quickly than a normal fire and wiped his hands.

"What do you see?" he asked quietly, in hopes of calming her. It took a moment for her to answer him.

"There are so many stars. I'd forgotten how beautiful they are. In the city, the light blocks them out."

"I thought you lived in the house by the forest."

"I lived in the city while I was going to school. I was visiting when the orcs took me. My parents live there. I hadn't been there in almost two years."

Calion frowned as he cleaned vegetables. "You had not been home in two years?

Talia heard the faint disapproval in his tone. It sent a single tear trickling down her cheek. "No, my parents and you have a lot in common."

"Indeed?" The disbelief and arrogance were easy to hear. It almost made her want to smile.

"Not in the regular ways. I mean you are a prince and all."

"Of course."

The arrogance came through even stronger, and this time she did smile. "It's just they're mad at me all the time, like you are. I can't seem to do anything right in either of our worlds."

He jerked his head up from his preparations and really looked at her. She was serious. He watched as a second tear followed an already wet path down her cheek, just before she turned away from him. He felt something twist hard in his gut.

Putting the knife down slowly, he walked over to her. "Explain yourself," he commanded as gently as he could.

Talia gave a start as she turned and saw him close behind her. "I'm going to put a bell on you. How do you walk so silently?"

Calion just raised an elegant black brow. "I *am* an elf." He reached out and took a tear from her cheek, rubbing it between his fingers. "Now explain."

"Just what I said." She turned back around. It was easier not to look at him. "My parents and I never got along. They wanted me to be something I wasn't. When I refused, it didn't go over well."

"I do not understand you."

"Have you ever felt like you just didn't belong? Like no matter what you did or where you were, it was off somehow?"

She glanced at him. He stared at her with a look of confusion on his handsome face. She turned back to the window. "No, I suppose you haven't. You probably know exactly what you're doing."

"I am heir to the throne of my kingdom. My destiny was set at my birth."

"How wonderful for you," Talia said without a trace of sarcasm in her voice. She meant every word. "I don't know where my destiny is."

She laid her forehead against the pane of glass, enjoying the coolness. Her voice throbbed with feeling. "I have searched as long as I can remember for my place in my world."

Calion felt his throat tighten. "And this makes you cry."

"I don't know if I can make someone like you understand." More tears formed and joined the others. "When the orcs took me I was terrified. It was right out of a nightmare. And then you came and saved me. A tall, handsome stranger, who just happened to be a figure out of a storybook. I don't know how to explain how you made me feel. You didn't even know me, yet you took an arrow to rescue me. Me." Talia closed her eyes for a moment before turning back to him.

She looked up at him. "Then we hid in the forest, and danger was all around us. Even though I was terrified, I was...happy."

He stepped even closer to her and gently took her face in his big hands, sweeping the tears away with his thumbs. "I am sorry, *Tia maer*... I still do not understand you."

She reached up and wrapped her fingers around his wrists. "Even though I'd been kidnapped and beaten, and was running for my life, for the first time, I felt right. I thought maybe I'd never been able to find a place in my world because...because maybe, I belonged in this one."

Her words swept through Calion like a wildfire. His hands tightened around her face and his heart raced, but she didn't notice. She squeezed his wrists and then pulling away, turned back to the window.

He dropped his hands, his mind in a whirl. He stared at the back of her fragrant neck where the ribbon was tied in a bow around her long hair.

"I know now it's silly to think like that." She sniffled a little. "I'm as much of an oddity here as I am in my world. I do nothing but make you angry."

Calion could only stand for a few moments as he digested her words. She didn't know why he was angry at her? Could she truly be so naive? He thought about what she'd said and what she hadn't. If she felt like an outcast, perhaps her relationships were few. How lonely it could be for a child who didn't know where she belonged. What kind of life did she have? His heart ached for the child *and* for the adult.

Talia sighed when his arms wrapped around her. He pulled her back against him, his chin resting on the top of her head. It gave her a tender, protected feeling.

"Can you do the things in your world you do in mine? Can you sense magick and make things appear?"

"No. I...I've just always felt like a square peg in a round hole. I don't fit."

He frowned. So she wasn't a true magician. That answered that question. He gave her a little squeeze. "I am not angry about your skills here. I am confused, frustrated and worried about what is happening, but I am not angry with you, even if I seem to be."

She gave an unladylike snort. "You sure act angry to me."

"How do I say this?" he wondered out loud. Shaking his head, he turned her so they faced each other. He traced her cheek with his fingers, ending up at the curve of her neck where he could see the beat of her heart as it raced beneath his touch. When his eyes finally met hers, she gasped at the heat she saw there.

"I desire you," he said quietly yet in a way that had her knees weakening. "I cannot breathe. I cannot think. I cannot move without wanting you. Even though we have just met. It matters not you are no elf, even though it should. My body wants you anyway. No matter what I tell myself, I want to kiss you, to touch you, to mate with you in every way possible I know."

He let her go and stalked back to where the food simmered, grasping the counter so hard his knuckles whitened. "But my kind is taught from birth the mating between humans and elves is forbidden. You have been our enemies for millennia."

He stared unseeingly at the gently bubbling pot. "Wanting you goes against everything that makes me who I am. I betray my land, my people and my throne just by my desire for you." He turned around, his face fierce. "Now do you understand my anger? It is not against you. It is against myself."

Talia was struck dumb by the intensity of the feelings facing her. To have such strong emotions pointed her way... She knew she attracted him, she wasn't stupid. But the heat that showed in his eyes now, that was something more. Something that made them glow with passion. She took a step back in instinctive defense.

"I frighten you," Calion said, his voice filled with astonishment. "You...who has so much power over me."

"It's hard for me to believe you." She blinked against tears as she tried to put her own feelings into words. "It doesn't make any sense. I'm just me. While you're gorgeous and brave, and a prince, for God sakes."

His laugh was full of self-mockery. "I thank you for the compliments, but none of those attributes will make wanting you disappear." He whirled away. "You wanted to know why I act as I do. You have your answer."

Talia took a step closer to him. While she didn't understand the fight, she did understand the importance. Thinking of how he made her feel, her pride died without a second thought. She took another step closer. "You know I wouldn't stop you," she whispered softly.

He closed his eyes as her hushed words shot through him. Jagged need cut through him once again. Ruthlessly, he battled it down. He knew she thought she understood, but she didn't, she couldn't. It was impossible.

He waited until he could speak. "I thank you, my lady, for your offer, but I must decline."

She sucked in her breath at his cool words. He sounded as if he were declining coffee instead of the offer of her body. It hurt more than she thought possible. Was it just sex with a human that bothered him, or was it something about her personally? Bowing her head, she turned back to the window in silence. She didn't know what else to say.

Calion almost went to her. He knew how cold his words sounded, but his inner turmoil was so great, they were all he could manage.

He finished preparing the meal in silence. After a few minutes, he placed the steaming *vardor* on the table, along with some cut-up root vegetables and fresh water. He wiped his hands off and pulled out one of the chairs. "Talia, the food is ready."

She turned, and he saw her face was a blank, as if she'd taken the time at the window to gain back her precious self-control. As she hobbled to the table he frowned. "What is wrong with you?"

Talia blinked at the loaded question, before seeing he was looking at how she was walking. "My feet are a little sore."

"*Shia si kydaer*!" he swore. "Sit down. Why did you not tell me?" He helped her into a chair and she wondered at how quickly his coldness could turn to concern.

"I'll be fine, Calion. They just need to rest."

Muttering in his own tongue impatiently, he grabbed the medicine pouch she'd used earlier. He picked up one of her feet, and when he saw the damage, he gave her a glare that should have toasted the tips of her hair. When she opened her mouth, he stopped her.

"Not a word. There is no reason for you to walk around in pain when this ointment will cure you." He covered both her feet in the medicine and then bandaged them as well, as impersonal as a doctor. "You will be well by morning."

"Thank you," she murmured. "I keep forgetting I'm not in Kansas anymore. You didn't pick that stuff up at a corner drugstore."

He chuckled reluctantly. "I know nothing of this Kansas, but I am sorry as well. I forgot your feet. You do not know about our medicines here...I do."

They smiled carefully at each other, fully recognizing a truce was being offered. Talia pointed at the *vardors* cooling on the table.

"Those look very tasty. Can we eat now? I'm starved."

They spent the rest of the evening talking together. Talia

told Calion about school and her travels, while he filled her in on elven history and some of the latest battles. Neither spoke much about their families, although he did tell her he was the oldest of three. He had a younger brother and sister. His sister, Eámanë, lived in the palace, and his brother traveled the faerie world.

Talia wanted to know everything about him. She learned his father was King Ërestor, and Calion had been heading home when he'd discovered the orcs had taken her. He told her he constantly traveled his kingdom, not content to rule only from the palace.

She yawned. "I think you'll be a good king. You seem to care about your people."

Calion watched her eyelids get lower and lower. He'd enjoyed the time with her so much, he didn't want to stop, but… He chuckled inwardly. If she slid down any further in her seat, he'd be picking her out of the plate.

Standing, he lifted her gently into his arms. "It is time for you to rest before you fall out of your chair." He carried her over and concentrated on the wall, and a door appeared again. Opening it, he set her inside. "I thought you might need this. I will clean up out here."

She blushed when she saw she was in an elvish bathroom. "Thanks," she murmured as he closed the door. Once in private, she took care of necessary business and then washed her face. When she opened the door she saw the room was clear of all the debris from their meal.

"That was fast," she commented as she looked around the room.

Calion grinned, and picking her up, he carried her the short distance to the bottom bunk. "One of the nicest things about *Malesia* trees is they clean up after everyone."

"Just think of what people would say back home about that. Housewives would go nuts." She smiled at the thought.

His amusement disappeared. That was one of the reasons the elven people feared the humans. Would they truly want to steal the magick for themselves? He ignored Talia's statement. "I have left a sleeping garment for you to wear. You may change while I take care of my nightly ablutions."

She studied him. He'd left her again. She reached out and sadly smoothed the fine silk with gentle fingers. "Thank you."

He vanished through the door, and Talia wasted no time in changing out of her gown. The fastenings still gave her trouble, but she wouldn't put him through having to undo them for her. Not after making it clear how he felt. She laid the gown on the end of the bunk and made herself comfortable.

She thought about her circumstances. Had it really only been one full day and a night since she'd been taken? A part of her felt like she'd been in the faerie world forever. She wondered if her parents even missed her yet. Would he take her home tomorrow?

Talia looked up as he came in. He'd removed his tunic and boots to sleep. His masculine beauty made her want to run her hands all over his chest, but remembering his earlier rejection, she just closed her eyes instead.

"Are you sleeping?" he whispered.

"No, not yet," she answered just as softly. She felt him leap up on the bunk above her.

"Lights!" he called. Immediately the room went pitch black.

Talia could sense it even behind her eyelids. Her eyes flew open. "I can't see anything."

"Hush, *Tia maer*... I will give you a light."

The soft glow of a candle filled the room. She saw it sitting on the table.

"Is that better?"

"Isn't that dangerous?" she asked. "You know...a lit candle inside a wooden tree."

"It is a magick light," he answered patiently. "It is not a real candle."

She sighed as her eyes began to close. "That's good then. I wouldn't want anything to hurt this lovely tree." Her breathing evened out, and soon she fell asleep.

Only Talia in her dreams heard the pleased humming of the *Malesia* tree as it pondered the human's words.

Chapter Four

Calion awoke to the sound of Talia's screams. Grabbing his sword, he leapt from the bunk, searching for danger. It took a moment before reality won out over sleep, and he realized he was still in the *Malesia* tree, and no one could attack them here.

Behind him, he heard her scream again, and whirling, he saw she was thrashing around on her bunk, caught in a nightmare. Clenching his jaw, he set the sword back up on his bunk and knowing he probably shouldn't, he slid in beside her. He couldn't let her continue to dream in fear.

Taking her in his arms, he spoke quietly, avoiding her flailing arms and legs. "Shhh...*Tia maer...* You are safe. It is only a nightmare. Talia...wake up now. No one harms you. I am here. Shhh..." Gradually, she quieted and he stroked the tousled hair from her face. "We are alone in the *Malesia* tree. Nothing can get to you."

Talia slowly opened her eyes and as reality hit, she buried her face in his naked chest, wrapping her arms tight around him. She started to shake violently. "I'm sorry." A sob tore from her throat. "It was happening all over again."

He held her while she cried, her copious tears wetting his shoulder. He rocked her back and forth in a soothing motion. "You are safe, *Tia maer...* I have you now."

She cried for a long while, all the emotion she'd experienced in the last two days, overwhelming her at last. Gradually, her tears abated.

"Can you tell me of your dream?" he asked. "It may help."

Shuddering, she tightened her hold on him, glad he was there. She needed to be held. "I was back in that horrible place.

It was dark and my hands were tied again." She felt his hands move soothingly up and down her back. "The orcan king came to me and he—" She swallowed heavily. Just the thought of the nightmare made her gorge rise.

"Shhh... Remember you are safe and here with me. What did he do, Talia?"

"He touched me," she burst out, her tears flowing again. "He touched me, and this time you weren't there to stop him."

Calion pulled her against him. He muttered soothing words as she wept. He cradled her, so she'd know he wouldn't let anything hurt her. "It was a dream, *Tia maer*... Just a dream. I did come for you. You are in my arms now. They cannot hurt you anymore." He kissed the top of her head and then her brow, and soon felt her tears lessen. As he stroked her arms gently, she began to relax against him. He brushed his mouth over her fragrant hair and her forehead again.

Unable to stop himself, he continued, his lips erasing the tears from the corners of her eyes and down her nose. He took her face in his hands, and kissed slowly over her eyelids, her soft cheeks, feeling her shudder in his arms until he couldn't fight himself any longer and captured her mouth with his own.

Oh, she wanted this. This joining of lips, the feel of his body sliding against hers. In the quiet of the night it felt so completely right. He was so gentle, so tender. His hands moved over her, touching...cherishing. Talia's open and seeking heart overflowed. Something moved within her, accepting...knowing.

She loved.

She'd loved him from the beginning, from the first moment his startling eyes looked into hers. She had been waiting for him all this time. It didn't bother her love came so quickly. She believed in love at first sight. And now she'd found it. After so many years of loneliness, she had found him at last.

It was a heady feeling and she lavishly gave him everything. She melted against him, and her surrender was like setting a flint to dry tinder.

Calion groaned, knowing he crossed an invisible line when he took her lips like a starving man. His tongue plunged into her mouth again and again, before he retreated, to nibble on her swollen lips. Muttering passionate words in his own tongue, he kissed down her smooth neck and then back up again. He nipped at her earlobe, causing her to cry out in surprise, but he gentled her with his lips, tracing the shell of her ear with his tongue, making her moan with pleasure. His hands were everywhere. He couldn't get enough of touching her.

He continued his assault on her senses, wanting to bring her to the same agony of need he himself was in. His people were sensual lovers, and he'd enough experience to know what he was feeling now surpassed anything he felt before.

It scared him, but the urgency in his body to make her his blinded him to everything else. He went back to her mouth, wanting the taste again, already addicted to the sweetness he found inside. Groaning, he moved over her, pressing his hard body against hers.

Talia floated in a world of sensation. Her body sang in arousal with every move he made. The world spun away, her whole being caught up in the touch of his heavenly mouth. She wanted to pull him to her, but her arms were useless and heavy with passion.

She instinctively responded to his demand, spreading her legs so his erection could fit between her thighs. The feel of him throbbing against her sent a pool of heat coiling in her loins. Unconsciously, she arched her back, pushing against him.

The movement tore at his barely held control. His body reacted for him, grinding his cock against her mound in an agony of need. Lifting off her, he dragged the sleeping gown from her body, his eyes feasting on the beautiful flesh he could see in the flickering candlelight.

She had high rounded breasts, with nipples the color of ripe peaches. They were drawn and pointed with arousal, and he bent and took one in his mouth, luxuriating in the feel of her. She cried out his name, pulling his head against her. He laved the bud, making it harder and more pointed as he sucked. She trembled beneath him as he kissed and nibbled. Moving to the other breast, he gave it the same loving attention, and soon she writhed beneath him, her body lost to the passion he stirred in her.

Calion too was lost, his body aching, his cock throbbing. His control slipped even further when she pulled his head back to her, joining him in a deep, searching kiss. Their tongues danced frantically, each seeking out the place that would bring most pleasure.

Talia wanted to stroke him like she'd thought of doing

earlier, but when she ran a trembling hand over his rock-hard chest and touched one of the flat male nipples, he came up off the bed. She watched, her mouth dry, as he bicycled his legs to get his breeches off. It was too dark to see anything, but his intense face showed his eyes beginning to glow in the flickering light. He was back on her in a flash, his hand taking hers before she could caress him again.

"No," he growled, his voice rough with desire.

She watched him as he fought for control. Wanting only more of what she was feeling, she began to kiss him wherever she could reach. She covered his face and shoulders with wet, passionate kisses. She heard him groan his need, as he lay back down on her, his knees edging her soft thighs apart.

There was nothing between them now as she felt him pulse against her. He dominated her with his size and strength, yet she felt no fear. She wanted it...wanted him.

Reaching down between their bodies, he stroked her gently. He ran his callused hand over her breasts and down her body, making her shiver with needs she barely understood. Taking her mouth again in a hard ravaging kiss, he carefully brought his hand down her hips and into the soft curls at the apex of her thighs. As his fingers made contact with her moist nether lips for the first time, Talia moaned into his mouth.

She felt him struggle for control, going still as he panted against her. Then, moving into her soft folds, he rubbed in circular motions as he parroted the action with his bulging shaft against her thigh. Going deeper, he discovered the small nubbin swollen from desire. Gently, he plucked at it, making her cry out in longing. She felt the coil in her loins, tightening higher and higher. Her body wasn't hers; it belonged to him, just as her heart did.

Abruptly, she couldn't stand it anymore, and reaching down she grasped him where he throbbed against her. Calion reacted as if he'd been struck. He jumped and grabbed her hand, growling her name as he felt her fingers move against him.

"Please," was all she could manage. "I want you."

His control snapped. The mating hunger blazed out of control, and he could only pray he wouldn't hurt her. Forcing her legs apart, he settled himself between them, groaning out loud as he felt the moist heat of her press against the head of his cock. He pushed and felt the head slip just inside.

The feeling was so exquisite he paused to relish it, fighting not to bury himself in her in just one thrust. He wanted this to last. She was his. He would be breaking *sardai* by lying with her, but she would be his. His body would allow nothing else.

Talia's eyes were closed tight as she felt him push just inside her body. Even that little bit stretched her. Could she do this? He felt so big, so thick and so alive. He moved again and her eyes flew open. His face was close to hers, his features drawn with the needs of his body. She moaned in delight at all the sensation. Calion's eyes opened, and she gasped in wonderment.

"Beautiful," she whispered in awe, her hands going up to frame his face. "Your eyes, Calion... Your eyes are on fire."

Calion froze at her words, the heat in his loins congealing into cold shock. All his doubts returned in an icy rush. He stared down at her and saw to his horror, the flames of his mating fire reflected in her eyes. Everything in him fought the revelation. He was elf, she was human. There could be no mating fire between them. It was impossible. With a roar of disbelief and denial, he pushed away from her in violent self-loathing.

Kneeling at the end of the bunk, Calion pressed his hands against his eyes. What had happened? What had he done? He felt a little sick at the knowledge he had almost shared mating fire with a human, even unknowingly. It was too significant an act to treat lightly.

When two elves were attracted enough to mate, that was only the first step. He had been with many females. All he'd enjoyed, many for long relationships, but none made him burn with the fire that signaled his readiness to do more than mate. When mating fire happened between a male and female, it was a sweet possibility. It meant you might have found something very, very special. If you shared mating fire, you may have discovered the one thing elves spent their lives looking for.

Mylari...soulmate.

Talia lay where he'd left her. After a moment, her mind spinning, her body still aching from Calion's aborted possession, she pulled herself into a sitting position, drawing her legs up instinctively for protection. She opened her eyes and watched him as he sat on the end of her bed. His face was furiously angry, his body language defensive. What had happened? All she'd done was admire his eyes.

He reluctantly turned to her. Staring at him from where she sat huddled against the wall, she watched in confusion as he reached to the floor, picking up her sleeping garment and tossing it to her. "Put this on."

She ignored the command, but took the gown and held it to her breasts. She stayed quiet as she watched him pull his breeches back on, his hard buttocks and thighs making her ache again for his touch.

Calion knew she'd barely moved, hadn't spoken a word. His guilt at hurting her made him surly. "Are you all right?"

She jumped at his harsh words. "No," she whispered brokenly. "I'm not. How can you even ask such a question?"

"*Thes*!" Calion swore, making her jump again. He got off the bed and paced over to the window. "I am sorry."

"What happened?" she asked softly, her knuckles white on her gown. "What did I do this time?"

Calion groaned. "It is not your fault." He stared out the darkened window, his jaw clenched. "I started it. I could not finish it."

"Because I told you about the flames I saw."

Calion's lips tightened. She was too perceptive. He looked at her and when their gazes met, he drew in his breath. While he expected pain, he hadn't been prepared for the shattered look that filled her green eyes. She'd done nothing but give herself to him. Remembering her responses to him made his mouth water, and he fought the lingering ache that filled him. She deserved to know the truth.

"My need for you outweighed my common sense," he said roughly, looking back out the window. "I would have taken you, forbidden or not, used your body for my release and given you pleasure in doing so. I had made that choice. But the flames meant something more. A thing important to all elves. Something I can never do with a human female. I am sorry I hurt you. I reacted...badly."

Talia listened incredulously. In a couple of short sentences he reduced making love with her to a basic animal act. She felt sullied, and a rush of anger went through her, driving out some of the hurt.

"So all this was just a way to get your rocks off? No

emotions involved. No harm, no foul?" Her voice thickened, and the pain in her eyes now mixed with anger.

Calion turned back to her, saw the emotions she couldn't hide. They moved him in a way he didn't understand, but he couldn't let them sway him. "I cannot give you feelings I do not have."

"You're going to have to do better than that," she said, edging forward, one long leg and creamy hip showing.

His lust spiked again, along with his temper. "Put the gown on! Do not make this any harder than it is."

She tossed her head, tears starting in her eyes. "Me, make it harder? I'm not the one who pulls back at the last second. I guess that's a pattern for you, isn't it?" She turned away and treated him to the sight of her beautifully curved naked back before she slipped the gown over her head. "It's easier to walk away than to deal with how you're feeling."

Knowing she spoke the truth didn't make it any more palatable to hear. "I did you a favor. You just do not know it as yet."

"Oh, please," Talia scoffed, scooting to the edge of the bunk. She swiped at the tears that slipped down her cheeks. "I've heard better rejections before."

"Do not do this to yourself," he growled. Everything in him wanted to go to her and soothe away the pain he'd caused. Even knowing he couldn't have her didn't make the wanting any easier. "Let it go."

"No. Make me understand. You tell me why we can't be together." Her eyes searched his for some kind of truth. "Tell me!"

He slammed his hand against the windowsill. "I do not have to tell you anything."

"Yes, you do." She raised her chin proudly. "You owe me that much!"

Calion whirled and faced her, infuriated with everything, hurting in body and mind. "You want the truth. Fine...here it is." He stepped closer to her so he could look her straight in the eye. "You are a beautiful, interesting female and I lusted after you. But as a fire mate? I do not want you in that way. The thought of making mating fire with you. That it might go even further..." He clenched his fists. "I cannot even stomach the thought."

"I don't—"

"I am an elf. A prince of my world. I cannot have and do not want a human female in my life. I would have mated with you so I could have gotten you out of my system, but I told you we have no future. I meant it."

Talia's face was paper white now, every word a dart against her heart. She didn't know what a fire mate was, but she knew it was something she wasn't.

He went on. "I thought I'd take you to my father so he could investigate this whole matter, but I see now that would be ridiculous. I do not want you here. I will take you home tomorrow and get you out of my realm. It will remove the temptation of doing something foolish, for both of us."

Calion crossed his arms over his chest, glaring at her. "I will take you to a part of the myst that is far away from your parents' house. You will be safe from orc attack there. It is a full day's travel through my domain on horseback."

"Why not just leave me in the forest? Why do you even care?" Talia's tone was low, her words dull.

"You are in my kingdom," Calion said flatly. "I am responsible for you."

"Now you *do* sound like my parents. I'm their responsibility too. They didn't want me either."

There was so much pain in her words, he almost reached for her. She turned away and Calion expected her to climb back in her bunk, but she spun back around and came to him.

"You think you are so honorable, protecting us like this, but you're not." Her chin went up and her eyes flashed as she poked him hard in the chest. "You're nothing but a coward who is afraid to try for something, because he doesn't know what will happen."

Calion went still with shock. "You dare...call me...coward."

"Yes," she nodded, her tone firm. "A coward. But don't worry about it. I promise I won't touch you anymore. Do you think I want to go through that again?" The anger faded from her eyes when she met his, and he once more could see the pain in them.

With a sigh, Talia reached up and ran a gentle finger across his lips.

Calion felt the impact all the way down to his bare feet, and his anger drained away as fast as it had come, leaving a dull, painful ache in its place.

"I'll leave you alone, just as you want. But I think that if we had loved together, it would have been wonderful."

Silently, she turned from him and climbed back in her bunk.

Calion sat in a chair, not trusting himself to go back to the beds. He sat there as the night waned, listening to Talia's muffled sobs, cursing the fact he had elven hearing.

She awoke the next morning to the sound of the outside door being pulled shut. She stretched, feeling every ache left over from yesterday's attack and run through the forest. Lifting her eyelashes just a bit, she looked around the room, pleased to see the slam of the door meant Calion was going out, not coming in.

She climbed out of the bed and going to the mirrored wall, wished for the bathing chamber. When the door appeared, she stepped in and immediately disrobed, climbing into the hot tub the tree provided for her.

Settling back into the warm water, she washed, trying to blank out her mind. She'd spent most of the night with her fist in her mouth to keep Calion from hearing her cry. Being rejected was bad enough, the thought he could hear her as she wept made her cringe. She loved him, and the knowledge that after today she would never see him again was intolerable.

She knew her eyes must be swollen, and the thought of facing him after last night, well, she didn't want to think about it. Talia shivered and felt the water around her become warmer.

"How do you do that?" she murmured. "How do you know what I need?" Opening her eyes, she looked around her. "Are you a tree or something more?"

A light breeze caressed her face, bringing with it the smell of home-baked bread. She smiled, and curious, she stepped out of the tub, drying herself off with another of the warm, fluffy towels.

"He's taking me home today, tree. What do you think of that?" Suddenly the bread smell went burned. Talia stopped drying her hair and looked up swiftly. "You do understand me, don't you?"

She wrapped the towel around her and stood in front of the mirror. "Okay then, tree, I'm going to be walking through the forest all day. That green gown won't work. And it wouldn't hurt to make him suffer a bit. Any ideas?" When the outfit appeared in front of her, she grinned. "I like the way you think."

As she put on her new clothes, she suddenly hesitated. "Wait a minute. Calion told me a *Malesia* tree is designed to give those inside exactly what they ask for, but I didn't ask for this. I asked for an opinion. If you're kind of like a magic computer, how did you do that?"

She finished dressing and then walked over to put her hand against one of the walls. "Can you talk to me?" she whispered, feeling slightly foolish. After all, she *was* talking to a tree and expecting it to answer. "Please, help me to understand you."

Suddenly, her mind was bombarded with pictures, feelings and sounds. Talia pressed her cheek against the tree and just listened, a smile growing on her face as she finally understood something the elves didn't. A *Malesia* tree was sentient.

Calion brushed Roch'mellon far longer than needed. He knew he was putting off going inside, but he couldn't help it. She'd been sleeping like an angel when he'd finally dragged himself out of the chair and checked on her. Breathing in, with jerky little breaths that told him she'd been crying, and his elven eyes could see the faint trail of tears on her face. The sight made him feel even worse.

He'd slept little, spending most of the night trying to figure out what was happening to him. It hadn't helped. He was just as confused as ever and now he was exhausted as well.

Roch'mellon nickered at him, bringing his thoughts back to the present. "Yes, my friend. We take the female home today." He ignored the dull ache the words gave him. "We will take her to the Whispering Falls area of the myst. It should be far enough from where the orcs originally found her that she should be safe."

Roch'mellon snorted, and Calion frowned back at him. "She will be safer in her own world." He put the curry comb back in his pack. "We will both be safer." When Roch'mellon snorted again, he gave him a slap on the rump. "No, I cannot change my mind. It is for the best."

When Roch'mellon just turned and looked at him with large, dark eyes, it reminded Calion of the look Talia had given him the night before, when she'd called him a coward.

"Whose side are you on, anyway?" he groused. He stomped over to the door. "I will go see if she is up yet."

The main room was empty, both beds made, and the chamber door was in the wall so he knew where she was. He busied himself laying out the remainder of the *vardor* from the night before.

"Talia," he called. "Breakfast is ready."

"I'll be right out."

So far, so good, he thought. *At least she is talking to me.* He heard the door open, turned and stood in shock.

She was wearing a tunic, somewhat like his, but green, just a shade lighter than her eyes. It had long flowing bell sleeves and laced up the front. Black breeches snugged her hips and fit her like a second skin. The soft boots she wore were identical to his. Her hair was pulled back in a tight intricate braid, with the green ribbon running through it. "Where did you get that?" he said, when he could make his voice work again. "Females do not wear breeches."

Talia gave a shrug and sat at the table. "This one does. The tree gave it to me." She pulled off a piece of *vardor* and began to chew. "It's a great help. Gave me lots of advice."

"That is impossible."

She sent him a look of pure dislike. "You know, you say that a lot."

He sat opposite her, trying not to stare at the curve of her breast that peeked out between the laces of her tunic. Picking up a *vardor* leg, he bit down, unable to believe he was having this conversation with her. "What I meant is a *Malesia* tree just follows orders."

"I guess you don't know everything, do you?"

"I beg your pardon?"

She giggled. "I love it when you get all disdainful and arrogant. Do you learn that in prince school?"

He felt himself flush. "I do not know what you are talking about."

"Never mind." She waved her hand carelessly. Taking a long drink of water, she smiled to herself. Her new knowledge about the tree made her confidence soar. She knew something he didn't. "When do we leave?"

"When you are ready," he answered. "I am sorry, *Tia maer*... But you will have to change back into the nightgown you were wearing when you got here. The *Malesia* tree will have cleaned and mended it, as it did mine." He gestured to his clothes.

"No," Talia disagreed lightly. "I'll wear this. The tree took the nightgown away."

He shook his head at her. "The tree can only provide supplies and materials while we are inside of it. If you try to wear that outside, it will disappear. You will be naked." He forced the picture of her soft, warm body out of his mind.

"The tree told me I could wear this."

Calion's lips tightened. "You will be bare the moment you leave the tree. Is that what you want?"

"What's the big deal?" Talia narrowed her eyes at him. "It's not like it would bother you. Remember, you don't want me."

"Fine!" Calion pushed his chair back with a screech as he lost his temper. "Do not weep to me when you find I am right."

She lost her smile. "You don't have to worry about that, Calion. I think I've wept enough, don't you?" They stared at each other for a long moment before he turned and stomped outside.

Talia blew out a ragged breath. "You better be right about this," she muttered out loud. The tree hummed its assurance.

A few minutes later, Calion stood in astonished surprise as Talia stepped outside in her new outfit. "I'm waiting," she said smugly as he walked over and rubbed one of her sleeves unbelievingly between his fingers. "For an apology."

"A what?" Shocked to the core, he stared at the tree and then back at Talia. He took her by the arm and led her further away to see if anything happened. When the clothes stayed real, he muttered under his breath and walked back into the tree.

"Is he always like this?" she asked Roch'mellon. She walked over to the horse and gently stroked his mane, introducing herself.

Roch'mellon answered with a snort and an obvious nod, making her laugh.

"Don't tell me you can talk to my horse." Calion glared at Roch'mellon, who tossed his great head. The elf was totally unsettled. Nothing made sense anymore.

"Not yet," she answered. "But someday I'll be able to understand what he says."

Calion relaxed. The thought of his opinionated horse mouthing off to this unpredictable female was frightening. He was discomfited enough. "Can we go?"

"I have to say goodbye." She walked back to the *Malesia* tree with him following. He watched as she laid her hands and then her cheek on the bark of the tree. After a few moments of whispered words, she pressed a kiss to the rough bark and stepped back, her eyes shining with emotion.

Shaken, Calion touched the tree himself. If what she said was true... "You have my gratitude as well." For a moment he swore he could hear humming. The hair stood up on the back of his neck. It was a thoughtful prince that walked back to Roch'mellon.

"Come. I will give you a leg up, and then I will swing up behind you."

Talia looked wide-eyed at him. "Shouldn't I sit behind you? Otherwise, won't I be in the way?"

He looked at her, just as puzzled. "Females always ride in front. For protection."

She thought of sitting between his outspread thighs, her bottom pressing against him, and began to smile.

His thoughts on the same path, Calion changed his mind. "Ahhh, perhaps, your way is for the best." He hurriedly jumped up on Roch'mellon and held out his hand.

"Will you be able to protect me this way?" she asked innocently.

"I will manage." He lifted her easily, and then sent Roch'mellon into an easy gallop. They rode silently for some time, both enjoying the fresh air, before Calion broke the silence.

"Tell me about the *Malesia* tree. What did you learn about it?"

"Well, I learned it has opinions and feelings, and it likes to be asked for advice about things. It also likes to be praised and it definitely appreciates being thanked. And it's got great clothes sense."

"I am not sure about that," he muttered as he digested what he heard. "Are you telling me the *Malesia* tree is...alive?"

"Of course, it's alive." Talia pinched him, making him jump and toss a glare over his shoulder. She glared right back. "It grows and breathes and eats, doesn't it?"

"Yes," he agreed. "But so does a bush and it cannot make a tunic for you."

"True, but a bush doesn't think. It just lives by instinct. A *Malesia* tree is more."

"You believe it is aware?" He felt rather than saw her nod. The motion caused her breasts to rub against his back and he groaned inwardly. This was going to be a long ride.

"I know it is. It spoke to me, Calion. I could see pictures of its life and I could feel what it was feeling. It told me it allowed your people to use it because you have a symbiotic relationship with the tree. It feeds off the magic of your people, so it allows you to use it as sanctuary."

"Why have my people never discovered this?" His elven pride bit at him. How could this human think she knew more than the wisest men in his kingdom?

"You never asked," Talia said simply. "You just assumed. I've noticed it's a very bad habit you have."

They rode in silence for a while longer. The shadows lengthened and Roch'mellon began to throw up little flecks of foam from his exertion. Calion pulled him to a jog to rest him.

"How much longer 'til we get to the myst?" Talia asked as the horse slowed.

"Finally in a hurry to get out of here?"

She didn't answer for so long, he turned to look at her. She stared at him with a look of deep sadness in her expressive eyes. "Don't do that, please."

"Talia?"

"Can we stop for a minute? I need to walk."

"Of course." Calion asked Roch'mellon to stop and then sliding off, helped her down. He sent the horse off to scout ahead. "I did not mean to offend you."

"It's okay. I've been doing my share of sniping at you too." She smiled sadly. "It's just... This is the last day I get to spend here in this beautiful place with you. I don't want to fight."

He reached out and took her hand. "I do not want to fight either, *Tia maer...*"

"I know you've made your decision and I respect it, even

though I don't agree with it. I just don't want to waste any more time angry at you, okay?"

"O...kay." For some reason, relief welled up in him. "I too would like to remember this day with happiness."

"Who knows," Talia said, her voice breaking slightly. "Someday this will be a great bedtime story for my kids."

The picture of her in another man's arms, creating those children, made Calion clench his teeth in rage. He felt as possessive as Roch'mellon did when his favorite mare came into heat. When he answered her, his voice was stiff with suppressed anger. "I wish it could be different."

She squeezed his hand. "I believe you do. I'm going to miss you, you know." Purposely, she tried to lighten the mood. "Even when you get uppity with me."

He raised an inquiring eyebrow. "Uppity?"

She grinned. "You know." She raised her chin and gave a convincing imitation of Calion at his haughtiest. Then she laughed out loud as he unconsciously mirrored her. "Yep, that's exactly what I'm talking about."

Seeing Roch'mellon at the end of the meadow, Talia grinned at Calion again and ran to the black horse, still giggling joyously.

He didn't go after her—his mind and heart were too full. Thinking of her comment about children, he clenched his fists. He wanted to be the one. Not to give her children. No offspring could come of a human/elf union. An impossibility, that.

But, he wanted to mate with her. He already knew what her body smelled, felt and tasted like. It was torture knowing she would leave him without his knowing how it felt to be deep inside her. Sweat broke out on his forehead. She'd been so tight last night. Remembering the pleasure of just the tip of his cock in her had him stallion-hard right now. He wanted to race across the glen and toss her on her back and show her the meaning of pleasure. If only she wasn't a human, then everything could have worked—

Calion stopped dead as a thought hit him. He stared blindly at the two figures romping on the other side of the meadow. How could he have been so stupid? Mating fire only happened when two elves came together physically. Talia wasn't an elf. Only he was. He began to walk again, his heart beating in sudden excitement.

He'd been thinking about this all wrong. He'd been so shocked to see himself with the fire in his eyes he hadn't thought things through clearly. She couldn't be his fire mate, even if he carried the glow in his eyes. She wasn't an elf! The glow must have come from something else. Mating with her would be safe after all! Against the *sardai*...but safe nonetheless.

He wanted to shout his good news to the sky. It didn't bother him anymore that he would be breaking *sardai*. He wanted her badly enough to justify that in a dozen ways. And since she would be leaving, no one would ever know about it. Now the only thing that could have kept them apart was if she was a maiden, and after last night, he knew for sure she wasn't. No maiden would have responded to him the way she had.

Looking at Roch'mellon and Talia playing tag, he frowned. Would it be too late for him? He'd said some pretty strong words to her last night. The fact he'd been trying to convince himself as well as her was no excuse. He'd seen her face. He'd heard her tears. He'd hurt her.

Calion rubbed his hands over his face. As the prince of this land, he could lift his finger and have any number of females in his bed. But the one he really wanted might still be out of his reach.

Chapter Five

Calion spent the rest of the afternoon trying to figure out a way to explain to Talia what a fool he'd been. With one chance to make up for his mistake, he wasn't sure just how to go about it, but he did try. When Talia and Roch'mellon came back from their play and they'd continued on their journey, he pulled her up in front of him. Even though he was sure he'd be hard as stone by day's end, he wanted her to feel him against her. To know that even after his foolish words of last night, he still wanted her.

He enjoyed every minute of it too. He held her in place with one arm, and if Roch'mellon made a sudden move, he would pull her back against him, his arm touching the underside of her breasts. The feeling of her rubbing against him was as exciting as he knew it would be, plus he had the added pleasure of being able to get glimpses of her soft breasts through the loose laces of her tunic.

He talked to her, telling her stories about himself, remembering her accusations of him not wanting the closeness of emotion. He would show her emotion…lots of it. All night long, if she'd let him.

They'd taken time to cook and eat a *vasodi* he'd shot, when no game could be called. It gave him time to sit close to her and make her laugh when he licked the juices from their fingers. He mind-talked Roch'mellon to take the long way so they would get there just before dusk. His plan was to talk her into going through the myst first thing tomorrow, when it was daylight and safe. That would give him the time he needed to explain everything.

Talia didn't know what to think. When she came back from

playing with Roch'mellon, it was like Calion was a different man. He talked to her, made her laugh, his touch unnerving but precious every time it happened. If he'd been any other guy, she'd think she was being courted. It was exciting and confusing, and she didn't want it to end.

Knowing *she* would never forget their time together, she was thankful he took her suggestion about their last day in such a positive way. Her love for him wanted to spill out. She wanted more than anything to throw her arms around him and beg him to let her stay...for another chance at getting to know each other. But she'd promised she wouldn't bother him and Talia always kept her promises.

Their arrival at the myst happened as Calion planned. It was just before dusk when they trotted into the grassy area by Whispering Falls. He slid off his horse then helped Talia down, holding on to her a little longer than necessary.

"The myst is just to the left of the falls," he said, pointing it out. It was invisible to the naked eye.

"Can you see it?" Talia asked, trying to be brave now that she knew the time was at hand.

"Yes, I can see a shimmer of light where the myst is. When I enter it, I use the light of my sword to protect me and shine my way." He pulled it from its sheath, the blue light spilling out as it again shouted its name.

"It's beautiful." She smiled faintly. "I can hear it say something." She listened carefully. "*Cylys?*"

He smiled ruefully. "It is its name. It means, *Honor*. But Talia...only faerie—"

"—are supposed to hear it. Yeah, sorry." She stood and stared at the invisible wall.

Calion shrugged. "I am getting used to it." After all the things he'd seen her do, hearing his magical sword didn't seem strange at all. "It is getting dark."

Talia swallowed, hard. "I guess I should be going."

He cleared his own throat. "You know, it would probably be safer to take you across tomorrow morning. That way you will come out on the other side when it is daytime. You can find your way around easier."

Hope filled her. Another night with him? She wanted to leap at the chance, but her stomach sank right back down as it remembered Calion's words of last night.

"I do not want you here. I will take you home tomorrow and get you out of my realm. It will remove the temptation of doing something foolish, for both of us."

Her heart broke as she shook her head. "No. I'll manage somehow. It would be best to get it over with."

He frowned. "In the morn, I can go with you and get you some money and clothing. I know your world is different from this one."

She bit her lip to hold back tears. He couldn't know how hard he was making this. "It's okay. I'll be fine."

Calion clenched his fists in frustration. He didn't know what else to say to change her mind. He turned to her and held out his hand. "But tomorrow..." He voice trailed off when he saw the single tear.

"*Tia maer...*" He pulled her to him, ignoring her feeble struggles. "Why do you weep?"

"Damn it, Calion. I'm trying to be brave here. Don't do this to me. I want to keep my promise to you."

He gently took her face in his hands and smiled slowly. Maybe he did have a chance after all. "What promise is that?"

"You're the one who wants to put me out of temptation's reach. I told you I wouldn't fight it."

The warmth of his lips against hers silenced Talia immediately. Passion flared. When he lifted his head, she just stared at him in shock and he smiled again. "What if I have changed my mind?"

Her heart beat faster in her chest. "I don't understand."

"Ahhh...I am a foolish and stupid male, Talia." He wiped the tear from her cheek and she remembered how he'd done the same thing last night.

"It seems I am always drying your tears," he mused as if reading her thoughts. "I cheated us out of our one night together because of my fear. I said things to you that were hurtful and untrue as I tried to convince myself my actions were just."

He pulled her close to him, reveling in the feel of her softness against him. "I am not a male who asks for forgiveness often, but I ask it of you. Please, forgive me for what I said and how I acted. I cannot change what happened, this I know, but I would like to have the chance to make you think of me with more than the pain I saw in your eyes last night."

"What are you asking me?" Talia pushed back and looked deep into Calion's eyes. The hope she felt wanted to burst from her.

Now that the time was here, Calion felt unaccountably nervous. He was unused to such a feeling, having never before begged a woman to stay with him. Pressing gamely on, he winced at the desperation he thought he heard in his voice.

"I am asking you to stay with me tonight. Let me mate with you the way I should have. Let me show you the pleasure I know we can have together. I want you to remember me as someone who gave you that delight, not just as the one who hurt you. Give us this one last night together, please."

Talia felt a rush of emotion so strong, she thought she would faint from it. She began to tremble. The sweetness of his words flowed through her. He wanted her!

"Talia?"

His tone was hesitant and she laughed inwardly. Was he actually afraid she'd say no? After everything that happened, she probably should walk away with her nose in the air. But the memories of how he'd made her feel, the security and pleasure she'd gotten just being held by him—those were stronger than her fears.

If only he knew how she truly felt. It meant nothing she'd only known him for a day. Talia always knew when she fell...she'd fall hard and fast. She was so much in love with him there was only one answer for her. She wanted to be with him for the rest of her life, but since that wasn't possible, she could only do one thing.

"Love me tonight, Calion. Give me those memories I will never forget."

Her breath left her in a great whoosh of air when he pulled her tight against him, wrapping his arms around her almost painfully.

"I swear to you, you will not be sorry," Calion said, his voice filled with relief. He could feel her tremble and exulted that he was the one responsible. *She would be his!* He bent and slanted his mouth over hers, sealing the promise of the night ahead.

When she was shaking in his arms, he ended the kiss. Deliberately, he turned her away from the myst and led her back to where Roch'mellon stood, his dark eyes wise and knowing.

"We will make camp there, by the waterfall. If we are lucky, when we have moonrise the falls will paint rainbows in the night sky. It is very beautiful."

"It sounds like it."

He rushed on. He suddenly felt like a youngling about to have his first female, all sweaty and bumbling. "I will find us something to eat then I have a surprise for you." His body tightened when Talia's smile bloomed.

"Really? I like surprises."

"Good." He jumped on his waiting steed and looked down at her. "If you gather some wood, I will start a fire when I return." At her smiling nod, he trotted away.

Twenty minutes later, Calion loped back into camp, wanting to get a fire started before it got any darker and Talia became frightened. He didn't expect to see a blaze burning merrily.

He swung down from his horse, grabbed the large *vardor* he'd caught and dropped it by the fire. "How did you do this? Do not tell me you used magick."

Talia had rolled several logs into a half square around the campfire and sat poking idly at the burning wood. She grinned up at him. "Not this time. I used a type of human *magick*. I'm an old girl scout." When he just stared at her blankly, she snickered. "I rubbed two sticks together. If you do it right, you can make fire."

"Ahhh, like a flint. How primitive."

"Oh, yeah?" She raised her eyebrows. "How would you do it?

He pointed his finger at the end of the log she was sitting on and said a single word. "*Tho'si...*" A spot on the log burst into flame.

She yelped and shot to her feet, staring at the fire for a minute before turning back to Calion, a disgusted look in her eyes. She flung herself back down on the log. "Showoff."

They spent the evening in idle conversation as they cooked the *vardor* on a spit over the fire. Like last night, they each shared their world with the other, answering questions and telling stories. Always, underneath the banter, was the knowledge of the night to come. They touched, and Calion would often drop a kiss on Talia's upturned mouth. Likewise, she would respond with a light touch on his hard thigh or chest. Need bloomed, desire simmered.

"Are you ready for your surprise?" Calion murmured. He wanted nothing more than to take her in his arms right now, but he wanted to give her this gift first. They'd finished with the clean-up, and Talia had packed away the *vardor* to break the morning fast.

She looked up at his words and smiled. "Oh yes."

He took her by the hand and together they walked towards the falls. "Look up," he instructed as they walked.

She did so. She gasped with awe at the shimmering rainbow of color undulating against the sky and surrounding trees. "Oh, you're right. It is beautiful. Where does it come from?"

"Our wise men say it is the light of the moon refracted through the water of the falls. There is something special in it." He turned to the right and led her up a stone pathway.

"We're going behind the falls?"

"Yes." His voice sounded hollow from the stone around them. Hearing the soft murmuring of the cascade above her, she knew how it came by the name Whispering Falls. Mist touched her skin, but Calion walked steadily on until they were behind the center of the fall of water. There before them was a pool, split in two by a stand of thick brush.

At her gasp, he smiled. "It gets better, *Tia maer...*" He brought her to the side. "Touch it."

She searched his face for clues, but then bent obediently and trailed her hand through the water. "Ohhh," she said in delight. "It's warm."

"I thought you would like it." He was more than pleased with her reaction. "You can bathe yourself over behind the bushes while I clean up here." His gaze heated and moved over her kneeling form. "I knew you would like to tidy up before we rested."

Talia was trapped by sapphire eyes already flickering with gold. She opened her mouth once and then shut it again as her insides melted with longing.

He helped her to her feet then grazed a kiss over her lips. "Call out when you are finished."

The feel of the hot pool was heaven after a full day on horseback. It had been a long time since she'd ridden, and her muscles were twinging a little. As she spread Calion's soap over her body, she felt the tingles of anticipation race over her nerve endings. She'd waited her whole life for this night, for this man.

Her hair coiled around her head in a sloppy knot, Talia used her pants to dry off. It felt wonderful to be clean again. She slipped her tunic back over her head, feeling the cool night air caress her naked body. Picking up the rest of her clothing, she called to Calion.

"You may come out, *Tia maer*... I too, am done."

She picked her way toward him noting he'd again left off his shirt and his breeches were on but unfastened. Calion's damp, long black hair lay in thick strands over his muscular shoulders. He looked like a pirate, standing there in the cave, his hands on his hips. A pirate looking for his treasure.

Calion watched as she came around the corner of the pool, her face flushed with heat. Her long legs were naked under the tunic, its dampened folds clinging to curved flesh. He went hard in an instant.

When she reached him, he took her hand and raised it to his lips. "When I first saw you, I thought you were the loveliest thing I could ever imagine. And now, seeing you like this...I am sure of it."

Without another word, he lifted her in his strong arms and carried her out of the waterfall and back to their camp. The fire burned low, but with enough light so they could see the thick pallet of blankets he'd magicked up for them to lie upon. Laying her gently down, Calion knelt and gazed at her beauty. The pale green tunic stopped at mid thigh, and her long legs gleamed in the firelight. The curves of her breasts showed though the unlaced tunic, and he longed to stretch out his hand and cup one of the perfect globes. Instead, he reached up and undid the topknot of her hair, taking the shimmering strands and spreading them out above her head.

"I have longed to see you like this," he said hoarsely, his hands shaking in need. "I have mated with you a dozen times in my mind."

His words washed over her, stirring her in ways she hadn't anticipated. She expected him to give her body pleasure, but she hadn't known he could seduce her mind. Her throat was too tight to speak. Her body trembled with love and desire. Her heart moved within her. All she could do was reach out to him.

Calion's eyes flared as he moved into her waiting arms. He knew if he went too fast, the fire within him would burn out of control and he would take her too quickly. He wanted this first time between them to last. His mouth touched hers lightly, his lips whisper-soft as he teased and nibbled. He followed its curve, brushing over it again and again until Talia moaned and arched up against him. The moan tore at Calion's self- control as he kissed her. With the tip of his tongue he traced the fullness of her bottom lip, dipping inside to tease. When Talia began to move her head restlessly, trying to capture his tormenting mouth, Calion moved to the upper lip, nibbling and licking it.

He was making her crazy. She wanted him to kiss her like he'd done last night, deeply, his mouth pressed hard against hers, but he wouldn't. His seducing tongue and teeth stripped her of any defense. Every stroke calculated to bring her to a higher level of need. Finally, when she was ready to scream with frustration, Calion took her head in his hands and brought his mouth to hers.

Oh, the sweetness. Could he have lived another moment without the taste of her? He dove back in for another...deeper. Slanting his mouth over hers, he devoured, knowing it would only fan the fire beginning to rage in his loins. His tongue swirled, taking the sweetness he'd tasted, searching for the spice he knew was there. Her hands gripped at him, clenching and unclenching on his arms. He was distracted just once, when he felt the scar on his arm throb and then cool as if a balm had been placed on it. Ignoring it, he dove in deeper, still wanting everything she had to offer.

He moved, trailing his lips down the curve of her neck to the shoulders. Pushing the laces aside with his mouth, he kissed the exposed curves of Talia's breasts. Her soft moans filled his ears as he pulled the tunic off one creamy shoulder to feast on the flesh beneath. She smelled like flowers, but the scent of his soap was on her too. Mine, was his thought. *All mine.*

His hands traced over her body, making her writhe. She was hot to the touch, and when he took both her covered breasts in his hands, she cried out and pushed them against him, her hard nipples poking against the fabric into his palms. Calion groaned in reaction, his cock straining against his breeches. He'd barely touched her and he was ready to explode.

Going with her instincts, Talia ran her hands down his arms. He was hard and strong and she reveled in the knowledge she could bring this powerful man to such a place of need. His hands on her made it hard to think, but she knew she wanted to touch him like she'd been unable to do last night. She put her hands on his chest and smoothed them over the tight skin, marveling in the strength and beauty before her. She ran her palm over his flat nipples, sensing his desire when they contracted and puckered, feeling her own heat flame higher when Calion groaned loudly, his body shaking.

He shot to his feet, keeping his eyes on hers as he finished unfastening his breeches and removed them. She saw him for the first time, his shaft standing tall and proud, huge to her inexperienced eyes. He looked like a pagan god standing in the moonlight. He dropped back down beside her, his jaw clenched with need.

"I swear to you," he growled as he took her hands and held them tightly. "You can touch me all you wish next time, but now...now you must not. I am close to losing control."

A thrill ran through her at his words. Her pulse raced as the heat in his eyes turned into the beginnings of fire. She arched her back so her nipples jutted against his naked chest. "Touch *me* then. I need to feel you touch me."

He kept his eyes on hers as he reached down with one hand and took hold of the tunic she wore. With one mighty tug, he split the garment in two and tossed it aside, leaving her naked to his gaze. Talia gasped as excitement poured through her. She wanted to cover herself, but the look on his face forbade it. Heat pooled between her legs at the flames in his eyes.

Calion let go of her hands, wanting to touch the flesh crying out for his possession. He nibbled down her neck and arms, nipping her earlobes until she shivered like a wraith under his touch. He used his fingers first, then his mouth as he moved his way from Talia's neck, over her breasts and down her stomach. His mouth teased the nipples dark with need, pulling and sucking on them until Talia cried out his name.

Not content to stop there, his mouth continued its sweet

torture while his hand moved down her stomach to the heat between her legs. He gently ran his fingers through her golden curls before tracing down over her soft outer lips. She shivered and shook in his arms, and he knew neither of them would last much longer. Carefully, he used his index finger to press inside her, stroking her, feeling the heat he held in his hand melt as her body's nectar began to flow and prepare the way for him.

Talia's inner flesh screamed. Too much sensation, too much feeling. She felt like she was going to implode. The yearning in her belly turned to molten lava and she didn't know how to stop it. All she could do was twist in Calion's arms until he chose to put out the fire. His mouth came up and ravaged hers as he closed his lids on the flames leaping in his eyes.

His nostrils flared as his elven senses caught the aroma of her heightened arousal, spinning his lust further out of control. He moved boldly over Talia, separating her thighs with his knees, while he used his finger to test the readiness of her body. Slowly, he pushed it deeper.

"Calion...please... Oh my God, Calion."

He growled, his body tightening so hard he wanted to shout with the pain of holding back his desire. He moved his finger in and out of her wet lips, feeling her body jerk against his hand. She cried out, her eyes wild from the pleasure of his touch. Faster and faster he went, until her body bucked against him with mindless need.

Hungry...needing her, he roughly spread her legs further apart and settled between them. Talia called his name when he stopped touching her, but he pressed the head of his cock to her and rubbed it against the insides of her hot, moist lips. She cried out again, this time with pleasure, her body straining against his.

His passion was a wild thing as he pressed his entire body to hers. Taking both of her hips in his hands, he pushed the head of his cock inside her.

Talia's eyes flew open at the sensation. God, it felt so good. He was huge, his shaft pulsating just inside her quim so hard she could feel it all the way to her toes. She felt his heart slamming in his chest. Felt his warm breath against her face. Looking up, she saw what she expected. His eyes were full of golden fire.

Calion moved just inside her, feeling an awareness of her, a connection, he hadn't before. His body was primed and aching to join with the female beneath him. When she arched up against him, his control snapped. The ache in his loins whipped into a blazing inferno, and he grasped Talia's hands, holding them next to her head.

Glorying in the flames raging against the sapphire of his eyes, Talia shivered with excitement. He was so beautiful to her, she wanted to tell him, but she had no words. Her throat was tight with desire, her body humming with need, her longing for him clearly written all over her.

With one hand Calion reached back down and rubbed the small nubbin, watching as her eyes went blind. He barely touched her, and her channel tightened fiercely around the tip of his cock. She came apart under him, her cries of fulfillment sparking the final fire in his soul. "You are mine," he ground out, the blaze in his eyes rivaling the campfire they lay beside. With a single thrust he buried himself inside of her. "*Mine!*"

Their cries of passion and pain intermingled in the night. Whatever control Calion had ended the second he plunged into Talia's tight channel. She was so small, only the momentum of his thrust allowed him to drive in as deep as he did. He worried for a moment about the tightness, before the feeling of her hot, wet quim clinging to his swollen cock drove everything from his mind.

He groaned deep in his throat as his body began to move on hers, long driving strokes that buried him deep. His body burned from the inside out, the only thing hotter—the sweet passage his cock was buried in. Dimly, he heard her crying out his name, but it only inflamed him more.

Talia's release was more than she expected. The pleasure just from his fingers made her cry his name over and over again, leaving her body shivering in reaction. But when he plunged inside her, she felt ripped apart, her pleasure overcome by pain. Too big, she thought desperately, her crying of his name changing to pleading for him to stop.

He didn't hear, too far gone in his own passion to understand. His thrusts continued and after a few moments the pain disappeared, and a remnant of the pleasure she'd known before flowered deep inside her. She moved instinctively with him, and as his strokes increased in speed, so did her desire.

Calion's faerie senses were filled with the female beneath

him. The sight of her beauty, the smell of her arousal, the feel of her tight body, all brought him to a fever pitch. He could barely think, he could only feel as he moved in and out of Talia's body. When she started to move with him, his mating fire burned hotter than ever before, reaching deep inside him, loosing a part of him never before used. Need spiraled so hard and fast, control over his mind, his body...even his faerie abilities were forgotten.

His magick rose around them, blanketing them in blue clouds, before spearing down into them both, bringing their pleasure to even higher peaks. Calion's mind closed down to everything but the gratification of his body, running on pure fire-mating instinct. His cock plunged faster and faster into Talia, his mansack slapping against her inner thighs.

Desire and need...lust and love. All came together when she screamed as she climaxed harder than she'd done before. Her explosion triggered his. With a hoarse shout of triumph, he buried his head in Talia's hair and poured her full of his seed.

Afterwards, Calion lay on top of her, his body shaking with reaction at the pleasure he received. He'd never come so hard, never gotten so much delight in being with a female before. He didn't want to move, he wanted to stay where he was forever, luxuriating in the satin feel of her body.

The scent of their mating clung to the air around them, sealing them both in a sensuous bubble of time. What they'd done touched him in a way he didn't understand yet. He'd lost control, even of his faerie abilities. Slowly, he lifted himself up on his elbows and looked down at Talia.

By the goddesses... She was even more beautiful now, lying beneath him, soft and satiated. Her breathing was slowing, her eyes half closed, her mouth swollen with his kisses, but her face glowed. He started to push the wisps of hair off her cheeks, but he frowned when he saw the tear stains.

Disquiet rose within him, and the worry that bothered him when he first entered her came to the fore. Calion's face took on a grim look as he remembered, and his gut twisted painfully. No...it could not be. He raised himself up a little further and reluctantly looked down at where their bodies still joined. There, stark against the paleness of their loins, combined with sweat and wetness, he saw flecks of blood red. He froze, staring in disbelief.

He went still and when she felt it, Talia's eyes opened fully. She lifted her hand to his face with an innocent, loving smile. "Calion?"

"What...have...you...done?" The words were dragged from him, his voice dark and angry. He said it again, this time his voice a roar. "*What have you done?*"

Talia's hand stopped midway to his face. She flinched away from him, her inner joy at their loving turning instantly to ashes. She stared in shock and confusion as his face changed from the intense satisfied look of a lover, to an ominous, frightening mask. He pushed himself off her, his body leaving hers in an agonizing lurch. Kneeling, he took her by the shoulders and shook her.

"Do you know what you have done?" This time he shouted it even louder.

Confusion was chased away by mingled fear and anger. It had happened again. They made love to each other and now he was angry with her. "Stop it," she cried as she fought his grasping hands. Flinging herself away, she accidentally fell against one of the nearby logs. There was a sharp crack as her cheek came in contact with the wood. She gave a stunned cry and slipped back down onto the blankets.

Calion stood, his naked body glowing like an enraged god's in the low firelight. Deliberately, he ran his hand over his loins then showed her his fingers, dripping with their combined mating juices and her blood. His voice was deadly.

"You have betrayed me."

Talia held her hand to her bruised face in dazed confusion. Her shocked eyes finally registered the blood dripping from his hand, and her brow furrowed. He was upset because she'd been a virgin? But he wasn't just upset, he was furious, his chest heaving with barely controlled rage. She stared up at him, tasting the salty warm taste of blood in her mouth, bewilderment written all over her face.

"You were a maiden." His harsh voice interrupted her bemused thoughts.

"Yes...but I don't—"

Calion growled angrily, cutting her off. "I should never have touched you. Why did you not tell me?"

Talia felt the pain of his statement go right through her

heart. She understood it might have been nice for her to tell him, but that would have been more for her comfort than for his. In her world a lot of men would take pride in being a woman's first lover.

"What does it matter?" She held her hand out to him. "It was wonderful. You were wonderful."

He never even felt the pride that rose up at her declaration. His anger was a living thing, his life now in shambles over this female's thoughtless action.

"You were a maiden. A maiden and I mated with you." Picking up one of the huge logs that surrounded the fire pit, he heaved it into the forest in his wrath. "Do you understand what that means? What you have done to me?"

"What does it mean?" Talia whispered, dread coloring every word. It was bad, whatever it was. The absolute fury in him showed her that.

"There are few rules for elves in mating. If both are willing, they can mate."

"I was willing—" she began.

"Be silent!" His command shook the forest. "Even though it is forbidden, I chose to mate with you. You were a female I wanted. I lusted after."

He took a step closer, and Talia pressed back against the blankets, her heart pounding in her breast.

"I did this because I was sending you back to your world tomorrow. Tonight would be our only night together. Do you understand what I am saying?"

"No, Calion." She spoke carefully, frightened of what she saw in his face. "I'm sorry. I don't."

"I mated with you because I could have you, and then you would leave. Go back to your own life. No one would ever know I broke the *sardai*...the taboo."

Talia drew in her breath. Her heart went numb. Suddenly she understood, and with that understanding came indescribable pain. "You're ashamed of me."

Arrogance filled his voice. "*I* am an elven prince. *You* are human. My life and duty you could never understand. A human female cannot be a fit companion for me. You are a lesser race."

She narrowed her eyes. She hurt inside, but now he was pissing her off. "A lesser race?"

"Why do you think I fought so hard against wanting you? Now you have trapped me and I have no choice."

"What are you talking about?" she cried, pushed beyond her endurance. "Nothing is changed. I'm still leaving tomorrow. No one will know what we've done. You can have your rosy little fantasy about finding your perfect elf female!" The pain of thinking of Calion with another woman speared through her.

"No, you have taken care of that. Now all will know what we did."

"How? How will anyone know unless you tell them?"

Calion ignored her question. "Why did you not tell me of your maidenhood, Talia? Why?"

Not comfortable with him looming over her, she picked up her torn tunic and wrapped it around her. Standing shakily, she wiped the blood from her mouth. She didn't see the awareness spring to his eyes when he saw the redness on her fingers.

"I would have at first. I didn't think it would matter so much. Last night things went so fast there wasn't time, and then when you stopped, I had no reason to."

"And tonight?" The words were dark and frighteningly quiet.

She sighed. "You put so many things up as obstacles between us I was frightened to. I wanted to tell you, but...I didn't want you to stop."

"If I had known this, I would never have touched you," Calion bit out. His rage swelled in him. "You lied to me."

"I never told you I wasn't a virgin. I just didn't say anything. I wanted you to make love with me." Her voice softened. "Even after all this, I still do."

Calion's temper snapped, and with an animal roar of rage, he picked up the other log and threw into the waterfall. The rainbow colors disappeared from the sky and the tremendous splash sent a spray of water over them, making the campfire hiss and wetting both their bodies.

"I...do...not...want...you...now!" he gritted out. He stepped closer so he towered over her. "Not anymore. You were to be a convenience, one quickly forgotten." He pushed away the knowledge that he lied to himself. "But I have taken your innocence. So now I have no choice."

"You said that before," Talia murmured, stepping back from

him. “What do you mean?”

“If an elven male,” he said in a too-level, too-calm voice, “takes a female who is a maiden, he is forevermore responsible for her.” He glared straight into her uncomprehending eyes. “Whether he wants her or not!”

Talia’s instinctive joy at the knowledge she could stay with Calion buried itself under the pain that he didn’t want anything to do with her. She met his furious eyes. Anger, sorrow and despair mixed in hers as they filled with tears.

“I’m sorry,” she whispered. “I didn’t know.”

This time her tears just infuriated him further. He didn’t have any self-control when he touched this female, and he wasn’t sure who he hated more at this moment, Talia or himself.

“No one needs to know, Calion,” she said. “I can still leave. Not being a virgin in my world is no big deal. Women go through several partners.”

“*Pas os aer*!” he swore. He grabbed her by the shoulders again, his fingers digging into her soft flesh. Thinking of Talia with another man made his rage burn hot.

“You would whore yourself with another? You would take from me my very honor? No one would know? *I* would know! It is bad enough I went against what is forbidden, that I could live with, but this? To walk away and leave you sullied? I am an honorable male!”

“You’re hurting me!” Talia wept, trying to twist away from him. “Let me go!”

“You will stay and you will listen.” He gave her an extra-hard shake that made her teeth rattle in her head. “I do not want you here! I wanted you out of my life. You have made it so I cannot get rid of you. And you think an apology will make things better?”

He shook her again and the tunic fell off of one creamy shoulder. The fury in Calion exploded again as he realized after everything that happened, his body still responded to hers. He let out a growl that made Talia flinch away.

“I hate you. My life is now ruined because of you and your betrayal. I am responsible for you whether I want to be or not. I cannot even pass you on to another because you are human, and no one would want you. My life will be a living nightmare. You will be a millstone around my neck for as long as you live!”

Talia sobbed openly, swaying in Calion's grasp like a willow tree whose roots have been torn from the ground by a harsh wind. Her mind, filled with the angry words he spoke could only focus on the three words that were deathly clear to her.

I hate you.

Her heart, so full of love, broke into tiny pieces and fell in glass shards at her feet. Now she was damned to spend the rest of her life with the only man she would ever love and he hated the very sight of her.

I love him, she thought as she stared at him. No matter what he says, no matter what he does, I can't help loving him. I won't let him ruin his life over a mistake I made, out of ignorance or not.

Suddenly, she remembered his last words: "*My life will be a living nightmare. You will be a millstone around my neck for as long as you live!*" Looking up at his beloved face, taking it in, imprinting it on her memory, she knew what she must do.

"Then I'll make it easy for you."

With strength that came from desperation, Talia shoved Calion away, knocking him to the ground. Turning, she sprinted away from him and ran straight into the unforgiving faerie myst.

Chapter Six

Calion sat in shock as she ran away from him. It wasn't until Talia disappeared that he realized what she was doing. "*Then I'll make it easy for you,*" she'd said.

He jumped to his feet and reached for his sword before the thought was completed. Cold fear erased every bit of rage within him. *What had he done?* He raced toward the faerie myst, his sword singing in his hand.

He hit the myst at full speed, not even remembering to protect himself. It came alive, sharp talons and teeth clawing at his naked body. He cried out in pain and then quickly shielded himself as he plunged forward. His mind numbed with fear. Talia had no defense against the cruel fog.

Lifting his sword above his head, he shone its light around him. She couldn't have gotten far. The myst wouldn't have given her time. He forged ahead, batting away the shapes that flew at him. The spirits here were always hostile, but never this aggressive.

Voices muttered in his ears, shouted in his face, battered his will. *She was the one. Go back... She is dead... You killed her.* He swore, wanting to cover his ears from the bedlam. The voices went on and on as he stumbled through the haze. Staring around him, he looked frantically for Talia, cursing himself as he ran. He'd heard the pain in her voice, yet he'd only cared about his own hurt and anger. He needed to find her before it was too late.

He stumbled over something and his heart went to his throat, but when he lowered the light of his sword, he saw the carcass of a *vol*, a pig-like creature of the forest.

"Talia!" Calion shouted, whirling around. He continued,

struggling against the darkness and cloying feel of the unrelenting wraiths that surrounded him. His panic grew as he realized Talia could have wandered in a hundred different directions and he would never find her.

The spirits laughed as they saw his fear. They pulled and teased at him, their very numbers overwhelming the shielding of his sword.

He turned again toward the outside human world, hoping Talia's instincts would lead her that way. A specter grabbed at his sword and it cost Calion precious time to wrench it away and hurry on. Fury at himself and what he'd done fueled his anger, and he swept the sword through the air, cutting a wide swath of light in the encroaching creatures.

Then, just at the edge of the light, he saw something on the ground. His heart leaped and he ran to the spot. He went to his knees with a cry of despair when he found her tunic ripped to shreds. Pressing the torn fabric against his face, he ignored the crowd of wraiths around him. It smelled of Talia, and his gut churned with regret and remorse. He needed to find her. She was running out of time.

Calion dropped the tunic and taking a deep breath, grasped his sword and pointed it above his head. He brought the pommel to his chest. The magick he called was as basic and as old as the mysts themselves. He used it without thinking, instinctively, his only thought to save Talia.

It was the spell to call...*Mylari.* When the spirits heard his words, they screamed aloud, thousands of voices shrieking into nothingness as Calion deepened the incantation. Searching within, he pulled a single instant of awareness from his thoughts and spun it out into a strand of sapphire blue light. The light contained the true essence of his connection with Talia.

Calion reached eagerly for it, hoping it would guide him to her, but the light moved off. He frowned. A spell of his design, it should obey him, but it danced away from his outstretched hand as if it didn't want him to know its secrets.

"Not...for you..." moved gently through his mind. *"You...haven't...the right."* The words made Calion's scar burn suddenly with molten fire.

Tears stung his eyes. *"Please,"* he begged the dancing light. *"If not for me...then for her."*

The light paused as if considering his words, flickering before him like a mad firefly. It circled his head, weighing him, judging his true intent. Suddenly, it sped away, so fast Calion almost missed where it headed.

He rose and sprinted after it, using the sword against the angry spirits in the myst. It flew in a straight line towards the far end of the boundary, shocking Calion that Talia made it so far. Abruptly, it turned to the left and headed back deep into the blackness, stopping just at the edge of his sight.

Calion rushed to the light, shouting her name as he saw Talia lying naked in a crumpled heap. The blue spell light hovered above her, driving back the angry wraiths enveloping her. Roaring in fury, he called to his sword.

"*Cylys!*"

The sword whistled through the horrible creatures, cutting them into ribbons, their second death cries echoing in his ears. He moved to Talia's side and enveloped her in his sword's shield. The spell winked out, knowing its job was done. The remaining wraiths screeched and spit, but they couldn't get to him.

Bending down, he turned her over, gasping as her torn, bloody face came into view. Welts and bruises covered her body. Long gashes from talons marred her flesh. Hurriedly, he took her into his arms and almost recoiled in shock.

She was as cold as ice.

He pressed his face against her, guilt and loss slashing into him. Touching his lips to her throat, he jerked in surprise when he felt the faint beat of her pulse. He scrambled to his feet, snatching her against him. It wasn't too late.

With his sword as his guide, he dashed back towards the elven domain. He battled unceasingly against the swirling wraiths. His sword dimmed for a moment as his strength failed and the creatures surged against them. He could feel the slash of frigid claws as the creatures of the myst moved in, but when one tried to pull Talia from his arms, he reacted, adrenaline flooding his whole body.

One more time the sword lifted, calling out for honor. It slashed at the wraiths, its renewed light pointing out of the myst. The spirits tried to come at the prince again, but they couldn't win out against his fury. Over and over again, he fought them. And then suddenly he was there, out of the myst, back in his forest.

Calion fell to his knees, taking deep panting breaths of oxygen. His vision was gray but he knew to help Talia, he needed to stay conscious. He smoothed back her hair and shivered at the icy feel of her body. So much damage. Spells and incantations would not be enough.

The prince felt a hard shove at his shoulder and he turned, ready to do battle, but Roch'mellon stood there. So confused and exhausted was Calion, he could barely hear his steed's mind-speech. When Roch'mellon knelt down beside them, he finally understood, and holding Talia in his arms, he climbed shakily astride.

The horse moved as quickly as he thought his partner could handle, heading straight toward the waterfall. Calion touched Talia, trying to bring life back into her. He didn't even notice the horse walk behind the waterfall to the pool within.

"My friend," Calion said, his voice broken. "This may warm her, but her wounds...even my magick cannot help her. The horse snorted and walked past the pond they had bathed in earlier. There, behind a stand of rocks Calion never paid attention to, he saw a second pool. Roch'mellon stopped and knelt. When the prince slid off, his precious bundle in his arms, the horse nudged him toward the water's edge.

Trusting his friend, Calion carried Talia into the pool. Fragrant, hot liquid swirled around him as he moved out far enough to submerge their bodies. Immediately, he felt the tiredness in his limbs fading. Surprised, he looked at one of the slashes on his leg and stopped breathing when it slowly closed up and vanished.

He whipped around and stared at Roch'mellon. "You, my friend have earned enough oats to last a lifetime. A healing pool. How did you know?"

The horse snorted modestly, but then he pointed his muzzle at the female, telling Calion to hurry. The elf needed no second urging. He turned with Talia and found a place to sit where he could hold her completely under the water, so only her face showed.

Calion cupped the healing water in his hand and it mingled with his tears as he gently poured the healing water over her mutilated face. "*Tia maer...*" he murmured, his voice rough with sorrow. "Please come back to me. Open those beautiful eyes."

He smoothed his wet hand down one of her naked shoulders and waited for the bruises to disappear. "I am truly sorry for what I did. Come back to me. Give me a chance to make it up to you once again."

He didn't know how long he sat spooning water onto her torn and tattered face, whispering words of regret and tenderness, before he saw a change. The bruises and welts began to fade, the tears and gashes on her soft skin, to mend and heal. Calion ran his fingers through her hair, combing out the dirt and matted blood until it was clean and golden again.

Soon, Talia's body healed completely. All the wounds disappeared...except for the mark he himself caused when she'd tried to escape from his anger and fallen against the log. It bloomed at the corner of her vulnerable mouth, a dark bruise no amount of healing water would take away.

Worse, the heated water did not take away the icy cold feel of her body. She was as chilled and as lifeless as a corpse.

"*Ai eis si paelor, eil si paelor air ti,*" Calion grieved. He pulled her close to his chest and began to rock her. "I have killed her."

Her head fell back onto his shoulder, and he stared down at her as he swayed. "I am so sorry. You did not deserve this. I was wrong. Such a fool." He bent his head and touched her cold lips with his, wishing with all his heart he'd done things differently. He pulled her hard against him, knowing he should sing the dirge that would send Talia's spirit to the afterlife. But he couldn't do it. No matter how hard he tried, he couldn't bring himself to sing those final words. He just held her and wept.

Suddenly, he stiffened and he jerked back up to stare down at her, determination on his face. "No!" He gave her a little shake. "I will not give up. *We* will not give up. We are not done fighting yet. You are stronger than this. I will not let you go." He took her head in his hands and kissed her, his lips hard against her cold ones.

"Do not give up, *Tia maer...* I do not want you dead. I want you alive. I want you in that bed of blankets, breathing and taking your turn to touch me. I did not mean the things I said. I lied to you. I could never hate you."

Crushing her lips beneath his own, Calion used his mouth to impart the truth in his heart. Truth he still wouldn't admit, even to himself. He poured his own life force into the kiss, sending all of his feelings—confusion, regret, passion, need and something more—deep into Talia's soul. He kissed her again and again, knowing this might be his last chance. Their last chance. He kissed her until his own lips hurt.

Were her lips warmer? Was her skin any less icy? Or was it his own need that heated them? Clenching his jaw, he kissed her again, this time gently, seducing her back to him with soft kisses of warmth and passion. He traced her mouth, her nose, her cheeks and her eyes. All of them treated to his lover's kiss.

A gentle puff of air surprised him. He pulled his head back slowly and studied Talia's face. Her mouth had parted under his gentle assault, and for the first time since finding her, a hint of color bloomed on her cheeks. Quickly, Calion put a hand on her breast. His eyes closed in furious relief. Her heart beat!

He kissed her again, feeling the warmth of her breath. "Talia? Can you hear me?" He smoothed more warm water over her. "*Tia maer...* Wake up, please."

Talia fought up through the fog in her mind, feeling as if she had been asleep for weeks. She opened heavy eyelids and looked up into Calion's strained face. She blinked a couple of times in confusion. "Cal...ion?"

He couldn't answer her. His throat tightened with unshed tears. Hoping he wasn't seeing things, he traced his fingers over Talia's face. He paused as he came to the bruise on her mouth and swallowed...hard. "I thought I had lost you."

She felt like her head was stuffed full of cotton and clouds. She moved gingerly, feeling nothing on her body to indicate what had happened to her. When she tried to sit up, Calion stopped her.

"Easy now," he said soothingly. "You have just been though a frightening ordeal. You are in a healing pool behind the waterfall." He took her hand in his and brought it to his lips.

The familiar gesture tickled a memory, and she stared at her hand against his mouth. Suddenly, she remembered him kissing her knuckles at the bathing pool. The memory of what happened afterwards rushed through her, leaving her pale again, her green eyes wide and wounded.

By the stiffness that arose in her body, he knew she remembered everything. Tears trickled down her face and her soft mouth trembled. His hand stroked her hair, and he continued to buss her hand with his lips. He wished he could tell her what was in his heart, but he didn't know how.

Talia didn't know what to think or feel. She'd gone into the myst to escape the pain of his hate, but she hadn't thought what would happen once she was inside. Even now, most of that was a blur. She could only remember the pain and heart-stopping cold—the knowledge of death.

But even that was preferable to what she knew awaited her now. Her voice thickened with her tears. "Why did you come after me? Why couldn't you just let me die?"

He snatched her back against him again as he shuddered. "You will not die!"

Confused, she lay in his arms. His rejection of her sliced her to pieces. It tore at the very essence of her womanhood. He hated her...didn't he? Then why was he holding her as if she were the most important thing in his life?

She lifted her arms and hesitantly put them around Calion, feeling his whole body shudder again at her touch. As he held her, the words he'd spoken to her when she was unconscious were placed in her mind, a last healing gift from the pool. It was Calion's strength of will that brought her back from the brink of death, not the water's healing touch. The pool could only heal the body. It could not bring hope or healing to the soul.

Her eyes again filled and overflowed. He cared for her. In a way he couldn't even acknowledge to himself. Knowing that, the pieces of her broken heart began to mend. She held him tighter. "You came after me. You saved my life."

Lifting his head, he looked somberly down at her. "My harsh words and lies sent you into that place. I did not mean what I said, *Tia maer...* I do not hate you. I lied to myself again." He kissed her gently.

"What happens between us... I do not expect to feel what I do. Learning that you were a maiden gave me an excuse to strike out at someone, reacting to the fear of what I feel for you." He put his forehead against hers and closed his eyes. He shuddered. "I did not know true fear until I saw you disappear into the myst."

"I'm sorry I scared you. It just hurt so badly. I didn't think about anything other than the fact you hated me. I can't let your honor force you to take care of me. You're right. It would be a nightmare. For both of us."

"Ahhh, *Tia maer...* I realized as I sat here waiting for you to wake up, I still look at you as an elven female. It is wrong of me. I cannot expect you, a human who does not know our ways, to know all the rules we have for our people. You did not know what taking your maidenhead would do to me."

"I can't be sorry I didn't tell you. I've tried, but all I can see is if I told you, you would never have made love to me."

"I know." Serious, he took her hand again. "Will you let me apologize? For all those horrible things I said," he touched the bruise on her mouth, "...and did? I find it hard to forgive myself. Can *you* forgive me?"

As she covered his hand with hers, Talia met his somber eyes. "In the struggle I was hurt. Both physically *and* emotionally. Worse than I've ever been hurt before. The things you said..." She swallowed. "They were painful. It won't be easy to forget them."

His jaw tightened. "I understand."

She jumped as the pool's empathic link reminded her again of what he'd done, of the real agony he'd gone through. Her heart couldn't help but soften. Her love for him was greater than any hurt or anger. She sighed. "It did hurt, but I can forgive you. The pool showed me you're sorry. That you really mean it."

Calion felt humbled. He didn't deserve this absolution. What he'd done... How could he make it up to her? Even if he had taken her maidenhood, she wasn't an elf, so he had no right to force her to stay. She'd be leaving at first light. And she probably wouldn't let him touch her. Not now. But her eyes forgave him. They were so filled with emotion as she looked at him, he needed to try.

"Talia," he said hoarsely. "Let me take you back to our blankets. I-I have a difficult time telling you of my feelings. Let me show you instead."

His heart dropped when she shook her head. "I am sorry," he mumbled, his jaw turning ruddy with color. "After everything...of course you would not want—"

"You're right," she interrupted softly, combing her fingers through his hair. "I don't. I don't want to wait." When his eyes narrowed in confusion, she smiled, feeling the power and rightness of her love bloom again. "I want you to make love to me right here."

He froze at her words, his eyes snapping back to hers. She smiled slowly, with unconscious seduction, and Calion felt every nerve ending in his body come to attention.

"Here?"

"Here." She pulled his head down to hers.

Their lips met. He tried to be careful, hesitating because of what he'd done, but she wanted none of that. She wanted the feel of him to wipe out what happened before. She might not be able to forget, but she could have other memories more precious to hold on to.

"Make love to me," she whispered. "Help me to know you won't change your mind."

He raised his head and searched her eyes for a long moment. "This making love...it is the same as mating, yes?"

"Yes."

Calion smiled and Talia felt the last of the chill melt away when she saw it.

"Then let us...make love. Let me show you I was wrong. I will not push you away again." His mouth came down on hers again, this time in hunger.

Talia moaned deep in her throat, the exquisite feeling of being in his arms again sending sparks of fire all over her body. I love you, she cried silently.

Calion's lips ravaged hers as his hands moved all over her body, searching out the areas he now knew gave her pleasure. He loved the feel of her, warm, wet and...alive. His fingers traced the path from her neck, to her breasts, to her thighs. Her response grew more frantic, and Calion felt the fire in his body begin to burn anew.

Knowing she belonged to him, Talia's body melted to his as if the last painful hour hadn't happened. She began to touch him as well, remembering his promise of before. Her hands smoothed water over his chest, lovingly touching those cuts the pool hadn't been able to reach. His face and neck were cut too, so she pulled back from his kisses and turned, straddling him so she could get to them easier

Feeling her softness against him, Calion stiffened, his erection already painfully hard. He pulled her closer and let her minister to him, the brush of her fingers against his body fanning his inner fire even higher. He groaned aloud when she scooped the healing water into her mouth and then touched her lips to the many wounds on his face. It was the most erotic thing he had ever felt. The embers in his eyes leapt into full flame.

One by one she kissed and licked the wounds, not moving on until each one completely healed. Her lips moved slowly over his face, firing nerve endings Calion didn't even know he owned. His chest heaved as she moved her hands over his flat male nipples, finally being able to touch him the way she wanted to. Clenching his hands to prevent himself from grabbing her, he throbbed, aching to be inside her. He was as hard as if their time earlier in the evening hadn't happened. Finally, he could take no more of the sweet torture.

Grabbing her hands, he put them around his neck. His mouth sought hers for a hungry kiss. Unable to wait a moment longer, Calion reached down and gently stroked his finger into Talia's quim. She was hot and wet and because of her position, wide open to him. He tested her, pushing a finger in deep, feeling her juices flow, even in the water. She moaned in his mouth and pressed herself against his hand.

Feeling her need, his instinct took over. His eyes glowed as he lifted her and brought her down on his hard, swollen cock. A heavy groan tore from his throat as she clenched around him. He lifted his head and met her warm, green eyes as he lowered her to him, one delicious inch at a time.

They both cried out when he gave one final thrust and buried himself deep in her. They sat panting, not moving, just reveling in the feel of their joined bodies. Tenderly, he kissed her, wanting to be joined with her in every way possible. When the throbbing of his body became too much, he began to move, putting his strong hands on Talia's hips and lifting her up and then down on his hot, turgid shaft.

Could she forget so quickly the way he could make her feel? She threw back her head, holding tight to Calion's shoulders. The sensations overwhelmed her. Her nipples tightened, her very breath began to back up in her chest. She climbed higher and higher with every stroke of his hard body.

Without them knowing it, the special magick of her unconditional love rose up around them covering them in a scented cocoon. Any lingering doubts, any leftover pain disappeared. All that existed was how they felt about each other...right at this moment in time.

Calion's whole body shook with the effort to control himself until Talia found her fulfillment. His eyes burned so bright the glow lit the darkened chamber. Faster and faster she moved, until he felt like his whole body would burst.

He cried out when Talia's quim clenched down on his cock, milking it with the contractions of her orgasm. Taking control, he slammed her body up and down on his until he exploded deep within her, his own climax adding to hers and driving her again up and over the cliff to fall with him.

Later, when they quieted, he covered her mouth with his and kissed her deeply. Murmuring low ardent words in Elvish, he rose out of the water, gently separated their bodies and carried her from the waterfall to their blankets by the campfire.

As the night passed they turned to each other again, seeking more of the closeness they'd experienced before. Soft kisses, warm caresses, bodies sliding smoothly over each other until need overcame them and they fused together in ecstasy.

As Talia drifted into sleep, Calion pillowed her head on his shoulder, his hands never ceasing the soft touches he so desperately needed. He pressed his lips to her forehead and heard her hum her contentment even as she slept. His eyes were heavy, but he couldn't go to sleep. Too many feelings raced through him. Too many emotions to name. He breathed another prayer of gratitude. She was alive. She was here. Here and in his arms, at least for the rest of the night.

Something moved inside him, twisting his heart painfully. Staring up at the night sky, he gazed at the stars that would soon fade with the coming of day. He still had a little more time with her. Why did it feel as if she were already gone?

Just before dawn, with the stars slowly growing fainter in the sky, Calion woke from his restless sleep. Talia lay snuggled next to him, her leg draped over his thigh, her hand lying gently on his chest. His cock stirred and his lips covered hers, gently sliding his tongue into her mouth to kiss her awake. When she opened sleepy green eyes, his heart turned over and he moved against her.

"Can you take me?" he whispered, his need already an urgent thing. His hands moved over her body.

She said nothing. She just smiled and lifted her leg higher on his thigh so he could slide into her. Their bodies were ready, their desire not abated from the night's loving. Calion intertwined Talia's fingers in his as he moved rhythmically against her. His mouth teased her skin, heightening her senses. Their breathing quickened and the need for closeness abruptly turned to the need for release.

Their hands clasped, they stared deeply into each other's eyes and something precious passed between them. It was not lost as their movements became more purposeful.

A deep awareness flooded him, the knowing of a question that defied all logic. He moved again, deeply, and Talia cried out in her pleasure. A few strokes later he followed, jetting into her hard and long. They both lay still, their bodies pulsating in the afterglow of lovemaking, overwhelmed at the emotions that filled them.

Calion lifted his head and brushed kisses gently over Talia's eyelashes. There would not be a more perfect time. He knew now what his heart ached for.

"Stay," he said quietly, bringing their clasped hands to his lips. "Do not go. Stay here with me."

She went still and then shuddered as tears of joy slid down her face. He took her face in his hands and kissed them away, trying to soothe. "*Tia maer...* Please..."

She looked fully at him then and he saw his answer in her eyes. His body flooded with relief and happiness as he took her in his arms again.

ꕥ

Much later, Calion hitched himself up on an elbow. The sun had risen and traveled halfway to its zenith when he looked down at Talia. She lay partially beneath him, her face rosy with the aftereffects of their time together. Her eyes were closed so he couldn't see her expression, but the slight smile on her lips told him everything. "You are happy?"

Her eyes opened, and he drew in his breath at the joy he saw there. She put her hand up to his cheek and caressed it lovingly. "I didn't want to leave you. I felt from the beginning, I belonged in this world."

"I do not understand why I fought so hard against you," he marveled, kissing the palm of her hand. His sapphire eyes darkened. "I hurt you."

Talia wouldn't lie to him. "Yes, you did. But it's over now. You want me to stay." The depth of her pleasure showed in that single sentence.

Her gaze wandered over to where Roch'mellon grazed near the waterfall. "Do you think we embarrassed him?"

Calion snorted, sounding much like his horse. "He is so disgustingly smug about knowing about the healing pool, he has not stopped strutting long enough to think about anything else." He grinned when she giggled. "Besides, he always walked away from us when things got...interesting."

He bent and kissed her again when she giggled harder. "This is the way it should have been, after that first night." He buried his nose in her neck and snuffled, bringing her to full laughter.

"I wanted to wake up with you." Her eyes clouded. "It would have been all I'd ever had."

Heat smoldered in his eyes. Would he ever stop wanting her? "You have me now. We have each other." Calion lowered his mouth to hers.

Talia answered him the only way she knew how. With everything that was in her. She didn't know how to play any of the games other women did. She knew she loved him. And because she loved him, her body belonged to him.

Calion pulled away and buried his face in her shoulder, his strong body shaking. Just a kiss and he found he wanted to bury himself deep inside her...again. "I cannot do this. You must be sore."

She looked at him with mischief in her eyes. "Then it's a good thing we're near a healing spring, isn't it?"

He stared at her in shocked surprise and then laughed out loud. "I guess it is," he agreed, rolling her back beneath him.

ℬ𝒪

"I'm hungry."

He chuckled. "*Tia maer...* I fear even one who wants you as much as I do cannot help you for a time. I am tired."

Talia punched him. Who would have known they could tease each other with such lighthearted abandon?

"I mean for food, Calion. It's mid afternoon." Her brows

furrowed as she rolled over and lay half on top of his chest to look up into his amused face. "You smashed everything when you threw your tantrum last night."

"Princes do not throw tantrums," he returned arrogantly, his eyebrow raised at such slander. The twinkle in his eyes belied his anger.

"You mean all elves throw eight-foot logs around?"

"Oh, that."

She rolled her eyes. "Yes, that. Our food was on one of those logs. I know they say we should be able to live on lo...on making love alone, but my tummy's growling."

He cocked his head, wondering why she'd hesitated. He gazed at her as she lay on his chest, her chin on folded hands. She looked perfectly content for a female who'd just given up her whole world.

"So, I am to leave the comfortable bed," he pointed around to the tangled blankets around them, "of my *torear* and go on the hunt."

Talia's eyes clouded at the term *torear*, wondering what it meant, but she shrugged it off. She wasn't sure she wanted to know. "Yes." She looked at him seductively from under gold-tipped lashes. "I think I've satisfied your hunger enough times today. So now it's your turn."

Calion sat straight up in mock protest, dislodging her from his chest. He could read the laughter in her eyes as he dove on top of her, tickling her until she cried out.

"You satisfied me? What about me satisfying you? Or are you saying all you really wanted from me is food?"

"Mercy!" Talia shouted, her laughter bubbling out of her. She threw her arms around his neck. "You know what I wanted. And it wasn't food."

"No," he said, his head bending to hers one more time. "Food is not what we want."

ஐ

When Talia walked out from behind the waterfall, she could see Calion working industriously over the fire. While she bathed, he'd gone into the forest to see if he could find anything close for their dinner. He wore just his breeches and soft boots, and his torso glistened in the last light.

She smiled to herself. It had been a glorious day. They'd done nothing but lie on the blankets and love the hours away. They made love, then talked and laughed and made love again. Even hunger couldn't get Calion out of bed. His hunger was for her. She hugged herself with joy. He didn't love her yet, but he wanted her. Enough to flout all his traditions and rules. That had to be something.

She walked towards him, noting again his strength and masculinity. He was hard all over, she knew that now. Not a spare bit of flesh on his beautiful body. When he turned toward her, she caught the flash of something in his eyes. But it disappeared before she could analyze it. The fire had left them for the moment, but they were warm with remembered heat.

Calion watched as she picked her way to him. She wasn't wearing shoes again. He now knew she didn't like them. She was a constant surprise to him. Full grown, yet with the curiosity of a child. He found himself wanting to constantly protect her, to keep her out of the scrapes he knew she could find herself in. He hadn't wanted to be away from her, even for the time it took to go on a hunt, knowing it would be a while before he would forget the memory of her lying helpless and alone in the myst.

"Did you enjoy your bath?"

"Yes. I used the healing pool. *All* my aches are gone."

He threw back his head and laughed heartily. "Then I suppose I must avail myself of it as well. I will not have you accuse me of slacking."

She smiled and knelt on the blankets to tidy them into a more comfortable mattress. Her cheeks pinked when she came across one with blood on it.

"I guess if you're going to lose your virginity, it's nice a healing pool is nearby." She moved to pick it up, but Calion's hand beat her there.

"I wish I had been gentler with you," he murmured regretfully.

Talia looked up quickly and took his hand…hard. "I didn't tell you. Don't you dare blame yourself!"

He blinked at her fierceness. His lady could be a tigress when she wanted to. "I only wish your first time could have been better."

That earned him a snort. "Don't go fishin' for compliments, Calion."

He narrowed his eyes. "And that means...?"

She blushed, her cheeks rivaling last night's sunset. She busied herself with the blankets, taking the stained one and rolling it to hide the blood. They could probably use it to lay their heads on. "I mean it was wonderful, okay?"

Calion grinned. Now his little tigress was embarrassed. "I did not hear you."

She threw him a scathing look. "Yes, you did." She continued to smooth out the blankets, not wanting to look at him.

"*Tia maer...*" he whispered close to her ear, chuckling when she jumped. "Tell me."

Talia squirmed uncomfortably. She didn't know how to tell him how he made her feel. "I never..."

He chuckled again. "Of that, I am now sure." He grunted when she put an elbow into his stomach. "Sorry."

"It may be easy for you. You probably know just how to sweet talk a lover." The thought made her frown.

Calion saw the frown and smiled tenderly. Moving, he knelt in front of her and placed his finger under her chin bringing her face up to his. "Do you think all I have said to you today, I have said to another female?"

"It's none of my business if you have!" She tried to look unconcerned and failed miserably.

"*Tia maer...* I will not lie to you and say I have been with no other. I have lived long and had my share of mating."

"Well," she huffed, trying to move away, but he held her securely.

"Talia." His firm tone made her look up into his eyes. "There is only one I have ever flamed for and that one is you." He saw she didn't understand and sighed. He hadn't wanted to go into this right now, but... "Do you remember in the *Malesia* tree, when I told you about fire mating?"

"Yes. I didn't understand what you meant, but you didn't want me because of it."

Calion grimaced. "That is partially correct, but let me explain further. You see, the elven people link for life. When an elf finds a member of the opposite sex he is attracted to, he will mate with her for both their pleasure. And sometimes you can find someone who is compatible enough to flame with...to make the fire you have seen in my eyes."

Talia nodded, interested.

"In some rare cases when both male and female flame, they can become fire mates. It is a very special linking."

"What is linking?"

"Linking is a relationship that extends through our lifetime. We share our lives, have children. Travel the journey of our days together."

Talia deliberately pushed down her pain, knowing he wasn't talking about her and him. "In my world, we call it marriage, although it seems very few do it for life anymore."

He nodded. "Many settle for a relationship that does not include a fire mate. They link and can have good lives, but they know something will always be missing. Some wait to see if they can find that special person who could be a fire mate, because only those can lead us to the person our very souls long for."

"Who is that?" she whispered.

Calion's eyes were far away as he answered. "*Mylari.*"

Chapter Seven

Talia said nothing for several minutes. Calion, lost in thought, didn't even notice. Finally, she touched his arm. "What is *Mylari*?"

His blue eyes met hers almost wistfully. "Soulmate."

She drew in her breath sharply. A soulmate. What she'd always longed for. Could she have been sent to this world to find hers? Her heart swelled, filling almost to the bursting. Joy mingled with desolation. She had found hers, but he was too stubborn and proud to ever allow her that part in his life. She almost wept with the knowledge her heart's desire was right in front of her, and she would never be able to reach out and take it. A human couldn't be an elf's soulmate.

Calion watched the emotions flicker across her face. The story he shared had touched her deeply. "Now you understand why we take fire mating so seriously. That night, when I realized my eyes flamed, I saw for the first time in my life a potential fire mate. You...a human. An impossibility. As I said before, I reacted badly."

He reached out and took her face in his hands. "I am not sorry I have broken the *sardai* and mated with you. Only that I have handled it so poorly."

Talia bit her lip. She knew she shouldn't ask, but she needed to know. "And you? Do you look for your *Mylari*?"

He smiled gently and kissed her. "I am one who seeks. But I am happy with who I have right here. Right now." He kissed her again, harder this time. "And I have never said the special things I say to you to anyone else. You are unique."

Pleasure battled with pain. He wanted her, but he would continue looking for his soulmate...his *Mylari*. The thought made her heart break.

Sadness filled her eyes. Mysteries Calion didn't know, and it bothered him. He was a private male and usually didn't care about secrets kept by another. But with Talia... He let the thoughts go with difficulty. "And now you must answer my question, *Tia maer...*"

"Question?" Confusion replaced the sadness.

He smiled temptingly. "What you meant exactly by—what did you say? *I was wonderful?*"

She blushed again. "*Calion.*"

"I shared my thoughts with you, now you must share yours with me."

Talia frowned at him, her hands fisted on her hips. Then she smiled, her dimples winking deeply. It charmed him without her even saying a word. She moved closer to him and put her arms around his neck. "If I have to do this, I'm going to do it my way!"

When he shrugged, she put her lips next to his ear, her body pressing against his to whisper her answer. Then she added all the things she liked him doing to her. When he groaned and shifted against her, she smiled and murmured all the things she wanted to do to him.

He closed his eyes, his body raging to an inferno just from listening to her sexy voice. When she finished, dropping her arms and smiling sweetly at him, he shook his head to clear it. Who, he wondered, came out on top in that contest?

"I best go clean up," he growled at her. He winced as he stood and adjusted himself. Her giggles followed him and he grinned, suddenly seeing the humor. "We will finish this, *Tia maer...* when I return. Until then, do not let the meat burn."

ꟹ

Calion took her advice and after he cleaned himself in the regular pool, he took a turn in the healing waters. He didn't want to admit it, but he was a little sore himself in places. He smiled widely as he thought of the previous night and day. Never had he mated so many times in such a short period of time. His need for her seemed unending and stronger than anything he felt before. He knew showing flame was one of the reasons the matings were so urgent and powerful.

Fire was a difficult element to control. He wished—not for the first time—that Talia was an elf. If she had been, would there be the possibility of a full linking? Could she have been his *Mylari*? He sighed, knowing wishes would not help him. Talia was a human and he knew his destiny.

Looking down at the scar on his wrist, he saw it was still red and inflamed, yet the pain was much less. Why did the healing spring not heal the bruise on Talia's face or his burning scar?

He shook the worry away. He'd thought it through and decided his original plan was the best. He would take her to his father. If he hadn't been distracted by wanting to mate with her, he already would have. It still bothered him about the prophecy the orcs spoke of. Perhaps his father or the wise men of the castle would know to what they were referring.

Back at the fire pit, Calion set down his packet and then strode into the woods. Talia watched then burst out laughing when she saw him coming back with the log he'd thrown the night before. Ignoring her, he set it up to the side of their blanket.

"Now we can be comfortable and lean back," he stated. "No matter how much you ask it of me, I will not redecorate."

"I think it's just fine," she murmured, drawing him down to her. She handed him a piece of cooked meat. "I don't know what this is, but it sure smells good."

"It is *paes*." He chewed a piece experimentally. "Good. You did not burn it."

Elbowing him a little, Talia took a piece for herself. "What's *paes*?"

"*Paes* is a four-legged animal that inhabits the forest. Like a horse, it grazes on grass. There are many of them, too many, so we take them for food when we need to."

She stared into the flames. "It's hard to believe two days ago, Mom sent me to the grocery store for steaks. It's a whole different world here."

He tensed. "It is different. Some things will be easier, others more difficult. I would understand if you have changed your mind."

Talia dropped her meat, fear in her green eyes. "Have *you*? Are you telling me to go?"

He bent and kissed her fiercely, tasting the *paes* on her lips. "*No*! I have not changed my mind." Tucking her under one arm, he leaned back on the log. "I find myself...insecure about you." He glared at her. "I do not like it."

Talia settled back against him and waited for her heart to slow down. He'd scared the hell out of her. "Well, I am too. And it's no more fun for me."

"What say we take this one day at a time? Perhaps then we will feel better about things. I know the feelings we have for each other are new and a little strange."

She giggled. "Yeah. I've just spent a glorious, decadent day making love to a being that doesn't even exist. That's strange!"

Calion narrowed his eyes at her. "Elves *do* exist."

"I know that and you know that, but humans don't. At least you knew humans were around. It gave me quite a start to see you land next to me with your pointy ears and sexy eyebrows."

He felt himself redden, as he did whenever she teased him like this. "I tracked you from the myst. Even knowing I would find a human female, I too was surprised to see you. You stole my breath with those green eyes of yours." He grinned. "And that position you were in..."

"My position?" Talia echoed.

"Oh, yes. As soon as I saw you, completely helpless, your arms stretched above your head." His eyes danced wickedly. "I wanted you. Just like that."

Talia stared at him, her mouth open. She couldn't decide whether to be appalled at him for making her remember what the orcs had done to her, or to go with the warm feeling that started between her legs and drag him against the nearest tree so he could make his fantasy come to life. She settled with a compromise.

"Since I wouldn't even want you to take me in a crowd of smelly orcs, we'll just have to find an appropriate stake you can tie me to later."

She did it again. Surprised him. The heat rose in his body. No female of his race would be so free in their mating. It was why he'd thought her experienced, when instead she'd been a maiden. Suddenly jealous, he frowned at her. "Do you speak of such things to your human males?"

She blinked at him. "As you should know by now, Calion, there were no human males. It's the type of things lovers talk about. I had no lovers."

Appeased, he sat back. "No, you did not," he said smugly. "I find I am pleased you were a maiden for me. I would have wanted to fight any males who tasted you before."

"Now you know how I felt when you let it drop about your past. *I have lived long and had my share of mating,*" Talia mimicked. "Puh-lease."

"I am not bragging, *Tia maer...* I am stating a fact."

"Well goody for you. Just don't state it anymore."

Calion smiled inwardly, thinking he liked her being jealous of his past relationships. She sounded almost...possessive.

ஐ

"I do have a question about something," Talia murmured. They'd packed up the food and carried it to the waterfall to stay cool. Now she sat in his arms as they watched the glow of the rainbow colors in the sky.

"I am all pointy ears, *Tia maer...*"

Her lips quirked in amusement. She kissed his chest and his arms tightened around her. "When your people link, is love ever in the equation? You never mentioned it."

"Love. You say this word often. Like in...making *love.* Or I *love* to do something. It seems to have varied meanings."

"Well..." Now Talia had to think. "Love means caring deeply for someone or something. So in the phrase making love, it means more than sex, sex with caring."

"Do your people often mate...have sex, without care of the other person?"

"Unfortunately, yes. It happens all the time. They do it just for the release."

"You did not."

"No." She swallowed. This was skirting dangerous ground. "I wanted to care about the person I was with. I never found one I cared enough about."

"Until me." He sounded smug again.

She laughed. "How I felt about you hit me like a ton of bricks. I didn't have a choice in the matter. Do you think you were the only one going crazy?"

Calion stopped himself from lunging at her. She made him rock hard by that last careless admission. She really had no idea what she did to him.

"But do your people love?"

He thought about her question. How to explain the complicated mating rituals of his race. His hand stroked her soft hair and he spoke. "My people do *love* but not in the same way as yours. We do not have a single word for it. There are different types of emotion you might term love."

"Go on," Talia urged him. She enjoyed it when he told her stories.

"There are the feelings you have for your family. For those you live with. That is *thastolor.* For friends and those you serve with, the word is *thaelyrdor.* For one you have linked with, if the affection is very strong, you may enjoy *thylaer.*"

"And *Mylari*? What is the term of love you use for them?

"Ahhh, that term is very different from the rest, because the feelings between *Mylari* are different. What a *Mylari* feels for their soulmate is indescribable. The closest term we have for it is *Varol thysi.* In your tongue it would mean...the force of passion."

"I see."

"No, *Tia maer...* It would be impossible for you to understand. There is nothing in your world that matches what happens between two *Mylari.* When they link, either formally or on their own, it is more than just a sharing of feelings or their bodies. When *Mylari* find each other they share their very life force."

"You're right. I don't understand."

"How can I explain?" Calion thought hard as Talia watched him, her eyes gleaming green with interest.

"I wonder... Can you see this?" He lifted one hand and held it palm up. He closed his eyes and called his magick. It formed in his hand. A swirling ball of blue light.

"It's beautiful."

"Another thing you are not supposed to be able to do. See magick." The prince shook his head in wry acceptance before continuing. "Every elf has magick within him." He spoke quietly as she watched the orb in awe.

"We are all born with it. It comes from the very soil on

which we now sit. Some, do nothing with the power, but use it as they need to live their lives. Others take that power and study, becoming wise men and sages, knowledgeable in all things. Still others, not content with just book learning, allow nature itself to become their teachers. They learn by doing. They are the strongest, the most powerful wielders of magick."

"That's what you are," Talia murmured. Her finger tips touched the cool, blue light gently.

"It is what I am." He closed his hand around her fingers and the blue light covered both their hands, flaring slightly. Not realizing the significance of what he did, Calion continued.

"*Mylari* share their life force...their power. The power that exists between two linked soulmates is the strongest power in all our world. Nothing can stand against it."

Talia's heart sank at the awe in his voice. "Were your parents *Mylari*?"

Calion shook his head. The blue orb blinked out of sight. "No, they did not seek them. Theirs was an arranged marriage. My mother came from another clan of elves, the Sky Elves. My mother never saw my father until the day of their linking."

He frowned. "While their time together was pleasant, neither knew the joy of having a *Mylari*. And the kingdom suffered for it. Their power was never strong. When my mother died in childbirth, even that was diminished."

And that is why you will never stop looking for your soulmate, Talia thought despairingly. *No matter how you feel about me. For the power.*

"But speaking of my father," he added, not knowing her internal struggle, "I have decided I will take you to him as I originally considered. He may be able to shed light on why the orcs abducted you. And I have a theory I want to run by the wise men."

Talia pushed her pain away. She needed to remember it was enough for her to be with him now. He'd told her to stay. She let the warmth of that memory chase away any lingering hurt.

"What theory?"

"As I have told you, all have a life force. Even humans. And this life force...this energy in you is doing magick." Calion pulled her to him and Talia snuggled closer, letting her last doubts wash away.

"You sense magick, you speak to the *Malesia* tree and you can hear my sword. All these in themselves bear investigation. But you went into the faerie myst and were not immediately destroyed. And just now..." He shook his head as he realized it. "My magick allowed your touch. I believe you have some of your own."

"And it just showed up when I came here?"

"Perhaps." He had another theory, one he wasn't sure he liked. She started using the magick after meeting him for the first time. "Anyway, we will know more once we see my father." Shrugging away his concerns, Calion grinned wickedly and rolled Talia into his arms, making her gasp.

"But not yet. I have no wish to share you with anyone. My father and the rest of them can wait." He reached down and unlaced her tunic slowly, one lace at a time, dusting Talia's face with kisses. When he was done, he pulled the laces out, and wrapping them around one of her wrists, lifted her as he stood. "We need to find that stake, *Tia maer...* or perhaps a tree will do. I promised we would finish what we started when I returned. And now I know just the way for us to do so." Laughing, he carried her off into the forest.

ᘐᘓ

They stayed at the waterfall for seven moonfalls. Calion told Talia it was so her face could finish healing. The bruise she'd received from striking the log hadn't been healed by the pool, even though she felt no pain from it. He thought privately the pool hadn't healed it so it could be a reminder to them both. As it turned the different colors of the rainbow before fading completely away, it constantly brought to memory Talia's lifeless body lying cold in the myst, as well his part in sending her there.

And as he'd said, he wanted them to be alone. Calion showed her the forest, teaching her about his land and the elves' empathy toward it. Those who didn't nurture the land soon sickened and died. The forest and his people were connected.

He taught her the names of the trees and the flowers. Those that could be used for making herb tonics and remedies as well as those that were dreadful poisons. He showed her the forest animals and she discovered she had a great affinity for them.

Calion was amazed when they came to her. Even the great *shyr*, the howling king of the mountains, came and laid his head in her lap. When the prince demonstrated how to call sick animals for their food, she wept, knowing the need for food but hating it at the same time. She came close to becoming a vegetarian that day.

On Roch'mellon, they traveled the paths near the waterfall, enjoying what they found and each other. Talia found the forests of the elven world were lush and healthier than those of the human world, whose people polluted their land and rivers. Everything was more. More colorful, more vibrant and more beautiful. She wanted to explore the whole country. She loved it here.

And she loved Calion. The time they shared together was the richest Talia ever spent with another person. Every day in his presence showed her why she was drawn to him in the first place. Her body had known what her heart was just discovering.

This was a man who made her soul fly whenever he touched her. Their lovemaking hadn't lessened, in fact it seemed that whenever they weren't doing something else, Calion had her on the ground, against a tree, over a rock. His favorite place was in the healing pool. It seemed moving against her in the water did something special for him.

But even without that, there was the joy of just talking to him. Of walking hand and hand, watching as the waterfall painted rainbows in the sky. She loved lying in the grass, gazing at the stars as they came out at night. All the teasing and laughing, even the arguments.

Sometimes he would drop into a gloomy, silent thoughtfulness that scared her. It was the one dark point in their days together. He wouldn't talk about it. If she asked him what was wrong, he immediately would pull himself up and distract her, usually in a way that felt too good to protest. But she knew, and that knowing hurt, because when he was in that despondent silence, his thoughts were of her.

On the eighth day after her healing, Calion woke her with a gentle kiss and a slap on the bottom. "It is time, *Tia maer*... As much as I would wish it, I cannot justify staying here any longer. We must go to my father."

She yawned and stretched, her naked body loose and limber after the week of rest and the night's lovemaking.

His eyes flared. He'd been inside her less than an hour ago, and just looking at her made him want her again. "If you keep doing that, I..." His brain shut down when she reached over and boldly took his cock in her hand. He hardened instantly.

"You'll what?" she asked, her smile broadening. "It seems like you're always telling me what to do. Eat this, Talia, drink this, Talia. Spend time in the pool, Talia."

She squeezed him gently, and Calion choked as the lump in his throat threatened to strangle him.

"And then you take me on the ground, on a log, in the grass. Always you, telling *me* what to do."

"I..." He trailed off into a moan when she stroked up and down on his shaft.

"You know what I think?" she murmured softly as she gently pushed him down on his back. "I think it is my turn to tell you what to do."

She never before wanted to take the initiative, he realized as his heart began to pound. He always was the one in control, as was his nature. But now, there was something staggeringly arousing in letting Talia take charge. Allowing her to push him down, he watched as she knelt beside him. Her long hair fell down around her breasts as she leaned forward and touched his mouth with hers. Taking his lower lip, she nipped him then sucked on it as if in apology. Letting go, she traced his mouth with the tip of her tongue, arousing him unmercifully.

She enjoyed this. Feeling Calion's powerful body beneath hers, knowing she would be able to touch all that gorgeous flesh, made her almost giddy. She continued to toy with his mouth, delighting in the taste of him.

Following her instincts, she covered his face with kisses, tracing down his strong neck to his shoulders. His scent was musky and exciting, his taste...delicious. Talia kissed and nibbled, refusing to miss any part of him. Her body reacted to his, her heart thumping, her skin flushing.

Calion's hands clenched the blanket beside him. She learned the lessons of seduction well, he thought foggily as he moved under her tender assault. When her lips pulled at the fine hairs under his arms, he groaned out loud at the kindling of the nerves there. She traveled across his chest licking and kissing, her caresses light and arousing.

He gritted his teeth as she found his nipples, tugging at them, bringing them to tight peaks. She went back and forth tirelessly between the small dark berries, until Calion cried out and took her head in his hands, trying to bring her up so his mouth could ravage hers.

"Don't!" Talia's hand pushed at his chest. "It's my turn, remember?" Her body loosened and her insides began to ache. She grew wet when she saw his need.

Panting wildly, he let her go, but the fire already burned hot in his eyes. "Do not push me too far, *tolí*."

She laughed softly, already bending back to his prone body. "I'm not afraid of you, big boy." She nibbled again at his chest before using her hair to stroke over the rest of his body.

His muscles clenched so hard, Calion thought he would surely break in two. Her hand reached back down and took his throbbing shaft in her hand, stroking his cock so his hips came up off the blankets.

"Tal...ia..."

"What do you want, Calion?" she responded silkily, her hand not stopping its motion. Her mouth still worked busily on his chest. "Do you want me to stop?"

He groaned, feeling his body burn out of control. Much more and he would fracture into a million pieces. His eyes shone solid gold as he stared at her. "Now...I want you...now!"

Talia lifted herself slowly as she stared down at him, seeing the flames, feeling the heat of his body. She ached to feel him inside her. She'd never felt so hot before. Not taking her eyes from his, she moved over him. Positioning his cock against her waiting nether lips, she slowly lowered herself down on him.

Calion knew he'd gone mad. She moved so slowly when he wanted—no, needed—her to go faster. His body shook as he tried to control himself. He knew she was exploring a side of herself new to her, but if she didn't hurry, she would kill him in the process. His hips began to move involuntarily against her, helping with her possession of him. Suddenly, she pressed herself hard against him and he slid deep inside her.

They both moaned in ecstasy at the feeling of their bodies joined as one. After a moment, she began to move. Throwing her head back, her hands on his shoulders for balance, she rode him up and down, passion burning inside her. Her hands clenched at him, and he knew she would find her satisfaction soon.

He grabbed her hips in his hands and began thrusting with her, the friction increasing both their pleasure. Undone, Talia screamed and climaxed violently, pulling at her hair in frenzied joy. Their eyes locked and for a moment Calion thought he saw fire burning in her green eyes. Then her clenching body ended all thought. Slamming her against him and wrapping his arms tightly around her, he erupted inside her.

"*Tolí!*" he shouted in triumph as they shuddered together.

"What did that mean?" Talia asked lazily. They'd reversed positions, and now Calion lay half on her, nuzzling her neck. His strong face was softened with satisfaction. "What you yelled at the end."

"Princes do not yell," he mumbled. He dropped soft kisses along her shoulder. "Neither do we bellow, holler nor screech." He raised himself up on his elbows. "We inform."

She tried to hide a giggle, but it escaped anyway. She loved it when he played the haughty royal. "Okay, then what did you inform me of so loudly?"

Calion chuckled and dropped a kiss on the end of her nose. "*Tolí.* It means mine." His eyes darkened. "You are mine."

"Oh," she said, touched beyond measure. She snuggled against him. "That's nice. I like it."

"And I liked the way you kept us from leaving. But it only delayed us. We must leave for my home today."

Carefully, he rolled and pulled himself to his feet, bringing Talia with him. "I suggest a last soak in the healing pool, and then we will be off. It will take us two days to get to my father's kingdom."

Calion saw the sadness in her face and lifted her into his arms. "Do not pout, *Tia maer...* We will try to return here again someday. This is a special place." Turning, he carried her towards the waterfall.

An hour later, packed and ready, Calion pulled Talia up in

front of him on Roch'mellon's back. She snuggled back against him with a little purr of contentment, her borrowed tunic top slipping off one shoulder.

"Behave," he said, his lips brushing her ear.

"I will if you will," came the tart rejoinder. He laughed as he nudged Roch'mellon into a gallop.

They traveled all day, stopping only when necessity intruded or Talia needed a break. She wasn't as used to riding as he was. Along the way Calion pointed out different things he thought might be of interest, but he wouldn't stop for her to really investigate anything. He acted like he was pointed in a specific direction and couldn't or wouldn't stop. They ate leftover *paes* as they rode, washing it down with cold water brought from the waterfall.

They made camp that night under a spreading *tadí* tree, its leaves burnished gold and red. Talia placed their blankets against the base of the trunk and sat quietly as she watched him making a fire. He poked at it, his face serious.

"Penny for your thoughts."

He looked over, his face comical in its confusion. "I do not know what that means."

She laughed. "Sorry. It means I want to know what you're thinking. I can see you're worried about something."

A shadow came and went in his eyes. "It is nothing, *Tia maer*... I am just thinking about tomorrow."

"It's more than thinking. You're concerned about something. Does it have to do with me?"

Calion sighed. How could he have forgotten how perceptive she was? Perhaps it was another part of her magick. "I do not want you to worry."

She kicked off her boots and lay down on the pallet, leaning on an elbow. "Saying that makes me worry. Come on, give."

He fought with himself and with a sense of guilt, chose the easy way. "I am concerned about the prophecy. The closer we get to the kingdom, the more danger you may be in if the orcs are not in their territory."

She felt a mixture of alarm and relief. "Can't you ask the trees?"

"You remember your training. Yes, I can ask the trees. Since I want to be beside you this night, I will ask them if all is safe before we sleep. They can keep watch for us."

"And if it isn't?"

He rose and came over to her. "Then we will keep on going until it is." He crouched and took her face in his hands. "They will not take you again. This I swear on my own life."

"No, don't." She reached up and grabbed his wrists. "Don't say that. I couldn't bear if something happened to you because of me."

"Shhh, Talia." Calion kissed her gently. "It is my right and duty to protect you. You are my..." He had to think for a moment on how to define what she was to him, before he said simply, "You are *tolí*, remember."

She felt a sense of disappointment at the description, but let it go. There were other things to worry about. "Then let's talk to the trees. The sooner you know, the better you'll feel. And then..." She smiled and ran her hand down his chest teasingly. "Then we can go to bed."

After that remark, Calion's kiss was not so gentle.

The night passed with no alarms raised. After eating a good meal, they both went right to bed. No sooner were they in the blankets than he pulled off her clothes, his movements rough and urgent. Their mating was hard and intense.

Afterwards, she fell asleep, but for Calion it seemed mating with her once wasn't enough. He woke her again and again, needing her. He loved her with a desperation she wondered at. The dawn was breaking when he came to her one last time, muttering soft words in Elvish that made her feel precious and wanted. He stayed inside her a long time, stopping when they got too close, needing the intimacy more than the release.

When he finally let them go, they came together with a glorious rush, their hearts singing and their pulses pounding.

They rose, cleaned up and got on the road before the sun reached the top of the distant mountains. They rode for about an hour before Calion spoke. "We are half a day's ride from the castle. Do not be surprised to see other elves soon. We are coming to a more populated area."

"I can't wait to meet other elves. I want to see if they are all as nice as you."

His face clouded. "We are all different, as your race is. Do not worry. I will be with you."

"I'm not worried," she said blithely. "I'm just excited."

He frowned. He worried enough for both of them. He'd kept some things from Talia, not wanting her to lose her lovely smile. Now, reality approached and he had no way to soften the blow.

They'd been riding for about an hour when Talia squealed and pointed off to the left. "Stop, Calion, stop! Are those apples?"

Roch'mellon stopped immediately before even being asked. Calion squinted over at the trees and nodded. "Yes, those are *eidaer*...apples."

"*Eidaer*," she repeated. "I'll remember." She turned and looked beseechingly at him. "Can we get some? Please?"

He smiled at her beauty. "Yes, *Tia maer*... Stop begging. It is unseemly for the companion of a prince to beg." He slid off the horse and helped her down.

"Oh." She narrowed her eyes at him, matching his amusement. "Heaven forbid I'm unseemly." Reaching down she pinched him in the butt. His startled yelp filled her with satisfaction. She whooped and ran for the apple trees. "You forgot," she shouted. "Princes don't yelp either."

She'd picked one apple before he caught up with her. Showing no mercy, Calion tackled her under one of the trees, rolling so he would take the brunt of the fall.

She laughed and wriggled when he pulled her under him, delighted to see his smile. When he pinched her back, she screamed for mercy, and laughing, he popped the apple into her mouth to quiet her. She bit down and moaned in pleasure at the sweet, crisp taste. As she swallowed, she gave him a bite and they both chewed the treat, their eyes on each other.

He kissed her then, tasting the tart apple on her lips and tongue. He enjoyed her company so much. She was refreshing to be with. It was why he'd hidden them away. He could have been back at the castle in an hour if he'd used the void. But like the day they left the *Malesia* tree, he'd wanted time with her all to himself.

He was not Prince Calion when they were together, but Calion the male. Talia didn't seem to care about his position, just him. She brought out a side of him never seen before. Even now he was lying in a field, playing tag and stealing apples.

What would she make him do next? The thought made him smile.

"So...you like my *eidaer*?" she asked saucily, her mouth brushing against him. "I have some others you may find to your liking." She rubbed her breasts against him.

"Stop it," he laughed. He moved so she lay on top of him. "I cannot ride when I am hard."

Grinning down at him, she couldn't help herself. He'd walked right into it. She carefully bounced her pelvis up and down on him. "Really? I thought that was the only way you could ride."

He swore and rolled again, taking her mouth in a hard kiss. She didn't give an inch, but wrapped her arms around him and kissed him back. Heat burst around them.

Suddenly Roch'mellon nickered a warning, and Calion swore again at his lack of control. He'd come perilously close to stripping his female and taking her in an open field. Roch'mellon nickered again, and this time Calion looked up and his gut tightened.

An elven male and female were walking across the field toward them.

Chapter Eight

Jumping to his feet, he pulled Talia up so he stood between her and the elves. Taking his cloak, he wrapped it around her, pulling the hood over her head to partially hide her face.

"Calion? What is it?"

He cursed. Of all the poor luck. "I do not have time to explain now. I want you to go over under that *eidaer* tree. Keep the hood up and stay there, no matter what happens."

She saw the couple walking their way. "Are they the owners of the trees? Are we in trouble? Oh, can I meet them?"

"No!" he almost shouted. Controlling himself, he gave her a push toward the tree. "Do not say a word."

Staring at him in shock, she finally turned and walked under the tree.

Breathing a sigh of relief, he used an illusion to change his features so the couple wouldn't recognize him. He walked to meet them, putting as much distance between Talia and the couple as possible.

"A good day to you, sir," said the male elf.

"And to you," Calion returned politely.

"I am Eo Miriel and this is my mate, Inwe."

Calion bowed politely to the lady. He used an alter ego. "I am Taurnil Ar-Feiniel." He waved at Talia, who waved hesitantly back. "My mate, Ireth. She is from another province and very shy."

"We heard a scream and came to investigate."

Calion didn't have to fake the red that crept up his neck. "My apologies. We are newly mated, and—"

Eo Miriel lifted a hand. "No need to explain, son." He leered at his wife, who smiled calmly. "We can still remember the days of our youth."

"Can you break bread with us?" Inwe asked, her gaze going to Talia's still figure. She hadn't moved since that first wave of her hand.

"My thanks, lady, but I have business at the castle. We only stopped when we saw the *eidaer.* I did not realize they belonged to anybody. Allow me to pay you for them."

"No need," Eo said benevolently. "There is plenty for all."

"I thank you." Calion bowed again. "Good day to you. I should get back to my mate before she worries any more."

The couple nodded, watching as Calion headed toward the tree. He felt rather than saw them turn and head back the way they'd come. As he reached Talia, he dropped the illusion spell. She still hadn't moved, hadn't removed the hood.

"It is all right. They have gone." When she still didn't budge, he reached over and pushed back the hood. His gut twisted when he saw the agony on her face.

"*Tia maer...* Let me explain," he began. He reached for her, but she stepped back, her wide eyes dark with hurt.

"You don't have to." Her voice was tight with pain. "I know why you didn't want me to meet them." She looked straight at him, and he knew by trying to protect her, he'd hurt her even more. "I was right before. You are ashamed of me."

He swore under his breath. "That is not the reason I hid you from those farmers! Let me explain."

"No need. What were you going to do? Hide me in your room so no one could see me? Have me service your needs at night, and then you could pretend I don't exist during the day?" Now her eyes held as much temper as hurt.

He grabbed her by the shoulders, his own temper flaring. "Do not cheapen what we have!"

"What do we have, Calion? You don't even know what to call me." Angrily, she brushed the wetness from her face. "Tell me now, straight to my face my being human isn't the problem."

When he didn't answer, she nodded. "I thought so. Damn you! Why did you even ask me to stay?" Twisting, she wrenched away from him, leaving the elf cloak in his hands. She ran through the orchard and never looked back.

Swearing, he threw the cloak over his shoulder and gave

chase. He'd forgotten how fast she was and his temper built as he ran after her. She'd made it out of the orchard and into the forest before he caught her.

"Talia, stop this!" he shouted. He grabbed her arm and pulled her to a stop. She fought him, using her fists and teeth to get away.

"*Kydaer pas air*!" he swore violently as a fist caught his chin. "Stop this, now!"

Talia took no notice. All the pain and hurt she'd felt narrowed down to this one moment. She wanted to get far away from him, and she didn't care if she hurt him to do it.

"That is it," Calion gritted as he finally captured her flying fists in his strong hands. He paid no attention to her swearing, but he was furious that she would strike him. His temper was so high, she was lucky he couldn't stomach hitting women, even to protect himself. Besides, the memory of that one bruise she'd received in their last struggle stopped him cold.

Instead, he pushed her back against the trunk of a large *shardyr* tree and kept her there with his strong body. "Enough, *Tia maer*... You will hurt yourself."

"Get...off me!" She squirmed against him, trying to escape. "I won't stay with someone who's ashamed of me! Let me go!"

Temper turned to desire as he held her there. Talia's struggling body inflamed his own, making him hard and ready in moments. He was done talking. He stopped her shouting simply by closing his mouth over hers.

Slowly, her struggles stopped as her body, so in tune to the feel of his, recognized his need and responded with its own. She was still angry, but persuaded by her love for him, she couldn't help but kiss him back, hesitantly at first and then harder, stroking her tongue into his mouth.

His body shuddered and one hand came up to cup her breast. Feeling it, she tore her mouth away from his. "No...I-I don't want this." But her protest was weak and they both knew it.

"You lie to yourself, Talia." His thumb brushed over her nipple and she fought back a shiver of pleasure. His lips caressed the side of her throat. "If you will not listen to what I say, you will listen to what we both feel."

She gave another half-hearted struggle, angrier with herself for still wanting him than with him for holding her immobile.

His hands moved over her, so familiar, so gentle, she had to fight not to respond. Her knees trembled at each touch, at each brush of his mouth and she knew that she wouldn't win this battle. No matter how angry she was, her love was stronger.

She held onto her control for as long as she could, but when his teeth fastened onto her earlobe, heat shot through her and her eyes closed in ecstasy. Forgetting their argument, forgetting the hurt she felt, Talia surrendered without another word.

As soon as he felt her response, Calion's lust soared. Pinning her hands above her head, he held her against the rough bark as he pulled her breeches down over her slim hips. Tearing open his own, he pulled out his cock and with a single thrust buried himself inside her. She cried out, and her eyes widened before she arched against him in unconscious invitation.

His body moved against hers, his desire for her making him want to finish quickly, but he knew if this was the only way he could communicate, he had to make sure she understood just what he was saying. He wanted her with him, no matter what.

When her body began moving along with his, his grip gentled, but his thrusts became more determined. Reaching down between their bodies, he slid his finger into her wet lips to find the sensitive nubbin hiding there. Within a few minutes, Talia cried out his name in satisfaction. Several grinding thrusts later, Calion joined her, jetting his seed into her so hard, his vision grayed.

Afterwards, he just held her against the tree as their hearts and breathing slowed. When she made a half-hearted attempt to get away, he said simply, "No...please," and covered her mouth with another soul-searching kiss.

Calion knew touch calmed the most fractious of females, so he kept her body pinned with his as he stroked her, feeling the fine trembling of her body.

Suddenly, she began to cry, her soft weeping striking at his heart.

"Please," he murmured, kissing the tears away gently. "Hear me out. If you choose afterwards to go back to your world, I will take you."

Talia let her head fall forward onto his chest. Now that her temper had left her, she was exhausted. She just wanted to close her eyes and pretend they were back at the waterfall. She hadn't realized she'd spoken it out loud until his arm tightened around her.

"I too, wish we were there. Back in a place where neither of us must concern ourselves with reality. But we are here. Will you allow me to explain what I should have told you before?"

At her slow nod, Calion let go of her arms and brought them back to her sides. Moving carefully, keeping their bodies joined, he lowered them both to his dropped cloak. He pulled her against him so they lay side by side. Once they were comfortable, he propped his head up on his hand.

"I did not keep you away from the farmers because I am ashamed of you," he began. "But the reason does have to do with you being a human." Feeling her tense, he soothed her with a gentle movement of his body against hers. "I did not tell you everything, because I knew when I did so you would be frightened and worried. I wanted you to stay happy as long as possible."

He frowned when he saw her disbelief. "It is true, Talia. I do not lie to you."

"What haven't you told me?" Her voice was whisper soft.

Calion sighed. "I told you I struggled with mating with you. I chose to do so in the beginning, knowing you would go home. I would tell no one I broke the *sardai.*" He bent and kissed her, pleased when she relaxed in his arms. "And then that morning, I knew I could not let you go. I wanted you with me."

He traced her lips with his finger. "At the waterfall, out there in the forest, there is no problem because there are no eyes to see what we are doing. But here, with others around us, they will see you are human."

"I don't understand." Talia searched his face worriedly. "You've already broken the...*sardai.* You didn't care I was human then. Why do you care now?"

He ran a hand through his loose hair. "Because of what will happen if anyone finds out."

"What can happen?" she asked in exasperation. "What are they going to do...kill me?" His expression made her close her eyes in horror. "You're saying they *will* kill me?"

"Not just you, *Tia maer...* Both of us."

She sat up, abruptly disengaging their bodies. "What?"

He sighed, pulling her back down beside him. She was

totally white. "I am sorry, Talia. I know now I have wronged you. I should have told you this back at the waterfall and given you the choice to go home. I was selfish and wanted you to stay with me, so I did not think it through, and now you will be in danger. Just having you with me puts us both at risk."

Talia stared up at him. "Are you saying if someone finds out we've made love—mated—you could be killed?"

"We could *both* be killed for disobeying the edict. There is also a chance I will be punished for bringing you—a human—to the castle."

"I don't understand. If you knew you could be killed over this, why did you bring me here? You could have had your fun at the waterfall and then sent me home. Why keep me?"

He frowned at the genuine puzzlement in her voice. "Have you not listened to anything I have said to you? I thought one night with you would be enough. It was not. Instead, the more I have you, the more I want you. Perhaps at first I thought I could get you out of my system, but now I know that is untrue. I could not let you go. It is not just your body I enjoy. It is you. I want you to stay with me."

Talia's heart swelled. She'd been so angry and hurt, but knowing he couldn't help himself, that he'd gone against everything just to be with her, made her love him even more. "You want me that much?"

He kissed her again, this time in relief, sensing she'd forgiven him. "Yes, that much. So much I put you in danger." He scowled suddenly. "Do you not understand you could be killed as well? It is not just me."

"I got that Calion, truly, I do."

"You seem more worried about me than yourself. This I do not understand."

"I got that too, you big idiot." Talia pulled his head down to hers and kissed him. "You're just going to have to deal with it, because I'm not going to explain it to you. But I'm not going anywhere."

As he held her closer, Calion knew he was missing something, but the relief he felt on hearing she was staying drove it out of his mind. When Talia pressed herself against him, his focus narrowed down to just one thing. Nudging her knees apart again, he slid inside her again, hearing her gasp of pleasure.

"As the day continues, things may occur that frighten or confuse you. I may not be able to act as I would wish. So remember this moment, *Tia maer...* Remember how we feel when our bodies are joined. When things get confusing, when you do not know what is happening, think of how we feel together. Do not forget how much I want you. Remember this."

They only took a few apples back with them. Somehow, their taste for them was gone. Talia fed a couple to Roch'mellon, who had waited patiently through all the drama. Then they mounted and rode towards the city. Talia wore the elven cloak now, her head and face covered from sight. It was his plan they ride straight to the castle without anyone seeing her.

They traveled through the afternoon, not stopping, rarely speaking, both lost in their thoughts. Incredibly, they were thinking the same thing: *How do I stop others from knowing how I feel?*

Calion knew if he showed his father or anyone close to him how he felt about Talia, she would immediately be put to death. And that could not happen. While his own life and destiny were important, so too was keeping this one unpredictable female alive. She must be allowed to tell her story. He had a gut feeling the prophecy had something to do with the elves. He just didn't know what.

Talia rode, enjoying the feeling of his body against hers. She struggled with the thought that simple pleasure would soon be taken from her. If they couldn't show how they felt, how could they touch? She berated herself for her earlier stupidity. Why she had thought his deciding he would break the *sardai* would automatically make everyone else okay with it, she didn't know. Pretending Calion was nothing special to her would be impossible. He'd saved her life so she could get away with acting grateful. She desperately hoped that would fool them all. Their lives were on the line.

They came to an area of tidy cottages and neatly laid out farmland. The land was more cultivated than where the apples had grown.

"This is the *thasals,*" Calion shared as he slowed Roch'mellon to a trot. He waved at the elves who stopped their chores and bowed, whispering among themselves when they saw a female with the prince. He ignored it. "This is where our people farm and raise animals. They bring their wares into market to sell."

They came to the top of a ridge and he leaned close to her ear. "Close your eyes." Obeying, she felt the horse came to a stop.

"This is the first look you will have of my kingdom, *Tia maer...* Welcome to *Osalai.* Open your eyes."

She did and her heart soared. Something deep inside her knew this place. It brought back faint memories of childhood dreams. I've found it, she thought, giving a gasp of pure pleasure. *Finally...this is home!*

Looking out into a shallow valley, she saw tall, stately trees rimming the valley edges, with fragrant lush meadows further within. Against the far side, sheer mountain walls to its back, lay the castle.

It was something straight out of a fairy tale. Cut gray stone, it was huge, with arched windows and turrets. Guarded watch stands dotted the tall outer walls. Black and gold flags waved in the afternoon breeze and smoke curled lazily from one of several chimneys. Talia could see soldiers practicing in the bailey, near the outbuildings that ran along the side of the castle.

The town clustered around it like chicks around an elegant mother hen. This too looked like something out of a storybook with its tiny cottages, shops and cobbled streets. Crowded and noisy, it was easy to hear the sounds of voices where they sat. A high wall surrounded the city, with a huge drawbridge that opened over the city's first defense...a wide rushing river.

"Many have tried to come against us." Calion spoke almost reverently as he gazed down upon his beloved home. "None have succeeded."

She bit her lip as she heard the pride and love in his voice. She would not let him lose this. "It is the most beautiful place I have ever seen. *Osalai.* What does it mean?"

"In your tongue, it means place of perfection."

"I can't argue with that." Talia could have stayed there for the rest of the afternoon drinking in the sight, but she sensed Calion becoming restless. "If for no other reason, I'm glad I got to see this."

He gave her a squeeze. "It will be all right. Be as brave as I know you can be. I will allow no harm to come to you."

Turning, she pressed her face against his chest. "Don't

make promises you can't keep, Calion. We both made the decision to follow this path."

"I will not let anyone hurt you. But do not forget what I told you back in the *eidaer* orchard, *Tia maer*... No matter what happens."

"I'll remember," she promised.

Bending his head, he gave her a quick, hard kiss. It burned them all the way to their toes, but it would have to suffice for now.

Pulling Talia's hood as far forward as possible, Calion clucked to Roch'mellon and started down the ridge. As soon as they hit the bottom of the trail, he left the dirt path, turning onto the wider road. They hadn't gone fifty yards when trumpets began to call, welcoming the prince home. Ignoring them, he galloped down the road and across the drawbridge.

There, many of his people alerted to his homecoming cheered and waved, but other than a regal nod and salute, he kept riding, wanting only to get to the castle with his precious cargo. He slowed when he came into the busy village streets but kept Roch'mellon at a trot.

Talia felt how tense he was. His body curved around hers like a shield. Suddenly, she realized what he'd meant about females being protected in this position. It made sense now.

She saw the faces of the elves as they cheered Calion. They loved their prince. And as they rode swiftly through the crowd, she could tell the moment the people saw he carried a passenger. They all gawked and whispered. Maybe he never brought women back from his travels. That thought made Talia feel better.

No, he would never have been able to keep her presence quiet. Calion laughed, but the sound held little amusement. With him riding through town, the gossip would spread like wildfire. The prince brought home a female...dressed like a male! Thank the goddesses they couldn't see under the hood. At least at the castle they would have a chance to tell Talia's story before rumors went wild.

Finally, they arrived at the inner wall. The gate to the castle proper opened and he rode through at a gallop, passing all who'd come to greet him. He headed straight to the stables and drew Roch'mellon to a sliding stop while stable hands scattered like mice at his approach. Leaning forward, he spoke softly.

"Keep your hood forward."

Talia trembled as she tugged the hood up to cover her face. What would happen now?

"Everyone out!" Calion gazed tensely around at workers in the stable. "Now!" Ten seconds later the stable was empty. He nodded decisively. "Now we wait."

"For what?" she whispered.

A few moments later, she heard the sound of approaching footsteps, and incredibly, he relaxed. "For back-up, *Tia maer...*"

Talia leaned back into him when the footsteps turned into the stable. Six large elven males, dressed in the same unrelieved black as the prince, walked inside. She saw they looked about the same age as Calion, as well as being brawny and well formed. It seemed as if a wall of muscle walked into the stable. They had hard, intelligent faces, but weary, as if they'd seen one too many battles to live as less experienced men. Their uniforms carried a crest. The same one emblazoned on the prince's cloak. Were these elves friend or foe?

Calion answered that question when he slipped off his horse and going to the largest of the men, clasped forearms. He then threw his arms around the man, pounding him heartily on the back. "My friend, it is good to see you."

The elf returned the embrace before stepping back to glare at the prince. "Your Highness."

Calion laughed. "Such formality!"

The elf didn't smile. "It is all I have when my prince goes off on a secret mission and forgets to take his Royal Guard with him."

The Royal Guard? Talia thought. Were these the back-up he had been waiting for? If so, he may want to rethink things. None of the elves looked happy with him.

"I sensed a disturbance when Roch'mellon and I went hunting. I sent word to you." Calion crossed his arms over his chest. "Did you not get it?"

"We received it," the elf admitted. "But how can we keep you safe if you will not allow us to accompany you?"

"You have been guarding my back for more years than I can count. I did not think I needed you. I checked the barrier."

"You worry too much about that thing," put in a brown-haired elf. "You always have."

"Peace, Celahir," returned Calion. "You are correct. I do worry about the myst barrier. This time it turns out my worry was justified."

He stepped back, touching Talia's leg gently, and then spoke, his tone very different from what it had been previously. This time he sounded like a prince. "I ask you to pledge your loyalty to me. The past is remembered, but I ask if you will stand for me now."

"My prince," the first elf gasped. He put his hand to his chest. "Why would you ask such a thing? What have we done to earn this condemnation? We are all your faithful servants."

"Maeglin," Calion said quietly. "You have done nothing to make me reproach you. But I wish to know. Will you stand with me now?"

Maeglin looked at his prince, and then his intelligent gaze moved over the still figure on the horse. "This has to do with the female."

"I await your answers," was all Calion would say.

Maeglin stared at his prince a moment longer and then silently went to one knee. The other five elves followed suit. He placed his fist against his heart. "Our loyalty is yours, Prince Calion of the Calen'taur Elves. We protect the heir to the throne."

"And you protect what is mine?"

Maeglin's eyes narrowed, but he answered the question readily enough. "You and yours...we protect them all with our lives."

"Good, good." Calion leaned forward and helped Maeglin back to his feet. "Celahir, Lólindir, Amroth, Valandil, Orophin. It is good to see all of you."

"My prince." The others bowed their heads.

"Prince Calion, may we ask—" Maeglin started.

"Maeglin," Calion put up his hand, "I will tell you why I asked you all to repeat your oath of loyalty. It is not as much for me but for someone else." He gave Talia's leg a brief, unseen squeeze. "I have found something that will challenge what you know, perhaps even the very beliefs you cherish. It is why I went into the myst. You will hear the full story when I tell my father, but all I ask of you right now is to have an open mind."

Calion turned to the cloaked figure. "Talia?"

Knowing what he wanted, she took a deep breath and pushed the hood off her head, revealing her beauty but also her rounded ears and flat eyebrows. She watched as the elves, almost as one, drew their swords.

"My prince," growled a redheaded man. His gaze went between Calion and the female. "It is a human!"

"Prince Calion!" Even Maeglin was shocked to the core. "What have you done?"

"Have you captured this human?" Celahir asked, his gray eyes flashing.

Calion felt Talia trembling where his hand rested on her leg. He wanted to reassure her but couldn't. Instead, he slowly drew his own sword and faced his men, protecting her himself. He knew his men wouldn't harm her, but she didn't understand their ways yet. It was why he'd requested they restate their pledge to him. She needed to hear it.

"You would lift your sword against us?" Maeglin asked, his tone astonished. He stared at the glowing, blue sword.

"This is Talia," Calion stated, his voice hard as stone. "She is under my protection and now under yours. I know of the legends and why you reacted in such a way. I will overlook the fact you drew your swords against something I call mine. But I expect your loyalty, the loyalty you just pledged. If you cannot honestly protect this female—this human—then say so now. You may walk away with no dishonor."

The elven Guard stood staring at the drawn sword. Their prince pulled it on *them*. They didn't know quite what to do with that fact.

Finally, Maeglin moved, breaking the silence. He dropped his sword. "I will do my duty, Calion. But I do not have to like it."

"I do not ask you to change your beliefs of a lifetime overnight, my friend. I understand the problem in doing so. Believe me when I say I went through much the same thing." He heard Talia give a small giggle and squeezed her leg in warning.

"But you are my Guard, and Talia is under my protection. She was stolen from the human world by the sons of Udaogong. The lady did not come here of her own will, but by the designs of another. She is as confused and frightened of this world as others will be when they see her."

Maeglin chewed on the information as he put his sword

away. The other elves reluctantly followed his lead. "How did she escape the orcs? Did they let her go?"

"Your prince released me," Talia spoke quickly. She wanted these men to know of Calion's bravery. "He came into the orcan stronghold and rescued me even though he was far out numbered."

All the elves jumped when she spoke. Calion moved to quiet her, but stopped. Better they know now that she was no shrinking elf maiden.

They stared at her like she had two heads. She stared back, her chin raised. "Don't your females talk here?"

The others seemed struck dumb, but Maeglin shook his head slowly. "We... You..." He finally looked back to Calion, not knowing how to answer the human. "Is she saying you went into *Grundlug* on your own?"

"I did. I had no time to call for help. We all know what orcs do to females...any female."

"But my prince," the redheaded man said angrily. "You put your life at risk for a human?"

Calion's temper slipped. Of all of them, he knew Valandil would be the one to give him trouble. He was his father's choice to the Guard. "No female deserves to be raped by an orc, Valandil. Even a human."

The elf reddened, knowing he'd stepped over the line. Moving back, he mumbled an apology, shifting side to side in his embarrassment. He glared at Talia from under bushy red eyebrows.

Maeglin ignored him. "You are all right?"

"Yes, Maeglin. I am—"

"He took an arrow in the shoulder," Talia interrupted. "It is healed now."

This time Calion did turn and look at her, commanding her to be silent. She just raised her chin higher. He sighed at her stubbornness and turned back to his men.

"All is well. A healing salve took care of any injuries." He purposely left out the part about the healing spring. "Not knowing the human female's physiology, I could not give her anything specific. We waited for her injuries to heal in a different way. That is why we are so long in returning."

Talia's eyebrow rose. He hadn't lied...exactly, but he hadn't told them the whole truth either.

"I ask again. Do any of you have a problem with keeping the Lady Talia safe? There are elves that will react as you did when they see her, with fear and even hatred. I will have her protected at all costs."

"Calion, no," Talia murmured quietly.

The elf prince turned back to her. "Yes...at all costs. Until we find out why Udaogong wants you, you must be watched at all times."

He looked at the Guard. "Well? What say you all?"

There was a long silence while Maeglin gave the elves a chance to bow out of Calion's service. When no one spoke, he pounded his right fist against his heart. "We serve the heir."

"You will protect what I call mine?"

"We will protect all you call yours." The elven men all took the pledge, mirroring Maeglin's actions.

"Then this..." Calion turned and held up his arms to help Talia down. She slid down against him, and he held her for a brief moment before turning her to his men. "This I call mine."

After a moment, he drew her away from his men. "I will go ahead to speak to my father. I must prepare him for seeing you. I want you to stay with my Guard. They will protect you."

"They don't want me here. They're afraid of me. How can I trust them?" Talia bit her lip, trying not to cry. His men's reaction to her was an eye-opener. If all the elven people felt the same way, she didn't want Calion out of her sight.

"Do not worry, *Tia maer...*" Calion caught himself before leaning down to kiss her. He straightened abruptly. "They have pledged themselves to protect you. No matter what they personally feel, they will do you no harm. They will give their life for you."

"I don't understand," she whispered forlornly.

Calion put his hands on her shoulders. "They are my men. I have their complete loyalty. Because you are under my protection, you are now under theirs. You will be fine." He dropped his hands, suddenly realizing what his actions implied. He would have to be far more circumspect.

Maeglin watched his prince touch the female, remembering the way he'd slid her down his body when she'd dismounted. Neither made the leader of the guards comfortable. It spoke of a closeness that should not be. He narrowed his eyes. Had the human female put a spell on the prince? If so, no matter what the pledge, he would protect the heir first. He'd barely finished the thought when Calion brought the female over to him.

"Maeglin, as leader of my guards, I put Talia in your care. Protect her, my friend."

"I will, my prince," Maeglin promised. He met the female's eyes and both saw the mute challenge in the other. "We will watch her as the hawk watches prey. She will be well defended."

Calion clasped Maeglin's arm and nodded to the other guard. "Come to the throne room, but slowly. I would speak to the king first." He looked at Talia, pulling her hood back up to hide her face. "Stay with them. And *remember...*"

She knew he referred to the apple orchard, and her lips quivered into a smile. "Please. Be careful."

His jaw tight with unexpressed emotion, Calion looked deep into her eyes before he bowed. Turning on his heel, he quickly left the stable.

Left alone, surrounded by a six foot wall of hostile elven males, Talia went as still as the *tyri*, the mouse-like creature Calion had shown her. She wanted to trust them, but she couldn't. Trust wasn't given, it was earned.

Finally, Maeglin spoke. He'd been unwillingly impressed at the concern she'd shown for Calion's wellbeing, but she was still an unknown. She would have to earn his trust. "Shall we go, my lady?"

Talia nodded and stepped forward to walk next to Maeglin. Celahir, the brown-haired elf with gray eyes took the lead. She was flanked by the blond, blue-eyed Maeglin on one side and a dark-haired elf with green eyes on the other. "What is your name?" she asked him.

The elf looked startled. Apparently female elves *didn't* talk a lot. Or maybe they thought all humans were dumb. "My name is Amroth, m'lady."

Talia nodded. She looked over her shoulder, not surprised to see the other three marching behind. She glanced at the redheaded elf. "I know you are Valandil." She looked at the other two. "But I don't know your names."

The two elves looked at each other. "I am Lólindir," said the one with sandy brown hair and chocolate-colored eyes. "And he is Orophin. He does not say much."

Talia looked at Orophin, with his long black hair and hazel eyes. Back home they would all be considered eye candy, even the sullen Valandil. But here they were warriors, and the only thing between her and a lot of angry elves. "I know you're not pleased to meet me, but I'm glad to meet you." She turned back around. "I've always wanted to meet faeries."

Maeglin frowned. "Humans know of us?"

Talia smiled, glad he would talk to her. "All we know are stories. I just happen to be one of the few that believe stories usually have a basis in fact. When I found myself in this place, I was shocked but not disbelieving."

Celahir led them through a tall doorway and into a courtyard. Talia saw servants going about their business, but they all stopped and stared when they saw the guards. Talia reached up and tugged her hood forward.

"Do not be afraid, m'lady. We have promised to protect you." Maeglin spoke softly so no one would hear.

"What would they do if they knew Calion had brought a human female into their home?" she fretted.

"In those clothes, you look like a youngling male."

Talia blinked. "I wonder if I should be insulted?" she teased.

Maeglin went ramrod straight in an instant. "No insult intended."

She sighed. "I'm just making a joke. I joke when I'm nervous."

As they left the courtyard and entered the castle, she glanced around her. There were high domed ceilings. The furnishings were ornate and beautifully taken care of. A soft white light lit the rooms. Talia could see tapestries and banners hanging in the hallways, and she longed for the time to look at them.

Celahir motioned down a long deserted hall. "This way."

Nerves whirled in her stomach—she was so sick with worry about Calion. Would his father punish him? Would he do worse? Fear crept up her spine. She was protected, but what about him? Shouldn't some of these men be with Calion? She put her hand on Maeglin's arm, making him jerk.

"M'lady?"

"Will he be safe?" she said urgently, squeezing his arm in

her fear. "Calion. Will he be safe?"

Maeglin stumbled. Her hooded face turned toward him, and he saw the fear in her eyes. As her words penetrated, he realized she was afraid for the prince and not for herself. "You are worried for him?"

Talia pulled on his arm, looking around at the others before leaning closer to him. "You are his friend. I could see that when we arrived. I know bringing me here is a risk. Calion thought his father should know what the orcs planned, but he didn't tell me he could be punished until too late."

Maeglin saw her in a new light. This was no sniveling human weakling he'd read about in stories. "I will not lie to you, Lady Talia. It is a risk."

"If seeing his father is a risk, shouldn't you be there with him? To protect him? Isn't that your duty?"

"We should be protecting him," Maeglin snarled, insulted by her words. "But he left us with you instead. We do not want it this way either."

"Then do something," Talia begged. "He must be kept safe. Send two of your men. All of you needn't stay with me."

Maeglin pondered her words as they left the dimly lit hallway and turned down another corridor. His prince would be angry, but then again, he hadn't been specific in how many should stay with the female. His respect for the lady increased.

He turned to Valandil and Orophin. "Run ahead and stand with the prince. He should not be alone."

"As you will." Valandil bowed, then he and Orophin passed by and ran up the corridor.

Talia sagged in relief. At least Calion would have someone to protect him now, *if* the stubborn idiot would allow it. "Thank you."

Maeglin ignored her, irritated he hadn't thought of the idea himself. "Celahir, fan out forward. Amroth, drop further back with Lólindir. Look alive, my friends. We do not know what may lie ahead."

Talia chewed her lip frantically as she thought of what might be happening in the throne room. She must protect Calion, no matter what. He would not lose his heritage or his life if she could help it.

"Maeglin," she said suddenly. "I wish to speak frankly with you."

Chapter Nine

At his nod, she took a deep breath. *I love you, Calion.*

"What Calion has done, bringing me here... It could be very bad, couldn't it?"

"Yes, m'lady. I am sorry, but it could be."

"You are responsible for his safety and his well being. I understand that. He is the most important thing in the world to you, right?"

Maeglin frowned. He couldn't tell where the female was headed with these questions. "That is correct. I have guarded him for many years. He is like a brother to me."

She gave a sigh of relief. "You may not believe it, but he is very important to me too. After all, he did save my life. That makes me, ummm, very grateful to the prince." Her intense green eyes met those of the blond elf. "He should not suffer because of me. Not in any way. Calion is too important to you...to his people. He will be the next king. Nothing can stand in the way of that, not even me."

Maeglin listened to her impassioned speech with surprise. What did this all mean? This human cared for Prince Calion? He looked down at the emotion Talia forgot to hide in her fear for Calion. Was it possible this human had feelings for his prince? What should he do with that knowledge?

She went on. "I want you to promise me if it looks like things are going to go bad for Calion, you will protect him."

"I do not need to make that promise, Lady Talia. I already have pledged my loyalty to the prince."

"Yes, but would you do anything to protect him?" She bit her lip. "Anything at all?

Maeglin nodded, his brow furrowed in confusion. "Anything

but high treason against my world."

"Then promise me, if it looks as if my presence here will cause the prince to lose his heritage or his life...then..." Talia swallowed and whispered, "I must die."

Maeglin did stop dead this time, thinking he heard the human wrong. He motioned the other elves away. "What did you say?"

"You heard me right. Calion must be kept safe. Promise me if it comes down to between me and him, I will be taken care of, before he can be hurt in *any* way."

Maeglin took her by the arm and continued walking. He took a deep breath. This human was not only strong, but brave. She would give her life so the prince would not be harmed or even shamed before his people. His animosity fell away. "You are not what I expected."

She brushed that off. "That's what Calion said. Please..." Her eyes beseeched him as she grasped his tunic sleeve. "Do we have a deal?"

He patted her hand. "Lady Talia, you are a unique female, and I understand now why Calion has risked himself to bring you here. Alas, I cannot do what you ask. First, because I have promised to protect you and I cannot break my word. But secondly, a female like you should not die. You have too much honor."

Her eyes filled with despair. "My honor will not keep him safe." She touched the blade he wore in his belt. "Then let me have your dagger. Give me the means to do it myself, if need be. Please, Maeglin. I will not be the one to bring harm to him!"

Maeglin just shook his head in wonder. Never had he met such a female. If she was elven, he would consider— He stopped himself cold. What was he thinking? Was this why Calion's face softened when he looked at Talia? Did he look beyond the hated humanity and see the strength and courage as well?

"I am sorry, Lady Talia. To give you my dagger would be breaking my vow. I must keep you safe, even from yourself."

Talia turned her head away, her heart aching. How could she keep Calion safe now? Her fear grew as they came to a large wooden door. Two liveried guards stood on either side, dressed in gold and black, holding long pointed spears. As Talia and the guards approached, they crossed the spears in front of the doors.

"We have come at the prince's request," stated Maeglin.

One of the guards nodded and stepped inside. Maeglin turned to Talia. "Obey your lord. Be brave and do not do anything foolish, but trust him to take care of you both."

Talia swallowed the knot in her throat and tried to smile, but the trembling made it impossible. She took a deep breath, trying to settle the butterflies in her stomach. As the door reopened, she adjusted her hood.

"Come forward," the sentry called.

Stepping into the throne room, she was immediately awed by the beauty of the place. It was an architect's dream. Wooden inlaid floors were polished to a high gleam, their mosaic patterns shining brightly in the sun that came through the tall, elegant windows. The walls and ceiling were all hand carved, with figures of woodland creatures and mystical runes. Magical torches burned, bringing light but no smoke. On each side of the room sat rows of tables set at a diagonal, leaving plenty of walking space between them.

At the far end of the large room were two other long tables, each lengthwise below a tall raised dais. Seated there were a smattering of elves, both male and female. She noticed immediately the beautiful gowns on the women, and suddenly felt plain and frumpy. She wondered if her face was dirty.

Tearing her gaze away from the clothes, Talia looked upwards. At the top of the dais were two thrones. One was empty, save a scepter leaning against its back. The fragility and beauty of the piece spoke of femininity—a queen's throne. Next to it sat a larger throne, more ornate and reeking of authority.

In it, sat an older elf, his robes bespeaking royalty. He had the black hair and sapphire eyes of the Sáralondë family and with his build and height, Talia knew without being told this was Calion's father, Ërestor, King of the Calen'taur Elves.

Calion saw the nerves in Talia's eyes. She was frightened but still aware enough to appreciate her surroundings. He wished he could let her know everything would be all right, but he knew the next few moments would hold the key to how Talia was treated by all. Would his father accept her? He watched as Maeglin brought her in front of the dais.

He smiled inwardly when he saw that Maeglin's previous

coldness had turned protective. How did she manage it in such short a time? He chuckled, thinking back to his own first meeting with her. She'd tied him up in knots from the second he saw her. The brief walk from the stable was plenty of time for her to work her magick on Maeglin.

The elves at the tables all craned their necks, curious as to who and what was going on. Maeglin halted and bowed to Calion and his king.

"Well, son. The room has been cleared as you requested. Is this the female you spoke of helping?" The king's voice boomed out in the quiet of the throne room. "Do you think you can dispense with the rest of the dramatics and just tell us what is going on?"

Calion frowned at his father. "I asked to clear the room of all but our most trusted associates because what I have to say is extremely important and must be handled discreetly."

"We are waiting."

"Yes, this is the female I rescued from the orcan stronghold." He turned and looked at the female elves at the tables. "We all know what would have happened to her if I hadn't."

The females all shuddered. Stories of rape and torture at the hands of the orcs were the stuff of nightmares for all of them.

"Are you well then, child?" the king asked gently. "They did not hurt you?"

Talia spoke softly from under the shaded hood. "No, King Ërestor. I was bruised but not broken. Your son is very brave."

Calion began his story, ignoring her comment. "As you know, my men and I were on a routine border search. We traveled over the western portion of our boundaries between orcan land and our own, making sure there had been no crossings. On our way home, I left my men to do some hunting. While out, I sensed a disturbance in the nearby faerie myst."

The king nodded, knowing full well his son's skill as a magician of nature. Calion was unsurpassed by any who lived, now or before. "Go on."

"I sent word to my men to go ahead home, and I went to investigate. I thought another *vol* or *paes* had wandered in, but it is my duty to check. However, when I went into the myst, I discovered not a stray animal, but a plot by our enemies."

The king sat forward, interested now. "A plot? What did you find, Calion?"

"I traced two orcs through the myst. Imagine my shock when I realized they'd gone into the human world." Gasps of amazement greeted this news. "I backtracked and found where they came back into the myst. I followed them."

Here he paused and looked over at Talia. "I hadn't gone very far when I realized they didn't come back alone."

Calion saw the moment realization hit his father. The king stiffened and then rose slowly from his chair. He stared down at the hooded figure.

"Remove the cloak," he ordered hoarsely.

Calion stepped forward and stopped in front of Talia. "Be strong, *Tia maer...*" he whispered. Gently he pushed back the hood, revealing Talia in all her human glory.

Cries of fear and dismay filled the room. His father's guards, sensing danger, pulled their swords and started toward her. They stopped immediately when Maeglin and the others drew their swords to protect Talia.

Several ladies at the table fainted, but one, a dark-haired beauty, stood and made to come closer. The king waved her back.

"Enough!" he shouted, giving lie to Calion's claim royalty didn't yell. Everyone froze where they stood. Ërestor turned to his son, steely anger in his eyes. "You have brought a human into our world?"

"Nay, father, I did not. The orcs brought her in. They spirited her away to *Grundlug*. I rescued her from there." Calion stood close to Talia. He felt her trembling and willed her some of his own courage. "I could not leave a female in the clutches of the orcs, human or not. My honor demanded it of me."

Ërestor walked down the stairs to stand in front of his son and the troubling female. She was a beauty in her own way, even with the deformed ears and even brows. She met his eyes with her own and even lifted her chin in defiance. He stared at her, unwillingly amused and impressed by her courage. "How do we know she is not a spy for the orcs?"

"They had her tied to a stake in their great hall. The orcs did not see me. They were eating." Calion looked over at Talia. "She was to be the after-dinner entertainment. I barely made it in time to prevent her ravishment. What she went through was bad enough."

Talia shuddered, remembering the feel of Udaogong's hands on her. Just the thought made her feel dirty again.

"Why did you not return her to her world after you rescued her? Why bring her here to contaminate our people?"

Calion knew he needed to make his father understand Talia's importance to the elven people. Unfortunately, he wasn't completely clear what that was.

"When we escaped, we could not outrun them. We were both injured. We made it into the elven forest, but they followed us."

There was another gasp at his words. This was unheard of. Orcs refused to come into elven trees. They thought the woods were haunted.

"They actually came onto our land?" Ërestor growled, his tone moving between outrage and disbelief.

"Yes, my father. For the first time in centuries. That showed me they wanted the female very badly. But why?" Calion shook his head. "When I heard them coming, I hid us under my cloak. We could hear them speaking, and what they said worried me enough I thought I should bring Talia here instead of sending her home."

"What did they say?"

Calion turned and looked at Talia. "It was Braduk and Modak, the sons of Udaogong, in the forest. They spoke of a prophecy. One that involved Talia. Only raping and keeping her away would stop it from happening."

"Keep her away from what?" The king stared at Talia, speculation on his handsome, lined face.

"On that they were not clear," admitted Calion. "But in the next breath they spoke of the elves. I did not like the coincidence." He allowed himself a touch on Talia's shoulder. She leaned unconsciously into him.

"I knew if I took her back to her world, they may go after her again. If the prophecy did have something to do with the elven people, I felt she should be brought here. She should be put under our protection until we find out what is going on."

"Hmmm..." The king stepped back from Talia. "Perhaps the wise men will know of this prophecy, if it exists."

"I believe the prophecy is real, and it concerns our people.

Talia is the key," Calion pointed out.

Ërestor turned and walked back toward the table. "It will be done. Until we find out what type of threat this female is, she will be watched."

"Father," said Calion quickly. He didn't like where this was going. "That is not what I meant. The Lady Talia is under my protection."

A few of the ladies at the table gasped, and the king turned back to Calion, piercing him with his blue eyes. "You would elevate this human? Make her the equal of an elven lady? Have you no shame?"

Calion stood his ground. "She possesses all the attributes that make a lady. So yes, I give her that name."

"Blasphemy!" squeaked one of the elven females at the table. She fanned herself frantically.

"We will talk of this no further. You are to speak to the wise men and find out what you can. If there is a prophecy for us concerning a human, they will know of it."

"Yes, Father," Calion agreed, his teeth clenched.

"Until then, guards, take the human to a holding cell."

Talia gasped. "Calion?"

"Father!" Calion struggled to keep his voice even. "She is not a prisoner. Talia is under my protection. She is my guest."

The female at the table squealed again, and the king brought his hand down hard on the table, making goblets jump. "She is human. Our enemy. She will be treated as such, under your protection or not."

"You take my honor from me," Calion gritted out. "I promised her she would be safe."

"And she will be no safer than in a cell." The king walked back over to his son and clapped him on the back. "Come, son. Eat with us and tell us of your travels. Forget this annoyance. She will be fine in the dungeon. In fact, she will probably be at home there."

Calion glared at his father. When he finally looked over at Talia, she was staring at him with eyes made dark green with fear. He knew if he pushed any harder, his father might suspect something and dig in his heels harder. Better they go along with him now and give him opportunity to change his mind.

"I will take her myself. And one of my men will stand guard

over her."

Ërestor shrugged. The human was an annoying diversion, but he was done with her. "Get her gone and hurry back. We have much to talk about." He looked smugly at his son. "Why, it is time for the annual *Tarol* festival. Perhaps you will find a mate this year."

Talia jerked against him, and Calion swore inwardly. Damn his father. The prince wanted to pull her into his arms to comfort her, but he knew he couldn't. What must she be thinking?

The answer to that was Talia wasn't thinking. When Calion went along with his father's edict about putting her in a cell, she'd gone numb. Not numb enough to block out the hurt of the king's remark about Calion finding a mate, but then what else had she expected? To be welcomed as a daughter-in-law? Only in her dreams.

"Come." Calion took her by the wrist and started out of the throne room. Once back in the hall, he spoke. "Maeglin, I want one of us to be with her at all times. No one is to have access to her but me. Is that clear?"

"Yes, Highness." Maeglin called to his men, looking carefully at the female. She'd gone bone white, not saying a word as she walked beside the prince.

Calion led them all down another long hallway to a dark door. When he opened it, Talia could smell the dankness of air far below. She swallowed back a whimper when he tugged on her wrist to go on. Following his lead, she stayed utterly silent as they traversed the long stairway that led to the dungeon. It felt like they walked forever before they came to a second door, this one stained with mildew and rot. Maeglin stepped ahead and banged on it. After a few moments, it creaked open slowly.

They stepped inside, finding a medium-sized room with a beat up table and two moldy chairs. The dungeon master stood off to the side, his piggy little eyes fixed on Talia. He might have looked like an elf once, but eons in this damp wretched hellhole had leeched all the life out of him. He was filthy and bent, his shapeless body rocking back and forth rhythmically. He grinned and showed blackened, broken teeth.

"My prince. You have a prisoner for me?"

"No," returned Calion, his voice hard. "This is the Lady Talia. She is not a prisoner, but the king wishes her down here to keep her safe."

"Not a prisoner. I see." The sneer in his voice was apparent to all.

"You will not be in charge of her, Aranil. My men will." Calion looked at Lólindir. "Find the biggest and cleanest of the cells."

When Lólindir moved off, he turned back to Aranil and gave his orders. "You will send for meals from the royal kitchen. She is to be treated with respect at all times. You are not allowed in her cell for any reason. My men are responsible for her and will protect her. You will have no say over her. Do you understand me?"

"But I am Dungeon Master, my prince. She should be in my care," the piggy little elf whined.

"She is not a prisoner! She is here only temporarily." When Lólindir returned after finding a cell, he nodded his thanks to the guard. "Amroth, you have first watch. Maeglin will set up the watches after that. I do not need to tell you no one is to have access to her but me."

"Your father?" asked Amroth quietly, very aware of the sneering elf at the table.

Calion snorted. "My father will not come here, but if he does, let me know. He may not speak to her without me present."

Turning, he led the trembling Talia into the cell. It was no bigger than a large closet, but the hay was fresh, and there was a tiny window up in the wall near the ceiling. He looked over his shoulder at Amroth. "Shut and lock the door."

When Calion heard the door lock, he immediately put a barrier up that prevented anyone outside from seeing or hearing in. He pulled Talia into his arms and held on tight, noting his wrist was burning again.

"I am sorry, *Tia maer*... This I did not expect. I hoped he would forgive us. But I must obey him. If I do not, it may turn out worse."

"What will happen to me?" she asked, her voice low and terrified.

"Nothing will happen to you. My father is reacting to the fear. When he is thinking clearer, he will realize what he has done." He pulled back and looked down at her frightened face. "I will get you out of here, this I promise."

"You're leaving me?" There was panic in her voice.

He bent and pressed his lips against her hair. He was afraid if he kissed her, he might never stop. "I must. The sooner I can convince my father of your innocence, the sooner I can get you out."

"The elf outside...he scares me."

"He will have nothing to do with you. Whichever of my Guard is on duty will bring you your meals and anything else you need. Aranil will not be allowed in the cell. I will be the only one who is allowed in here with you."

Talia couldn't help it. She clung to Calion, burying her face against his chest. She knew she wasn't being the brave female he wanted, but she needed to feel his strong heart against hers, just for a moment.

"*O eisi tia maelor oli,*" he murmured comfortingly in his own tongue. "*Ai cyro tyri sai tia caes.*" He held her as long as he could, but he knew his father would be wondering about him. "I must go."

She took a deep breath, wanting to hold him until she woke up from this terrible dream and they were back at the waterfall, but she knew better. She had to let him go. Curving her lips up into a trembling smile, she backed away and let her arms fall.

When Calion saw her brave attempt, his gut twisted. Anger at his father swelled inside him. He hated to leave her in such a place. Giving into his need, he kissed her, hard and deep. "It will not be long, *Tia maer*... I will have you out soon."

ꟗ

Talia cried the first night. The sounds and smells of her cell frightened her almost as much as the orcan stronghold. Only the knowledge one of Calion's Royal Guard stood outside made it possible of her to sleep at all. She prayed she would have to spend only the one night in this place.

But that night passed and the next. And even though Talia was treated well, with plenty of food, water, blankets and other necessities, it did not make up for the terror she went through each and every moment. Fear that the guard outside wouldn't be enough and someone would get in to hurt her. Fear that Calion would say something he shouldn't and be punished or killed for breaking the *sardai.* Fear that the orcs would find her and Calion wouldn't be there to protect her this time.

And her biggest fear—the one that preyed on her more and more as days passed with no visit from him—the fear that he was finished with her.

He sent word with whatever guard came on duty, but she never saw him. Doubts began to creep in. Had he changed his mind? Were all his words to her a terrible lie?

Talia stopped eating and she had terrible nightmares. Her skin began to itch and burn and she worried she had caught some horrid disease by staying in the cell. She paced during the day, feeling like she was going crazy. As the days went by, the only thing Talia could hold on to were his final words. "*Remember...*"

Calion went straight to his father. He tried to talk to Ërestor about Talia, but the king was adamant. The human would stay in the cells until further notice. At first the prince just played along, thinking he would eventually be able to talk his father into letting Talia out, but after the first day passed, he realized the king was going to be stubborn.

So he spent the days with the archivists, trying to find the prophecy the orcs spoke of. If the king could see she wasn't a threat, he would let her go.

He wanted to visit her, but he knew if his father heard about it, things would go badly for them both. He was sure she'd be worried about him and wondering why he hadn't visited. But it would be better if the king felt Calion was angry because the prince had been forced to break his word. Everyone knew how Calion felt about a vow.

An elf is known by the word he keeps.

It was a better excuse than everyone finding out the truth. He was going out of his mind without Talia. As each day passed, Calion's self-control bled slowly away. He became restless, finding it difficult to sit through a meal or study parchments in the archives.

His eyes began to hurt and no amount of rubbing or healing magick would help. His body switched between being too hot and too cool, and the scar on his arm burned so badly, he was tempted to cut it from his arm for relief. He even tried some of the healing water he'd brought from the spring, but it did nothing for him.

The castle began preparations for the *Festival of Tarol*, the summer mating time, but he wanted nothing to do with it. Each night his father placed an eligible female at his side for dinner. Each night, Calion left the table before dessert, ignoring his father's choice.

When Ërestor asked him to help him judge some local land disputes, Calion agreed but spoke not a word during the whole proceeding. When the king called him on it, he was told if he wouldn't trust his son's judgment about the human female, he shouldn't trust him with anything at all. It was obvious to all a stalemate had been called.

By the fifth day, Calion was climbing the walls. He had given up any hope of working in the archives, he was just too restless for that. His body temperature settled down into a steady blistering heat, causing him to sweat all the time. His scar was so painful any accidental touch set him flying. His eyes were so bloodshot and sore, they hurt to look at. His temper lashed out frequently, and all knew to step lightly when they were around the prince.

The king finally admitted defeat. He'd known the female posed no danger to the crown or its people, but he felt he needed to make a strong show so the castle folk wouldn't be frightened. But by doing so, and disparaging Calion's honor in the process, he had created something else they were more afraid of. A Sáralondë in a temper is an awesome thing.

Ërestor called his son to him in private and apologized. They would put out the word Talia was not a threat but a guest of the prince. All would have the opportunity to see what a human was really like. But she would be Calion's responsibility. The female would be released that very day.

Since he hated to be at odds with him, Calion took the time to quickly thank his father, but his need to make sure Talia was all right overrode everything else. His whole body cried out for her. He could barely keep himself from running as he made his way down to the dungeon.

Pulling open the door, he saw the dungeon master, Aranil over at Talia's door, trying to talk Valandil into letting him have a peek at her. It appeared Valandil was considering it.

Calion moved so fast neither Valandil nor Aranil saw him. He grabbed Aranil by the neck and flung him across the room onto the table. It broke beneath the smaller elf's considerable weight, but he didn't even look back to see if the creature moved. He gazed fiercely at the red-haired guard, and Valandil flushed in shame. He pointed at the lock on the door.

"Open it."

Inside, Talia listened to the door open and scrambled to her feet. She'd heard the nasty little Dungeon Master bargaining with Valandil to get in, and she was suddenly afraid he'd talked the elf into it. While the other guards talked to her, helping stave away loneliness, Valandil refused to speak at all. She came to dread the times he watched her. Did he betray her now? Looking around, she grabbed the only thing she could to defend herself and faced the door.

When Calion walked in, he saw Talia standing unsteadily by the wall, a large stick upraised in her hand. He swore aloud at the fear he saw in her thin, tired face. When she saw him she cried out, and dropping the stick, she ran to him as fast as her feet could move. Just before she got there, she seemed to remember herself and she stopped, her hands clenched at her side, but nothing could prevent the hope that leapt into her eyes.

He wanted to pull her to him and banish the look of fear and worry he saw there, but he knew it wouldn't be enough. Reaching down, he picked up the cloak she'd worn into the cell and placed it around her, pulling the hood into place. He put one finger under her chin, knowing it was all he could dare with the fire burning inside him. "It is time to leave, Talia. Come with me."

They were out of the castle and into the courtyard faster than either of them thought possible. Calion held her hand in his, almost running to the stable where Roch'mellon waited. He ignored the open-mouthed looks and whispers as he tossed her up on the horse and then leaped up himself. Not even bothering with reins or pad, he turned his steed and galloped out over the drawbridge.

Maneuvering swiftly, he rode through the village at breakneck speed, elves hurrying away from Roch'mellon's hooves. When they got to the other side of town, Calion shouted, "Hold on!" He drew his sword, pointing it to the sky.

Talia stared in wonder as a huge vortex sprang into

existence before them. She screamed when Roch'mellon rose up on his back feet and lunged inside.

Her world turned upside down. Closing her eyes, she could only press back against Calion and grab tightly to the horse's mane. The pressure of the void threatened to pull her off, but the prince's strong arm kept her pressed against him. She found it hard to breathe in the swirling, wild maelstrom, and she choked as the wind tossed her hair into her face.

"Breathe through your mouth," he whispered in her ear. "It will soon be over."

She did so and found that even though uncomfortable, she could now manage to take in air. Not long after, she felt the winds lessen and as suddenly as it started, the vortex mouth opened, and they jumped out.

He offered no explanation as he turned Roch'mellon to the east and kept riding. After almost a week of being without him, Talia soaked up his presence and very touch. Tears of joy ran down her cheeks, and the wind picked them up and flung them back at Calion, whose mouth firmed when he felt them. After about five minutes of steady riding, he turned Roch'mellon onto a tiny path. They trotted down it until they came to a beautiful cove next to a small lake.

Dismounting hurriedly, he pulled her down with him. He stared at her for a long moment before groaning deeply, and crushing her against him, he brought his mouth down on hers. Her taste... He had needed it, craved it. It was as wonderfully sweet as the nectar of the goddesses. His passion was a wild, howling thing as he devoured her soft lips. His hands ran demandingly over her trembling body. The burning in his body increased and his eyes blazed.

His cock throbbed, his skin tight and painful. The very air around them shimmered with lust and desire. As he struggled to control himself, Calion suddenly realized that human or not, Talia had brought him to the full flame of a mating fire.

She met his urgency with surrender. Her own passion clawed at her, her need for his touch a living thing. As soon as his mouth met hers, all the pain of his abandonment disappeared. There would be time enough for recriminations later, now she just wanted him. She threw her arms around his neck, sliding her hands up to fist in his hair, and pressed her body against his, cradling his hard erection in the notch of her thighs.

His mouth demanded more. Frustrated desire, controlled passion and lingering anger all mixed up in the taste of her. Swearing under his breath, he pulled her to the ground, not even noticing when Roch'mellon danced away, shaking his head at the dramatics. Her clothes fell away under his searching hands, and he groaned as his mouth tasted the bounty of her breasts. "I...need...you. By the goddesses..."

Driven by the burning of her body, Talia met his demands with those of her own. Her hands moved, exploring the sculptured planes of Calion's body. Hard, male, strong. His reaction electrified her. With another muffled curse, he tore at the fastening of his pants, freeing himself. She reached down and took him in her hand, feeling his strength...feeling the heat of him blaze through her.

He growled as the madness of his need overwhelmed him. He moved between her thighs. Lust surged up and out of control when he felt the warmth of her scald him.

"I can't wait. I need you so much," he muttered hoarsely against her lips. When she arched to him in response, he let go of his control and drove himself into her.

Even as she gasped for air, his thrust drove her up and over into an uncontrollable climax. Talia screamed, her body imploding into a rainbow of sensation. She vibrated against him as he plunged into her again and again, until his own explosion sent him flying into the maelstrom as well.

"Did I hurt you?"

Talia opened her eyes and looked up into Calion's. They were no longer bloodshot, but clear again. Clear and worried. Their hearts still pounded together, but were slowing, gently drifting into complete relaxation. She smiled. "No, of course not." She reached up and kissed the corner of his mouth. "It was wonderful."

"I took you on the ground with all the finesse of a *vol*!" he said with self-disgust.

She pulled his face around to look at her. "Do you hear me complaining? Don't you know how exciting it is to be wanted so much? And I wanted you. The last five days without you were horrible."

Calion rolled so they could lay together in more comfort,

with her head pillowed on his shoulder. For the first time in nearly a week, he felt in control of his body once more. "I tried to get you out sooner, *Tia maer*... This I swear, but my father... He is very stubborn."

"I thought you'd changed your mind."

Chapter Ten

In that single sentence Calion heard all the fear and hurt she'd struggled with. His arms tightened around her. "Do not say such a thing. Do not even think it. I went mad trying to get him to see reason."

"You didn't come to see me."

"I was afraid if my father saw my concern for you, he would know my feelings were not altruistic but more personal." His hand played with her soft hair. "I wanted to."

"I was so frightened." She sighed and snuggled against him. "Even when you sent me a message, I thought you'd changed your mind about wanting me with you."

He snorted. "As you can see, I have not changed my mind. Do you think this behavior is normal for me? You make me feel things I cannot control."

She thought of the beautiful elven women at the table. "There are so many others here you could be with. I saw them look at you."

He gave the curl he toyed with a sharp tug. "If I wanted any of those females, I would have approached them many years ago. I am prince of this land and have been offered their bodies for my pleasure." He moved, pulling Talia underneath him so he could look her in the eyes.

"When we were separated I burned with the need to mate, but when I looked at them I could not touch them. None of them make me feel as you do. No one else can ease the fire within me. *You* are the female I want."

"I tried to remember that. Just like you told me. But that place...it's so cold and dark. I hate closed spaces." She shivered. "And I kept thinking about you out with all the other women, how they would be so much easier for you to be with."

"*Tia maer*... we are together now. That is what matters."

"Do I have to go back?"

"No," Calion groaned, wanting to kick himself when he heard the return of fear in her voice. "I am sorry. I should have told you immediately. My father gave his permission to release you. You are now my responsibility and a guest of my house."

Relief flowed over Talia like a smooth caress. "Are we going back to the waterfall?"

He shook his head. "I am sorry. As much as I would like to return there, we cannot. Even taking you from the castle was a risk. I needed to know you were well." He bent and teased her lips with his, needing the contact. His body stirred again.

"We must go back to my home so other elves can get to know you. I want them to see a human is not our enemy. And if we can discover the prophecy the orcs spoke of, we can understand why they wanted you. It may help to keep you safe."

"We will be able to be together?"

He moved, and his cock hardened inside her as he grinned wickedly. "Not as we are right now." His face sobered. "While we are safe for the moment, if anyone found out we have broken *sardai*, there would still be trouble. No...we must continue as we started. Once we get back to the castle, we must hide our feelings."

"I'm not very good at that."

Calion frowned, remembering what she had said to bring his head guard to her side. "You shared your feelings with Maeglin with the request you made of him. I should beat you for asking such a thing!"

"I—"

"Do you know what it did to me to hear that you offered your life for mine? When will you begin to trust me? I will take care of you." He grew angrier the more he thought of the sacrifice Talia might have made.

She frowned up at him, her green eyes sparkling. Even though he was still hard inside her, he argued with her. And his anger excited her. "I can take care of myself. I'm not one of your clinging lady elves."

"I am charged with your care and safety. It is my honor to do so. Why do you think I fought so hard to get you out of the cell?" His voice gentled as he ran a finger down her cheek. "And more so, you are important to me. In ways I still do not understand. Obey me in this."

Talia pushed down the natural inclination to defy him. He would learn soon enough what she meant, but until then, she'd obey him...when she felt like it. I love you, Talia thought as he covered her mouth with his own. *Whether that suits you or not.*

They arrived back at the castle just as the shadows lengthened into night. They spent the whole day by the lake, rediscovering each other. Talia's fears of the last few days lightened as Calion worshipped her with his body, showing her without words how he felt about her.

Calion looked healthy and strong again, refreshed from the time in the forest. Afterwards, they bathed in the lake, laughing and splashing each other like children because he worried with their highly tuned senses other elves would pick up their scents on each other.

After leaving Roch'mellon at the stable, Calion led Talia back into the castle. They were met at the door by a very disgruntled Maeglin.

"I see you are angry with me again."

Maeglin bowed. "As usual my prince, you are very observant."

Talia giggled, and both men slanted her a look. It just made her giggle harder. She looked mischievously at them. "You aren't just a prince and his guard...you're friends. What was the word? *Thaelyrdor*?"

Calion smiled. "You remember well. Yes, Maeglin and I have known each other since we were boys. We are *thaelyrdor.*"

"And as *friends*, I would think you would be more thoughtful. This is the second time in as many weeks you have disappeared," Maeglin chastised him. "Although you do look refreshed."

The change in the elf was obvious. The prince's whole attitude seemed happier. His face was almost content.

Calion shrugged, unconcerned. "I needed the time away from my father. Talia needed the fresh air." He narrowed his eyes at Maeglin. "Do not make too much of this."

"You were noticed," Maeglin said sharply. He looked from his prince to the tousled female next to him. "Your sister."

Calion tensed. “She is to stay out of this. Leave her to me.” He pulled his lover closer. “I am taking Talia to her quarters. Send Amroth to stand watch outside. She is to be guarded at all times.”

Maeglin bowed again, sending the mind-command. “As you wish, Your Highness.”

“Let us go.” Holding her hand, he led her into the castle, Maeglin following in silence. Calion escorted Talia down a hall and once again she was treated to the beauty of the castle. She craned her neck, looking this way and that.

“I will get so lost,” she muttered under her breath. She stared in awe as they passed a huge room that looked like a chapel.

Calion chuckled, squeezing her hand. “Once you get to know the place, it will be easier for you. Our family quarters are up those stairs and to the left.” He pointed up a twisting staircase. “We are not so far apart.” He stopped before a large, ornate door. “This will be your living space.” Throwing open the door, he guided Talia into a large room.

Her new quarters were spacious and beautiful, with arched windows and skylights that opened to the stars at night. A huge bed sat in one corner, partially hidden behind a screen painted with the pictures of the forest animals she loved. Near the window sat a table and four chairs carved out of a wood that shimmered in different colors. A sofa and two comfortable armchairs sat in a cozy circle around the fireplace.

“It’s beautiful,” she managed as she walked with him around the room. “All this for me?”

Calion chuckled again, and some of the tenseness left his shoulders. “Yes, *Tia maer...*”

Neither noticed Maeglin stiffen at the endearment as the prince went on.

“You will have free run of the castle, but you must have one of the guards with you at all times. This is for your safety, especially until others are used to seeing you about.” He turned and walked to where Maeglin stood at the door with Amroth, who had just arrived.

“I will have some hot water brought for your bath.” His eyes fired suddenly, his gaze traveling over her body. Talia’s cheeks warmed as she remembered the feel of his hands on her. “You will need something to wear. I will arrange for a clothier tomorrow, but until then, I will find a dress for you."

Talia removed the elven cloak from her shoulders, feeling a pang of regret. She'd become attached to it. "Here, this belongs to you."

Calion took it and tossed it over his shoulder. "I will return with the dress."

"I'll be here."

Calion and Maeglin headed down the hallway. "My sister. I will ask her for a dress. They are close to the same size."

"I would speak to you, Calion"

The prince raised an eyebrow at the seriousness of Maeglin's tone. "Speak."

"You have feelings for the human." He saw Calion tense and went on quickly. "You are my prince and my friend. I see what others may not. I will not betray you, but I worry. Do you know what you are doing?"

Calion laughed shortly. "My friend, I do not know anything. But you are correct. I do have feelings for Talia, ones I should not have." He took a deep breath. This was the male he had gotten drunk with the first time. When his mother died, Maeglin had been there for him. They had protected each other's back in more battles than he could count. If he couldn't trust him... He sighed.

"I flame for her."

Maeglin stumbled. "Calion!"

Calion stopped and faced his best friend. "Do you think I planned this? That I even want it? I know the *sardai*...I know the legends. I am heir to the throne. The last thing I need is to flame for a human. But I cannot help it. I want her. So much I burn."

"You should have taken her home."

Calion just looked at his friend, and Maeglin sucked in his breath at what he saw in the prince's face.

"I could not."

They parted at the door of the princess. Calion knocked and flashed a smile when his sister Eámanë opened the door.

"Calion!" she exclaimed, grabbing his wrist and pulling him inside. "You are back. Where is the female...Talia?"

"Leave me be, *shar.*" He laughed as he gave her a hug. He had nicknamed her *brat* the first time she'd stolen his sword. "I will answer your questions without the mauling."

"Where did you go?"

"I wanted Talia to get some fresh air. She needed it after her time in the cell." Calion tweaked his sister's nose. "And I took her back to her room to get ready for dinner."

"You are going to bring her to dinner?" Eámanë's blue eyes, several shades darker than Calion's, widened. "Oh, I cannot wait to see that."

"It is for that reason I came to see you. She needs a proper dress to wear."

Eámanë pursed her lips as she considered. "I think we can figure out something." She went to her wardrobe and threw open the doors. "Let's see..."

Calion followed her. "She needs something in green. She looks good in that color." He began to paw through the closet.

Eámanë watched her brother speculatively. Since when did Calion care about dress color? "What shade are her eyes?"

Calion rejected one dress after another. "What? Oh, they are green. The green of new grass in a spring meadow."

"That is so poetic."

Calion glared at his sister. "It is hardly poetry. It is her eye color."

"Like a spring meadow..." Eámanë repeated in a lilting voice. She ducked expertly when her brother swatted at her and giggled. Then she sobered.

"She is a human, Calion."

Calion went still. "What are you saying, Eámanë?"

His sister cocked her head at him. "You care for her. I know you better than anyone, Calion. You care for this human."

Ignoring his sister, Calion pulled a soft green gown from the closet. "This one will be fine. Do you have slippers for her as well?"

"Calion. I am not going to go away."

Suddenly, Calion slammed his hand against the closet door. Having Maeglin and now his sister expose his secret...it was too much.

"What do you want me to say, Eámanë?" He turned and glared at his sister. "I owe you no explanation."

Eámanë's eyes filled. "I am not asking for an explanation. You are my brother. I care about what happens to you."

Calion rubbed his eyes. "Let it go. If you care for me, just let it go."

They stared at each other before Eámanë lifted both hands in a gesture of capitulation. "How can I help?" It was a peace offering.

Calion sighed and looked at his determined sister. "You are so stubborn."

"It is in the Sáralondë genes."

They both grinned.

"If you really want to help me, then get to know Talia. You are not afraid, are you?"

Eámanë stiffened. "I am not afraid of anything...even a human."

"She is special. Try and look past the humanity and see the soul within. She is all alone in a new world and will need a friend."

"I will try, for your sake." Eámanë took the gown from her brother. "You need to dress for dinner as well. And..." She sniffed loudly. "You stink like your horse."

She laughed at his outraged look. "I will take the dress to your lady and perhaps I will learn why she is so important to you."

As Calion walked toward the door, she cleared her throat. "And brother?" She waited until he turned, his brow raised in question. "Talia is not alone here. She has you."

When Talia heard the knock at the door, she expected Calion to enter. But instead of her prince, she recognized the dark-haired female she'd seen in the throne room. As the beauty got closer, Talia recognized the facial features and blue eyes of Sáralondë royalty. Butterflies started doing circles in her stomach.

Calion's sister was probably the most beautiful woman she'd ever seen, with her short cap of raven black hair and pale skin. Her eyes were a darker shade of blue than her brother's, almost the color of a stormy sea. She was small like Talia and in her dark blue and white lace dress, her figure was shapely.

She saw curiosity in the elven woman's eyes and smiled

inwardly. It seemed no matter what the race, inquisitiveness was a female trait. "You must be Princess Eámanë."

Eámanë studied the human female in front of her. She was very pretty, even in the awful male clothing. But the way she held herself intrigued the princess. The human stood straight, and her eyes met Eámanë's with no fear in them. She may have been nervous, but she hid it well. The princess held out the garments she'd brought with her.

"I brought you a dress. You expected Calion I suppose, but I sent him to clean up. He smelled like Roch'mellon."

"Thank you," Talia said, her voice cautious. "If you could put them in the chair? I smell a bit like a horse myself."

Eámanë laid the dress out carefully and then sat, studying Talia some more. "Do all humans look like you?"

"No," Talia returned. "We're as different as your kind is. All different colors, sizes and shapes."

"Will you tell me about it?"

Talia laughed a little. "That would take a long time. But if you want we can get together and talk some. We could compare our worlds."

"I would like that. I have always been curious about the human world. I want to visit it some day, but my father..." She shrugged.

"He doesn't trust humans...yes, I know. Has there always been this hatred of my kind?"

"You are our enemies. I have read the legends. But there has been no contact with the human world in centuries. It is an old feud." Eámanë shrugged again. "I think it is silly."

"On that we both agree."

"Do you miss your home?" Eámanë leaned forward in her chair.

Talia shook her head and began to undo her braided hair. "I am happy here. I love how beautiful it is, how clean and bright. And the magic... It's amazing. I'm very glad I got to see the faerie world." Her face softened. "If it hadn't been for your brother, I wouldn't have seen it. I would be dead."

Eámanë stilled as she deciphered the look on Talia's face. By the goddesses. It looked as if her brother wasn't the only one who cared. The human had feelings for him too.

She waited for the disgust she expected to sense, but

nothing came. This Talia...this human, with her funny-looking ears and odd eyes didn't seem any different than some of her female friends. Why then was there such fear of the race?

"My brother is a wonderful prince and a strong male," she said, watching the other female closely. "He is well liked by all his people."

Talia smiled fully this time. "He is the bravest man I've ever known. He came into a room full of orcs to save me. His people are lucky to have him."

"He is heir to the throne."

"I know." Talia sighed in relief when her hair finally came free. "I think he will be a wonderful king."

"You are more than friends," Eámanë mentioned casually. She saw Talia stiffen and for the first time, the princess saw fear in the human. "He is my brother. I do not want him to be hurt."

"Believe me when I say I want the same thing," Talia returned quickly. "We have learned a lot about each other since he rescued me. We've been able to get by the prejudice and become friends."

"Calion wants me to be your friend too."

Talia looked warily at the beautiful princess. "And what do you want, Eámanë?"

"I want to know that my brother is all right. I do not want him in any trouble. I see the way he acts around you, and it worries me because of all the old hatreds. You may be a wonderful person, but you are a human."

Talia's throat tightened. Unbeknownst to her, her feelings were clear for the princess to see. "I would cut out my heart before hurting Calion. He saved my life. He could have left me with those filthy creatures, but he risked himself to help me. Even his reputation is threatened by bringing me here so I could be safe. I don't want any harm coming to him. I would do anything to protect him."

"Anything?" Eámanë pounced on that.

Looking straight into the elven princess' eyes, Talia nodded. "Believe me, he is as important to me as he is to you. He must be kept safe, no matter what." She reached out and took Eámanë's soft hand. "No cost is too high, do you understand me?"

Eámanë wasn't sure what to say. She had her answer all

right. Talia did care about Calion. A great deal. She thought about how Calion had acted all week when the human was imprisoned. He'd been like a prisoner himself, his temper raging out of control.

She squeezed Talia's hand. "He cares about you too. I know neither of you is going to admit anything to me, but I know my brother and I am getting to know you, so I will just say this. Be careful. Not everyone is as open-minded as I am."

Talia sighed. "Thank you, but we are just friends."

Eámanë sighed too. "You are loyal. That I can see. I think I would like to be your friend, Talia of the humans. Would you allow me that pleasure?"

"It would be fun. I've never had a close friend before." Talia grinned mischievously. "And you can give me all the dirt on your brother!"

"Dirt?" Eámanë frowned in bewilderment. "He is taking a bath now. Why would you want dirt?"

Talia laughed and proceeded to give the princess her first lesson in human slang.

Maeglin came to get her for dinner. Talia hoped it would be Calion so she could ask him how she looked. She felt so strange in these elven garments.

She'd taken her hot bath, although her very presence scared the elf maids so badly they couldn't even speak. They scurried out before she could ask any questions at all. She dressed and then set about doing something with her hair.

Remembering all the ornate styles she'd briefly seen on that first night at the castle, but knowing her limitations, she worked the golden tresses into a French braid chignon. Looking in her mirror, she still felt plain, but the knock on the door gave her no time to change anything.

"Come in," she called.

Maeglin felt like he'd been punched in the stomach and his mouth went dry as he stared at her. Suddenly he realized just how beautiful his prince's lady was.

Calion's choice of gown was pale green, its skirts shimmering with shades of the same color. The bodice was much higher than the one Calion had described Talia wearing at the *Malesia* tree, but it still showed a nice amount of cleavage. It had long flowing sleeves and crystal beading around the neckline.

She wore matching slippers and her hair was braided with green and gold ribbon. If it hadn't been for her ears and eyes, she'd look like any other lady of his acquaintance.

Talia cleared her throat self-consciously. "Either I look really, really bad or really, really good."

Maeglin blinked as if coming out of a trance. "M'lady, you may outshine them all tonight. It will be my pleasure to escort you to the dining chamber."

"Thank you." Talia blushed in pleasure at his words. "Where is Calion?"

A frown marred Maeglin's handsome face. "He has some...business to attend to. He will meet you at supper."

Talia sighed, reading Maeglin's face accurately. "He's in trouble about me coming, isn't he? Maybe I should stay here."

"You are not such a coward."

"Of course not," Talia said, bristling. "But I told you I don't want to be a problem for him."

"Lady Talia..." Maeglin bowed. "It is already too late for that." Taking her arm, he led her from the room.

They heard the argument all the way outside the closed chamber door. Talia hesitated only briefly before raising her chin and continuing forward. They stopped outside, and Maeglin nodded to the sentry.

Inside, Calion wanted to strangle his father. The king balked at Talia's presence, even suggesting she should be sent back to the dungeon. It didn't help that many of the others at the table felt the same way.

"She is our guest, Father. By your own words."

"That does not mean I want to have her around me. Her supper habits may be so bad we cannot stomach her at the table."

Calion rolled his eyes. "I have seen her table manners. She would put many of us to shame. I have invited her. She will eat here."

"She is very nice, Father," Eámanë put in. "I spent some time with her today. I like her. She is interesting."

"So is a *polyras*," the king retorted, referring to the lizard beast that roamed the troll caves to the north. "But I would not invite it to dinner."

"She is already invited," Calion bit out, his blue eyes snapping in his anger. "Would you have me break my word again?"

Ërestor frowned at his son, not liking the reminder. "I will not go into this again. My word is final. The human will..." His words trailed off when the outer door swung open and the lady in question walked in.

Calion had known Talia was beautiful before, but now... He walked forward as if in a dream, not even seeing the look of astonishment on his father's face as he looked at the human female. The others at the table were all struck dumb—except for Eámanë, who smiled widely.

When he reached her, he held out his hand and Maeglin placed Talia's hand on top of it. The guard sent Calion a warning look. *Be careful.*

Calion needed no reminder. His body tightened with need as he caught the scent of her in his nostrils. He knew this night would make a huge difference in Talia's future in his world. He would have to be very, very careful. Smiling, he gave a courtly bow. "You make the stars look plain, my lady."

She blushed. "Thank you." Her eyes teased him as she took in his handsome dinner jacket. "You clean up pretty good yourself." She looked at the table behind him, her eyes a little wary. "Is everything all right?"

He quirked his lips in a half smile. "Everything is fine." He turned to his father, challenge written all over his face. "Is that not right, Father?"

Ërestor stared at the human. This was no animal. Her refinement was unmistakable. To toss her out now would make him look a fool. "Please join us. We are just about ready to start."

Talia murmured her thanks as Calion led her to a chair next to him. He sat to the right of his father, who was at the head of the table with Eámanë on his left, across from her brother. Most of the others at the table said nothing, but the female elf at the end of the table opposite the king tossed her head.

"I do not know if I can eat now." She fanned herself quickly.

"There is an odd smell in here."

Talia recognized the female as the one who had mouthed off the night she'd stood before the king. Here was an enemy.

Calion's eyes darkened with temper. The lady Nienna had been after him for years. She was trying to pay him back for his disinterest. He wanted to grab her by the scrawny neck and drop her out the window. When Maeglin stepped forward threateningly, the prince motioned him back. He knew how to deal with this *shor.*

He turned to Nienna. "I am sorry to hear that. Would you care to go to your chamber? I will send a maid with supper for you."

Nienna stiffened. She thought her disapproval would force Ërestor to send the human away. After all, she was the king's hostess. She believed if she played her cards right, she would someday be Calion's bride. Didn't her wishes mean anything?

She looked into the prince's face and saw only anger there. She backtracked quickly, pouting. "No, thank you. I suppose I will have to manage."

"Yes, you will." Calion turned away from the female so quickly it was an insult in itself. Nienna went white with shock and anger.

"Thank you for the dress," Talia whispered softly to Eámanë. She smoothed the gown nervously. "I've never worn anything so fine."

"Well, you wear it better than I, that is certain." Eámanë grinned and tossed her short, dark hair. "You might as well keep it." Talia's look of shock made the princess laugh. "You cannot wear those breeches to the table." She glanced down the table to Nienna. "Some might not like it."

"I couldn't accept..."

"Yes, you can," Eámanë said blithely. "We are friends, are we not?"

"I... Yes...but..."

"She was much more coherent earlier, Father. We had a very interesting discussion about our worlds."

Ërestor still had trouble with the loveliness and sophistication of the human. "A discussion?"

"Yes." Eámanë grinned as she sipped the fragrant soup she'd been served. "We talked about the differences between our two worlds."

"Are they much different?" asked a male elf sitting on Talia's right. He introduced himself as Finrod, the king's financial advisor.

Talia smiled, showing her dimples. All the males at the table blinked in appreciation. Calion chuckled into his soup. He wavered between amusement and jealousy at the display.

"There are a lot of differences and a lot of similarities," Talia responded, tasting the food curiously. "The people look different, and the customs aren't the same, but you seem to do the things we do. You live, raise families, eat dinner, worry about the future. Not so different from us."

"Humans are said to be killers," the king put in carefully. Her gentle tone and speech were already making him reconsider some of his ideas of humans.

Talia's eyes flashed. "Some could say the same about faerie." Their gazes met and Talia's chin lifted in challenge.

Ërestor lifted a considering brow. The female had spunk as well. An interesting combination. "That is true. You are saying no matter what the race, there are those that give them a bad name." When Talia inclined her head in agreement, he went on. "Our legends are filled with the wars of your people. In the early days they spilled over into our realm."

"Calion told me some of the history of your people." She looked at her lover next to her, finding his warm eyes on her face. "I think that is where many of the human stories of your kind come from."

"What is the biggest difference?" asked a plump little elven woman. Her voice wasn't exactly friendly, but it wasn't cold either.

"Oh, that's easy." Talia looked again at Calion. "The magic. If there ever was magic in my world, it's long since been suppressed. Here, it's everywhere. In the land, the forest, the people. You can feel it no matter where you go."

The table went quiet at her words and Talia stopped speaking. Her eyes widened as she saw the looks on the elven faces.

Ërestor spoke, his voice tight with shock. "You can sense the magick?"

Chapter Eleven

Talia nodded slowly and Calion swore under his breath. "I cannot believe I forgot." He turned to Talia, his eyes eloquent in apology. "I was so worried about the prophecy, I did not tell my father of your skill. I am so sorry. The dungeon might have been avoided."

"Son, what say you? What skill does she have?"

Calion sighed and pressed Talia's hand under the cover of the table. He was furious with himself. "After I rescued the Lady Talia, we spent time in the forest...while she healed. I was as surprised as you when she told me she could sense the magick all around her."

All eyes turned to Talia and she squirmed uncomfortably. "I can just feel it. I'm not sure I can explain."

"Is there anything else?" Ërestor questioned.

Calion nodded. "Watch..." Concentrating, he caused his magick to appear in a glowing orb above his hand. "Tell us what you see, Talia."

"I see your magic. A bright, sapphire blue ball of swirling light. It floats above your hand." She reached out and touched it gently. "It's quite lovely."

"She can see your magick?" asked Eámanë, her mouth open with shock. "And touch it?"

Calion nodded, almost enjoying the others' shock. He knew just how they felt. He ended his magick and picked up a forkful of flaky *malyl*, looking over at his father who was eyeing Talia in confusion. The others at the table seemed to be struck mute.

"This is the other reason I brought her here. Talia can sense and see magick. She can also hear my sword speak when I draw it from the sheath. Add to that, she can talk to *Malesia* trees. The animals in the forest, even the mighty *shyr*, treat her as their own. Plus, she went into the faerie myst by herself and survived until I rescued her."

Calion looked around at the astonished and speechless faces around him. "For any one of these things, I felt Talia is special and should be studied further. That she can do all of them is...extraordinary."

"Humans cannot talk to *Malesia* trees. Only elven folk can!" Ërestor objected, pointing his own fork at Calion.

"That is what I thought, Father. But I saw her open a tree with my own eyes. And that is not all. She could speak with it. Ask it questions and receive answers. Just by a touch."

"That is impossible," gasped Finrod.

Talia cleared her throat. "Actually, it's very possible," she said bravely. "I asked a specific question and it put the answer in my mind. Not by words, but in pictures. Once, I almost thought I heard humming." She looked around the table.

In for a penny, in for a pound, she thought. "I think the *Malesia* trees are sentient."

Ërestor gazed in shock and irritation at the female. "Do you know what you are saying? Do you think you know more than all the elven wise men? If the trees are alive and thinking, would we not have discovered it by now?"

Calion jumped in quickly. "Did we ever try asking it, Father? Or did we just assume the things we believe?"

No one could answer that. *Malesia* trees had been around since the beginning of the world. They were what they were. To have a human come in and tell them something different, well, no one knew just how to take that.

"If Talia can do magick, it may not be so hard to believe she can talk to a *Malesia* tree too," Eámanë said finally.

"How do we know she is not just repeating what you have told her about your magick, my prince?" Lady Nienna sneered spitefully. "Can she see others?"

Talia turned and looked at the elven woman. "I don't know. I've never tried. Would you like to test me?"

That took Nienna aback. Her magick was not very strong, and she couldn't manufacture a light ball like Calion's. Her mouth opened and closed before she shook her head. "I do not trust the human. What if she harms or tries to steal my magick?"

"What magick?" muttered Eámanë under her breath.

Talia stifled a giggle.

"I would ask you to look for mine." This came from a tall, elegant male sitting across from her. He looked about the same age as the king, with long graying hair, but his face was intense and a little frightening.

"No," Calion objected. "I will not allow her to be subjected to a formal testing by Círdan." He could still remember being examined as a child. He'd hated it. The memory of having the control of his magick wrested away by the older, stronger male had never left him. And the last thing he needed was to have Círdan in Talia's head. By probing her mind, he might discover their secret and then all would be lost. No, it was better to keep them far, far apart.

Ërestor frowned. "He is the magick finder, Calion. If the human is gifted in any way, he will find it."

"What is a *magick* finder?" Talia looked back and forth between Calion and the king.

Calion touched her shoulder. "Círdan is skilled in reading the aura of another. He can tell the type of magick an elf has. For example, my talents are both as a natural magician and as a strategist. They are my strongest skills."

"Whereas I," put in Eámanë, "I am a truthsayer. Alassë there," she pointed to the plump woman who'd questioned Talia earlier, "she is an herbalist."

"All elven folk have a little of every type of magick," the elegant Círdan explained, his black eyes fixed on Talia. "But most have a specific type that defines them."

Talia chewed her lip. She was very curious as to what Círdan might have to say, but Calion seemed against it. "I must bow to my lord Calion's wishes. He would prefer I not."

Calion shot her a surprised look. He'd not expected her to defer to him, but it warmed him she did. He had never liked Círdan, and he didn't want him touching Talia's aura or her mind. Not now, or anytime soon.

They went on to other topics of interest as they ate the delicious food before them. Finally, Ërestor leaned back in his chair, swirling his after-dinner drink in his hand. "I would like you to reconsider being tested, Lady Talia. Do you not wish to find out more about the magick you carry within you?"

"I admit to being curious."

"Calion?"

Calion scowled. He didn't enjoy feeling pressured, but there was a part of him that *did* wonder if a name could be put to Talia's skills. "I will not agree to a formal testing, not at this time. But perhaps Círdan can do something now. Something not so intrusive."

Lord Círdan narrowed his eyes at the prince, obviously displeased with the royal's hesitation. But finally, after a little thought, he nodded. Stretching out his hand, he made his own magick appear. "What do you see, human?"

Talia gazed at him. His magic wasn't as bright as the prince's, but she could see something. "It's not as easy to see as Calion's, but... It looks golden in color. It is in the shape of...an eye?"

Círdan curled his hand up, shutting off his magick. He looked at Talia speculatively. He held out his hand again. "Give me your hand."

Talia looked at Calion for permission. When he nodded, she put her small hand in the tester's old one. Círdan smoothed her hand between his own, closing his eyes and cocking his head in concentration. After a few moments, Talia felt a pressure just behind her eyelids. It built steadily, moving up over her entire head. She frowned and blinked, but the heaviness increased.

He's in my head! she thought in amazement. Instinctively, she shielded her mind from him and the tension lessened.

Círdan opened his eyes, surprised. He stared at her, as if willing her to let go the barrier.

Talia raised her chin in defiance. Her mind belonged to her.

After several uncomfortable moments, Círdan seemed to accept her choice. He rubbed his thumb over her palm. "I sense in you many things. You carry fragments of another magick, one that has blended with your essence, so I cannot identify where it came from. You do have magick of your own, Lady Talia, but it is not elven. I have never felt its kind before, but I do know what type it is."

"What form of magick has she?" Ërestor asked eagerly.

"The Lady Talia is a natural empath. She's probably always had the gift, but didn't know how to use it." He looked at Talia. "When in your world, was it uncomfortable to be in crowds? Did you prefer to be on your own? Did you often feel strong emotion for no reason?"

She nodded at him, wide-eyed.

"Then I suspect you have been an empath your whole life. It is just here, where the magick is stronger, your gift began to flourish."

Círdan dropped her hand and turned to the king. "The fact she can sense our magicks—and yes, my magick shows itself as a golden eye—leads me to this belief."

"What exactly *is* an empath?" Talia asked softly.

"An empath is someone with the inherent ability to discern the feelings and emotions from someone or something else. They can take those emotions upon themselves. Those with this intuitive skill are able to communicate without words. Some use this talent to heal, knowing just by sense what is wrong. Others are remarkable trainers of animals. From what I sensed in the Lady Talia, she leans more to the natural world—trees, animals and such. Somewhat like our prince."

"Then how can she sense our magick?" Calion questioned.

Círdan shrugged. "All our magick is pulled from the land and forest around us. It is part of being elven folk." He looked at Talia. "She can sense it because the base of that magick is in nature."

"How can I learn more about this?" Talia asked in fascination. "I would like to study and maybe improve my gift."

"I will show you the archives," responded Calion. "There is much to learn there. You can also search for the prophecy that involves you."

"Thank you, Lord Círdan, for showing me that to me. It's nice to know I'm not going crazy." Talia smiled sweetly at the older elf.

"You are welcome. I am curious as to where your gift came from. It is said empathy is in our bloodlines. If you change your mind about having a deeper search done, please inform me."

"She won't," Calion said firmly.

ഇ

The days passed swiftly. Calion kept his promise and showed Talia the elven archives, a room full of documents and scrolls carefully kept from ages past. There was an area of learning that touched on everything from simple mathematics to the reading of runes. That was where Talia found the information about being an empath.

Calion spent some of the time with her, showing her how to search through the musty parchments to look for the prophecy. The wise librarians never heard of such a written vision, so they narrowed it down to parchments over a millennia old. It was slow, time-consuming work.

After that, Talia and Calion spent few hours together, partly due to Calion picking up his royal duties. The only time they really saw each other was during mealtimes. They hadn't been alone together since the day Talia had been released from the dungeon.

Eámanë helped keep Talia busy with tours around the castle and by visits to the clothier, where Calion bought her a new wardrobe. But she had her duties also, so the majority of Talia's time was spent alone.

She discovered the castle gardens and spent many hours there, either thinking or practicing her empathic magic. Some of the pets of the castle found their way to her. It got to be wherever Talia was, so also would be a herd of dogs, cats, birds and the occasional mouse.

The king also spent time with her. He was getting over his unreasonable hatred of humans, and while he still was hesitant about her place in his kingdom, Ërestor found Talia's humanity fascinating. They spent time each day discussing the differences between their two races. He found the female well spoken and intelligent, always ready to argue her point but courteous enough to admit when she was wrong.

Talia managed to make friends with her maids once they realized the legends about humans eating elves were false. Talia's honesty and humor helped them to come to accept her quicker than she could have hoped.

Gilraen and Silmarwín were excellent sources of information about the castle and the village. Sometimes they even went with her when she explored her new surroundings. The village elves were standoffish with the human at first, but as the days passed and they got to know Talia, they began to treat her like they would any other noblewoman. If anything, they treated her humanity like an unfortunate accident.

Always she was followed by one of Calion's royal entourage. All of this kept her busy, but it didn't keep her from missing

Calion. That was a deep ache inside of her, and it only seemed to grow worse the longer she was kept from his side.

Calion hated the time away from Talia. He wanted to help her find that prophecy. Everything in him knew it had something to do with the elves, *and* it was very, very important.

His duties always interested him, but while the appeal was still there, his need to discover her future gnawed at him. He couldn't seem to get it or her out of his mind. The few moments they were allowed at dinner just whetted his appetite for more.

Just touching her hand under the cover of the table made him stallion hard and aching in a moment. The time spent mating at the lake seemed months past, rather than days.

Now that they were back at the castle, his illness returned. The burning in his eyes, the sweats, the constant itching under his skin. It seemed to grow worse day by day, making him tense and irritable. He didn't say anything to anyone...he hated being sick. After a week, he tried the healing water from the waterfall again. It soothed his eyes some, but the itching didn't change. He began to wonder if he'd developed an allergy to something.

To make matters worse, the castle was filled with elven nobles there for the *Tarol* Festival. It had started several days before, just another thing making it difficult for Calion and Talia to spend any time together. His duties kept him busy escorting different females to the various functions. Even though his guest, it was decreed because she was human, Talia was not important enough to warrant his attentions in that way. Instead, Finrod, the royal advisor, had the honor of being her escort.

Seeing her on another man's arm didn't improve Calion's temper. He was barely civil to the females he was escorting, not even noticing their attempts to impress or attract him. He had eyes for one female only.

If Lord Finrod touched Talia's waist to guide her or took her arm to steady her, his temper flared. He barely managed to keep control of himself. Each night the burning of his illness worsened.

As for Talia, watching Calion each night with another woman struck deep at the ugly insecurity she tried to hide. She knew the king hoped for a match from one of these ladies. Night after night, she pretended to feel nothing, but she loved him, and knowing she wasn't considered good enough to touch him or be with him hurt her in too many ways to count. It got to be so bad she had to force herself down to supper and then out to whatever party going on that night. She stayed just long enough to put in an appearance before going back to the safety of her room. There, she could cry her eyes out and no one would hear.

While she thought Lord Finrod nice, she hated the feel of his hand on hers. It literally made her shudder. The itching under her skin made her feel like bugs were crawling all over her. She tried to be kind...it wasn't his fault he wasn't the man she loved. It wasn't his fault he wasn't Calion.

She was treated with politeness from most of the elven nobles. They knew she was under Prince Calion's protection, so they made the appearance of civility. Unfortunately, ladies such as Nienna all smiled to her face but gossiped nastily behind her back.

The male nobles seemed nicer. They were curious about the beautiful female, even though she was human. So they looked, sometimes even spoke to her, but they knew better than to touch.

Calion didn't see Talia's anguish. He was too caught up in his own agony, losing control of his own body. The burning of his skin and the pain in his eyes was overwhelming. The females he was around just exacerbated it when they touched him. Having to do his duty to them and his father was slowly destroying him. All he wanted was to go back to the forest. At least there the illness seemed to disappear.

He wanted to be with Talia. She didn't make his flesh hurt, *she* soothed it. He fought battles with himself every night when he saw her leaving early. He wanted to sneak into her room and take her, hard and fast, just the way he'd done before. Knowing he didn't dare made his agony only worse.

On the seventh day of the *Tarol* Festival, exactly a week after Talia had been released from her prison cell, she noticed Calion didn't appear at supper or later at the gathering held that night. Troubled, she made her way through the crowded room to the king. He stood in a group of ladies, all dressed in their best gowns. In his staid blue robes, he looked like an eagle surrounded by a flock of colorful tropical birds.

"My king," she said softly, curtsying low before him, noting the nasty looks sent her way by the females on his arms. "If I may beg a moment of your time."

Ërestor smiled at her, admiring the beautiful peach-color gown she wore. Cut low over her breasts, the bodice sparkled with crystal light. The snug waist showed off a trim figure as it flowed out into the long beautiful layers of skirt. He sighed. Even though he couldn't admit it, the human was easily one of the most beautiful females in the room.

"What is it, child?"

She moistened her lips. "I don't see Prince Calion anywhere. Is he gone from the castle?"

Something came and went in Ërestor's eyes. "He is here. Just not feeling well."

Her heart sank into her stomach. "He's sick?

"Just a little under the weather." The king smiled smugly, and Talia felt her nerves begin to jump. "He will soon be as right as rain."

"Perhaps I should go see him...to cheer him up. No one likes to be sick."

"*No*!" the king disagreed firmly. "That will not be necessary. He is better off alone." Forcing a smile, Ërestor patted Talia's shoulder gently. "Do not worry, child. It will soon be over."

Talia watched as the king and his flock of females wandered off. The concern she felt now grew into worry. What was going on? Where was Calion? What would be over soon? She looked around blankly until her gaze fell on Eámanë.

The princess was holding her own court with a crowd of handsome males. Firming her lips, Talia marched over to her.

"Excuse me," she muttered as she grabbed her dark-haired friend from a chair. "Be right back." She dragged the protesting Eámanë over to a corner of the room, out of the king's sight.

"Talia!" Eámanë grumbled, straightening her ice-blue gown. "What is the matter with you?"

Talia wanted to shake her. "I thought you were my friend." When she saw the princess' blank look, she did. "Why didn't you tell me about Calion?"

"Oh." Eámanë bit her lip and a shadow flickered in her eyes. "How do you know about him?"

"I'm not blind! He's not here, so I asked your father where he was. What's going on? What is the king not telling me?"

Eámanë sighed. "My father keeps the truth from you because he does not think it concerns you. I did not say anything because...I did not want to hurt you."

Talia's stomach lurched. She grabbed Eámanë's hand. "What's wrong with Calion?"

The princess put her other hand over their clasped ones. "I know how you feel about Calion, even though you try to hide it. I am a truthsayer and care about both of you. I was afraid if you found out what was happening, you would be hurt."

Icy fear knifed through Talia's body. It was her worst nightmare come true. Her eyes filled as she looked at Eámanë. "He's with another woman."

"No!" Eámanë pressed Talia's hands. "No! He is not with another female. But what I have to say may be hard for you to understand."

"Go ahead," Talia muttered hoarsely. Anything to free herself from this horrible fear.

The princess sighed again. "Calion is in what we call...a fire fever. It causes painful itching eyes, burning under the skin and other symptoms. It is very rare. Very few get it. In fact, none of us have ever seen it. All we have are legends to go on."

"Legends?" Talia shook her head. Her mind involuntarily flew back to their day by the lake. Calion's eyes had been bloodshot and his body like a furnace, but he'd been fine later on in the day. What did it mean?

"Do you know anything about the relationships between female and male elves?" Eámanë asked.

She frowned in confusion. What did relationships have to do with Calion being sick? "Just what Calion told me. He explained about your traditions. Linkings and such."

"Did he ever tell you about fire mating?"

Talia's head came up, and she paled. "Yes, he told me a little."

Eámanë nodded. "Then you know fire mating is very important to the elven people. For several reasons. It is a passion that is strong and lasting. It can breed power between the two, and most importantly, it can lead to—"

"To *Mylari*," Talia said dully. Her heart was breaking again.

"Yes, *Mylari*."

"Has he...has he..." Talia could barely speak the words. "Has he found his soulmate?"

Eámanë shook her head. "We do not know. Fire fever is

what happens when an elf, most often male, comes in contact with a female who is a potential fire mate. One who could be *Mylari*. It is said if he does not act on the attraction, he can sicken. Or even die."

Talia sat on a nearby couch before her weak knees caused her to sink to the floor. "He could die?"

Eámanë frowned and quickly sat next to her friend. "Do not worry, Talia. If he is in a fire fever, then he has found someone. I did not want to hurt you with this, knowing how you feel about him, but once he seeks her out, he will return to his old self."

Talia wondered if she would ever have the strength to walk again. She was literally frozen in fear. Was she the one he fevered for, or was it someone else? "You don't know who she is?" she asked hesitantly.

The princess shrugged. "Father says it is someone in the castle. Here is where the symptoms started." Eámanë narrowed her eyes in thought. "Was he all right in the forest?"

Talia thought about his behavior up until the time he mated with her the first time. He'd been antsy, but in control. After that, he'd just been insatiable. But she couldn't tell his sister that. "He was fine. He had none of the symptoms you describe."

"Then all will be satisfactory. He is confined to his room because the symptoms are so powerful. Tomorrow, Calion will seek out the female and if he is lucky, he will have discovered his *Mylari* as well."

Talia stared at her friend. She wondered what Eámanë would say if she told her the female Calion flamed for was sitting right in front of her.

ꙮ

The next few days were the worst of Talia's life. Even though she knew it was probably herself Calion needed, she suffered the torments of the damned, imagining him finding another female he flamed for. She wanted to see him, but was balked at every turn. The king, Eámanë, her own guards, even Calion himself prevented it. It was an elven thing, she was told over and over again.

So she paced and prayed and paced some more. She haunted the corridors trying to get a glimpse of him. She tried to use her gift to find out things, but her knowledge was still too sketchy. She could sense concern in those around her that grew as the days went by. Once, when she took the king's hand, she felt his anger and strong frustration, but what she wanted to feel was Calion. Was he all right? Was he whole? Did he still want her? What good was this skill if she couldn't communicate with the one person she loved most of all?

Finally, totally frustrated, she sent a songbird to his window. She waited, chewing her lower lip in anticipation as she paced the now familiar track around her room. An hour later the bird came back. Rushing to it, she gently offered a bit of fruit as a snack. The little bird cocked his head and gave a little chirp of thanks before greedily gobbling it down. Once finished, he stepped up on her finger.

She took a deep breath and closed her eyes. Talia was just getting the hang of dropping into an animal's mind. Like the *Malesia* tree, animals couldn't really speak to her, but used word pictures to communicate. If she was lucky, the songbird would tell her what she longed to know.

The picture was cloudy at first but then cleared as the bird concentrated on what he'd seen. The room was dark. The only light came from the windows where the bird stood. She could see a figure lying on the bed. Was it Calion?

Off the windowsill and onto the table next to the bed, the bird hopped closer. Its eyes adjusted easily to the lack of light, and Calion's face came into view.

Talia gasped and squeezed her eyes against the tears that welled up in her. His face was ravaged with pain and an anger that was frightening, even to her. Moving restlessly, he tossed in the bed, his sheets tangling around him. He was naked to the waist and she cried out when she saw the raised welts on his skin. It looked as if he'd been beaten...from the inside.

He muttered in his sleep, elven words that were low and dark. She wanted to reach out and soothe his troubled brow. He needed her and she couldn't get to him.

Later that night, she sat at the supper table, her mind barely registering the talk going on around her. She sat several seats away from the king tonight, closer than usual. For the third night in a row, Calion was nowhere to be seen. She looked distractedly around her. Everyone was talking about the day's hunt, but no one seemed concerned the heir to the throne lay in his room, writhing in pain. Suddenly, she couldn't take it anymore. She pushed her dessert away.

"Your Majesty, how is Prince Calion?"

Heavy silence fell in the room. She was reminded of the fable in her world about the emperor's new clothes. No one wanted to be the one to bring that problem up either. She looked at the king and raised her chin. This time she would not be put off.

King Ërestor froze, his after-dinner *shalia* halfway to his mouth. He stared at her, shock hardening his face. His mouth opened once and then closed. "He is...fine. A few more days and all will be well."

Talia wasn't having any of it. "That's what you said three days ago." She bit her lip. Asking this question was so difficult. "Hasn't he found her yet?"

Ërestor choked on his drink. "What do you know of it?" he demanded. "You are not elven!"

"No, I'm not," she said, holding onto her temper. She refused to get Eámanë in trouble. "But I live here and I *am* empathic. It wasn't hard to sense what is happening. I know there is something wrong."

All conversation stopped. No one pretended not to listen. They all were curious as to what was happening with the prince.

Ërestor's mouth firmed. To Talia, it was like looking at Calion. The movement chased away her anger.

"Please..." she whispered, knowing her heart must show in her eyes.

The king didn't see her heart, but he did see fear and honest concern. His irritation at her pushiness vanished. He made his decision and stood. "I would like to speak to my advisory staff in the library." When they rose to leave, he looked at her.

"Lady Talia, would you join us, please." There was a murmur of disbelief as the others at the table heard his words. The human was to be allowed in an advisory session? How could this be?

Talia didn't care how. She would find out the truth. That

was all she wanted. She put her hand on the king's arm. "Thank you."

Ërestor patted her hand and then tucked it in his arm, leading her out of the room. "You are my son's friend. I should have told you, but it is an elven matter. I'd forgotten just how persistent you can be."

With a smile, Talia walked into the library. "Majesty, you have no idea."

When they were all seated with fresh drinks in their hands, the king spoke. "Lady Talia asked a question. But the information I am about to impart must stay in this room. I will not have the nobles and the populace gossiping about my son."

There was a murmur of agreement before the king went on.

"Calion refuses to name the female he is attracted to. In fact, he will not admit to being in a fire fever at all. He says he is allergic to something."

"Could this be true?" Finrod asked. "None of us has ever seen a fire fever. Perhaps we are wrong."

Círdan shook his head. "You do not have to have firsthand experience to know the symptoms."

Ërestor nodded sadly. "Even the healers agree. It is a fire fever."

"Then what do we do?" Eámanë asked. "I have seen him. He does not look good. I fear for him."

"I gave him three days to name the female. There is no reason why he did not do so." Ërestor took a long sip of his *shalia.* "The only conclusion is he does not know who it is yet."

Lady Nienna sat up straight. "Are you saying it could be any female? Even those he knows?"

Círdan frowned. "It is most probable one of the females who arrived at the *Tarol* Festival sent him into this fever. He does not have to know her. Calion may have just brushed up against her in the castle."

Talia sucked in her breath. He hadn't even looked for another woman. The sheer relief speared all the way down to her toes. Did he really think it just an allergy? Or was he protecting their secret? What should she do now? He was so sick.

"So how do we get him to find this mystery female?" Eámanë questioned. "If he will not admit to the fever, how will we get him to search for her?"

"We will not," the king stated grimly. "As of tomorrow morning, every elven female in the castle will be brought before Calion. Legend states when he is confronted with the female he needs, it will be clear to all. He will not be able to control himself."

"And if she is not in the castle?" asked the king's military advisor, Amras. "Will we bring them in from the village and surrounding countryside as well?"

Ërestor looked at everyone in the room. "We will search everywhere until we find the elven female who set off the prince's fire fever. I will not rest until she is found."

Talia woke to Calion's bellow of rage. She nearly fell out of bed, her own body reacting to the pure outrage in his. Breaking out in a light sweat, she pulled on her silk robe and raced from her room, almost running into Amroth in her hurry.

"What is it," she gasped as she knotted the belt at her waist. "What is wrong with Calion?"

"M'lady." Amroth stopped her as she made to step past him. "By the prince's command, you cannot go up there."

"Don't be ridiculous!" she scoffed. "I know what's happening to him. He has the fire fever. But why did he scream? Calion doesn't yell."

"I am aware you know of our prince's condition, but he specifically asked you not be allowed upstairs. He does not want you in the family quarters." Amroth flinched when he saw Talia's face. "I am sorry."

She stood very still. "I'm still not welcome," she whispered, dropping her hands in defeat. "Even now."

Amroth didn't know what to say, so he stayed quiet.

"Can you at least tell me what's happened? Is Calion okay?"

The guard nodded warily. The female looked like she might burst into tears. He could slay the mighty *jhol* and bring its mane and claws back as prizes, but the thought of a female in tears scared him speechless.

"The prince is meeting the females in the castle as the king decreed last night." Amroth looked up when another bellow shook the walls around them. "Apparently, it is not going well."

Talia didn't say another word but turned and walked back into her room, shutting the door behind her. She walked straight to the bed and threw herself down on it. Another shout of anger filled the castle, and she shuddered.

Oh, my love, she thought. *What have we done?*

Chapter Twelve

She didn't leave her room that day. The thought of the parade of women being shown to Calion made her sick to her stomach. Would he stand firm, or would the pain cause him to break down and take one of the females for his own? Every time he roared, her own skin would shiver and crawl, and by the end of the day, her eyes were sore from all her tears.

She didn't go to supper that night. She couldn't even think about food, knowing what the man she loved was going through.

When the guards changed, Lolíndir, who'd been up with Calion, passed on the latest news. "They brought every female in the castle. From the highest-born noble to the lowliest scullery maid. He would not even look at them. Their presence seemed to infuriate him." The elf rubbed his eyes tiredly. "He started throwing furniture around."

Talia, who remembered his strength when he was angry enough to toss two tree trunks, shuddered. "Is he safe?"

Lolíndir looked at her sorrowfully. "We chained him to the wall."

She gasped aloud. "You chained him." Her eyes flashed in outrage. "He is your prince! How could you?"

Lolíndir slammed his fist into the wall outside her door. "There was no choice. He began to act irrationally. Going after the females."

Her heart stopped. "He found a fire mate?"

"No," Lolíndir snorted. "Calion was angry we brought females into his room. He chased them out, scaring them badly. The prince cared not for his father's decision. Even the king could not make him see reason."

"What happens now?" Talia asked faintly.

"It starts all over again tomorrow. The king wants every female in *Osalai* brought before him. Chained, he can do them no harm."

No one slept that night. Calion raged against his bonds as well as what had been done to him that day. He'd never been so angry before. His body burned as hot as fire, and he swore his very blood was boiling. He pulled so hard against the chains his wrists were bloody, his scar weeping puss and poison.

He wanted Talia. His whole body focused on her and her alone. He knew he was in a mating fever, and he knew who he needed to mate with. But he also had enough control to know if he gave his father her name, she would be killed. He'd even spelled himself so he couldn't utter her name when asked who he flamed for.

When they brought the line of women in, his entire being cringed away. He couldn't bear to be in the same room as them, knowing they were there hoping to be chosen as his mate. He'd frightened them and it pleased him. Perhaps it would show them he would not give in.

He didn't believe he would die, even though the healers told him he would. Calion knew his own strengths, and his will to survive was great. He would get through this and everything would get back to normal.

He'd take Talia back to the waterfall and they would—how had she put it?—make love until neither of them could walk straight. Then they would go to the healing pool and start all over again.

Two more days went by. The nobles staying in the castle gave their regrets and escaped, knowing since none of their females pulled Calion out of his fever, their presence wasn't necessary. It wasn't long until the castle was empty again, with only the family and regular tenants around.

Calion's howls grew louder the longer the king continued to parade females through his room. Ërestor watched helplessly as his son's mind began to go. Whatever control the prince had slowly disappeared. His eyes turned from sapphire to bright gold, blinding him to everything but his own need. His skin, already burning, began to split open in long, tearing strips.

He pulled at his chains, screaming for release so he could find the female his body craved. His father pleaded with him, but Calion refused to give the female's name.

Talia knew she was going crazy. She hadn't slept in two days, and she barely nibbled on the trays that were brought to her. The knowledge she might be comfortable while Calion was chained in a hell of her making was unbearable. She should have gone home. Then none of this would have happened. His shouts followed her wherever she went, whether in the garden or in her room. No matter where she was, she couldn't escape him.

She was in the rose garden, seated on a marble bench, when the king came to see her. Pity stirred when she saw the strain and worry on Ërestor's face. As she started to rise, he waved her back down.

"Lady Talia, I needed some fresh air. How do you during this horrible time?"

Shaking her head, she shuddered as another howl rent the air. "How can you bear it? We have to do something!"

The king sat next to her, hunched and miserable. "I have done everything I know to do. Every elven female in my kingdom he has seen, and he wants none of them. Wherever she is, she has not come forward."

Talia eyes misted. "Perhaps she can't."

"Then it would be better she leave completely," Ërestor bit out. "If she went out of his scent range, then Calion would return to normal."

"Is that part of the legend?" she whispered.

"It is said fire mating is brought on by pheromones." The king rose, agitated. He paced over to a rosebush and plucked a single rose, twirling it in his fingers. "If the female is far enough away, he will not be able to scent her."

She stared at him, her world crumbling around her. Up until that moment, she'd held onto the hope that Calion would get better and they would be able to be together, if not as mates then as secret lovers whenever the opportunity presented itself. It wasn't what she really wanted, but she loved him enough to take whatever he could give her.

Now she knew as long as she was around him, Calion would get the fever again. Her presence wouldn't matter if he loved her and wanted her enough to defy his father and the *sardai*, but he'd shown her by his silence that wasn't so. While he might want her, even care for her in his own way, his first priority would always be his heritage.

Talia sat silently when the king finally left, listening to the inhuman raging and mourning her broken dreams. She knew now what she must do. When she calmed herself, she walked back to her quarters and turned to Celahir, the guard on duty.

"Please, I must speak to Maeglin."

Celahir frowned. "He is with the prince. I dare not take him away from him."

She swallowed back fresh tears. "It's necessary I speak to him. It's about the prince. I think I may be able to help."

Those words sent the guard racing for the stairs. It wasn't long until Maeglin knocked at her door. When she bade him enter, the leader of the Royal Guard glared at her.

"I do not have time for this!" he growled. "My prince needs me."

Talia looked at the elf. His face was haggard and worried. Dark circles dusted his eyes, making him look like he hadn't slept in months. Calion's illness had been hard on everyone, no one more so than the male who was his closest friend. She knew Maeglin was the only one who could help her.

"M'lady..." The elf tried hard to be civil. "Why did you call me here? You said you could help Prince Calion."

She swallowed hard. Now the time had come, she was terrified. "M-Maeglin," she stuttered. "You love your prince. More than that, you are loyal to him and his best friend, right?"

"Lady Talia—"

"Please...hear me out." She took a deep breath as Maeglin reluctantly subsided. "I have to trust you. If I don't, then Calion could die. I can't let that happen." It was now or never. She lifted her chin and looked into his pale blue eyes.

"It's me. I'm the one Calion is flaming for."

He blinked once and then swore. "I do not have time for the fantasies of a crazy female. You are a human. Only an elf can be a fire mate."

"Think, Maeglin," she insisted. "The king brought every female in the kingdom to see him and nothing worked. Who is left?"

The guard stared at her, suddenly remembering his prince's quiet confession. *I flame for her.* He'd hoped it had been an exaggeration. Still, he didn't want to believe it. "We missed someone. Calion has been with a female. His mating fever is too strong for him not to know her. When we find her, he will be all right."

"You *have* found her. I've been right under your nose all the time, but no one will let me near him."

"Ridiculous!" he charged, turning and pacing over to the bed. "It is impossible. He would have had to mate with you already to have brought him into the full flame of a mating fire."

There was silence in the room, and he turned and looked back at her. His face paled when he saw the truth written for all to see.

"*Shia si kydaer!*" He sat heavily on the edge of the bed.

"It is a secret, one you now share." Talia's voice broke a little as she went on. "If he wanted anyone to know, he would say something. I know he doesn't want me anywhere near him."

Pain touched the human's face, and sympathy welled up in Maeglin. The prince would rather die than claim her as his own. How that must hurt. "I am sorry."

"I have to leave."

He blinked. "What?"

She brushed a tear from her cheek. "The king told me if the female Calion is flaming for goes out of his scent range, then he would recover."

"So they say."

"Then help me. Take me back to my world. If I am there, then he can't scent me, and he will get better. I should have left before, but...but I wanted to be with him. I was selfish and look what's happened."

The elf tried to keep up. "You want me to take you back to the human world? What about the orcs?"

She paled a little. "If you take me through the myst far away from my home, they won't be able to find me. That's what Calion was going to do."

"You would leave him. Put yourself back in danger."

"I told you once before. He's what's important. I can't let him die." Tears flowed freely now. "I listen to him screaming and my flesh crawls too. I can feel everything he does, and I know it's my fault. Please, help me."

The guard rose from the bed and walked to where the human stood. She was such a little thing to have such a big heart. Maeglin found he couldn't be angry with her, even after all the trouble she caused.

He would lay odds most of the fault lay with his stubborn prince. He'd seen a female he wanted, and although it meant breaking *sardai*, he would have her, no matter what the cost. He found the thought of Calion and this human didn't bother him as much as he thought it would. He knew the Lady Talia. She was beautiful inside and out.

Her plan was sound. Getting her out of the faerie world would help Calion. He wasn't sure how much longer the prince had. There was just one problem. He'd promised Calion before his mind left him that he would protect Talia, and sending her back to her own world would be suicide. Orcs were some of the best trackers around. If they found her once, they would find her again.

"I am sorry, Lady Talia. I cannot help you. I made a promise to the prince."

She looked stricken. "Your promise could kill him. I can't get to the myst by myself. Please...I need your help."

His jaw clenched. "I cannot and neither will anyone else in the guard. Besides, the king closed the border until the female is found. I could not take you even if I wanted to."

"We could sneak out. You have the ability. I know you made him a promise, but what good does it do him if he's dead?"

"I will not go against my prince! I have my honor."

Talia broke. She threw herself against him, pounding his chest with her fists. "Honor! Honor! I'm sick of hearing about honor. Your honor won't keep him alive." She burst into tears as Maeglin held her away from him.

"You are distraught." The elven man spoke calmly even though his guts twisted. "I understand you are concerned, but we do not even know for sure it is you. You and Calion may have...mated, but only an elf can be his fire mate."

"You're being a fool, Maeglin." She pulled away and stalked to the window. "You see the evidence right before your eyes and ignore it."

He bowed. "I can only do what my prince asks of me." He

walked to the door of her chamber. "If it could be different, I would help."

She swore as the door closed behind him, knowing her only way of getting back to the human world had just walked out. Talia wasn't even sure how to get around the village, let alone the countryside. Turning, she stared out the window, shivering as Calion let loose with another shout of rage. What should she do now?

Her answer came when Eámanë knocked on her door late the next afternoon. The princess looked as tired and worried as everyone else, but she was still the prettiest woman Talia had ever seen. Dressed in a soft silver-blue tea gown, her friend looked fresh and young.

"Even with everything that is going on, you still look gorgeous."

Eámanë snorted. "I do not. I am old and ugly and so tired." She gazed at Talia with fear in her blue eyes. "He is not getting any better. They think he is going to die. They say that tomorrow—" The princess broke off.

Talia's heart dropped to her stomach. "That can't be true. He can't die."

"No one seems to be able to pull him out of the fever. It is as if she does not really exist." Eámanë walked over to Talia's favorite window, missing the look on her friend's face. "I do not know how my father will handle it if Calion dies."

"He's not going to die," Talia almost shouted. She thought about the long days and nights when her skin crawled and her eyes ached. Impossible though it may seem, she knew it was the fever sickness, and if what she felt was even a portion of what Calion was going through... She squeezed her eyes tight shut.

The sun dipped below the horizon, sending shadows into Talia's room. Eámanë sighed, wishing her brother could enjoy the beauty of the sunset, but his mind was so far gone he didn't even remember his own sister. The healers and the learned men all believed the same. If the female wasn't found soon, the heir to the throne would die.

The princess turned back to her friend. "I am sorry. I do not mean to—" She stopped dead, her hand going to her throat.

"Talia?"

"Eámanë? What's wrong?"

The princess just stared. Talia stood by her bed, her face in the shadows cast by the evening sun. Her dark gown blended in with the surroundings, leaving only her golden hair easily seen. But what shocked Eámanë down to her toes, was when the human opened her eyes, soft, dancing flames flickered.

"It is you!"

Talia gazed at her friend in confusion. "What are you talking about?"

Eámanë walked over to her, taking Talia's chin firmly in her hand. "Your eyes. How can this be? They are on fire. *You* are the female Calion is flaming for!"

When the human blushed, all the pieces of the puzzle came together. The princess dug deep, using her gift of truthsaying to discover what was hidden. Her stomach sank when all was revealed.

She slapped Talia across the face. "How could you?"

Talia staggered from the blow and stepped back, ready to defend herself. "Stop it, Eámanë. That will get us nowhere!"

"How could you do that to him?" Eámanë hissed. "I thought you cared about him."

Talia rubbed her cheek. The princess packed a punch. "It's because I care that it happened. I'm sorry, but I couldn't tell you. Calion made me promise."

"Do not lie to me!" Eámanë snarled. "You have not seen him since his illness. He could not have told you to hide from us."

Talia blinked. "What are you talking about?

"You leave him to suffer? He should have left you with the orcs!"

"You're crazy. I don't want him to suffer!" Talia cried. "I'm talking about what happened with your brother and me before, not what is going on now."

"Then tell me...how could this happen?" Eámanë shouted.

"I have wanted to be with him since he rescued me," Talia shouted back. "We fought it, but those feelings wouldn't go away. We spent a week sharing our bodies in the forest. I know what the flames look like in his eyes. When he asked me to stay, I grabbed onto the chance to be with him. Do you think I would have come here if I'd known what would happen to him? I fell in love with him."

When she saw Eámanë's shocked look, she sat heavily on the bed.

"I love him."

The princess had been with Talia enough to hear stories about her world, and she knew what she meant. She took a deep breath and sat next to her. "You have mated with my brother...broken the *sardai*?"

Talia nodded sadly. "Yes. I don't care who or what he is. I love him."

"But he does not claim you."

The human's eyes filled and overflowed. "No. He knew how your father would react. His heritage is what is important to him."

"But now—"

"Now is no different. He would rather flirt with death than admit to needing me...a human." She whirled and her eyes flashed in a quick shift of mood. "Do you think I want it this way? I would shout how I feel from the ramparts. I love him." Her shoulders slumped. "But he doesn't love me. He's made his choice."

"And so you are just going to let him die? Why did you not leave? It would have cured him," Eámanë cried.

"I tried!" Talia shouted again. "I tried to leave, but they wouldn't let me go." She rubbed her smarting eyes. "It hurts, Eámanë. All the time. The burning, the itching. It's driving me crazy. If the fever is doing this to me, what must it be doing to him?"

"By the goddesses..." Eámanë murmured. Shoving back one of Talia's long sleeves, she saw the long, deep scratches on her friend's arm. She looked up at her in amazement. "You are in the fever too. It should be impossible."

"I don't know and I don't care," answered Talia shortly. "What I care about is Calion." She pushed the sleeve back down. "I've got to help him."

"How?" Eámanë questioned.

Talia took a deep breath. She'd known it would come to this. "If I can't leave so he will be better, there is only one other choice." She met the wary eyes of her friend.

"I have to mate with him."

Eámanë argued long and hard with Talia. There were logistical problems to figure out, such as how to get her in and what Calion might do once she was there. But overshadowing all of that was one thing. If she mated with Calion, everyone would know. The king would find out and her life would be forfeit. Because the prince was in the fever, he would probably be forgiven for breaking the *sardai*. But not Talia—she would have no excuse.

Talia didn't care. She'd watched the man she loved suffer long enough. If he wasn't going to save himself, she would. She understood making this choice would most likely cost her life, but to choose between her life and his? That was the easiest choice she would ever make.

"You cannot do this," Eámanë fretted. "We will both talk to Maeglin. I will order him to take you out of here."

Shaking her head, Talia pulled on the bell cord. "You know it won't work. He still thinks he must obey Calion."

"My brother told you to obey him too, but you are not."

Talia smiled grimly. "I'm not a royal guard. I'm the woman who loves him." When Gilraen came to the door, Talia asked for a hot bath. After the maid left, she turned back to Eámanë. "I will go to him clean. It will be easier for him to get my scent."

The princess frowned. "If you go through with this crazy scheme, it may also be the last bath you have."

"Oh, I'm going through with it, all right, and you're going to help me."

The bells tolled the midnight hour when Eámanë slipped back in Talia's door. "Are you sure about this?" she hissed.

Talia nodded. "I'm sure. Who's outside?"

"Lolíndir. He's just about asleep."

"Did he see you?"

Eámanë laughed. She pulled out an elven cloak similar to Calion's. "No one sees me unless I want them too."

Talia took a deep breath. "Okay, let's do this."

Nodding, Eámanë flipped the cloak over them both. Carefully, they cracked open the door and watched as Lolíndir adjusted himself against the stone wall. He dropped his chin to his chest and closed his eyes.

Talia knew he wasn't sleeping, but it gave them a slight advantage. Moving silently, they eased by the guard and tiptoed up the hall. When they were out of his sight, they both blew out their breath in relief.

"That's one."

"The next one is going to be more difficult." Eámanë answered. "Getting both the outside guard and Maeglin away from Calion's room..."

"You can do it, Eámanë." Talia smiled at her partner in crime. "If anyone can draw them away it would be you."

"Keep the cloak on tight," the princess instructed as she slipped out from under it and became visible. "We will have only one chance at this."

"I know," Talia responded grimly. She reached out an invisible hand and took Eámanë's. "Thank you. I couldn't have done this without you."

Eámanë shrugged. "I hate what you are doing, but I understand why you have to do it. We both l...ove Calion."

Talia knew the princess couldn't see her, but she smiled at the way Eámanë said *love.* "Yes. And that's why I have to go through with this. I do love him."

"Good luck, my friend." With a final squeeze of her hand, Eámanë headed up the stairs to Calion's quarters. Talia gave her until the count of ten before following. She walked carefully up the stairs until she could see the guard, Valandil, outside Calion's door. The prince's howls grew even louder as she drew nearer.

Suddenly, a scream rang out. The guard shot upright and looked around, trying to find the source of the noise. A second scream sent him sprinting toward the king's room, where he met Eámanë running toward him.

"Help! Help!" the princess screamed. "The king is injured. I need help!"

Valandil made to run past her, but Eámanë grabbed his arm. "No, something fell on him. You will need someone else. Get Maeglin." When the elf hesitated, she gave him a push. "Hurry! My father could die."

The guard inclined his head and raced over to Calion's door where he unlocked it. There was a muffled conversation before Maeglin ran out followed by Valandil. They looked over to

Eámanë, who wrung her hands and wept. "Please…hurry!"

Both males swept by her and headed to Ërestor's room. As soon as they moved out of sight, Eámanë motioned to the invisible Talia. "If you are there, now is the time!"

Talia pulled the cloak from her shoulders as she ran to the door. She knew once the guards saw there was nothing wrong, they would be back in an instant. She tossed it to her friend and embraced her.

"Thank you."

"Go on!" Eámanë urged, looking over her shoulder. "You do not have much time." She pulled open the unlocked door and moved out of the way. A roar from inside the room met her efforts, and she shuddered. "May the goddesses be with you."

Talia stepped inside, gazing around frantically. Where was he? She moved further into the room, quiet and as slim as a wraith in her white silk nightgown. She had never been in Calion's quarters before, but the set-up was somewhat like Eámanë's. She glanced toward the raised dais that held the bed and moaned in distress at the sight that met her eyes.

Calion stood against the wall, his body hunched forward, his unbound and matted hair covering his face and torso. He was naked, pieces of clothing torn and scattered around the room. They had chained his wrists, his arms slightly above his shoulders, but the bonds were bloody as if he'd tried to tear them from him.

His body was ripped and torn, great gouges where he'd tried to scratch out the burning itch. Her eyes filled with tears. Had she come to him too late?

The being that had been Calion heard the sounds in his room. He knew it was someone different. Not the male who stayed with him constantly, telling him stories about his life. He'd appreciated the tales. They kept him grounded for a long time. But now…now he was slipping over the edge into pure instinct.

He was crazed by the scent of the female he needed. It was always there, just at the edge of his awareness. He spent hours begging to be released to find her, but everyone was afraid of him now. So they chained him, fearing he would rampage around the kingdom looking for his female.

And rightly so. He would have done whatever it took to get

to that scent. What the others didn't understand was that it was close by.

Now it was closer still. Was it a trick? He pulled against the chain angrily, swaying back and forth as he scented the air. Yes. He growled menacingly. It was nearer than ever before. Taking a deep breath, he let out a bellow that rocked the room. He pulled hard against his chains, causing his wounds to open and bleed. Where was she?

Talia moved closer to Calion. The prince breathed hard, muttering in his own tongue. She couldn't see his face—it was still covered by his long hair. But trails of blood streamed onto his chest. Her tears overflowed as she sensed his agony. Stepping closer, she raised her hand and pushed back the sweat-matted hair. "Calion?"

She was there. His head shot up as he breathed in the scent that haunted him. The female stood close, her hand touching him. His whole body reacted. He flung back his head, his long hair flying behind him as he pulled against the chains that held him. Flame-filled eyes met hers, burning her with their intensity.

Talia almost stepped back at what she saw. Calion wasn't Calion anymore. He looked almost primitive. His face was harder and sharper, brows tilted twice as high as before, lips stretched tight over pointed teeth. Golden eyes glowed so hotly she could almost feel them where she stood. His body had bulked up and changed, with huge corded muscles and a fine layer of hair.

What had happened to him? She blushed when she saw his shaft, already half hard, swell to full arousal at her presence, the tip brushing his stomach in its urgency.

Even with all the changes, she knew him. His scent. The feel of his energy. Even his golden eyes. Her heart pounded in a mixture of excitement and fear. Calion wouldn't hurt her, but this wasn't her Calion anymore. Suddenly, she heard a sound behind her. Turning, she saw Maeglin and Valandil come into the room.

The leader of the Guard was furious. He'd been taken in by a child's trick. Never mind it had been the princess, someone he trusted. Maeglin blamed himself. He strode into the room and stopped dead, seeing his prince straining toward the human female.

"Lady Talia," he said commandingly. "Come away from there. It is too dangerous. You know what will happen if you stay with him."

She looked at Maeglin. "I know exactly what will happen to me. I tried to get you to let me go, but you wouldn't. I have no choice now. This is his only hope. It doesn't matter about me."

"Do not make me take you by force. I must keep you safe. I must keep *both* of you safe." The guard moved stealthily closer.

"I'm not leaving him." Talia turned back around and stared into Calion's wild eyes. "He needs me." She stroked her hand down the prince's hard face. "I'm here for you if you want me. It's up to you." Without another word, she snuggled herself against him, wrapping her slim arms around his waist.

When the female touched him, Calion's entire being shrieked with pleasure. He knew this female. She carried the scent he'd been chasing. The mating fever fanned high, fueling his need and emotions. As she pressed herself to him, he could feel every line of her body against his. His cock jumped hard, pushing itself into her soft stomach. He let out a roar that was unlike any heard before.

He'd found her.

Listening to her argue with the other male, it suddenly became clear to him. The other male was trying to take her away. He shouted in anger. He would not let that happen.

Using all his strength, assisted by the fear of losing her, he strained against his chains one more time. His muscles bulged and knotted, but with a mighty heave, he pulled himself free from the wall, showering himself and Talia with broken masonry and dust.

Wrapping himself around the female, he breathed in the sweet scent of her. He crushed her to him, wanting nothing more than to bury himself in her body. He glared at Valandil and Maeglin, who stood near the door, staring in disbelief. Showing pointed white teeth, he snarled and held her closer still.

"*Toli!*" he hissed at them both. "*Toli!*"

Chapter Thirteen

Ërestor hurried down the hall. He'd been awoken by the two guards rushing into his bedchamber. Their faces, when they saw him lying comfortably in bed, set off warning bells, and the fact they both turned and ran from his room without a word made him jump out of bed and shrug into his robe in seconds.

He heard his son's scream as he stepped from his room, and the back of his neck prickled. This was not the sound of a man in agony, but the sound of triumph.

Turning into the hallway, he found several of Calion's elven Guard standing by the door. His daughter leaned against the wall, softly weeping. "He found a female?"

"Yes, Majesty," Amroth said, but his face didn't look happy.

"Then why the tears? Why the alarm? This should be a cause for celebration." At the grim shakes of the heads, Ërestor's heart pounded in trepidation. Who was in with his son? He stepped through the door just as Maeglin and Valandil came out.

"Your Highness, you should not go in." Maeglin's jaw clenched.

"He found a female?" the king asked. The guard nodded. "Who is it?"

"Majesty—" Valandil began.

"I do not understand your hesitation," Ërestor interrupted as he pushed past the two guards. "My son will be healed." He peered through the open door, seeing Calion holding a female in his arms.

"He is not rejecting..." His voice trailed off as Calion swung the female around to the wall and long golden hair flew out around him. He gasped in disbelief. "No! It cannot be!"

The king staggered back into the hallway, and Maeglin closed the prince's door and locked it, putting the key in his pocket. Ërestor blinked at the action. "What are you doing? You must get her out of there. It was Talia. He cannot mate with a...a human!"

"It is too late, my king." Maeglin bowed. "He has her now. If I try to stop him, he might kill himself or her."

Ërestor pulled at his hair. "This cannot be happening. He cannot want her. It must be because she was all that was available to him. Calion is too far gone to notice." He whirled and glared at the guard. "Who allowed this? How did she get in?"

The guards said nothing and Eámanë pushed herself off the wall. "I let her in."

The king gaped at his daughter. "You what? Do you know what you have done?"

Eámanë nodded, her blue eyes flashing. She faced down her father with no fear. "I have saved his life. He was dying and we all know it. Talia was the only one we had not tried. She is the one who can save him, and he has accepted her."

"She is a human!" Ërestor shouted at her. "No proper fire mate. You have forced your brother to break *sardai.*"

"Maybe," responded the princess, her chin in the air. "But at least he is alive."

The king paced up and down the hall. "What will everyone think? The prince mated with a human. It is disgusting."

"She will stop the fever. He needed her!"

"She will pay for this outrage," Ërestor growled as he stared at the closed door. "I will protect him from her."

"Father, you are being ridiculous."

"Go to your room, Eámanë. You have done enough!" Ërestor pointed down the hall towards the princess' room. He watched as she flounced off to her room then turned to the guards. "No one may know of this. We must protect his reputation. He did not choose to mate with this female. She forced him."

"Majesty..." Maeglin began, thinking of the times in the forest Calion chose to be with Talia.

"It is my wish no one finds out about this. We will tell

everyone the female was found and Calion was healed, but in the mating she died." The king tossed a glare at the door. "It may be true soon enough. If not, well, I will find another way to deal with the female."

"Your Majesty," Maeglin interjected, not liking where his king was headed. "Talia knew she might die by going in there. She cared enough about the prince to risk that. When you decide to deal with the female, you may want to remember she saved his life."

Talia heard the door close behind them and she sighed in relief. No matter what happened now, Calion would be safe. He hadn't moved since the men backed out, accepting his claim on her. He still held her in a crushing grip, breathing in her scent.

"I'm here, Calion," she whispered, softly stroking him where she could. "It's okay now. I'm here."

He could hear her trying to soothe him, but his need was too great. He'd waited too long to touch her. She was here, in his grasp...his now. The fire inside him could not be denied any longer. The burning was an agony and an ecstasy knowing he would soon be one with her. Everything else shut down, his whole consciousness focused on the slim female before him. The lust gripped him, feeding the need so hard he began to shake.

Somewhere deep inside him, the part of him that was still Calion tried to slow down. He knew in his present state of mind, he would hurt Talia, maybe even kill her. He dug up through the fog of the fire fever, struggling to make himself heard.

She sensed the battle going on inside him, and pressed herself closer. "I'm not going anywhere. I'm not afraid of you. You need me, Calion. You need me to stay alive. Please...take me. Mate with me and make me yours again."

Her words seemed to snap whatever control the prince was holding on to. Pulling back from her, he stared at her, panting heavily. She stood motionless except for the pulse beating in her throat.

Suddenly, he growled, making her jump when he reached out a single thick finger and ripped her gown from neckline to hem. Tossing it aside, he picked her up and shoved her against the wall.

"*Toli*!" he growled again as he drove himself into her.

Talia cried out. She was ready for him, her own fever making her quim wet and aching, but the force of his cock as it hammered into her was huge and bruising. Wriggling for a moment in pure feminine distress, the pain of his possession speared through her. After a few moments, her body adjusted to the driving force of his. Knowing there was nothing more she could do, she slid her arms around Calion's neck and just held on.

Relief…blessed relief. He was inside her, joined as he always was meant to be. The haze began to lift, but the need never lessened as he plunged deeper and deeper into her soft channel. The exquisite feel of her body began to calm him, pushing away the fog and pain, leaving pleasure and awareness in its place. The burning lightened, the itching receded as if it had never been. He lowered his head onto the female's shoulder and grasping her hips in his hands, thrust harder.

She moaned as his movements became stronger. He pushed her against the wall, her skin bruised by the stones behind her. Calion's panting became louder, his breath hot on her exposed neck as he reached down and hitched her up higher, wrapping her legs around him. In that position, she felt him go deeper still as he pulsed within her, signaling his release was imminent.

Pulling him tight against her, she kissed him, nibbling up to his ear. "I love you, Calion," she whispered, giving him everything in her heart. "I love you."

Her caresses, her words, both sent him over the edge. Moving hard and fast, he slammed into her until his roar of completion filled the room. He came in a long rush, jetting streams of life seed into her body. His body shuddered and shook as the worst of the fever left with his climax.

Talia lay limp in his arms. She'd not found her release, hadn't expected to, and her whole body ached from a combination of desire and the pain of mating with Calion. He stood, shaking against her, his breathing hard and hot.

As they stood there, leaning against the wall, she was aware of him changing. His body decreased in size, back to his pre-fever muscle and form. The hair that had covered him drifted to the floor. Gently, Talia lifted his head from her shoulder, smiling when she saw his face was back to the handsome one she'd always known.

He moved against her, and she felt him, still hard inside her. His eyes opened and she looked deep into them, past the gold fire that still flickered. She could see blue, and better yet, she could see him.

"Ta...li...a?"

Tears wet her lashes as she pulled him to her. "It's me, Calion. I'm here. Everything is okay now."

"Ta...lia." The words were stronger, and she gasped as he began to move in her again. He was gentler this time, but no less determined to have her. Minutes passed, turning into hours as he held her pinned against the wall. She lost count of the amount of times he shuddered and climaxed inside her.

Calion felt like he'd come back from being deep underwater. He could see things above him, but couldn't reach them...couldn't communicate. His body worked on instinct alone as he mated over and over, until the last of the fever left his body.

It was early in the morning when he finally lifted his head and stared blearily down at the female he held. What was Talia doing here, in his room? His thoughts were fuzzy and clouded as he looked at her.

She lifted a shaking hand to his cheek. She was so tired. Exhausted by everything that had been done to her. But it was worth it to see him look at her with recognition in his eyes.

"Are you all right?" she asked softly. He frowned at her, and she could see the confusion on his face. "It's okay, love. Everything is okay."

He pushed away from the wall, reeling with the weakness in his legs. He caught Talia as he slipped from her body, his need for her finally satiated. Carrying her in his arms, he stumbled to the bed and they both fell on it. In a natural move that made her heart ache, Calion tucked her against him. Knowing this may be the last time she would ever touch him, Talia snuggled herself to him, listening as he dropped into a heavy, healing sleep. As tired as she was, it was a long time before she followed.

Calion woke to the sound of birds singing. He immediately became aware he wasn't alone. Looking down, he saw Talia sprawled across his chest, her breathing deep and regular. Need spiraled up in him, so fast it was as if the fever had taken him again. Without thinking, he rolled her over and drove himself into her body. She was as tight and hot as she had been the first time.

She awoke in a rush of sensation. Her whole being shook with desire, and before she was even truly awake, her body began to move in time with Calion's thrusts. Heat built quickly. Talia hadn't found release at all last night, concentrating only on making sure Calion got what he needed to break the fever, so she was more than ready to mate with him, no matter how sore she was. She moaned, arching against him when his mouth covered one of her breasts. His hands moved over her body and the need flamed up inside her to meet Calion's fire.

He moved faster, feeling the faint twinges that told him she was close to her release. He reared back and stared down at her as he sent her over the edge, crying out his name. Watching her climax triggered his own, and he plunged into her until he too exploded in orgasm.

They lay like that for a long time, until their breathing returned to normal and awareness returned. All hope Calion would understand what she had done ended when he stiffened and rolled off of her. In the past he would have pulled her to him, but not this time.

Refusing to look at her, he rose and walking to his wardrobe, pulled out a pair of breeches and slipped them on. Grabbing a tunic, he tossed it at Talia. "Dress yourself," he said, his voice rusty from disuse.

She struggled to a sitting position, pressing the tunic to her chest. "You're angry with me. I hoped you wouldn't be."

Calion gritted his teeth as he looked at her. She looked so right sitting in his bed. But he knew what had happened last night. Her hair was still tangled from his hands, and he flinched when he saw the bruises on her arms, legs and hips. Her lips were swollen from his possession, and from what he could remember, that wasn't the only place where she would be sore. She had been his salvation. Now she would be his downfall.

"Won't you even talk to me?"

"What do you want me to say?" he bit out. He walked over to the window. The sun was just coming up. He could just see red coloring the horizon. "You have done what I asked you not to do."

"I saved your life," she whispered. "They said you were dying. I couldn't let that happen to you. I love you."

Calion turned swiftly, his eyes angry. "Do not say that."

Talia narrowed her eyes at him. "Say what? That you were dying or I love you?"

He swore under his breath. "I do not believe I was dying, so your actions were unnecessary. And as far as your declaration of human love...save it. I do not want to hear it."

Talia lowered her eyes so he couldn't see the pain in them. He threw her love right back in her face even after she saved his life. "All right, I won't say it again. But not saying it won't make it any less true."

The prince ignored the statement. "Do you realize what you have done by coming to me last night? You did not even try to come in secret."

"There was no other way to get in. Everyone was very good at keeping me away from you. You included. Eámanë finally helped me. She knew your time was almost up."

"You brought my sister into it?"

She flinched at the deadly look he gave her. "I didn't give her much choice. She won't get into trouble."

"You should have left it alone. Now all I tried to conceal is brought to light." Calion rubbed his eyes. They were still a little sore. "Everyone will know we have mated."

"Only if you tell them," Talia retorted. "I realized you didn't want anyone to know about us. You literally would have rather died than reveal we'd been together before." Her eyes filled with tears, and she blinked rapidly. She wouldn't cry in front of him, no matter how much he hurt her. "I'm not stupid, Calion. I know what that means."

"What do you think it means?" Calion's tone was caustic.

"It means," she raised her chin defiantly, "I will never have a place in your life."

"I gave you what I could."

She stared at him. "I know that's what you believe. And you'll never go against your traditions to change it."

"In that you are correct." Calion's eyes flashed. "But you now have stolen that choice from me. I have broken *sardai*, and all who know will despise me for it."

Talia laughed, but there was no amusement in it. “I finally figured it out,” she murmured and her eyes were sad as she looked up at him. “It’s you who despises yourself. Just like you told me when we were in the *Malesia* tree. You hate yourself for wanting me. I should have listened to you then.” She turned her head away. “I made the mistake of listening to my heart.”

He struggled with the emotions tearing through him. She was right. His problem had always been she was human, and no matter what had happened between them, it continued to be a problem. “I cannot change who I am.”

Talia didn’t speak. She heard the finality in his words, knowing there was nothing more to be said. She slipped on the tunic top and crawled out of bed. The pain in her lower body was acute, but she didn’t say a word.

Calion watched her. He knew she must be hurting. He’d taken her like an animal last night and she’d never tried to stop him. Even though he wouldn’t admit it out loud, he knew there was truth in the idea she’d saved him, but by doing so, she brought their secret to light, and that he could not abide. “Go to your room. I will send healers to you.”

Talia blushed at his words. “No, thank you.” She thought of the punishment she knew was awaiting her. You couldn’t feel pain when you were dead. “It isn’t necessary.”

“Nevertheless—”

“Calion…just stop,” she cried, her heart aching. “I know it’s over. You aren’t responsible for me anymore. Please, don’t pretend you care. I can take a lot of things from you, but that I can’t bear. Leave me my pride, at least.”

He stared at her as she swayed next to his bed. Everything in him still longed for her. His blood fired just at the sight of her naked legs. He did care…too much. That was the problem. He’d wanted her, believing he could cheat and not have to pay the cost. He’d been wrong, and now they both suffered. In trying to help him, she’d betrayed him. He could see nothing but that. There could be nothing left between them.

He heard a sound at the door, and they turned as it swung open. Maeglin stepped in first, his sword drawn, but when he saw his prince standing healthy and whole before him, his face spilt into a huge grin and he sheathed the sword immediately. He walked forward and grasped Calion’s arm. “It is good to see you, my prince.”

Calion pressed his hand. "I too am pleased to see you. You kept me sane, Maeglin. I owe you my thanks."

There was no time to say more as Ërestor walked in the door. Calion immediately knelt. "Father."

Ërestor's eyes filled with tears as he pulled his son up and embraced him. "My son, my son. You are alive and well." He pushed back and looked searchingly at Calion. The prince looked tired, but his features were normal, his body slim and muscular. There was no sign of any flames in his eyes. The fire fever was gone. "We were very concerned about you."

"I hope never to put you through that kind of worry again, Father."

Ërestor turned to Talia, who stood silently throughout the whole reunion. "Lady Talia."

Talia curtsied painfully. "My king."

"You know I cannot condone what happened here last night." The king's eyes snapped in anger. "You know our laws. The prince was out of his mind in fever, but you have no excuse for what you did. I know you wanted to help him, but how you did it...it cannot be tolerated. You and you alone broke the *sardai*."

"Father," gasped Calion. He hadn't expected a full pardon.

"No, Calion," Ërestor said, lifting his hand to stop his son's objection. "You are a survivor. You finally gave in to a female, knowing if you did not, you might die. You did it instinctively. I cannot punish you for your instincts taking over."

"But I mated with her. *I* mated with a human."

"Not by your own choice. She came to you. It is her fault, and she knows the consequences." The king turned to Valandil. "Take the human and put her back in the cell."

"Father." Calion took a step forward in protest. Talia, back in that cell? "Not there, please."

"It's all right, Calion," Talia said softly. She looked at the king, and there was acceptance of her fate in her eyes. "I made my choice last night knowing how it might end." She walked over to where Valandil was standing, refusing to give in to the weakness that threatened her.

She looked back at Calion and tried to smile, her heart breaking. "If I had to do it all over again I would change nothing, because you are alive."

Calion wanted to go and take her in his arms. There could be nothing more between them, but as he looked at her standing there, his heart cried out in protest. All the time they spent at the falls came back to him. It had felt so right...so wonderful. Their bodies had fit together perfectly. And now? How could he push away the female who'd given him back his life?

Then he remembered the *sardai* and shuddered at the thought of everyone finding out what he had done. So all he said was, "At least allow her to go to her room. We are not animals."

Ërestor waved his hand at his son. "No one but the family and your Guard knows of what happened here. It can all be swept under the rug if the female is out of sight. And it is not like you have made a habit of mating with her, right?"

Talia turned and looked at Calion, her eyes dark and wondering. She went very still, waiting for his answer.

There was silence as Calion struggled with his father's question. He looked at Talia, seeing both hope and fear lighting up those beautiful eyes. She was as lovely now as she'd been the first time he'd seen her. And just as brave. He wanted her desperately, but knew it could never be. He was the prince. As much as he wished he could toss that aside and go to her, he knew he couldn't. His guts twisted in anguish, but he had no choice. His way of life depended on what he said now. Swallowing down the sickness of his answer, he turned to the king.

"No, Father. Never would I do such a thing."

Talia gave a pained gasp and her shoulders drooped, all the life going out of her green eyes. He'd denied her completely, choosing who he was over what they had together. What was left of her heart splintered into tiny pieces. Tears overflowed, running unchecked down her cheeks. Death would be a relief right now.

Valandil grabbed her arm and started to drag her from the room. She was so numb with hurt, she didn't even feel it. She ran into Maeglin and he barked a command at his guard to be gentle with her.

She came out of the fog long enough to look up at the dark-haired guard. "Please," she choked out, her voice thick with tears, "take care of him."

Maeglin nodded, not trusting his own voice. Anger at the prince welled up inside of him. Couldn't they see what a jewel Talia was? She had healed him. Calion was denying his own fire mate, maybe even his *Mylari*. Did it really matter she was human? It made him furious.

"Take her down and then return," the king finished. "We must decide what our story will be."

"Are you removing Lady Talia's protection, Prince Calion?" Maeglin asked his friend incredulously. Calion didn't answer. He had turned away from the sight of Talia and stood staring blankly out the window.

"You need to bathe," said the king, ignoring the by-play. "A good soak in your hot pool will get rid of all those aches. I will see you in the throne room when it is time." He gave his son another hug, startling Calion out of his reverie.

When the king left, Maeglin turned furiously to Calion. "You didn't answer my question...*prince*. Are you removing your protection?"

Calion's mind whirled and he couldn't make himself think properly. Finally, he looked back at Talia. Her long legs made his mouth water. She stood so small next to his men and he frowned as he saw Valandil's hand on her. He wanted still to go to her. To protect... He turned away again, unable to look at her and think straight. Rubbing at the odd aching pain in his chest, he sighed. He hated the thought of it, but he had to obey his father. The cell, even though nasty, would keep her safe and out of the way until he could figure out just what to do with her.

"Do as my father asks, Maeglin. I am going to bathe her smell from my nostrils. Maybe then I can think clearly."

They all watched as Calion opened the bathing chamber door and disappeared inside. Maeglin looked at Talia. She was white as a ghost, trembling so violently he could see her knees shaking. Her eyes were dark and wounded as if she'd watched something precious die right before her. They had all been worried about the prince, but what had *she* gone through last night? There was no way he was going to leave her to Aranil's tender mercies.

He turned to Orophin. "I want you to take the Lady Talia to the cells. Find her a clean place and stay with her. She is not to be touched by anyone. Do you understand?"

"What are you doing?" Valandil objected. "The king doesn't

want her coddled. She is nothing but a prisoner now. Even the prince is in agreement."

"The prince is not in his right mind yet. When he is, then I will obey him. Until then I will follow his edict and protect Talia."

"The king should hear of this!"

Maeglin grabbed the rebellious guard by the throat. "Are you the prince's guard or the king's? Choose now, Valandil. You have made me wonder long enough."

Valandil flushed an ugly red. "I am the prince's, but I do not believe what you are doing is right. She is nothing. She is human!"

"Orophin, take Talia now." After the other guard had helped the human out of the room, he turned back to Valandil. "Do you have a problem with the chain of command? This is not the first time you have questioned me." When the redheaded elf made no reply, Maeglin nodded. "Good, then get out and guard the door. I will wait for the prince."

When Calion left the bathing chamber, he was surprised to see Maeglin pacing by the bed. His pale-haired friend wore the look of a thundercloud. Saying nothing, he moved to the wardrobe and pulled out another pair of breeches and tunic. It made him think of Talia and how she looked in them. His blood warmed instantly. Cursing, he drew on his breeches before his erection would make it difficult. He was surprised after the night that his flesh would even rise.

He pulled the dark tunic over his head before speaking. "You have something to say, Maeglin?"

His friend stopped pacing. "I told Orophin to stay with the Lady Talia. I did not want Aranil to have charge of her."

Calion had forgotten the nasty elf in the dungeon. The thought of him touching Talia made his skin crawl. "That is good. She should still be kept safe."

Maeglin surprised him with a harsh laugh. "Oh, by all means, let us make sure she is safe."

Calion turned and looked at his guard. The anger on Maeglin's face was unmistakable. "What is the matter with you?"

"You have to ask?" Maeglin shook his head and strode over to his friend. "I have watched your back for many years. I have seen you do all kinds of things. I may not have agreed with all of them, but I respected you anyway." He glared at Calion. "But today... After watching how you treated her? Today you lost my respect."

The words hit Calion like blows. He stared at his friend. "I-I do not understand. I have no choice but to accept my father's wishes."

"She saved your life!" Maeglin shouted. "And you repay her loyalty by having her tossed in the dungeon. Not even mentioning destroying her soul in the process. And you dare hide behind your father?"

Calion's temper flared. "I hide behind no one. And what do you mean, I destroyed her soul?"

Maeglin looked at the prince in pure disgust. "You denied her in front of everyone. You have made her a whore, when she cares so much she risked her life for you."

Calion felt the words spear through him. "Of course she is no whore. What she did last night does not make her so."

"And what about all the other nights, Calion? You have mated with her before and now when it becomes inconvenient, you pretend like she doesn't exist? What is that, if not the treatment of a whore?"

Embarrassment fueled Calion's wrath. "She told you. She was not to tell anyone. I should never have trusted her."

Only Maeglin's deep love for his friend kept him from knocking the prince on his ass. "You fool," he hissed. "She only told me so I would understand the need to get her out of here. She found out if she was out of your scent range, you would go back to normal." He glared at him. "She wanted me to take her back to the human world."

Calion pushed away from his friend. Talia had tried to go back home? Pain reared up inside of him. She hadn't said anything to him about that when he was accusing her. Guilt curled greasily in his stomach. "Why did you not you take her?"

Maeglin shrugged. "Because you made me promise to protect her. If she goes back to her world, the orcs will find her again." He glared at Calion. "I wish now I had broken that vow. Anywhere would be better for her than here with you."

"Then why are you here?" retorted Calion, stung. "If I am as bad as you say, why do you not resign from my guard?"

Maeglin stiffened. "Your actions have disgusted me enough

I would gladly withdraw, but I am bound by another promise." He straightened his sword. "I promised the Lady Talia I would take care of *you*."

Calion's emotions churned within him. His best friend looked at him with revulsion in his eyes, something he thought he'd never see. What he had done to Talia was the cause, but she was the one at fault.

"She should not have come here last night. I know she was trying to help, but what she did has ruined me."

"Ruined you? Pah!" Maeglin spit on the floor. "If a brave female's actions for the male she cares for can ruin you, then your life is not worth much anyway. I thought you stronger than that!"

"I am the heir to the throne," Calion shouted angrily. "No matter how I feel about her, I am to be above reproach. Because she came to me last night, that has changed. How else am I to react?"

Maeglin whirled away, striding to the door. "The king insured no one will know of what happened here. Your sterling reputation is intact. But you will have to live with yourself and what you are doing to Lady Talia. Can you do that?"

"All I have done is allow my father to put her in the dungeon until I decide what to do with her."

"You are not such a fool, Calion," Maeglin snorted. "You sent her away like she was trash, bruised and hurting from your mating. You forced her to walk half naked across the castle with your seed still running down her legs. You humiliated and then abandoned her, not even caring about what she would face. She is not a possession. She is a living, breathing female."

Calion felt sick when he heard his actions spoken so coldly, so brutally. Had he really done all that? He thought of Talia's face when he'd agreed to send her to the cells. It had been not just hurt, but shattered. She'd been barely able to walk and he had allowed his father... He groaned out loud. He had done it. His mind had been in such turmoil, he'd selfishly ignored her pain. No matter how angry he was at her, she didn't deserve that.

"She was your fire mate. She may have been your *Mylari*. How could you toss that precious gift away?" Maeglin spoke softly but his words hit with the force of an arrow.

"She is a human," Calion protested weakly. His heart pounded in his chest at the thought. It was impossible...wasn't it? He shook his head at his friend. "There could be no chance of that."

Maeglin narrowed his eyes. "Are you certain? Stranger things have happened lately. But if that is true, then your fire fever will not come back. It will not matter what happens to Talia. She will be free." He smiled fiercely at Calion. "And you will not mind if I take her for my own."

Pure outrage drove every other thought from Calion's mind. He moved across the room and had Maeglin by the throat before his guard even saw him move. "*You will not touch her!*"

Maeglin bared his teeth at the prince. "Why do you care? She means nothing to you, remember? You made sure everyone knows that. At least allow her to find someone who can care for her the way she deserves. If not me, then back in her own world."

Calion felt sick. He let the guard go, pressing his hands to his eyes. Nothing was making sense. "This is insane! I do not know what to do. I cannot have her, but I cannot think of her with anyone else." He looked at his friend with tortured eyes.

"I still want her."

Maeglin grabbed his arm. "Then stand up to your father. Take her as your mate."

Pulling away, Calion walked over to the window to stare out at the beauty of his world. Why must he choose between it and her? He clenched his fists in frustration. "My father would disown me. All my life I have waited to be king. Am I to give that up for the need of a female?"

"She is an extraordinary female. She stood before you last night without fear. She allowed you to do whatever needed to be done so you could come back to us. The elven females we brought took one look at you and ran for their lives."

Maeglin ran a hand through his long hair. "Should they be considered more appropriate, because they have elven blood, than the one female who stood for you? The one with tainted human blood?"

"I do not know. I cannot think." He remembered again how Talia looked when leaving his room. His gut clenched in sickness at his actions. She'd been dead white, her lips pinched with pain.

"I wanted to bring her healers," he said hoarsely. "She refused."

"She knows she has no need of healers where she is going." Maeglin shook his head at the prince.

Calion jerked his head around to look at Maeglin. "What is that supposed to mean? She went to the dungeon. When I go meet my father, I will arrange for her to be taken to her quarters. She need not be in a cell."

"Why do you think you are going to your father, Calion? It is not to discuss the latest farm taxes." Maeglin glared hotly at the prince. "The Lady Talia is to be executed this afternoon."

Chapter Fourteen

Even in her numbed state, Talia was glad it was Orophin with her and not the horrible Valandil. Where the redheaded guard would have dragged her, Orophin carefully helped her down to the dungeon as if he knew her legs were about to give out. She watched through a fog as he dealt with Aranil and found her a somewhat clean cell to rest in. He even found a blanket for her to sit on.

"I don't understand," Talia said in the childlike tone of a person in shock. She looked up at him with wide eyes. "Why are you being so nice to me? Didn't what I do disgust you? Calion said it would disgust you."

Orophin clamped down on his temper. He had admired the Lady Talia from the first day she arrived. She was so beautiful and as the days passed and he got to know her better, he found many other things to admire as well. And after what she had done for Calion, well, he would gladly die for her. For the first time in his life, he wanted to take up arms against his own prince.

"You do not disgust me." He brushed back her hair. "You are the most perfect female I have ever seen. You are loyal and brave and beautiful. You may be human," he touched his callused palm to her breast, "but your heart...your heart is elven."

She stared at him with her mouth open. Orophin had never said more than a few words to her. When he decided to talk, he certainly made up for lost time. His words reached deep inside her frozen soul and warmed her.

He wrapped a second blanket around her shaking shoulders and gazed at her eyes. Her pupils were fully dilated, meaning she was in shock. He grunted, obviously finished with being talkative. Leaving the cell, he returned almost immediately with some dried fruit and water. Setting it on the blanket beside her, he pointed at it. "Eat."

After he left to stand guard outside the door, Talia picked up a little of the fruit and nibbled at it. She wasn't really hungry, but since Orophin was kind enough to get it for her, she had to try. Sipping at the tepid water, she was afraid her uneasy stomach wouldn't let her keep it down.

As she sat, she felt some of the numbness wear off and pain took over. It was kind of like having Novocain at the dentist's—it wore off slowly, bit by bit.

Then realization hit. She was going to be killed. She'd seen the look in the king's eyes. The only one who might have been able to stop her execution didn't care enough to fight for her. Maybe he'd be glad to see her go.

That thought was particularly painful, so she took a deep breath to center herself. She couldn't panic. If she was going to die, it would be with dignity. Closing her eyes, she flowed into a meditation that helped her use her empathic awareness. It had always calmed her in the past.

Talia wasn't sure how long she'd sat there before she became aware of a presence. Quickly, she opened her eyes, thinking someone had sneaked into the cell, but she was alone. She frowned, positive she'd felt something. Curious now, she slipped back into the meditative trance to look again.

She stilled her mind, opening up her awareness to the presence she'd felt before. Ahhh, there it was. Cocking her head, she tracked it. It was faint, barely readable, but it was there. As she drew closer, she recognized it as a life force. It felt elven, but that wasn't quite right. Was she feeling the old emanations of a long-dead prisoner?

Gently, softly, the life force called to her. It was close, very close. It was... Talia's eyes popped open in surprise. Slowly, with the utmost care, she pressed a hand to her flat stomach. The life she felt was...inside her. Tears flowed as understanding came.

Last night, Calion had given her his child.

Calion reacted to Maeglin's announcement with icy cold terror. He didn't doubt his friend's word. At one time he'd expected this punishment. But when his father had pardoned him, he'd been sure that death wouldn't touch either of them. "When?"

As if in answer, Valandil poked his head through the door. "My prince, the king requests your presence." The guard grinned. "He says you are not to miss it."

Calion's eyes flashed. Quickly, he pulled on his boots and strapped on his sword. He motioned Maeglin out ahead of him. "I will put a stop to this."

When he entered the throne room he was greeted by applause. Calion looked around him in horror. The higher tables were full of his father's advisors. Had all these folks witnessed his shame? He firmed his jaw and strode forward to the king.

"Father, please. I must speak to you."

Ërestor smiled and waved his hand at his son. "Come Calion, stand beside me. It is good to have you back with us." He looked benevolently out over the crowd. "Does he not look good?"

Calion ignored the cheers and turned to his father. "I must speak to you about Talia. She should not—"

"Do not worry, son. She is taken care of. In fact, I think she is joining us now. This will soon be no more than a bad memory." He inclined his head toward the door.

Turning, Calion cursed as he saw Talia being brought in. She still wore only his tunic, her hair straggling down her back. Ugly bruises could be seen on her naked legs and arms. Her mouth was still swollen from his kisses, and she could barely walk. His eyes narrowed when he saw her hands were bound in front of her. He turned to his father. "Those are not necessary!"

Ërestor frowned. "It is traditional for the accused to be brought before me in such a manner. You know this."

"It is unseemly!" Grabbing a cloak from a nearby sentry, he walked down and put it around her shoulders, covering her nakedness. When he fastened it under Talia's chin, he looked down and saw the trails of dried semen left on her. They hadn't even allowed her to clean up, and it was his fault because he hadn't protected her.

Self-loathing filled him. Maeglin was right. He *had* sent her away from him in such a state. Calion wanted to kick himself. He may have been groggy due to the fire fever, but he was still responsible for her, no matter what she'd done to him.

She looked up at him, surprised at his ministrations. "Thank you, Calion."

The prince nodded, his jaw ticking in anger. "I am sorry. This, I never meant to happen."

"I knew what I was getting myself into," she responded softly. She put her bound hands up on his hard chest. "I'm not sorry."

He stepped back quickly. The feel of her hands sent lust curling up inside him. That shouldn't be happening. He had finished with her. The fever was over. He shouldn't be feeling so out of control.

"My son!" Ërestor watched them unhappily. "Come away from her."

Calion didn't move. He was trapped in the beautiful green of Talia's eyes. What had happened? She was lovelier now than she'd ever been. Her face was glowing, her eyes shone with a secret joy. Her whole manner was calm and serene. It made no more sense than anything else did.

Talia had been ready to die. She'd expected it, had accepted it, but that was before she had another life to worry about. Her child, her son if she read the signs correctly, deserved to live. Now she would fight to stay alive. She didn't want to yet, but if she must, she would tell them all about the baby.

She met the prince's gaze. "He is going to kill me, Calion. Is that what you want?"

"No," he growled angrily, keeping his voice low. "Of course not."

"It would be easier. Don't you think?"

His jaw dropped in utter surprise. "I know we cannot be together any longer, but do not be foolish. I do not want you to die."

She smiled. A secret smile that made him wonder about her sanity. "Good. I don't want to die either. In fact it's very important now that I live."

"Calion!" This time the king stood. "It is time now. Come back up here."

The prince stared hard at the beautiful female in front of him. No matter what happened between them, no matter what he thought she'd done, he couldn't let her die. He turned and looked at the king. "I am sorry, Father. I cannot allow you to execute her."

Ërestor gaped at him. "What say you? She must be executed. She broke the *sardai*—I mean she committed high treason against the crown."

"How?" he demanded loudly. "By saving my life? I will not hide behind her, Father." He turned and looked at the crowd around him, knowing what he said next would change his life forever.

"She is the female that broke the fire fever. Talia is the one I mated with."

There was a loud gasp around the room, and then the whispers started. Calion ignored them all and turned back to his furious king. "I will not live a lie, and I will not kill her for being brave enough to do what no elven female could. I owe her my life."

Ërestor was almost apoplectic with rage. He hurried down to stand next to his son. "What are you doing? I had everything fixed. She would die and then you would be safe."

Calion stared at his father. "You would kill an innocent to keep a secret? How could you do such a thing?"

Talia stared in fascination at the king's face. If he turned any redder, he might have a stroke. Then her attention was drawn to the crowd where Eámanë sat. Her friend sat weeping as she watched the tableau before her. She smiled at the princess, wishing she could tell her she was going to be an aunt. But that discovery must stay a secret for a while.

"Would you defy me in this? Does this female mean more to you than I?" Ërestor demanded, bringing her gaze back to him. "I am your king."

Calion stiffened. "You taught me from birth to do what is right and true. I have always honored those teachings. Would you have me stop now?"

Ërestor clenched his fists. "She is human. She dishonored you."

"Nay, Father," Calion answered. Suddenly, a lot of things were clear to him. "If anyone has been dishonored, it is the lady." Turning, he used his dagger to cut Talia's bonds. "She has saved the heir to the throne and has been treated with nothing but disrespect. I brought her here to be safe." He put his hand on his father's stiff shoulder.

"I understand you are trying to protect me, Father. But what kind of king would I be if I allowed her death, knowing she was the one who gave me life."

Ërestor stared at his son. Part of him rejoiced at his son's strength of character, while the other was furious he was putting his life and reputation on the line for a mere human.

Talia sensed the king's internal struggle. She didn't really blame him. He was motivated by superstition and fear, but he didn't understand everything had changed.

First, she had been brought to the faerie world, then the discovery of her aptitude for magic, and now her ability to tame the fire fever in Calion. And then the greatest miracle of all...a child. Would he believe it? Would he accept it? There was still hope. It looked like the prince might have changed his mind.

"Your Majesty." She laid a gentle hand on his arm. "I don't want to hurt your family. I care about each of you and I love your son." She looked up at Calion with all the feeling inside her showing on her face. "I will do whatever it takes to prove to you I'm telling the truth, but please, don't be angry with each other. You are family. *Thastolor.* There is nothing more important than that."

Calion stiffened, hearing her proclaim her feelings for him to his father. What was she doing? Her words might make the king believe there was something more between them than the one night. He sought a way to distract him.

"Perhaps Father, instead of an execution, we can take this time to publicly thank the Lady Talia for her service to the crown. These folk," Calion gestured to all those who sat avidly watching, "will follow whatever cues you give them. Make her a heroine and let them leave knowing she has our gratitude and continued protection."

Ërestor knew his son was making sense. While the idea of letting the human female get away with befouling his son's name made him ill, he knew if he punished her, he'd now have to punish Calion, and that he would not do.

"So be it," he said softly. "You will be a heroine to the people for saving our prince. But know this." The king bent and stared straight into Talia's eyes. "I will not forget what you have done and neither will my son. You have broken the *sardai*...an unconscionable thing. Your time here is coming to an end."

Her eyes widened and she unconsciously put her hand on

her stomach in a protective movement. Her gaze went to Calion, and she blinked when she saw the same stiffness in him she saw in his father. Her heart sank when they stepped away from her and climbed the dais. They both turned and looked back over the crowd.

"My friends," the king began. "Tonight we bring you a heroine. She may be human, but she is as brave and as loyal as an elven female. I give you Lady Talia, savior of my son." He started to clap and after a moment Calion joined in. Slowly, the others in the room stood and also applauded. The efforts were only halfhearted, but it was a start.

Talia kept her eyes on Calion. His face was impersonal, very unlike the man who had stood up for her just a few minutes earlier. Lifting her chin, she refused to let him see her confusion. She gave a stiff curtsey. "My thanks to you. As I have said before, there is nothing I would not do for you, Calion, Prince of Calen'taur."

She smiled, thinking of the tiny life inside her. "You could say I have a vested interest in your continued good health."

"Perhaps you would like to retire to your room and refresh yourself," Calion stated. "I know it has been a difficult day."

Tears stung her eyes and she wrapped her arms around herself for warmth. He sounded so cold, she knew now he'd made his choice. He would ignore what they had together. "Would that be in my old quarters, my lord, or my new ones?"

Calion's gut twisted in pain, knowing he deserved her bitterness. He wished with all his heart things could be different, but he'd told her the truth. He could not change who he was, no matter how much he sometimes wanted to. Pushing the pain away, he turned to Orophin. The guard hadn't moved more than a few feet from Talia the whole time.

"Escort the Lady Talia back to her living quarters." He looked over to Maeglin who watched him with an unreadable look. "She is still under my protection."

Talia spent the rest of the day alone in her room. She bathed, wishing she could be back in the healing pool. Her bruises hurt, but they were manageable. As long as she didn't move quickly, the rest of her body didn't complain too much either. She spent most of the time shifting between the grief of losing Calion, and the utter joy of knowing she would have his son.

She heard nothing from the prince. No note, not a visit, nothing. The urge to go to him was overwhelming, but she fought it. The last time she had done so she'd saved him, but her actions had changed everything.

She loved him. Loved him so much, knowing he didn't want her was a pain without ending. If only she could find a way to get through to him. She thought about telling him about the baby but discarded that idea. She wanted Calion to love her for herself, not for the child she could give him.

Her thoughts went back to the prophecy. It had started all this, maybe it could end it too. She spent the next few days back in the archives, searching for something that would help her.

Surreptitiously, she pored over documents on elven birthing. She knew it wasn't only her gift that made things seem different—she was just a few days pregnant, and she already was having some morning sickness. Looking through the parchments, she found an elven pregnancy only lasted six months. She carried a half-elven child. Since she was human, what did that mean for her?

Eámanë visited her whenever she could, but their relationship was strained. The princess was caught in the middle, between Calion and Talia. So Talia didn't bother her, although it would have been nice to share her secret with another female. Most of the time she chose to be alone, delving deep into the archives, desperate for answers.

As the weeks passed, she was sadly amused at the return of some of her fever symptoms. Her skin started to itch again, and when she looked in the mirror, her eyes glowed a green-gold. She worried about what it would mean for the baby. There was no information in any of the elven birthing parchments about fire fever.

She was on her way to the archives one afternoon when she felt his presence. Stopping, she waited until he appeared in the dark hallway beside her. She drank him in, seeing the strain on his face, noting the bloodshot golden eyes and scratches on his arms.

"Talia." He bowed politely to her, as if they had never loved each other. It made her want to scream.

"How have you been?" She wanted to leap into his arms,

her need to touch him was so great. But if he wanted to play it cool, so could she. She stepped closer and her eyes flickered gold.

Calion drew in his breath at the sight. He shook his head in shocked amazement. "You have the fever as well."

"Just as I did last time."

He didn't bother to tell her it was impossible. He was tired of pretending she was a normal human female. She was different and he needed her. All he wanted was to take her into the nearest room and have his way with her. She wouldn't stop him—she needed him too. His jaw clenched and he had to fight to keep control of himself.

"I have spoken to my father. He sees the fire has returned to my eyes, and he knows something must be done."

Hope leapt up in her. "What are you going to do?"

He firmed his lips and looked over her shoulder. "I will leave tomorrow for the eastern edge of our boundary. When we are out of each other's scent range, the fever will end."

Her heart fell and her eyes burned with tears. "You're leaving?"

"Yes," he agreed. "It is the only choice we have."

Talia wondered if he knew how much he hurt her with that simple statement. Angry with herself for continuing to hope, Talia just stared at him. Suddenly, she realized if he left this might be the only chance she had to talk to him.

"It's not the only way, Calion. Why can't you see that?" She put her small hand on his arm, and felt him go tense beneath her fingers. "Go to your father. Claim me for your own. If we were linked, we could mate and the fever would end. You wouldn't have to leave."

He stared at her in shock. "Are you crazy? We cannot link. You are a human. It is forbidden."

"Can't you see things are different now?" Her eyes pleaded with him to understand. "They have been since I got here. It doesn't have to be forbidden for us to be together. I love you. I want to be your mate."

"You being in my world does not change the basic rules and traditions of my people, whether I wish it or not. It is believed you are not fit to be my mate."

She drew in her breath at his cruel words. Would he think

she wasn't fit to be the mother of his son? At that moment, she swore to herself unless he came to her with the same commitment she had for him, he would never know of the pregnancy.

"If I'm not fit to be your mate, then why does your body crave mine? Why am I a fire mate for you?"

Hearing the pain in her voice, knowing he was hurting her with his words, his gaze shifted away. He was as confused as she, but he still had his world to think of. Even if pushing her away was tearing him apart. "I do not know, but it matters not."

"It should matter," she cried. "I know how long you've searched. I've searched too! I know how precious it is to you. I saw your face when you first told me. You and I have been given a great gift. We are *Mylari*...soulmates. How can you throw our only chance away?"

A wave of emotion welled up in him at her words. *Mylari*. It was his dream to find the other half of himself. He *had* searched his whole life. But to find it in a human? Even one such as Talia? That was beyond his understanding. Even with all that happened between them, with how he felt about her, he couldn't see it as anything but wrong.

"You cannot be my *Mylari*. The *sardai* against you has been around for millennia."

"You can change the rules, Calion," she whispered, trying again to convince him. "I know you care about me. Why won't you admit it? We could be happy together. We could be a family."

He reached out and cupped her soft cheek in his hand. His jaw worked as he tried to contain his emotions. "I do care for you. I will admit it. I long to have you in my arms at night as we were in the forest. Do you think I want to let you go?" His hand tightened. "What we had together...I will never forget it. But as much as I would like to, I cannot give you what you want. We cannot be together." His hand dropped away and he felt the loss keenly. "My destiny was set at my birth. You are not a part of it."

Her shoulders slumped. "So you will just pack up and leave your home?"

He nodded, his handsome face grim. Seeing the pain on her face almost destroyed him, but he forced himself to step back from her. "Yes, the healers feel once I cannot scent you, I will recover. You will stay here until we know for sure."

"Know what for sure?"

"Whether it works or not."

She frowned, not understanding him. "And if it doesn't work?"

He straightened his shoulders. "Then I will come back here to you. I will mate with you until the fever is gone."

Talia took a step back in shock. "You're saying you will mate with me only whenever you need to stop the fever."

"Yes. We would have to be discreet, but if it is the only way to keep ourselves healthy, it is what must be done."

"And this arrangement will last how long?"

"Until we no longer flame for each other." As he spoke, he couldn't believe he would ever feel that way. She was still too important to him...too necessary. The thought of losing her made his stomach churn.

"Do not worry." He sighed as he watched a tear trickle down her cheek. He hated seeing her cry. "I will protect you and take care of you. You will be my *torear*."

Talia could barely speak, her throat was so tight. "You called me that once before. What does it mean?"

Calion shuffled his feet as if embarrassed. "It means in your tongue...mistress."

She closed her eyes. "You want me to be your whore." She'd thought there was nothing left of her heart to break.

He took her by the shoulders. "Not a whore. If you are my *torear* you are protected, taken care of. A whore has no such protection."

Talia stepped back, making his hands drop. She thought of what her son would think of her if she accepted that. How could she face him? She stared up at Calion's beloved face and knew she couldn't do it. "But it's not a mate, is it?" she whispered, her voice breaking. "I wouldn't have your name. I wouldn't have your love."

Watching the emotions playing over Talia's face, Calion knew what she was thinking. His own heart ached too. He wanted to hold her, to make her understand he had no choice. He knew he was being selfish, but there was a part of him that actually hoped the fever wouldn't go away. That way he could keep Talia with him.

Of course, he'd have to link with an elven female to keep his bloodline going, but there would be no true soulmate mating. He couldn't imagine ever feeling about someone else the way he felt about Talia.

But now he had to be strong and do his duty to his people. "As my *torear* you will want for nothing. It is all I can give you. I plan to leave first thing tomorrow morning. I will visit you tonight so I can leave with no fever."

Talia just stared at him for a long moment. "Excuse me?"

"We will mate tonight so I can leave in good health. Once I am gone, the fever will not come back. You will do this for me."

Anger welled up inside of her. "I won't do it! Don't you dare try and come to me. I won't be your whore."

"I will come and you will accept me."

"You would take me by force?"

Calion burned with a mixture of anger and thwarted desire. His body ached just by being in her presence. The hurt and anger on her face was a living thing, and a part of him despised himself for what he was doing, but he had no choice. He knew his duty and it didn't matter how agonizing it was. Controlling himself with an effort, he reached out and ran a finger over her lips.

"I will not need to."

Talia thought about barring the door. She thought about ordering the guards not to let him in. She even thought about leaving so he couldn't find her. But none of those ideas were really feasible since the men who guarded her wouldn't let her do any of them. Telling herself she wouldn't wait up for him, she still found herself pacing by the window in her nightgown. She knew she would fight him, but in her heart, she wasn't sure of the outcome of the battle.

When Calion stepped through the door and saw the empty bed, his heart dropped. Had she flown from him? Looking around desperately, he finally saw her standing next to the window, poised as if to run.

"Don't do this, Calion," she warned him.

His entire being cried out for her. His heart, his mind and his body wanted her. He wished with all his soul things could be different, wanting peace between them, tired of the constant struggle. It would be so much simpler if she would only give in to his wishes.

But she would fight him. He could see it on her face. Crossing slowly to her, he watched her chin go up in the way he knew bespoke defiance. She was so beautiful and so angry. "Do not run from me, Talia. You need me as much as I do you. Come to me and let us have this last night together."

"When you mated with me before, it was different," she cried passionately. "You may not love me, but I knew you cared about me. If you do this, it will be only because I'm a means to an end. You'll turn me into a whore, just to stop your fever." Her eyes filled with tears. "Don't you understand? I love you. I have loved you since the beginning. Don't do this to me, Calion. If I ever meant anything to you...don't do this."

He stepped closer, his gut twisting at her pleading, but he forced himself to ignore it. "Just standing in the same room with you makes me burn. I cannot change the fact my body needs yours. I will not even try. But as for the rest," he said, referring to her declaration of love, "it is an impossibility. Do not ask for what I do not have."

She took a step back as he came closer, watching as the prince's eyes flared. She didn't think she could hurt any more if she tried. "I will hate you for this. I will hate you forever."

He laughed harshly and swept her struggling body into his arms, his own heart agonizing over what he was doing. "Then I will take your hate. At least it...I understand." With that sad declaration, he carried her to the bed.

When Talia awoke the next morning, she knew before she opened her eyes he was gone. Tears burned and seeped from under her tightly closed lids as hot shame rose over her like a prickly tide. He'd been right. Once she was in his arms, she had accepted him. Sure, she'd struggled for a while, but once his lips touched hers, her flesh took over. It needed...it took.

Her body was satiated now, the fever gone, but her mind and heart were in turmoil. For the first time, she felt dirty after Calion's touch. Before, she'd been able to tell herself he cared about her, but not this time. All he had done was slake his lust. Her own love mattered not. He'd taken her self-respect from her last night.

Her hand crept down to lay over her bare stomach. Their child rested there. She could sense the life force throbbing within her. It gave her a measure of peace to know her son had been conceived when there had been some emotion between Calion and herself.

Opening her eyes, she turned her head to look at the pillow beside her where his head had rested. Her eyes widened, and she burst into tears. Reaching out her shaking hand, she picked up the long-stemmed, peach-colored rose he'd left behind. Attached to it was a note that said simply…

Remember…

ꕥ

After Calion left, it was easier for Eámanë to come to visit. She wanted to explain, but Talia just shook her head. "He's your brother."

That was all the explanation needed.

The king however, did not change his mind. Talia was forbidden to mingle with anyone else in the castle. No more cozy suppers or advisory meetings. It was clear she was *persona non grata* now.

Her meals were brought to her by Amroth or one of the two guards Calion left to watch her. They at least didn't treat her badly. In fact, both Orophin and Amroth came close to worshipping her for what she had done for their prince. But not the third guard, not Valandil. His enmity grew daily. She hated it when it was his turn to guard her.

Days passed into weeks, but she was little bothered by the symptoms she knew pointed to fire fever. She grew used to looking in the mirror and seeing little flickers of light. Her eyes hurt and her skin itched, but none of it was unmanageable. She was glad, having enough to worry about with her pregnancy. Just a few weeks into it and she was already losing her waistline. Soon her gowns wouldn't fit her anymore, and her secret would be out.

She spent most of her time in the archives. She hadn't given up hope the prophecy would help bring her lover back to her. The rose he left on her pillow showed her he did care, even against his own better judgment. She hoped the prophecy would make him realize the caring he felt for her was not an evil he had to fight.

Two weeks went by, then three without any luck. She'd read more of the old parchments than many of the wise men. As her son grew stronger within her, she became more and more convinced than ever that the prophecy was the key to everything.

It was almost anticlimactic when she found it. Talia had spent the whole day in the stacks, reading legends and stories until her eyes blurred from fatigue. She'd just turned over a page having to do with an ancient king and the kingdom he'd built, when it jumped out at her.

...human female will be the one.

Her heart leaped and she moved the magic candle closer, scanning the page until she found the prophecy's beginning.

Chapter Fifteen

You ask for help, I give to thee,
a message from the goddesses three.
Spears without, a knife within,
treachery will seek to win.
Death, despair, and pain will come,
all your work will be undone.
A mighty war, your people's end,
will come, on that you can depend.
Unless true passion can guide the day,
and give to you a stronger way.
A human female will be the one,
to save the kingdom, you've begun.
She will be the first of three,
to break the hold fortune has on thee.
Varol thysi...passion's force come true,
breaks through traditions old and new.
Only in acceptance can salvation be,
one of your blood holds the key.
An heir to the throne will this create,
he will win out over fate.
His father's heart, destiny will kiss,
he will carry your mark upon his wrist.

Talia read it a second time, feeling the joy flow through her. She'd found it! This had to be the prophecy. It touched on everything. Her humanity, the child she and Calion made together. Even the scar on his wrist. There were other things she didn't understand, but still this must be it. She knew it in the deepest part of her soul.

She'd take it to the king. No! She shook her head. That wouldn't help. He wouldn't listen to her. She'd have to get a copy to Calion. Smiling widely, she hugged herself in her joy. She'd been right.

Carefully she made three copies of the precious prophecy. At the top of one, she penned a special note to the prince she loved.

Calion,

I found it. You'll see it explains everything. I love you so much. Come home to me.

Talia

"This will have to work," she whispered to herself, covering her slightly rounded tummy with a trembling hand. "This will bring your daddy back to us."

She gave the precious note to Orophin. "Take this to Calion," she pleaded as she pressed it into his big hand. "It is very important he gets it immediately."

Orophin looked at the human. Her eyes glistened with happiness, and her smile put the magick candles to shame. Whatever was in the missive was very important to her. He nodded and departed, leaving her pacing with both anticipation and excitement.

Hours passed. Talia was so worked up she couldn't eat. When dusk fell, she forced herself to nibble on the tray Amroth brought for her. Her whole being was tuned to listen for Orophin's return. Would Calion come with him? Or would he have to wait until the morning to settle things in the east?

When she heard the door open, she rose quickly, dropping her tray to the floor. She ran to Orophin, her questioning eyes searching his face. "What did the prince say?"

The guard swallowed. He pulled his hand from his pocket and handed her a piece of paper.

"What's this? He sent me a message?" She smoothed open the paper, and froze when she saw her own writing. All color bled out of her face, and she lifted shattered eyes to Orophin's.

"He didn't read it?"

Orophin looked at her tragic face and wanted to strangle his own prince. He hadn't read the note himself, but he could tell what it meant to her. "No."

Talia whirled away, fighting for control. She crushed the note in her fist, feeling as though she crushed any hope left in her. Her son's spirit within her moved restlessly, as if knowing the deathblow dealt to his mother. Closing her eyes, she prayed for the strength she needed. She heard Orophin leave and like an old woman, walked stiffly over and sat on the bed.

It was finished. Her last chance to make Calion see the truth had been vanquished by his own stubbornness and fear. Her heart went numb with the agony of her loss. There was only one thing left to do now.

She waited until Orophin went off duty and Valandil took his place. She knew the red-haired guard would do whatever necessary to get her out of Calion's life. He was the one to approach.

Calling him inside, she steeled herself against the look of hatred in his eyes. "I have a request of you, Valandil."

"What do you want of me, human?"

Talia firmed her lips. "I know my being in this world is harming your prince. The only way I can help him is to go home. I want you to take me."

Valandil froze. "You wish me to take you to the human world?"

"Yes." She swallowed hard as the pain of leaving speared through her, but she shook it off. She needed to get his cooperation, so she'd appeal to his ego. "You are the best of the trackers. Calion always said so. I know you can get me there safely."

"Do you have Prince Calion's permission?"

This was the tricky part. "No, I don't. But you know as well as I do I don't belong here. I should never have come. I am hurting Calion. If I leave, then everything will go back to normal."

Valandil narrowed his eyes craftily. He wanted her gone, all right. He'd take her away from his prince. And he'd make sure she was never found again. "As you wish, human. When do we leave?"

"As soon as possible. I will take tomorrow to say my

farewells. I have to say goodbye to Eámanë, but not to the king. He may try to stop me."

"I will escort you to the myst," the red-haired guard decided. "Orophin and Amroth will stay here, to make it look as if you are still in your room. We will leave in two days, at first light."

"I know you hate me, Valandil, but you have my thanks."

"I do not want your thanks, human," the guard sneered. "All I want is to see you gone."

Talia spent the next day getting ready for her departure. She didn't pack much, just a few things that meant something to her. The first gown Calion chose for her and a set of hair combs he'd surprised her with. The rose he'd left her was now pressed between the pages of a favorite book. She also took several of the elven birthing parchments, stolen from the archives. She would need them in her world, being pretty sure the average midwife wouldn't know how to deliver an elven baby. Her only worry now was how the baby would fare in the myst, even safe in an elven-made portal.

She sneaked into Calion's room and borrowed some pants and a tunic. Riding though the woods in a long gown wasn't her idea of a comfortable trip. Besides, all her gowns were getting too small to fasten. The pants could be adjusted easier.

Once everything was packed, she wandered through the castle saying a silent farewell to everyone. She loved this place, would always treasure the memory. She'd only been a couple of months in this world, but leaving it would be like tearing out her heart. If she hadn't been so convinced it would be best for both her son and herself, she would stay and let the chips fall where they may.

She only needed to do two more things, and then she would be ready to leave in the morning. The first she took care of immediately. She found Orophin grooming his horse in the stable. She knew he disapproved of what she was doing and refused to even look at her.

"I want you to take this," she said to him without preamble. She handed him the smoothed out missive she'd entrusted him with before. "There may be a time where he will want to read it."

He took the note and stuffed it in his pocket. He glared at

her with angry, hazel eyes. "You should not go."

"I have to, Orophin. Maybe someday you'll understand why. I'll miss you." Tears clouding her eyes, she hugged him tightly.

He went rigid with embarrassment, awkwardly patting her back.

After a few minutes, Talia controlled herself and pulled away. "You take care of him for me, promise?"

Orophin nodded gravely, his own eyes suspiciously damp.

Wiping her eyes, she headed toward her last destination. This one was the hardest of all. She knocked on Eámanë's door.

Eámanë's face lit up when she saw Talia. "Come in. I was just thinking about you." She ushered her to a seat. "I am taking a trip into the village tomorrow. I want you to come with me. It will do you good to get out of the castle."

Talia smiled. "It sounds like fun."

"I could smack my brother for what he is doing to you," Eámanë hissed suddenly, making Talia's eyes widen. "Oh, I know I have not said anything before, family loyalty and all, but he is wrong. I think...I think you are his *Mylari*."

Talia gasped. "You can accept that?"

"With all that is happening? I may be slow, but I am not stupid." The princess narrowed her eyes. "My brother, however..." She tapped her forehead. "He is stupid."

"It means a lot to me to know you believe that." Talia removed a sealed copy of the prophecy from her gown pocket and handed it to Eámanë.

"What is this?" she asked, turning it curiously in her hands. "A note?"

Talia smiled sadly at her friend. "I want you to keep it. When Calion comes back, I want you to give it to him for me."

Eámanë frowned. "Why can you not give it to him yourself?"

"He won't take it from me."

The princess swore under her breath. It made Talia giggle, even with the soreness of her heart. "Does your father know you say those words?"

The princess blushed. "The king does not know I *know* those words." She put the note for Calion on her bed table. "I will see the foolish male gets your note."

"Thanks." She leaned forward and hugged Eámanë.

"What is that for?" her friend asked.

Talia's smile wobbled. "You are the best friend I have ever had." I will miss you so much, she added to herself.

"I care for you as well. You are *thastolor*...family."

Talia lost the battle with tears. "Oh, Eámanë. You have no idea how much I needed to hear that."

Eámanë frowned. "Talia? What is wrong?"

Suddenly, she knew she couldn't tell the princess she was leaving. She intuitively knew her friend would try to stop her. If Calion had said she was *thastolor*, she would be overjoyed. Now it was bittersweet. Eámanë would never know her brother's child. She would never know they really were...family.

She was awoken before the sun came up by a soft knock on the door. Valandil poked his head in. "It is time."

Talia blinked. She barely slept last night, and now her head pounded from a combination of the tears she'd shed and exhaustion. Stumbling out of bed, she quickly washed her face, hoping it would chase some of the cobwebs away. It cleared her mind a little, but her heart ached with the knowledge she was leaving.

She'd escaped Eámanë the previous day with an excuse about it being her monthly flow time. It covered the crying jag in the princess' quarters. Now, as she dressed, she wished she'd told Eámanë the truth. She wanted to say goodbye.

Looking around her room one last time, she picked up her pack. Tears threatened as she opened the door to find Amroth, Valandil and Orophin waiting.

"Amroth has decided to accompany us," the redheaded guard said sullenly. He glared at his confederate.

"One guard is not enough," Amroth stated. "Are you ready, m'lady?"

"As I'll ever be." Talia turned to Orophin. "Thank you for everything. Your friendship meant a lot to me."

The guard regarded her with cool, multicolored eyes. "Reconsider."

Talia's own green eyes overflowed. "I can't."

"We must go," Valandil put in quickly, as if he was afraid she might be talked out of going. "Before it is light."

They left Orophin at the door and made their way carefully to the stable. Their horses were already saddled, and it was quick work to tie Talia's bundle to her horse. They left the castle before the first cock crowed.

"We are heading to where the myst lies the closest." Valandil motioned to the horizon. "It will take just a few hours.

Talia nodded. Now that she had started her journey, she only wanted it to be over. Everything in her wanted to turn around and go back, but the memory of Calion's last rejection kept her pointing forward. She would be no man's whore.

No one spoke as they followed the faint trail towards the western edge of the faerie world. Lost in her own thoughts, Talia remembered the times she and Calion spent in the forest. Tears pricked her eyes. She wasn't even gone yet and she missed him.

The early morning sun colored the forest. Birds began to sing, and Talia opened herself up to all the feelings that surrounded her. She wanted to memorize it all so someday she could tell her son about the beautiful world he was conceived in. It broke her heart anew to know he would never see it.

Steadily, the path led them away from *Osalai* and through the valleys. It was well after lunch when they ventured deep into a darkened forest. Here the trees grew close together, stunted by their proximity to each other. Talia had never seen the like in the faerie world before. The trees' voices were muted, as if drugged and hidden away. She turned to Amroth.

"What is this place?" she asked.

"*Mysyr*," the green-eyed elf answered. "It is an old forest. Full of secrets." He frowned at Valandil. "The trees are hard to communicate with. Even the prince has trouble. We do not often come this way."

"It is the quickest path," said Valandil shortly. "Do not blame me. It is what the human wanted."

Talia shivered as she looked around her. There was no birdsong. The air was stifling. A heaviness weighed in the trees. Closing her eyes, she opened herself up to her gifting, wanting to understand what she felt. She took a deep breath.

Danger...danger...run...run... The words came to her with such suddenness she almost fell. The trees spoke, their voices ragged and faint. Her eyes popped open. "Amroth? I sense—"

She got no further. Screams and howls came from all sides. Talia pulled up her horse, watching in horror as orcs poured from the woods around them. She screamed and heard Amroth call her name. As she turned to him, he reached for his sword.

Suddenly, an arrow caught him straight through the chest, piercing his heart and knocking him off his horse. Orcan swords slashed at his mount, dropping it in a bloody tangle of limbs as it squealed in agony.

"No!" Talia screamed. She looked for Valandil and was struck speechless in terror as the guard carefully notched a second arrow and let it fly, hitting his friend and comrade right between the eyes.

Talia didn't see the orcan arm that swept her off her own mount before sending her sweet mare to the ground with a severed neck. She fought and bit, knowing this time there would be no one to save her. The orc who had her cursed and slapped her face, sending her reeling to the ground. Picking herself up, she ran, only to be brought down by the very guard who was supposed to be protecting her.

Valandil laughed as he knocked her back to the ground. Talia glared up at him, wiping the blood from her mouth.

"You see, human. I am keeping my promise to you. I have taken you to where you can do no more harm to my prince."

"You killed Amroth! He was your friend!"

The red-haired elf shrugged. "An unfortunate sacrifice. I tried to get him to stay with Orophin, but he was too loyal to you. So you are the one who killed him."

He reached down and hauled her up roughly. "You will not be returning to your world." He gestured behind her. "I think you three have met before."

Talia turned and felt her stomach lurch in protest. Behind her stood Braduk and Modak, the sons of Udaogong.

"No!" she breathed. "You can't do this."

"I think you have some unfinished business with these two." Valandil bowed to the creatures and then smiled maliciously. "I told you I would take care of you." He laughed and threw her against the orcs.

Braduk grabbed her by the arm. "Pretty human. Prophecy over. We fuck."

Talia pulled against his grasp. If she'd been frightened the first time, it was nothing compared to how she felt now. Her child's life was at stake. He would be killed if they raped her, torn apart by their invasion.

"Let me go!" She looked back at Valandil. "You won't get away with it. Amroth will be missed."

Valandil laughed. "Oh, did I not tell you? You, Amroth and your horses will all be lost in a tragic accident. Once I clean this mess up and spend some time unprotected in the portal myself, I will be the brave hero who tried to save his brother and his prince's lady from the faerie myst."

He smiled evilly at her. "Calion will hate you even more for killing one of his own."

Talia stared at the elf. He was mad...his loathing of her sending him over the edge. "They will know. Somehow they will find out. You can't hide from the truth."

Valandil sneered at her. He turned to the orcan brothers. "Get going. I will clean up here. The sooner she is away, the better it is for all of us."

Back at the castle, Orophin brushed his horse. He'd stood by Talia's door for several hours, but then he came here, taking out his anger and frustration by cleaning the stable. The lady shouldn't have left. He felt that deep in his bones. The prince was being stubborn...granted. But that was no excuse to leave. Orophin wished for the thousandth time he was better with words. Maybe he could have stopped her.

He frowned, thinking there was something she hadn't told him. His mind went to the missive she had given him. What if there was something in that? She'd gotten the idea to leave just after Calion refused to read it.

Orophin pulled the note out of his pocket. He smoothed it with one callused finger. Should he read it? It wasn't for his eyes, but what if it could help both the lady and the prince? Shrugging, he unfolded it. He blushed a little at the endearments at the beginning, but hurrying through that, he came to the meat of the message.

His eyes widened when he realized he was looking at the prophecy they had searched for. As he read it, his heart started to beat wildly.

Orophin growled aloud. His prince *should* have read it before. If he had, she would still be here. Cursing, anger welling up inside him, he threw his riding pad on his horse. Calion would read the note. He would make sure of it.

"Orophin...Orophin." He turned as he heard his name

called. Eámanë hurried up to him. "I have looked all over for Talia. I have to talk to her. Where is she?" The princess looked down and saw Talia's note in his hand. Her eyes sharpened. "You have one too?" She held up her own prophecy, now open. "She gave this to me to give to Calion, but she acted so funny I opened it." Eámanë looked up at the guard. "Where is she?"

Orophin stuffed the note back in his pocket. "Gone."

Eámanë rolled her eyes at the taciturn guard. "Gone? Gone where?"

"Home."

"That cannot be," Eámanë whispered, clutching the note to her breast. She bit her lip, remembering the hug Talia gave her the night before. She'd felt something, but it took her half the day to distinguish the truth Talia inadvertently revealed. "You *must* bring her back."

Orophin swung up onto his horse. "Calion." With that succinct thought, he was gone.

Eámanë stared after him, her Sáralondë eyes lit with anger. "Yes, bring my brother back. I have a few things to say to him."

ꕥ

"My prince...you must rest." Maeglin stood inside Calion's tent watching as the prince paced back and forth, wearing a path in the soft dirt. They'd been at the eastern boundary for almost a month, but instead of making him better, Calion's health had deteriorated. The fever hadn't taken him as fast, but it came. Slowly, inexorably, no matter what Calion did to prevent it.

"I cannot rest. You know that. It is only if I keep going that I stay ahead of the pain." Calion scratched at his arms. "She is too far away for me to scent. Why is this happening?"

Maeglin sighed. The prince asked that every night. His mind was going, along with his body. His features sharpened and his form changed rapidly. Soon he would be the primitive they had seen before. During the day, he was covered by battle robes and helmet, so the soldiers couldn't see anything happening, but at night... That was the worst time. There was nothing to keep his mind off of the lady he'd left behind.

"Maybe if you ate something."

Calion laughed harshly. "What I hunger for, is not here. *Thes*... I have even tried to be with another female, but I could not bear her presence." He looked at Maeglin with rich disgust. "Nothing would work. Yet when I think of Talia..." He looked down at the erection that bulged in his breeches. "I am as ready as a stallion for a mare."

"She is your fire mate...your *Mylari*."

The prince swore at him. "Do not say that. It is impossible. We have been through this before."

"And I will continue to speak the truth until you recognize it. You must claim her for your own!"

Calion just growled. The subject was an unwelcome one, yet Maeglin harped on it again and again. The commotion outside was an appreciated interruption. "See what is happening."

Before Maeglin could leave the tent, the flap swung open and Orophin stepped in. He bowed quickly.

The prince stopped pacing. "Why are you not at the castle? You are supposed to be with Talia."

Orophin stared at him, seeing the scratches that covered Calion's arms. The fever had grown much worse in the last few days. His gaze slid to Maeglin, who shrugged. Orophin frowned. If the elf was this far gone, it might be hard to reason with him.

"I asked a question. Why are you here?"

Pulling the note out of his pocket, he tossed it at the prince. "Read."

Calion caught it automatically. But when he looked down at it, he snarled. "I told you I do not want to read anything from her." He started to crumple it in his hand, but stopped when Orophin slammed his body into him, knocking the prince against the wall.

Calion stared with utter shock at the usually quiet guard he called his friend. Orophin took his dagger out of his waistband and pressed it to the prince's neck. He warned Maeglin off with a look and then turned back to Calion. "Kill me later. Read now!"

Calion's mouth opened and then shut again. Whatever the contents, they must be important if Orophin was willing to die for the note to be seen. Standing very still, the dagger still pointed at his throat, he opened the note.

He read the first part of Talia's message, feeling the longing clutch him. He needed her still, wanted to go home to her, but he knew he couldn't. Duty and honor still stood between them, no matter how he felt or what he wanted. What could she have found that would change that? He looked up into Orophin's eyes. The elf lowered his dagger, but the sharpness of his gaze did not abate. Calion dropped his gaze and continued reading.

When he saw what it was, he gasped and read the note out loud.

"You ask for help, I give to thee,
a message from the goddesses three.
Spears without, a knife within,
treachery will seek to win.
Death, despair, and pain will come,
all your work will be undone.
A mighty war, your people's end,
will come, on that you can depend.
Unless true passion can guide the day,
and give to you a stronger way.
A human female will be the one,
to save the kingdom, you've begun.
She will be the first of three,
to break the hold fortune has on thee.
Varol thysi...passion's force come true,
breaks through traditions old and new.
Only in acceptance can salvation be,
one of your blood holds the key.
An heir to the throne will this create,
he will win out over fate.
His father's heart, destiny will kiss,
he will carry your mark upon his wrist."

There was utter silence in the tent when Calion finished. He stood completely still for a long time before he crumpled the paper, his hands going to his chalky face.

"What have I done?"

Orophin stepped back and tossed his dagger at the prince's feet. "My life is forfeit." When Calion just looked blankly at him, the guard unbuckled his sword and threw it down as well. "I raised my hand against you."

Calion stared down at the weapons. His mind was in such turmoil, he didn't react immediately. Finally, he looked at the guard.

"Do not be absurd. Pick them up." When Orophin didn't respond, he bent and picked them up himself, tossing them back to the startled elf. "I admit to being a fool, Orophin, but I am not foolish enough to kill someone who is as loyal to me and my lady as you are."

"Calion," Maeglin sheathed his sword as Orophin buckled his own back onto his waist, "what are you saying?"

"She found the prophecy." The prince held up the missive in his clenched hand. "All this time I tried to keep our traditions. To obey my father. I ignored how I felt about someone who would have made me complete. I hurt myself and destroyed Talia in the process." He gave a loud groan.

"Now I discover she is the only one who can save our people from a horrible war, and it is our passion for each other that will keep our kingdom safe. I should have more than a dagger pressed to my throat!"

"At least now you know why the orcs wanted her. To keep her away from you." Maeglin took the message from Calion and read it himself. "I do not understand all this, but parts are clear."

Calion ran his hands through his hair. "It is clear enough to me. I denied my destiny. If I am to save my kingdom, I have to...what does the prophecy say? *Only in acceptance can salvation be.* I have to claim Talia as my own."

Maeglin frowned. "My friend, are you accepting her for yourself? Or for your kingdom?"

"For both. Now I have a reason to break the *sardai*, and not even my father can counsel me against it." The prince clapped his best friend on the back. "Do not worry. Now everything will work out. I will go home and claim Talia—"

"Cannot."

Stopping dead in his tracks, Calion looked over at Orophin. "What are you talking about?"

"Gone, gone home."

Calion literally staggered. "What?"

Orophin looked steadily at him. "You not read. Lady cried.

Left."

The prince's gut twisted in guilt and fear. Talia...gone? He grabbed Orophin by the vest. "When? Where?"

"This morning."

Calion felt his whole life crashing around him. He couldn't lose her. He couldn't. Not when he'd just been given a reason to be with her. Rubbing his head, he fought the fever. It was still so hard to think. He looked at the paper in Maeglin's hand. The prophecy provided the means, but his heart cried out he could claim her. He had to get her back.

"Prepare the horses. We ride after them."

They followed the sign of Talia's party. They didn't even stop at the castle, because the prince was terrified he would miss her. If he must go into the human world he would, but the thought of Talia going through the myst without him scared him to death. The closer Calion got to Talia's scent, the hotter his fever burned. He was jumping out of his skin by the time they made it through the lower valleys.

"Why did they come this way?" Maeglin asked Orophin over his shoulder.

"Shorter."

Calion sighed. Orophin wasn't the best communicator, but he'd done Calion a service by letting him know Talia had left. As he rode, he kept replaying the prophecy in his mind. It was the last part that confused him. He knew it was about him. Didn't he have the mark on his wrist? And he was the heir. But how would he win out over fate?

He shook his head. It was too confusing. He'd stick to what did know. He needed Talia with him. Their fire would help save the world. That part of the prophecy, he was glad to accept.

They entered the *Mysyr* forest, walking carefully through the twisted roots. Lolíndir shuddered. "I do not like this place. I smell death."

Thinking much the same thing, Calion drew his sword. *Cylys'* light was muted here, the song deadened. "The trees are too quiet. Something is wrong."

Suddenly, from out of the forest came a horse. It almost ran past them before Lolíndir grabbed its reins. He looked over at the prince, worry on his face. "He belongs to Valandil."

Calion's blood turned to ice. No elf willingly abandoned their steed unless there was trouble. "Something has happened to Talia." Kicking Roch'mellon into a gallop, dodging between trees, he followed the stray horse's wandering path. He came around a corner blocked by a large tree and burst into a small clearing. The prince cried out as he saw the horror that awaited him.

Chapter Sixteen

The grassy area was covered in blood. The air stank of it. From where he was, Calion could see two horses down. He raced forward, Roch'mellon sliding to a stop, and the prince sprang to the ground. Tears slid down his cheeks when he discovered the body of his childhood friend.

Amroth lay close to his horse, his chest hacked open by the ragged blade of the ax. His face was mutilated, his long hair pulled away from his bleeding scalp. Blood soaked into the ground under him.

"By the goddesses," breathed Maeglin, who also dismounted. "Amroth!"

"Who did this?" shouted Celahir, his eyes wide and angry. "Who could have done such a thing?"

Calion whipped around, staring at the other horse. It was the mare Talia usually rode. He ran over and stood beside it. The pretty little mare had been hacked to pieces, her head lying away from the rest of the body. Her legs were broken, and it looked to Calion as if something had cut large pieces of flesh off the carcass. But of Talia there was no sign. Calion didn't know whether to be overjoyed or afraid.

"Calion, I have found Valandil," Lolíndir called.

The elf was covered in blood, his arm twisted in an unnatural position. What looked like an ax wound showed on his left shoulder. "My prince," he gasped.

"Valandil..." Calion knelt and held his guard's undamaged hand. "What happened here? Where is Talia?"

In truth, Valandil had been cleaning up the clearing when he heard the prince's party coming. Thinking quickly, he let go his horse and then wounded himself to look as if he'd survived an attack. It wasn't the original plan, but Valandil was a smart elf. He would adapt.

"They took her, Calion. I tried to stop them."

"Who took her, Val? Who?" Calion was afraid he already knew. There was only one being that delighted in the butchery he saw in this tiny glade.

"Orcs. So many of them. It felt like the whole orcan army attacked us." Valandil struggled to sit. "Amroth? They hit him first."

"He did not make it." Maeglin's voice was full of sorrow as he efficiently bound his friend's wounds until they could get him to the healers. "He has gone to the goddesses."

Calion came abruptly to his feet and walked back to Talia's slain mount. He knelt next to the dead horse, stroking its hide where the blood did not corrupt it. He shook with fear and fury.

Talia was gone. The orcs had taken her again. A howl of grief left his throat. He'd promised she would be safe and he'd not kept his vow to her. The prophecy, the kingdom, his father, all disappeared in a wave of pain that almost buckled him. Tears poured down his cheeks. What good was his vaunted heritage when he didn't have the female he needed? *No,* he corrected himself. He should be honest here. It was more than that.

"Soulmate," he whispered, bowing his head in shame. "I denied my *Mylari.*"

Looking up, he saw Talia's saddle pack. A bit of silk hung out of one of the sides. Pulling it out, he recognized the green dress he'd nagged his sister for. Crumpling it against his face, he breathed in her scent. The fire flamed up hot, burning him with his need, but he ignored it. He *should* go through the pain of the myst itself. He deserved it for tossing her away like he'd done.

Calion remembered her at the waterfall, so giving, so loving. Guilt twisted in greasy knots at the thought of all the times he pushed her away since.

Cringing, he remembered their last time together. He dared to call her his *torear.* She'd been right. He might as well have named her whore. He'd left her the rose because he couldn't bear walking away from her that way.

Telling her to remember was the only way he could show her he wouldn't forget. But hadn't he? He'd been too afraid to even read a note from her, thinking the temptation to be near her would be too great for him to handle. So he'd dismissed her and she'd left him.

By the goddesses, if she were here right now he would—

Calion lifted his head. What *would* he do? Realization hit him. Truth lit up his mind like a starry summer sky. He had fought so hard against it, and now...now it seemed so foolish. He finally understood everything she'd been trying to tell him. She loved him and by the goddesses...

He...loved...her.

He wept again, his heart clearing out all the poison of hatred and fear. All the words he remembered tossing at Talia shredded him, slicing deep into his soul. He'd had to lose the female he loved and needed above all else before he would admit to himself how he felt. He'd been so stupid, so afraid. His lady had far more courage than he.

She'd loved him and was willing to risk her life to protect and be with him. He wanted to laugh. It was so clear now. All he had done. All he must do. His heart expanded, his soul rejoiced. Loving Talia would not be easy, but it would be worth it.

She was the other half of his soul.

Acceptance came and with it strength unlike any he'd ever known. Feeling it fill him, he finally realized what he must do. No matter what his father may say, he would link with Talia. She would be his mate. Take his name. Never again would she wonder what he felt for her. He would cry it from the roof of the castle if need be. He would do this not to protect the kingdom or his people, but because of a very selfish, personal need.

Without her love, he was incomplete.

He laid his hand on the broken body of Talia's horse and spoke aloud. "I vow to the goddesses, I will bring her back. They will pay for the lives they took here. They will die for taking from me the female I...love. For taking my *Mylari*."

Summoning his magick, he drew his sword. This time *Cylys* called out for honor in a voice that rang clear and strong, its blue light shining up into the sky. Closing his eyes, Calion placed the sword against his chest, its tip pointing upwards. As he had done once before instinctively, he now did deliberately. He thrust his sword up into the air and shouted it aloud. "*Mylari...*"

The soulmate spell didn't hesitate this time. It shot hard and fast into the sky, tracking its other half. As Calion knelt there, his sword in hand, his guards saw to their amazement his body and face were back to normal.

His fire fever was gone.

Far away, unconscious, facedown on the back of a *volai*, Talia stirred as she heard the ancient call. Her heart answered and her own soulmate magick burst into life.

ꟸ

They went back to the castle. Calion knew no matter how badly he wanted to leave quickly, they were only six and one was badly injured. The soulmate spell showed him Talia's location. She was alive and being taken back to *Grundlug*. The full force of the orcan army was there. Calion would need more troops to rescue his *Mylari*.

They also could not leave the wood that way. To ignore the mystical pain left behind from the murders would destroy both the wood and any elf that came in contact with it. Orophin, since he had specific talents with that type of thing, was left behind to purify the ground and dispose of the dead horses. Amroth's body would be brought back with honor.

Calion and his guards arrived back in *Osalai* just before dusk. Maeglin and the others immediately went to put together the soldiers needed for the raid and get Valandil to a healer. The prince went to speak to the king. As he stepped out of the courtyard he was met by his sister, her face streaked with wetness.

As soon as she saw her brother's face, Eámanë burst into tears again. "You did not find her. She is gone?"

Calion pulled her into his arms and hugged her fiercely. "Come with me. I must speak to Father. I would only say this once."

"By the goddesses, Calion," Eámanë moaned tearfully. "You are frightening me."

Calion didn't respond. He needed to speak to the king. It was not a conversation he was looking forward to. Together, they walked into the library where their father entertained several of his advisors. When the king caught sight of Calion, he beamed in satisfaction.

My boy," he crowed in delight. "It worked. Sending you to the east broke the fever around you."

Calion stared at him. He'd totally forgotten about his fever. He looked in a mirror and saw to his surprise his face was back to normal. He pulled back a sleeve, noting the scratches and cuts were healed and his body sound. He smiled, knowing the distance between Talia and him had meant nothing.

It was his acceptance of his love for Talia that had restored him.

"No, Father. It was not the east that cured me, but the truth."

Ërestor frowned in confusion. "What truth is that?"

Calion left his sister's side. "I mean the truth about my destiny. The truth about what my future holds."

The king sighed as he sat. "You are being dramatic again, son. What do you really mean?"

Calion pulled the note Talia sent him from his pocket. Smoothing it out, he handed it to his father. "Talia found the prophecy. Unfortunately, I refused to listen to her and now she is gone."

Ërestor sat up straight. "The human left? She didn't have permission to do so." He relaxed again. "But she is not needed now. You are healthy."

Calion looked straight at his father, ignoring everyone else in the room. "I do need her. She is my *Mylari*...my other half. And I love her."

As shocked murmurs filled the room, Ërestor almost fell out of his chair. "What? What?" He leaped to his feet and came to Calion. "You still must be ill."

Calion shook his head. He smiled when he saw Eámanë weeping tears of joy at his words. "I am not sick. Talia is my destiny. I will not fight it any longer. We belong together."

"I will call the healers. This is a symptom of the fever." Ërestor wrung his hands in agitation.

"No, Father." Calion stopped the king from pulling on the bell cord. "I love her. I was wrong to push her away...to treat her as I did. Talia is who I have searched for my whole life. She will be my mate. This you have to accept."

He turned and looked at his sister. "I have been a fool for a long time. Tradition-bound and afraid to change. I am sorry for what I put this house through."

Eámanë nodded through her tears. "You have seen the prophecy?

"Yes, she tried to give it to me before, but I refused to see it. I broke her spirit and she fled from me." Calion put his hand on his sister's shoulder, his face turning grim. "I went after her, but I was too late. In the forest of *Mysyr*, the orcs took her."

Eámanë gasped. "No." Her knees gave out and she lowered herself into a chair. Her face went pale with fear.

Calion looked back at his father. "Amroth is dead, as well as two of our horses. The orcs took Talia to *Grundlug*."

"Amroth...dead?" Ërestor squeaked in shock. The other advisors in the room broke into agitated conversation. "Killed by the orcs? Are you sure?"

"Yes," Calion nodded. "There was orc sign all over the woods. Orophin is bringing his body back." He turned to his sister. "Will you care for him?"

Eámanë swallowed her tears. "Of course. I will treat him as you would."

"We must have the ceremony immediately," Ërestor muttered. "His spirit will be sent to his fathers."

The prince shook his head. "Nay, my king. I am leaving soon for *Grundlug*. I will get Talia back and avenge Amroth."

"What?" Ërestor shouted. "Are you mad? You cannot go. I will not have you risk your life for that human. She is *vyryl*...poison."

Calion stepped up close to his father so they stood nose to nose. "Be very careful of how you speak. I did not stand for her before when I should have, but by the goddesses, I will stand for her now. She will be treated with the honor and respect she deserves. Talia is my *Mylari*. She is my mate in everything but name. I love her. "

Ërestor was furious. His son, his beautiful son, choosing to link with a human, to break the *sardai*... It was disgusting, it was abhorrent.

"What is this...love? A pathetic human term? I will not allow it. If you leave this castle, you leave your heritage behind. You will be my son no longer."

"Father!" Eámanë gasped, standing and going to her father. The others in the room all gaped. "You cannot mean such a thing. Calion is your heir. Please, read the prophecy. Then you will understand."

Ërestor folded his arms across his chest. "There is no prophecy that can change my mind. No human will ever link with a Sáralondë."

Calion pointed to the paper his father still held. The prince was very pale, but his face was determined. He would never turn away from Talia again. If he had to hold a dagger to his father's throat, as had been done to him, he would. "Read it, Father."

Ërestor stared at his son's implacable face. He looked into his daughter's pleading eyes. "I will do so, but do not expect me to support you in this decision." Bending his head, he began to read.

Since Valandil was still with the healer, it was only the four royal guards who came into the room. They were dressed in full battle armor and Lolíndir pulled a floating pallet on which the body of Amroth lay. Eámanë stood and walked over to him. She'd liked Amroth, he'd always had a smile and a joke for her.

"My prince," Maeglin motioned him over. "Orophin found something in the Lady Talia's pack. I think you should take a look at it.

The silent guard held a roll of parchments in his hand. He handed them to Calion with a small smile.

"What is it?" the prince inquired. "Is it the original prophecy?" He glanced up at his father, who was staring at Talia's note with a look of stupefied wonder on his face.

"No," Orophin stated. "Read."

Calion opened the parchments. Talia had taken them from the archives, but why would she have stolen anything but the prophecy? He read the title on the first page. *The Care and Birthing of an Elven Child.* He frowned and turned the page. *Carrying Your Child to Term.* He turned another page, still not comprehending.

Suddenly, the pages slipped though lifeless fingers, as understanding came and his mind went numb. *The Care and Birthing...? Carrying Your Child...?* His heart began to pound within him. He stared at Maeglin and Orophin, seeing the grins on their faces. His legs gave out on him and he would have collapsed if they hadn't held him upright. He couldn't believe it. Could this really be happening? Tears of joy wet his face. It was another miracle.

"She carries...my child."

The room went absolutely still at his announcement.

Calion let go of his friends and gathering up the parchments, walked over to his father, thrusting them under the king's nose. "Well Father, what of this? Talia is pregnant. Another impossibility, but a miracle. Does it not say it is possible in the prophecy?

An heir to the throne will this create,
He will win out over fate.
His father's heart, destiny will kiss,
he will carry your mark upon his wrist.

I thought I was the heir, but I am not." Calion rolled up his sleeve and showed his father the scar. For the first time in two months it did not burn. "I am the one who carries the scar. Do you not see, Father?" His azure eyes shone with joy and sudden understanding.

"This child, created by Talia and myself...a human female and an elven male. This miracle will be the salvation of our world."

Even Ërestor could not stand against such logic. His father subdued, Calion set to preparing his troops. Eighty brave elves saddled their horses and donned battle armor. Calion swung up on Roch'mellon and turned to his soldiers.

"We go to *Grundlug* to rescue the Lady Talia and avenge the death of Amroth. She is an innocent, taken because of a prophecy that gives her to me as *Mylari.* Amroth died valiantly, trying to protect my lady. These monsters have no honor, butchering both the animals and the males they left behind. The orcs have a full regiment, but we are elven. We will not be defeated."

He turned to Maeglin. "Use the time void. She has already been in their hands too long. Bring all the troops to the meadow just outside of the swamp." Turning, Calion was surprised to see Valandil with them. He trotted over to the guard. "Should you be up? You were badly wounded."

"I must avenge my brother," Valandil said with a fierce smile. *And cover my tracks.* He had to get to the human before Calion did, or all would be lost.

"Calion?" He turned to see his sister standing in the courtyard, her skirts blowing in the breeze. She walked up and put a hand on his leg. Roch'mellon snorted, wanting to be gone.

"Just hold on." Eámanë smiled as she scratched the horse's nose. "I want you to know I checked Amroth's body. It is prepared for burial."

"I thank you, sister."

"Calion...something is wrong with the wounds."

The prince hesitated. "Wrong?"

"I used my gift to scry if there was anything we could learn from the attack. I am not getting much, but there is something off about the wounds. I do not think they were made by orcs."

Calion shook his head. "But Eámanë, they were made by an ax. It was in his chest."

"I know, I know," the princess returned with a frustrated sigh. "But it is not right. I cannot tell you more. Just be careful."

Calion thought of Maeglin's words earlier when he spoke of the attack. Amroth hadn't even pulled his sword. "I will be careful." He touched the top of his sister's head gently.

"Bring her back to us, Calion. I want to rock my nephew."

Calion started. "You knew."

"I felt it too late. She was already gone."

"Why did she not tell me?" That question had been eating at him the whole time he prepared to go. It was the one thing that really hurt him.

"Oh, Calion." Eámanë squeezed her brother's leg to take the sting from her words. "Why would she, with the way you were treating her? You did not see her face the day she came to me. She had no dreams left. She left because not even the prophecy could bring you back to her."

Calion felt the pain and loss all the way to his toes. How long had Talia been pregnant? Going through everything alone.

"I have made a mess of things. If she is hurt..."

Eámanë shuddered. "Do not even say that. You will find

her and everything will be fine. You two are supposed to be together. Now go get her!"

Calion grinned at the optimism. He clucked to Roch'mellon and they trotted forward. After a few steps, he turned back to his sister, a smug look on his face. "A son, huh?"

Eámanë laughed. "A son." A beautiful smile lit her face. "Even in the midst of all the pain, I felt Talia's joy in him."

They rendezvoused at the swamp. By the time Calion arrived, Orophin and Lolíndir were scouting for any sentries between the wood and *Grundlug.* He gathered his other guards around him. "Maeglin, you are with me. The rest of you each take a unit of soldiers and surround the fortress. When I go in after Talia, I may need a diversion, so listen for my signal. When it comes, fire at will."

Valandil pushed forward. "Your Highness, allow me to accompany you. I have unfinished business with these creatures."

Calion nodded. "I know you do, but you will serve me better by attacking in another area. Take out as many orcs as you can. If the prophecy is true, this is only the beginning."

Valandil started to protest again, but the arrival of the other two guards interrupted him.

"It is clear to *Grundlug.*" Lolíndir shook his head in amazement. "Not a single sentry outside."

Orophin shook his head in disbelief, grunting at the creatures' lack of foresight. "None seen."

The prince breathed a sigh of relief. "They did not learn anything from the last time I was here. The fools. Do they think I would give her up so easily?"

Only Valandil knew the orcs weren't worried at all. As far as they knew, the elves were mourning the loss of their people in the myst, not readying to attack the fortress. He began to sweat, the reality of his position suddenly hitting home.

"Take your people and go to your position. I will give you twenty minutes, and then I go in."

"Do you know where to go?" Celahir questioned as he readied his bow.

Calion got a faraway look on his face. "They have put her in a safer location this time. I sense her nearby but not exactly where she is. The locator spell will pinpoint the way when I am close enough." He frowned and looked at Maeglin.

"Talia is frightened and despairing, and does not believe I would come for her. Have I destroyed her...love for me by my ill treatment of her?" His face filled with pain. "She must believe I do not care about her at all." He shook his head and his eyes glowed angrily. "But she will soon see she is wrong."

The group fanned out, each heading to their own assigned areas. Calion and the guards, Maeglin, Orophin and Lolíndir, headed to the far side of the fortress following the soulmate sign. As they crept through the dank woods, they could hear the sounds of orcan revelry going on inside. It frightened Calion to think about what they might be celebrating.

They found their way to a small clearing beneath the eastern wall. Closing his eyes, Calion traced the locator spell. He swore softly. "She is on the top floor, in the tower."

"She will not be easy to get to," Lolíndir commented.

Calion smiled grimly. "I have experience climbing these walls. My friends...this is what we will do."

&

Talia woke with the same feeling of dread she'd had once before. She knew where she was by the smell. She was back in the orcan castle. But what was she doing here? How did she get here? Her head pounded as she drew her breath in fearfully. She couldn't remember anything.

Opening her eyes, she found herself in a small room, lying on a ragged bed. There was nothing else in the room but an empty chamber pot against the wall. Her clothes were torn and dirty and her hands were bound. She swung her legs over the side of the bed and carefully stood, swaying unsteadily for a moment as she fought to keep her stomach from being sick. Worriedly, she checked on the baby, letting out a sigh of relief when she sensed his strong presence moving within her.

She looked around the small room. At least this time they hadn't staked her in the main hall, but she wasn't sure if that was better or worse. The room was no bigger than the cell she'd been in at *Osalai*, but it had a window. A huge one.

Running over, she stood on her tiptoes to look out. There

were bars, as big around as her arm, but the spaces between them were easily wide enough for a man to get through. Talia's heart leapt in hope, until she actually peered outside and saw how high up she was. It was as tall as a twenty-story building and she had no magick rope. She slumped back, knowing there was no way she could get down on her own.

Suddenly, she heard something clatter against the wall, and her heart leaped again. Under her tunic was her dagger. They hadn't taken it from her. Quickly, she reached to get it but stopped when she heard something outside her door. She froze in fear as the door was flung open and Modak came inside.

He looked around the room until he caught sight of her and then grinned, his ugly face creasing into even uglier lines. He shuffled to her, his hand outstretched. "Pretty human. Mine now."

Talia's throat constricted in fear. How had he captured her? Why couldn't she remember anything? There was no way she was going to let this filthy creature touch her. "Get away from me!"

Modak chortled as if it were a game. "Mine...mine...all mine," he caroled in a singsong voice.

She dodged away from him, putting the bed between her and the orc. "What about your father?" she asked, desperately trying to distract him. "I thought I belonged to him. He'll be mad if you touch me."

Modak stopped, considering her words. He scratched his head, and her stomach churned when she saw bugs leaping for safety.

"Father no care. Prophecy broken."

"Then if it's broken you don't need me. You can let me go back to my world." She tried to remember something...anything that would help her, but the blank spot in her mind made it difficult to think at all.

The orc scratched his head again, and more insects abandoned ship. "You with elf. No mate. No prophecy. You no danger. I want. I fuck." He reached out a hand again.

Talia thought she understood. For some reason the orcs thought she wasn't a danger to them anymore. A memory moved through the haziness of what happened to her, but it disappeared before she could grasp it.

She dodged away from his hand again. The orc was

becoming aroused by her flight. He laughed, sending shivers down her neck. His foul breath had quickened and he was rubbing the bulge in his crotch. He lumbered after her, only her quick reactions keeping her safe. He chased her around the room for several minutes before stopping and eyeing her balefully.

"No run," he panted.

"Yes...run," she retorted. She dodged to the left but this time the orc was ready for her. He grabbed her by her long hair and dragged her back to him. "Ha, ha, ha!" he chortled as he bent her head back. His putrid breath made her gag. Modak stroked her body with one rough hand. "Pretty human. All mine. Fuck now."

With a quick grab, he ripped the tunic off her shoulder and pressed his fat lips to the soft skin exposed. Talia thought she'd pass out, his touch was so sickening. She struggled as the orc fumbled at her breast. Somehow she thrust her bound hands down between their bodies, and digging under her tunic, she pulled out her dagger.

Modak tried to root at her breast, his hands grasping her waist to hold her to him, and she knew she'd only have one chance. Her small knife wouldn't do much damage. It would have to be a death blow. She remembered a story on TV about a man dying from his neck being stabbed. It seemed like the best choice now.

Swinging her arms out to the right, she aimed her dagger at the blubbery skin at the side of his neck. Modak saw the telltale movement and ducked. Instead of her knife driving into the vein at the side of his neck, it plunged into the soft tissue of his left eye.

Modak screamed. A high-pitched sound that shook the stone walls. Blood and gore spewed out, covering Talia's tunic. She screamed as well and fought her way from him. Modak screeched again, going to his knees, tears mixing with the blood that ran down his chest. She backed away, terror congealing in her veins. She hadn't killed him, only blinded him.

The door opened on Braduk. Modak rolled on the floor, weeping and cursing. The dagger still protruded from his ruined eye. The orcan heir took in the scene, seeing Talia standing in the corner. He grunted and stood next to his fallen brother, kicking him in the side with his heavy boot. "Stupid."

He knelt and viciously pulled the dagger from Modak's eye. The orc screamed as more blood and torn flesh tumbled out. "Deserve," Braduk growled as he kicked his brother again. "Female mine."

He went to the door and called out in his own tongue. Two big creatures came in. They grunted when they saw Modak lying in a pool of blood, screaming in pain. When they glanced at Talia, she was shocked to see a glimmer of respect in their eyes.

"Out," Braduk grunted, and the two dragged the sobbing Modak out of the room. The door closed behind them and she swallowed. Would this be a replay of before?

"Good stab," Braduk told her.

She blinked. Had he really given her a compliment on disfiguring his brother? What type of animals were they?

"You mine. Modak wrong."

Great. They were fighting over her. If she was lucky, maybe they'd kill each other. Talia backed away. Braduk had her weapon now.

As if divining her thoughts the big orc laughed. "I keep." He tucked her dagger in his own breeches and then stood staring at her.

"What are you going to do with me?" Talia asked.

Braduk grinned. "Fuck you soon. Merging ritual coming."

She began to shake. "What are you talking about?"

Braduk walked to the door. "Merging. You strong. We mate. Destroy prophecy. Give Braduk son."

Talia's stomach heaved. She clapped her hand over her mouth. He wanted to mate with her so she could bear his child. Her unruly belly gave way and rushing over, she vomited in the chamber pot.

Oh God, she thought. This can't happen. She touched her stomach. If Braduk knew she already carried a child, both of their lives would be forfeit.

Braduk laughed at her as he opened the door and shouted something down the hall. A few minutes later two slatternly female orcs came in dragging a small tub. "You wash." He touched the tip of her dagger with his finger, watching his brother's blood drip. "No brother smell."

He crossed his arms over his massive chest and waited.

Her stomach lurched again when she realized he wanted to watch her bathe. She almost panicked. The orc might see the rounding of her tummy. "Not with you here!"

The heir grinned. "You mine. I watch."

She put her chin in the air. "If you don't want me to smell like your brother...get out!"

The two slatterns snickered as the orcan male glared at her, but she held her ground. "I mean it. *Get out!*"

Braduk reached in the pack at his waist and pulled out a silk cloth. "Wear!" He tossed it at Talia as he stepped up close to her, and using her own dagger, cut the rope that tied her hands. His stink was incredible.

"You mine. I go. Be back. Fuck you hard." He cuffed one of the females on his way out. After grabbing the fouled chamber pot, they followed him, laughing coarsely.

When the door closed, Talia sank to her knees. What could she do? He would come back, and after whatever ritual he'd talked about, he would mate with her. Even if she could handle it, she knew the baby she carried couldn't. Braduk's body would destroy Calion's child to make room for his own.

She got to her feet and walked to the tub. She needed time and she needed to hide the fact she was pregnant. That meant she had to go along with them and bathe and change her clothes. She couldn't afford for them to see her naked.

Talia set the record for a bath. She scrubbed Modak's blood from her body so fast she left marks behind. Cringing a little, she used the ragged blanket from the bed to dry off and slipped on her soft shoes and the white gown. It reminded her of the nightgown she'd worn the night they'd first taken her.

Full circle.

Standing, she gazed around the room. She was clean and clothed, but those wouldn't help her when Braduk came back into the room. Tears filled her eyes. There would be no Calion flying to the rescue this time. He thought she'd gone back to her world. There would be no reason for him to come after her.

Again the memory tickled, but still nothing. She sighed, knowing she was on her own. How could she get out? The window wasn't an option. Too high. Through the door? No. She didn't know what was out there.

She needed to find a weapon. Looking around the room, she saw nothing that would help her. The tub and the bed were all there was. Chewing her lip, she walked over to the bed. When she'd removed the ratty blanket she'd exposed the bottom, made of wood slats. Leaning over, she took one in her hands and pulled. It broke with a harsh crack that had Talia looking over her shoulder in fear that it had been heard outside.

She turned it in her hands. The break was sharp but not sharp enough. Grimly, Talia began rubbing the edge against the rough stone floor. If she could sharpen it, she might have a chance.

Talia lost track of time as she hurried to sharpen the slat. She wasn't sure how much longer she had left. If she could get it pointed enough, she could use it to protect herself. It was the only thing left for her to do. Her hands were sore, her fingers splintered when she raised it up to look.

The hand covered her mouth a heartbeat before she sensed it. Terror filled her. Had Braduk sneaked in and she hadn't seen? She struggled against the arm that banded around her waist. Her nails raked at the fingers on her face.

"Be easy, *Tia maer...* It is me."

Chapter Seventeen

Talia froze. That voice. She knew it. Tears filled her eyes. The pressure around her waist lessened, and she whipped around.

"You came after me."

With a muffled cry of joy, she threw herself against him. His arms came around her and he hugged her to him. She began to shake, her relief at his presence overwhelming her. She pressed her face against his chest trying hard not to cry.

Calion shook as well. His mind had painted terrible pictures of how he might find his beloved. Seeing her healthy and whole in front of him, he sent prayers of thanksgiving lifting to the goddesses. Having her in his arms, he could only do one thing. He raised her chin and crushed her mouth with his.

She moaned at the contact. It had been so long. She'd given up believing she would ever touch him again. His mouth wasn't gentle. It had been too long for both of them. His tongue delved deep into her mouth searching...seeking.

Her taste... He had missed it, needed it. The fire flared up in his body and he groaned, knowing he was being rough, but he could do nothing else as his hands clutched her to him. The need to mate was a fever in his blood. How could he have thought he could do without her?

Their bodies strained together as they filled the need that battered at them. When Calion finally pulled away, they both were breathing hard. He ran a shaky hand over Talia's unbound hair. "Are you all right? Did they touch you?"

"I'm fine," she assured him. "They didn't have a chance yet."

"The blood—"

"It's not mine." Her eyes glinted and her chin went up. "I put my dagger in Modak's eye when he tried to touch me."

He drew her back to him, his heart beating in relief. He wasn't too late. "My bloodthirsty lady," he chuckled. "Thank the goddesses, you had it with you." When he remembered why, he pulled back and took her by the shoulders, giving her a little shake.

"You did not have my permission to leave. You put everything at risk by doing so. What were you thinking?"

So much for him coming after her because he cared. She'd just messed up his plan to have her as his mistress. She stiffened and tried to turn away. "I'm sorry you had to bother. As soon as possible, I will—"

Calion groaned. She'd misunderstood him. Cursing his temper, he covered her mouth again with his own.

Talia's knees went weak. It wasn't fair he could do this to her. Her flesh trembled, her body ached, just from the beauty of his kiss. She couldn't let him hurt her again. Tearing her mouth from his, she struggled against him. "No!"

He held her closely, feeling the tremors of her body. He needed to get her out of here, but he had to deal with this first. "*Tia maer...* Please... Let me explain." He moved to hold her face in his hands. "I read the prophecy."

She stopped trying to push out of his arms. "You did?"

"Yes." The prince smoothed back her tangled hair. "I should have read it the first time you gave it to me. I was a fool, too afraid of what I felt for you. I am so sorry. If I had read it, you would not be here."

Talia forgot to breathe. "I wouldn't?"

"I would have been home and in your bed before an hour had passed." He frowned and let his gaze touch her beautiful face. "But even in that I would have been wrong."

He was rejecting her again? She pushed at him. "Don't Calion. I can't bear it."

"*Tia maer...* I am making a hash of this. You misunderstand me." His eyes stared into hers. "If I had come back, I would have done exactly what the prophecy said to do. Admitted I needed you...linked with you and we would have mated. Our fever would be gone and my kingdom safe, because I had the human female that would save us all."

Talia shuddered. It sounded so cold.

"But that was just the bones of the prophecy, not the heart. You were not sent to me so I could save my people. You were sent to me to save my soul."

Her heart pounded. Calion could feel it beating against his hard chest. She stared up at him, and he could see fear warring with hope. "What are you saying?"

He pressed a kiss to her forehead, and then another gentle one on her lips. "It was not until I lost you that I truly understood. The prophecy speaks of acceptance. I thought it meant I had to accept a human for my mate so my kingdom would be saved. To break through centuries of *sardai.*" He kissed her again, his lips caressing hers with a little more heat. "But I was wrong. The prophecy did not mean that at all."

"What does it mean?" she asked, holding her breath.

"It meant I must accept what I felt for you. I had to accept that you are...my *Mylari*. The other half I have searched for my entire life." He ran a loving finger down her cheek.

"I had to admit I had fallen in love with you."

Talia just stared at him, her heart in her eyes. After a moment, her lashes fluttered and she swallowed, hard. She lifted a trembling hand and touched his face.

"What did you say?"

Calion laughed softly. "I love you." He repeated it in his own tongue as he brushed his lips over hers. "*Ai jhyli osu.*" He kissed her again. "I have probably loved you since I first saw you, standing so bravely, surrounded by monsters. You destroyed me with a single look from those dreamy, green eyes. You changed my life."

She grabbed his face in her hands. "Say it again. I need you to say it again."

He smiled. It was easier than he expected. All he had to do was open his heart and let the feelings flow. "I love you. You are *Mylari*...mine. I have come for you now, not for the sake of my kingdom, but because I need you. I need your laughter, I need your touch, I need your beauty, but most of all I need your love."

He reached up and covered one of her hands. "Tell me it is not too late."

Talia let the tears go. They cleansed and healed. She looked up at him. He stared at her with a vulnerability she'd never before seen in him. "Calion—" she began before her voice broke. She stared at him helplessly. She could not mess up the most important moment of her life. What had he said? Taking a deep breath, she took his hand and held it against her beating heart.

"*Ai jhyli osu...* I love you."

Calion pulled her back to him, the joy in his heart at her words swamping him. *She loved him!* Even after everything he'd done to her...she loved him. He didn't deserve it, but he'd make sure from this moment forward, she would never regret it. "*O Eisi tia maelor oli. Ai cyro tyri sai tia caes. Ai jhyli osu...*" He spoke to her in Elvish, giving her the love words in his own tongue. Then, he covered her mouth in another hard kiss that drained all the thoughts from his head.

He loved her! She gave him everything back in the kiss, wrapping her arms around him and pressing herself to him. Their bodies, their hearts, their very souls released by the power of love. Soulmate magick, born from that release, swirled around them, binding them together. It burned gold, filling the room with translucent light.

Far below, Maeglin laughed as he saw the light come pouring out into the night. "He found her," he told his fellow guards, satisfaction wreathing his face. "This thing humans call love has made their prophecy complete."

Calion wanted to go on kissing Talia until their bodies joined in the most natural of ways. He'd almost forgotten their surroundings when a noise at the window made him stiffen. He lifted his head from hers, and looking around, saw the enchanted rope he'd bespelled twitch frantically, reminding him of his need to flee.

Reluctantly, he sighed, gazing down into her love-filled face. It was time to go. There was just one more thing he needed to know.

He slid his hand down to her slightly rounded tummy. "I found the parchments, *Tia maer...* Do you have something to tell me?

Talia went still in his arms. She lifted her eyes to his, suddenly frightened of what she might see.

A chuckle escaped him. "After that kiss do you really still worry how I feel about you?" He lifted one of her hands to his lips. "You are carrying my child. My son."

She heard the pride and joy in his voice and relaxed. "You're pleased?"

"Talia, the fact the goddesses have smiled on us and made a miracle happen by giving our love life is most pleasing to me. I loved you before I knew of this blessing. I did not expect it. Now I can only love you more." He squeezed her hand, suddenly serious. "You are well...both of you?"

She nodded. "Yes, so far it hasn't been difficult for me. The baby got a little shaken up on the ride here, but he seems fine now." She smiled smugly at him. "You know, it was supposed to be impossible."

Stroking his hand over her stomach, the prince chuckled. "You have made a calling out of making the impossible possible." He frowned suddenly. "But you would have taken him from me."

She bit her lip. "I didn't know what else to do. I couldn't stay with you, knowing the way you felt—"

His gentle finger across her mouth stopped her.

"I was a fool. I should never have treated you the way I did. It was my arrogance that made you leave me. I made you believe you and the child would be unwelcome. But I am no longer that fool." He grinned wickedly. "And, if our past performance is any clue, this child will be one of many."

"Calion," she gasped, blushing furiously. "Let me have this one first!"

He sobered. "To do that, we have to get out of here." He looked toward the door. "What is going on out there?"

"They're getting ready for Braduk's merging ceremony."

He frowned. "A merging? Who?" He narrowed his eyes. "Do not tell me..." At her slow nod, he snarled. "He thinks he is merging with you? With my *Mylari*?" His eyes flashed. "I will kill him where he stands."

She put her arms around him. "Please, Calion. Just take me home to *Osalai*."

The prince reined in his temper. He would take her to safety and then he would kill the *sharas*. "We have men all around the fortress. We have come to rescue you and avenge Amroth."

Talia grabbed his arm. "What happened to Amroth?"

He hesitated. "Do you not remember the attack?"

"I don't remember anything after leaving the castle. What happened to us?"

"You were attacked in the dark forest. Amroth was killed. Orcs slaughtered your mounts." He didn't go into detail. She didn't need to hear it."

Her eyes overflowed. "I'm sorry. If I hadn't left the castle, he'd still be alive. It's my fault."

"He died doing his duty...protecting you. Do not take his honor from him."

"Is that how you found me? I didn't think you would come after me."

"You were wrong." He kissed her again. "I would follow you into the human world if I needed to. Once I knew my feelings, I had to bring you back to me. When I realized you had been taken by orcs, my heart froze in my body. I had promised to protect you."

"It's over and you're here now."

He squeezed her gently. "Yes, it is over, and I swear I will keep you both safe." Pulling her to the window, he stepped up on the windowsill. "I am worried about the child. Can you do this?"

She nodded. "I'll be fine. It's not like we have a choice. I just want to get out of here!"

Calion wrapped the line around bars on the window. "I think you still know what to do, *Tia maer...*" He helped her up, putting her arms around his neck.

Talia smiled weakly. "We have to stop meeting like this." She kissed him, pressing herself close and murmuring softly in his ear. "But I do like this part."

He couldn't help grinning even as his body heated. Here they were fighting for their lives again, and they were teasing each other. He hadn't realized until now how much he'd missed the carefree banter they'd had at the beginning. It was one of the reasons he'd fallen for her in the first place, so he teased her back. "I find it sweet you wore the same gown for me."

Talia looked down at her dress and snorted. "I guess Braduk liked me in white too." She gave a little shrug. "It was for the ceremony."

"That ceremony will never happen," Calion gritted out as he

stepped off the window sill. "Hold on."

Down below, Maeglin saw the two figures step outside the window. "They are coming," he said in relief. It felt like hours since the prince climbed up to rescue Talia. So far it had been quiet, but Maeglin didn't trust it would stay that way. "Orophin," he ordered, "scout to the right. Lolíndir, to the left. I do not want any surprises waiting for them at the bottom." The elves nodded and melted into the darkness.

Talia felt Calion's muscles ripple as he lowered them carefully down the fortress wall. This climb was three times longer than the first one had been, but at least he hadn't been shot this time. She burrowed against him, feeling the strong beating of his heart. "What happens when we get to the ground?"

He grunted. "If all goes well, we spirit you away without trouble. The horses are waiting in the meadow by the swamp."

She thought of the sweet mare that lost her life in the attack. Knowing the orcs were the cause made her doubly glad she'd blinded Modak.

"Look below us," Calion instructed. "Can you see anything?"

She craned her neck, staring down at the ground. "I don't think so. It's so dark. If your elves are there, I can't see them."

He blew out a breath. They were more than halfway down, but his arms were tiring. "You would not see my guards, *Tia maer*... They are too well hidden. It is the orcs I am concerned with."

"Nope...nothing."

He grunted in acknowledgment and they continued to descend.

Unexpectedly, they heard a commotion above them. They both looked up and she saw the two slatternly female orcs staring out the window. The maids cried out an alarm and she gasped. They were discovered.

"Hold on. I must hurry before they cut the rope." Hand over hand he went, his gloved hands moving faster than she could see. Still, they were about thirty feet above the ground when they felt the rope give. Suddenly, they began to fall.

Calion twisted so his body protected Talia and the baby. Struggling, he removed his sword and pointed it down at the ground. He prayed the spell he read about but never tried wouldn't fail him now. "*Taji ti ei baer...*"

Talia gasped as she was pulled closer to Calion. She knew he was trying to cushion their fall. She wanted to close her eyes, but her gaze was inexorably drawn to the ground that rushed up to meet them. When she heard him shout something in Elvish, she thought he was calling for help. She watched in stunned silence as a glistening web of blue fire appeared below them. It sparkled and snapped, its power shining in the twisted woods.

They hit the web net, Calion cradling her slim form with his own. They bounced once and then lay still. He rolled and leaned over her, his face dark with concern. "Are you all right?"

She'd had the breath knocked out of her, but otherwise, she was fine. Talia gave him a tremulous smile. "That was fun. Can we do it again?"

He shook his head in amusement and helped her to her feet. "Perhaps another time, when you do not carry my son."

Orophin stood at the edge of the net and held out his arms to Talia. Gratefully, she hugged him as he set her on the ground. "I'm so happy to see you." She looked around at them. "All of you."

"We are going to have company in a minute." Calion stepped off the blue web. It vanished with a wave of his sword.

All around them they could hear the sounds of battle. The orcan army had been called out. Braduk wanted his bride back.

"Everyone is fighting," Lolíndir said. "When the alarm was called, they all poured outside. They are heading this way. If we are to save the Lady Talia, we have to leave now."

The prince nodded. "Then let us escape the way we planned. If we are lucky, they will all follow the main path. This one side is less used." Taking Talia by the hand, he pulled her away from the castle.

Maeglin led the way, with Orophin and Lolíndir guarding their backs. The few elven soldiers that accompanied them fanned out around the party.

Silently, they picked their way through the wood. Talia could hear only the sound of her own breathing as the sounds of battle fell behind them. The wood was dark, the tangled trees so close together, they walked single file to get through. There were no other night sounds. The orcan land seemed as silent and dead as the swamp that dominated it.

As they got further from the fortress, they began to think they'd escaped undiscovered. Calion searched the darkness, his mind was already working on the plan as to how they would get back to *Osalai.*

When the attack came, it was from all sides. Orcs crashed out of the trees, surrounding them in seconds. Calion cursed. How had they gotten here so fast, so quietly? Orcs were not known for their stealth. Steel rang upon steel as elven blades met orcan axes. Shouting, struggling, bleeding, the battle churned over the swampy ground.

Calion dragged Talia behind him as the other guards set up a circle surrounding her. He pulled his sword, the blue magick shooting into the darkness as it screamed its name: *Cylys!* An orc came lumbering at him, its teeth bared in a battle snarl. The creature lifted its bloodstained ax, intending to part Calion's head from his body. An arrow caught him through the neck, and the light went out of the orc's eyes as the creature tumbled to the ground.

Turning, Calion saw Celahir running from the woods, nocking another arrow in his bow. Letting it fly, he killed an orc who'd sliced through an elven soldier. Panting, he joined the prince.

"It is bad, Calion. All my soldiers are down. There must be a hundred orcs in the forest."

"How did they know we would be here?" Maeglin demanded. He used his sword to drive off an orcan blade. "It makes no sense."

Talia stood by helplessly as the men around her battled on. She had no weapon, no way to fight. It soon became clear they were outnumbered. The circle around her tightened as the elven soldiers died one by one. Soon all that was left was the Royal Guard, standing firm in the blood-soaked woods.

Lolíndir gasped as an orcan sword stabbed into his chest. He went down, his own sword clattering to the ground. Talia screamed as the orc stepped over the fallen elf to reach her. His hate-filled eyes seared her as he lifted his sword and snarled.

Calion twisted, his own sword flashing blue as he met and deflected that of the orc's. The fight pushed him back out of the circle as he parried one blow after another. Sweat ran down Calion's face, but his fear wasn't for himself. It was for his beloved who'd been left without his protection in the circle. He tried to battle back to her, but the orc was too strong. Suddenly, Calion's foot caught in a root, and he slipped, going down on one knee. The orc shouted in triumph as it pulled back its sword for the killing blow.

Calion put his own sword up in defense, but the blow never came. He watched in amazement as the life went out of the orc's eyes and the sword slipped from its hands. The creature fell face downward onto the ground mere inches from him. Stunned, Calion looked up.

There, standing just behind where the orc had been was Talia, holding Lolíndir's sword. It was covered in orcan blood.

Her eyes, wild with fright, met Calion's. He staggered back to her, pressing her to him in a brief embrace before taking up his place again in the circle. He shook with the realization that she had saved his life.

Lolíndir was still down, surrounded now by his elven brothers. The orcan rabble continued to press closer. To the side, Calion saw movement. His heart leaped when he saw Valandil creeping along the tree line. The elven unit he would bring with him would be a welcome help. He killed another orc who'd gotten too close to Talia.

The ground was littered with the dead, but there were more where that one came from. He called to Valandil, hoping to get his attention. When Valandil notched his bow, Calion smiled. The orcs would be the ones surrounded now.

When the arrow pierced his shoulder, Calion was flung back against Talia. He stared in pain and shock as Valandil strode closer, the orcs ignoring him as if he wasn't even there.

"I missed my target," Valandil said as he pulled his sword from its sheath. He stepped closer to the wounded prince, his lip curling in disgust as he saw Talia frantically try to stem the flow of blood. "The arrow was meant for her."

Maeglin snarled loudly, his own shock bleeding into understanding. "*Shaeras*...betrayer!"

Talia moaned as her memory came back in a flood, filling her mind with horrifying sights and sounds. "Oh God, I remember now. It wasn't orcs. It was him. *He* killed Amroth!"

Valandil started. "You mean you did not remember what happened?" He spat angrily. "*Thes*... I could have prevented this had I known. I could have killed you at my leisure and stayed true to my prince."

"Your honor ended the moment you betrayed Talia and killed Amroth," Calion rasped out. His gut churned with anger and pain. One of his own.

"Prophecy." Orophin stated the one word furiously as he warily kept an eye on the now-silent orcs. They watched the scene with interest, their weapons down.

Calion shook his head in self-disgust, recalling the words too late. *Spears without, a knife within, treachery will seek to win.* "The prophecy warned us of this. I just did not see it."

"I am not the betrayer," Valandil shouted. "It is you, Calion, who would betray your people. Taking a human as your mate. It is an abomination." His eyes flickered wildly. "I will kill her and save you. You have been under her spell from the beginning."

Calion shoved Talia behind him. "You will not touch her. You are no protector of me, Valandil, or the elven people if you wish to see their salvation destroyed. Think...the prophecy is true."

"The prophecy is a lie!" Valandil wiped his mouth shakily. "It talks of things that cannot be. An heir to the throne? Pah! All know that is impossible."

"But it isn't, Valandil." Calion suddenly remembered Valandil had been with the healer when the truth of Talia's pregnancy had been revealed. "The prophecy is true...all of it. The lady Talia carries my son within her body. My heir."

"*Noooo*!" Valandil screamed. "You lie! It cannot be." His sword dipped to the ground.

"It is true, you pile of orc dung. You have betrayed your prince and us. I will kill you myself." Maeglin snarled and lunged at the red-haired elf while his guard was down. Valandil's sword came up barely in time to save himself. Maeglin's righteous anger gave him strength as he hammered at the elf he once called friend. That the traitor had been under his command was doubly infuriating. He hacked away at Valandil.

Calion stepped forward, his sword in his hand, but Orophin stopped him. "Not for you."

The prince gritted his teeth. It was all he could do to stand there and watch. He knew Maeglin needed this, but...by the goddesses, he wanted to kill the guard himself. He pulled Talia against him as she watched, her eyes filled with fear.

Valandil's gaze darted around the wood as he searched for a way out. He knew he couldn't take Maeglin in battle, and he was tiring fast. Maeglin, on the other hand showed no sign of stopping, his pale blue eyes promising death. Using both of his hands, Valandil hit Maeglin's sword with a crushing blow. When his leader staggered, he used the opportunity to turn and run. Maeglin's furious bellow sounded behind him, but the coward didn't hesitate. He ran for his life into the safety of the woods.

The arrows hit him square in the back, lifting him off his feet and slamming him to the ground. He died, never even seeing who dealt the final blow.

Maeglin turned back to his guards, seeing they held bows in their hands just as he did. He glanced over his shoulder, counting the shafts in Valandil's body. There were three of them. "Amroth is avenged."

The orcs, who up until then had been quiet, began to stir. The one who'd brought them there was gone, and they had no direction.

Calion, looking around, saw they were still hopelessly outnumbered. Once the orcs figured out what to do, his elves would all be slaughtered. Staggering from pain and loss of blood, he pulled Talia against him. "We must retreat. Help Lolíndir. Everyone stay close to me."

Lifting his sword above his head with his good arm, he shouted an incantation to the sky. "*Stars at night, shining bright...hide us from our enemy's sight.*"

Talia felt a great wind, as if she'd been pulled up into a tornado. She cried out as someone bumped into her, but she realized it was Celahir carrying Lolíndir. The stars shifted and then blinked out. Their feet left the ground and they were yanked out of the clearing and into the sky. Minutes later they came down on a small knoll, tumbling to the earth in a pile of tangled bodies.

She struggled out from under Orophin and knelt next to Calion. His skin was waxy gray and his breathing ragged. "Calion?"

The prince's eyes opened. "How far?" he croaked.

Maeglin moved to his other side. "Just on the other side of the wood." He looked grimly at Calion. "We are back within sight of the fortress.

Calion swore and closed his eyes wearily. "Not far enough and in the wrong direction. My strength is gone and the spell relies on my energy to make it work. I am sorry."

"We have to get the arrow out," Talia muttered. She muscled Calion to a sitting position, not noticing the surprised looks of the men around her. She stripped away his battle gear and tore the tunic away from the wound.

Calion chuckled weakly. "My...tigress...is back."

She ignored him. "Maeglin, hold onto the shaft. It didn't go all the way through this time, so we will just have to pull it out." She lifted her eyes to his and swallowed. "You'll have to do it. I'm not strong enough."

Maeglin obeyed her, holding the shaft in one hand and placing his other on Calion's chest. He looked at his prince. "This is going to hurt."

Calion nodded grimly. He closed his eyes, smiling when Talia crushed his hand in hers. "Go ahead."

With a grunt, Maeglin jerked the shaft from Calion's shoulder. The prince let out a hiss of pain as blood poured from the torn flesh. Talia swore as she ripped off a piece of her gown, stanching the blood as best she could. "I'm getting tired of doing this."

Orophin leaned over and handed her a vial of clear liquid. "Use."

Talia opened the bottle and sniffed. "What is it?"

"Stops blood."

"How is Lolíndir?" Calion panted. He could see his friend's body lying still on the ground. He jerked when Talia began to clean his shoulder.

"He lives." Celahir pulled the armor off the elf and examined the damage. "It was a clean blade, but he has lost a lot of blood."

"Use the potion on him," Calion ordered. "He needs it more than I."

"In a pig's eye!" Talia snarled as she pulled a bit of scarlet cloth from Calion's wound. "You've lost a lot of blood too."

Calion glared at her. "He is mine. He comes first."

She let loose with a string of Elvish swear words that had all the men staring at her in disbelief.

"Where did you learn...?" Calion was momentarily diverted from his pain. He stared at his lady in shock.

"Oh, for God's sake." Talia rolled her eyes. "As if we don't have anything else to worry about." She blew out a breath. "Eámanë taught them to me."

"The princess?" squeaked Celahir, his mouth hanging open.

She rolled her eyes again at their reactions. "Boy, if you could hear the women in my world." She opened the vial and made to pour it on Calion's wound.

"No." The prince put his hand on hers. "Lolíndir first."

When she opened her mouth to argue with him, Orophin took the vial away from her. "Both," he said simply.

Upending the bottle, he poured half the medicine on Calion's wound, then moving to Lolíndir, emptied the rest of the potion on him.

Talia glared at him, not giving an inch. "It better work."

Sounds coming from the woods around them caught Maeglin's attention. He pulled himself up and cursed as he saw a horde of orcs marching toward them. "They are here."

Calion looked around quickly. "We must get lower. We can use this hill as a barricade. It may buy us some time." He staggered to his feet and took Talia's hand. "Hurry."

They moved to the bottom of the knoll where a large group of rocks made an adequate hiding spot. The elves all hunkered down behind them.

"We all have our swords and our bows." Maeglin counted as he spoke. "But we only have a few arrows apiece. We will have to rely on hand-to-hand combat to get us out of here."

Calion rubbed his eyes. He knew the chances of that were slim to none. He was wounded, Lolíndir unconscious. There were hundreds of orcs surrounding them. Any surviving elves were on the other side of the fortress fighting the army there. And as brave and strong as Talia was, she was no match for an orc in a face-to-face fight, so she would be of little help.

Sighing, he lifted Talia's hand to his lips. "I am sorry, beloved. This time the plan was not so good."

Talia tossed her head. "Don't be ridiculous. We'd have made it if that fool hadn't told the orcs where to find us. If you want to blame someone, blame me. I forgot what he did back in the woods!"

"Or me," Maeglin put in. "He was under my command."

"I knew there was something wrong about the attack." This came from Celahir.

Orophin grunted. "Smelled wrong."

Calion laughed. "All right. I will stop feeling sorry for myself." He pulled Talia down to him, kissing her until she collapsed on his chest. Maeglin and the others discreetly moved away.

When he finished, the prince sighed. "It will be difficult to get out of this, *Tia maer...* I will not lie to you." He laid a hand on her belly. "I am sorry."

Talia snuggled against him. "I love you and I trust you. You'll get us out."

Calion wished he could feel the same optimism as she did. They were outnumbered and out-weaponed. And he, their strongest magician, was exhausted from pain and loss of blood. They needed more strength, but that wouldn't be found in an orcan swamp. He closed his eyes, just enjoying for the moment Talia's body against his. He could smell her sweet scent and his eyes burned at the knowledge they could be lost to each other and his son taken before he could be born. He ran through different scenarios, trying to find a way out.

Suddenly, he stiffened. A phrase from the prophecy jumped into his mind.

Unless true passion can guide the day,
and give to you a stronger way.

Calion opened his eyes slowly. Could this be the answer? Turning to Talia, he saw she watched him with serious green eyes. He smoothed her hair away from her face. "Do you trust me?"

Smiling, she remembered the last time he'd asked her that. She put her hand on his. "Of course." Heat entered his eyes and she saw he remembered too.

The prince kissed her hand. "I have an idea."

Chapter Eighteen

"I think it will work, but I will need your help."

Talia cocked her head. "What is it?"

He sat up slowly, ignoring the pain in his shoulder. "I wanted to do this a different way. One you would remember and treasure for our whole lives together. A way you could share with our daughters when it came time for them to find a mate of their own."

She shook her head. "I don't understand."

Calion swallowed, hearing the sounds of orcs on the other side of the hill. Out of the corner of his eye, he could see Maeglin and the others preparing for a siege. He didn't have much time. Bringing his gaze back to hers, he took her hands in his.

"Do you believe I love you?"

She gripped his hands tightly. "Yes."

"All right then." He knelt before her, moving her so she was kneeling, facing him. Taking one of Talia's hands, he put it over his heart, while he placed his own on her soft breast. He held her other hand tightly in his.

Maeglin and the others came to sudden attention at the other end of the hollow, seeing what he intended.

He looked deep into her beautiful eyes. "Do you believe you are my fire mate?"

Talia quit breathing. Something was happening. She could feel it moving within her. "Yes."

"Do you believe we are *Mylari*...soulmates? Destined to be together from before our births?"

Her eyes smarted. The air seemed heavier. "Yes."

"Do you come to me without reservation, willingly, knowing once we are linked, it is forever?

Her heart pounded against Calion's strong hand. She trembled in joy and anticipation. "Oh, yes."

"Then I, Calion Sáralondë of the Calen'taur Elves, heir to the throne of *Osalai*, take you Talia of the humans, to be my mate. To link with me forever. To share our bodies, our minds and our souls. Our life forces will mingle and a new power will be born. A force of passion. *Varol thysi*—the power of soulmates." He smiled and raising her hand to his lips, kissed the palm of her hand, before adding, "The power of love."

Talia felt the change now. The air thickened so it was hard to breathe. An invisible wind lifted her hair and played with her skirt. The very ground seemed to tremble beneath them.

"*Tia maer...* Will you link with me?"

She looked at him and saw her future in his eyes. Bringing his hand up to her mouth, she kissed it in turn. "I have been yours since I drew my first breath. All I've done in my life pointed me to you, to this moment in time. You are my love, my prince and the father of my child. I belong to you."

His eyes flared as fire began to paint them a hot gold. The flame of soulmate passion that would never again be denied. She didn't need to be told the same glow lit her own green eyes.

Releasing her hand, Calion pulled the dagger he wore from his breeches. He looked at Talia with such pride and love, her throat closed up on her. "I love you. You are my soul." With a slash of the dagger, he cut down the center of her palm.

She gasped at the pain, but took the dagger when he offered it to her. The beauty of the ritual warmed her heart as she gave him the words back. "You are my soul. *Ai jhyli osu.*" Carefully, she drew the blade down his extended palm.

Taking her bloody hand, he grasped it with his own, mingling their blood together. The prince felt the pain of his wounds leave him as the power of soulmate passion filled his body. Groaning, he let that desire rule as he claimed her mouth as he'd just claimed her heart.

The glade lit with a golden fire that made everyone cover their eyes. Maeglin, Orophin and Celahir dropped to the ground, feeling the power flow over them with bruising strength. The wind howled, sending leaves and debris flying all over the wood.

Orcs on the other side of the hill cried out as the light went through them with the pain of a bolt of lightning. Scrambling, screaming, they ran back the way they had come, fleeing from the force of passion that was released.

Talia and Calion clung together, their hearts and minds empty of all but the power that claimed them. Their life forces mingled, making their separate powers into a new one, a stronger one. Secret truths were whispered only true lovers can understand. Two hearts became one as their lives changed and the two halves of their soul merged. *Mylari*...soulmates. *Varol thysi*...now complete.

Calion came back to himself slowly. His heart and head struggled with all the new sensations he felt. He could feel his own desire, his own need, but holding Talia as she struggled for breath, he realized he could also feel hers.

Lifting his head, he gazed down at his new mate. *"You are so beautiful."*

Her soft mouth trembled into a smile. "Thank you."

He gasped. She heard him? Wonderingly, he tried again.

"I want to take your clothes off and lick your—" He laughed as Talia's eyes popped open, green still flickering with gold. She looked around, color rising in her cheeks.

"Shhh," she whispered, covering his lips with her fingers.

He grinned. That wouldn't stop him now. *"Then what if I turn you over and kiss down your..."*

Talia's eyes widened in shock as he spoke to her without words. He saw the moment she understood. Her eyebrow lifted, and she got a mischievous look on her face.

"Two can play at that game, mister. I want to run my hands down your chest to the soft hair you have on..." Her eyes lit with laughter as she heard him groan.

"Enough, you win." He pulled her close to him. "But you must admit it will come in handy."

"How did it happen?"

Calion shook his head. "I am not sure. Most assuredly the linking of two soulmates is stronger than that of a normal couple." He took her face in his hands. "Do you know why I did it? Here, in this loathsome wood?"

Talia nodded. She'd seen his heart and mind in the linking. "You told me once soulmate linkings have power beyond compare. We needed the edge."

Calion's hands were hard on her face. "I would have linked with you anyway. This I swear."

She put her hands on his wrists. "I know, Calion," she said gently. "I saw your heart. I feel your love for me. I didn't have any doubts before, but if I had, they'd be gone now. You chose this place to gain the power to save us all. I know. I love you."

He kissed her hard. "We have to put together a new plan. I must check with the others to see..." His voice trailed off as he looked over Talia's shoulder.

Frightened, she twisted around and gasped in shock.

"Lolíndir?" Calion got to his feet and walked forward. "You are walking."

The other elf laughed. "I must thank you, my prince, and you as well...princess." He grinned as Talia blushed at the title. "I have been healed."

Maeglin stepped forward. "I think if you check your own wound, it too will be gone. There is much power in a soulmate linking."

Calion circled his wounded shoulder and grinned in amazement. "I am fine. In fact, I feel better than I have in a long time. Better than I ever have before."

Talia rose to her feet. She opened her fist and gazed at where Calion and she had mingled their blood. The cut had healed, leaving a thin scar behind. "Then it worked."

As one, all the guards went to their knees before her. Maeglin put his fist to his heart as he had done once before with Calion.

"Princess, our loyalty is yours from this day forward. You are the prince's mate. You carry a crown prince. We protect both heirs to the throne."

Her eyes filled with tears. She looked for help from Calion, but he stood silently, gazing proudly at her. She looked back at the kneeling men. "I thank you. You've all shown your loyalty for me and my child already. You are my friends." She smiled suddenly. "What would we do without you?"

"What Talia says is true. You will be richly rewarded for what you do here." Calion reached down and helped Maeglin to his feet. "But we've got to get out of here in order for me to do that. Any ideas?"

"Go scout." Orophin pointed toward the fortress. At Calion's nod, he hefted his sword and faded into the darkness.

"The linking light sent most of them running. While it healed and strengthened us, it was torture for them." Celahir motioned to the woods to their left. "They ran screaming into the swamp. But there is still a large contingent between us and freedom."

Calion pondered that. "If we cannot go back into the forest, then we must skirt around the walls. Perhaps they will not expect that."

"Go closer to them?" Talia shuddered. "Isn't there another way?"

Calion draped his arm over her shoulders and squeezed. He spoke to her in their new mind-speech. *"Be brave, my love. I will get us out of here."*

Out loud he said, "When Orophin comes back we will take the route that has the least resistance. But if we have to fight, we now have an advantage." He smiled at Talia. "The power of soulmates."

Orophin found a path empty of orcs. It skirted close to the fortress, but there were fewer orcs there than in the forest. In the same formation as before, they crept along the path. Joining Maeglin in the lead, Celahir took point, determined to get his lord and lady to safety.

They had just reached the side of the fortress, when a crowd of orcs came boiling out of the woods. They were led by Braduk himself. Modak followed, sporting a filthy bandage over his ruined eye.

Calion stopped, and the elves all gathered in a protective circle around Talia. Swearing to herself, she gently eased Calion's dagger from his waistband.

"I won't be caught without a weapon again," she mind-spoke him when he raised a questioning eyebrow.

"Stay back." The words were spoken quietly, but they had the power of command in them.

Talia gritted her teeth. She had the baby to think of, but if he thought she'd leave him to fight alone, he had another thing coming.

Braduk stepped forward, his brother trailing after him. He pointed at Talia. "Human mine. Elf give."

Calion's temper burned. "You have no right. She is mine."

Braduk turned and motioned up at the balcony above them. High up on the fortress, watching, stood King Udaogong. "Father give. She mate. I fuck. Give son."

Calion's eyes burned with golden fire. In response, Talia's eyes also began to glow. "She has belonged to me since the beginning of time. You cannot have her. I have already claimed her."

Braduk cocked his huge head. He frowned, showing anger for the first time. "Not yours. No fuck. No claim."

Talia cringed at his crudeness. In her mind she began to list all the ways she would make him pay for her discomfiture. She heard Calion's chuckle in her head.

He turned to the orcan prince. "If the elf traitor told you that, then he lied to you, Braduk. Talia is my mate. She was my mate two days after I rescued her from you. She belongs to me."

Talia went rosy with embarrassment. Great, now everyone knew how easy she was. What would the men think of her now?

Braduk finally understood he'd been deceived. He shook his flail at Calion, its chain clanking with the motion. He pointed his sharpened war hammer at the prince. "Then I take. Kill. No prophecy!"

"Come on then," Calion invited. "Just you and me, Braduk. I challenge you." He heard Talia's strangled gasp behind him. *"Be easy, love. No harm will come to you. This I swear."*

Calion moved forward out of the circle. The other elves closed in behind him.

"No." She elbowed them partially out of the way. "I must be able to see him."

Braduk trudged forward, accepting the challenge. He spit on the ground and leered in Talia's direction. "Kill you. Fuck pretty human."

Calion laughed. "You will never get that close. By taking her, you signed your death warrant. Say your prayers, princeling. I will send you to your fathers."

Braduk's face changed, growing hard and angry at his words. Lifting his flail, he swung it around his head. He pointed his war hammer at Calion and charged.

The elf prince met him halfway across the clearing, his sword swinging in a fierce arc as he slashed at his enemy.

Braduk's flail parried it, the spiked ball coming close to Calion's head in the process.

Calion felt Talia's alarm in his head, but muffled, as if she knew it would distract him. He rolled as the war hammer came sweeping down on him, bringing his sword up and hitting Braduk hard behind the knees with the flat of his blade.

The orc howled in pain, but he rolled as Calion had, swinging the flail in a deadly circle. Calion deflected the blow, but it cost him, sending him reeling backwards. The elf staggered for a moment and then leaped aside as the war hammer whistled by his head.

The two warriors circled each other, breathing hard. Grunting with the effort it took, Braduk swung both hammer and flail, catching Calion off guard. The prince avoided the hammer, but the deadly flail pounded into his shoulder with lethal force.

Pain shot through Calion. It had been a glancing blow, but true enough to send him flying. He hit the ground, spitting out dirt, but rose quickly to his knees. His left arm was numb and blood trickled down his arm.

Talia's scream rent the air, and instinctively, he raised his sword and parried the slash of the hammer he'd seen through her eyes. Grunting, he pushed backwards, tripping the orc. Steel rang on steel, with a shock that sent agony through both of their bodies.

Shouting a violent curse, Braduk swung again at Calion. The war hammer shone in the moonlight as it descended towards Calion's head. With a strength born of the fire within, the elf roared his defiance and slashed his sword up at his enemy. Braduk wasn't expecting the blow, and the tip of Calion's blade caught him in the thigh. The orc screamed and blood flowed over the sword's pommel, making it slippery to hold.

Calion pressed forward, intent on taking advantage. He sliced down at Braduk's exposed side but paused at the sound of Talia's scream in his head.

"Treachery!"

He turned quickly to see Modak coming at him with sword drawn. He turned back to Braduk, just in time to deflect a killing blow to his head. When he heard an orcan bellow of pain, he turned again to see Talia's dagger find a place in

Modak's sword hand. The other elves turned their swords to him, but his mate had reacted first, piercing the orc's hand and sending his sword tumbling to the ground.

Calion snarled and blocked an arrow sent flying towards his lady by an orcan soldier. Fury flashed inside him. Passion's fire blazed and power called. His eyes went solid gold. Behind him, Talia gasped as she felt the demand. Her eyes flamed as she sent all the power inside her to her mate.

Calion turned to Braduk, the inferno within him raging so brightly, the orc recoiled from it. "You have no honor. This was between you and me. You *dare* attack my mate." Calion bared his teeth at the orc. "A very bad idea. Never anger an elf. We have very long memories."

He leaned closer to the orcan prince and whispered, "It is too late for you, anyway. She already carries my son." Calion turned to his elves, and there was doom in his eyes. "Kill them all."

Braduk swallowed. He desperately wanted to tell his father the prophecy had been fulfilled, but he was looking death in the face and he knew it.

All around them, the battle began, his orcs being cut down left and right, the power from Calion and Talia a living thing around them. Braduk swung his flail one more time, trying to catch Calion unaware, but the elf grabbed the chain with his hand and wrenched it out of his hand. Howling, the orc swung his war hammer with all his might. Calion again ducked and rolled, and with a cry of triumph, Braduk lifted the hammer for a killing blow.

Too late the orc realized he couldn't protect himself from the sword that pierced his throat from below. Before he could even cry out...Braduk was dead.

Calion rose and stood panting over him. He heard a sound to his back, but only held out his hand as he sensed his mate running over to him. He folded her against him in a practiced move, pressing his lips to her hair. "It is over, love. They are defeated."

Above them they heard the grieving roar of the orcan king. His son, his heir was dead. The elves had won.

ஐ

They rendezvoused in the meadow. Roch'mellon was waiting, snorting joyously when he saw Talia. They had a whispered conversation that made Calion groan. Just as she'd warned him long ago, she could now understand what his horse had to say. It was enough to frighten the strongest of males.

It had been simple to get away from the orcan stronghold. The orcs left had been too dispirited by the death of Braduk to do much of anything. Modak disappeared like the coward he was, and the king stood on the balcony swearing insults at the elves as they retreated back to their own land.

Maeglin and the other guards arranged to transport the injured elves back to *Osalai*. The dead were magicked back, since the orcan swamp was still too unsafe to traverse. Calion's wound had been bound by Talia, who wept over the shattered flesh. He'd taken a spike directly to his shoulder and couldn't lift his arm above his waist.

So now the war had truly begun. Calion wouldn't soon forget how he felt when he stood over the butchered body of Talia's horse. Just as Modak would not forget the twin wounds given to him by a puny female, and Udaogong wouldn't forget the death of his son.

The prophecy was true, and they were just beginning to understand it. What would happen in the future would be up to destiny and the three goddesses.

As Calion stood, cradling his broken arm, Maeglin walked up to him. "All are ready, my prince. We await you and the princess."

Calion grinned. He liked having a princess. "I have been talking to my mate. In her world, when a male and a female are married...linked, they go on what is called a hooneymon. It is a time to be alone together, to get to know each other. This idea pleases me."

Maeglin snorted. "You are soulmate linked. I would think you know each other quite well." He raised his eyebrow at Calion. "Two days after?"

Calion's face warmed. He'd blurted that secret out in the heat of battle anger. He wasn't sure what Talia thought about it. "What can I say? I was under her spell from the beginning." He leaned close to Maeglin.

"If I had not been so stubborn, I could have had her two

hours afterwards."

"I heard that." Talia's amused voice sounded in his head.

Calion flinched. "I guess I will have to learn to monitor my words, since you can now hear all my thoughts."

"Well," she giggled as she walked up to him and tucked herself under his good arm, "it's pretty certain you'll know if I'm angry with you."

"I think we will go on this hooneymon, Maeglin, if only overnight. There is much to be done at home, and Amroth..." Calion's eyes went dark. "He will deserve a hero's burial."

"Valandil doesn't." Talia tossed her head, her eyes flashing angrily. "He should burn in hell."

Calion pressed a soft kiss against his mate's lips. "I do not know this hell, but his soul is that of a traitor. He will go to where all betrayers go. To wander through eternity in the faerie myst."

They watched as the last elf was transported back to *Osalai* through the time void. Finally, it was only the guards and the royal couple.

Maeglin was again unhappy about leaving the prince. "Someone should be with you," he argued for the fifth time. "These are unsettling times. We should protect you...all three of you."

"I appreciate that, my friend. But hooneymons are just for the linked. It would not be the same with you there. Plus, where we are going is private and safe."

"I'll take care of him." Talia drew the dagger she'd picked up after the battle. "No one will get by me."

Maeglin grinned. He believed her. "You are sure of this?" he asked, staring at the prince.

"Very." Calion pounded his friend's shoulder. "As soon as you are gone, we will leave. It is only one time jump away."

"Only one?" Talia's eyebrow raised.

Calion smiled crookedly. "Aye, love. The first time I took you the long way. I wanted more time with you." His smile widened when he saw her eyes soften.

They watched the guard disappear, and then, true to his word, they left as well. Talia hadn't asked where they were going, but he figured she knew. On the other side of the time void, she blew out her breath and smoothed her hair. "I hope those things won't hurt the baby."

Calion tickled her. "They are harmless. Females use them all the time. However," he touched his heels to Roch'mellon to move him forward, "I think during the later months of carrying you may want to reconsider."

She thought of how bumpy the ride was and silently agreed.

A few minutes later, Whispering Falls came into view. Through their link, Calion felt Talia's joy at being back in this place. He himself felt like he was coming home. "Perhaps we should build a home here," he thought out loud.

"Wouldn't that ruin the beauty of the place?" She frowned, looking around. "I wish there was a *Malesia* tree here. Now *that* would be perfect."

He laughed, thinking of the many Sanctuary trees he coaxed into being in his lifetime. With her skills, he was sure he could train her to do the same. "I will see if I can arrange it."

"Okay Roch'mellon, you know what to do," Talia ordered. She moved on to the more important task of getting Calion well. With a snort, the horse headed for the waterfall.

The prince raised an eyebrow. "Now you tell my horse what to do? I am not sure this linking is what it should be."

"Oh, please." She rolled her eyes at him. "First priority is to get you healed. I hope we didn't wait too long."

"Your wounds were older than mine the first time we were here, *Tia maer*... I will heal just fine."

His words were truth. As soon as he hit the healing pool, pausing only to remove his boots, she was there, ripping his tunic off and then ladling the water over his shoulder. She hadn't even bothered to remove her gown.

He gritted his teeth, but it didn't take long for his wound to close up and flesh over. He raised his arm slowly and rotated it over his head. It was a little stiff, but the healing waters had restored his shattered shoulder.

Pulling his mate to him, Calion molded her wet body to his. Desire rose in him as he bent his head, his lips teasing hers. Loving her in the pool was one of his favorite things to do. "*O eisi tia maelor oli. Ai cyro tyri sai tia caes. Ai jhyli osu.*"

"You've said that before," she whispered, fisting her hands in his hair. "What does it mean?"

Lovingly, he traced his fingers down over her face and across her trembling lips. "It means...you are my special one, and I hold you close to my heart. You already know, I love you."

Tears burned in her eyes. "You first told me that when I sat in the cell. I wish I'd known what it meant then."

He kissed her again, this time lingeringly as he tried to decide whether to love her now, or wait until they went to bed so he could see her naked body in the firelight. It was a difficult decision.

"Why must it be one or the other?" came Talia's mind-voice. She moved against him seductively, and his already aroused body went hard as stone.

"Indeed," he growled. "Why choose at all?"

It had been over a month since they'd been together, and their hunger was great, but mixed in was a new tenderness. This would be the first time they made love, knowing they loved each other.

Calion's mouth glided over Talia's, barely touching, setting off explosions in all of the nerve endings in her mouth. She moaned, trying to capture his torturing mouth with her own, but instead he nibbled on her lips, bringing even more heat to her body.

She nibbled back, catching his bottom lip in her teeth, rejoicing at his indrawn breath, and then gliding her tongue over the bite, she made him growl in reaction.

Taking charge again, he took her head between his strong hands and covered her mouth with his own, dipping in with his tongue, testing, tasting, finding the sweet spots so she trembled in his arms. The little sounds she made in the back of her throat made him wild.

Oh God, what he was doing to her. Every nerve in her body screamed and he hadn't even touched her yet. She shivered, wanting more, wanting everything.

"You are cold?" he whispered as he stroked her wet body. "Let me take care of that for you. Perhaps you will be warmer this way." Taking the hem of her gown, he pulled it up over her head. Her pale body shone in the soft light of the cave.

"You are more beautiful every time I see you." He ran a gentle hand down her side until his hand covered her barely rounded stomach. His eyes darkened.

"The child, how long have you carried him? How long did

you suffer in silence?"

Talia cupped his chin in her hand. "You gave me our son the night I came to your room. He was conceived in passion and in love."

Calion closed his eyes. They had created a life because she'd been brave enough to save his. "Just when I think I cannot love you any more."

She smiled, pure joy showing in her eyes. "I knew I was pregnant when I sat in that cell waiting to die. I felt your son, and I had a reason to live."

He crushed her to him, feeling his eyes burn with unshed tears. "I was not there when you needed me. I let you go through so much alone."

Talia soothed him with loving hands. "You're here now. That's what matters." She pulled his head back to hers. "Show me now. Show me you love me."

His eyes flared. Lifting her into his arms, he walked to the side of the pool where the water lapped gently. Murmuring an incantation, he swept from the air a sapphire blue mat, its fabric soft and silky to the touch. He spread it out at the side of the pool, half in, half out of the water, kissing her again as he lowered her down.

Looking at her, Calion caught his breath. She was perfect. Her breasts, slightly larger than he remembered, glowed white in the pale light of the grotto. Her waist was barely thickened, her legs long and slender as he watched the water lap gently against her. "You put the Moon Goddess to shame, *Tia maer...*"

Talia smiled, her green eyes already glowing in golden desire. "If I am a goddess, then you are my god. Show me yourself, so I may worship you."

Her words set fire to his blood. He stripped off his clothes quickly, tossing them up on the bank. Soon he stood before her, his whole being pulsing with the need he sought to control.

He did look like a god as he stood there, his body perfectly carved. He seemed to her like one of the marble statues of the Olympic gods she'd studied back home, but he was flesh and blood. Sitting up, she reached out her hand and took hold of him gently.

He groaned, his knees almost buckling under him. "Have a care, love, or it will all be over much too fast."

"Really?" Feminine power welled up in Talia. She scratched

her nails gently down the underside of his shaft, feeling him leap and throb.

He caught her hand with his, his eyes almost desperate. "You are destroying my control." Pushing her back down on the soft cloth, he covered her body with his own. "Will the babe be all right?" he whispered in her ear.

She nodded and moved against him, reveling in the feel of his strong body. "He already knows his father. You will not hurt either of us."

That was all the permission Calion needed. His hunger for her overwhelmed him. He threaded his fingers through her soft hair and crushed his mouth to hers. The kiss was wet and carnal, showing her silently how much he wanted and needed her. Their tongues dueled together, each moving in love's fiery dance.

Talia's hands moved over him. Re-exploring the male form she'd missed for so long. Muscles, flesh, the pounding of his heart, she remembered them all. Her flesh, already warmed by his hands, burned hotter as she caressed him. His cock throbbed against her, showing her she wasn't the only one affected.

He wanted her with a need that made him shake. No female but her could make him tremble. He touched her, fanning his own fires as well as her own. Her passion seduced him, her love enchanted him. Looking into her flaming green eyes, he saw his destiny.

He kissed down her body. First her breasts, one at a time swirling his tongue around the nipples until she begged him to put out the fire he started. Instead, he moved further down, trailing his mouth down her ticklish sides until he came to the small indentation in her belly. He twisted his tongue in the small dent, causing her to arch up off the pallet and cry out his name. His own desire stabbed hard, telling him to cover and plunge.

Controlling himself with difficulty, he kissed the small hollow, whispering words of love to the son who slept below.

Talia whimpered. She wanted to grab him by the hair and drag him up to her, but her arms were so heavy. This type of passion she'd never before felt. It was hot and drugging, and every time he touched her it pulled her deeper and deeper into the whirling eddy of desire. Her skin felt tight and sensitized…her blood heavy and hot. She wanted him like she'd never wanted him before.

Calion rejoiced at what he sensed from her. Their linking made it possible for him to feel not only his need but hers as well. When he ran his fingers down her thighs and into her curly blonde hair, touching her, the scream of desire in her head made him break out into a sweat. He buried his face against her stomach, fighting for control. Did loving her make these feelings so much stronger?

"I love you," he whispered, understanding for the first time how true it really was. Her body sang its siren song to him. He couldn't help it. He had to worship her fully. Moving down, he kissed her belly again and then her thighs, trying to ready her for what he intended next. She moaned, pressing against him as she tried to get closer. His lips flowed over her, stopping at the junction of her thighs, breathing in the spicy scent of her arousal.

His mouth watered. Suddenly, he needed to taste her like he'd never needed anything before. He nuzzled down through the soft curls. It wasn't until he lipped at her softness, that she realized what he was doing.

"Calion!" Her voice was choked by shock and desire as she tried to push his face away.

"Trust me," he mind-spoke her as he licked at the slick opening. *"I love you."*

He continued to kiss and lick, until her hand fell away, grasping at the pad instead. Her soft moans were like music to his ears.

Gently, he separated the folds of skin that held her passion. Running his tongue down them had her arching off the pad, his name a strangled gasp in her throat.

His own need beat at him, a steady throb in his loins. His cock was so hard he knew one touch of her hand would send him flying.

He continued to suck and nibble until her tiny bud swelled with desire. Her quim dripped with her own nectar. When she began to shake with the need for release, he gently took the pulsating piece of flesh and squeezed it between his lips.

Talia screamed as her soul imploded, all the sensation in her body traveling to the one spot where his lips held her. The fire that filled her flared out of control. Her body shook and shivered, her cries filling the cave. Her screams of completion seemed to fuel Calion's lust for more.

"Again," he told her as his mouth covered her again. His tongue swept back and forth over the hard nubbin. Her second release came a few moments later, leaving her sobbing.

Moving up her body, Calion kissed her panting mouth. She could taste herself on his lips, and it aroused her all over again.

The fire in her eyes still burned as steady as the one in his cock. His body shook as he fitted himself to her, parting her legs to ease himself, groaning, into the warm, wet depths.

The soulmate fire erupted within them, burning so hot they both cried out in pleasure and delight. Never had it felt like this. They stayed that way, staring into each other's eyes as their bodies throbbed in rhythm with their hearts.

Finally, Calion bent and slanted his mouth across hers, kissing her with tender passion. He began to move in her, slowly at first, and then faster as his desire rose higher and higher. Talia moaned against his mouth, her hips rising and falling in rhythm with his thrusts. His heart pounded against hers as his body took what it had been craving for so long. The past was forgotten, new love covering all the foolish mistakes of before.

He erupted inside her, his release hurtling her into another. Their life forces combined, sending power screaming up into the air, showering them with blue and green light. Burning passion...flame and fire, filling their bodies. It seemed to last forever before they were allowed to drift slowly, quietly back to earth. Their one soul, finally at peace, curled around them, giving them the full strength and love of soulmate power.

It was much later, as they lay in the darkness by the fire that Calion spoke, his voice heavy with masculine satisfaction. "I find I am pleased with this hooneymon. I think we should do it at least once a month."

Talia smiled in the darkness. She opened her mouth to correct him and then stopped. Somehow, "hooneymon" sounded just right to her. It was as different and unusual as her new life. So, instead of saying anything, she let her body tell Calion just how much she liked the idea.

Epilogue

"Talia, if you do not hurry, they will start the linking ceremony without you," Eámanë fretted as she paced around the bedchamber. "What would Calion say then?"

Talia appeared from behind a screen, her hands holding a white gown covered in green crystals that matched her eyes. "Probably the same thing he said when I told him we didn't have to have a big fancy ritual." She laid the gown gently on the bed and moved to the vanity.

"I have a soulmate and everyone is going to know it." She spoke in Calion's deep masculine voice. "Just because we linked in some far-off woods does not mean we are not going to have a proper ceremony."

Eámanë giggled. "Yes, and then he said he wasn't ashamed of either you or his son and that if you didn't let him have his way with the ceremony, he would stand on the parapets and shout the news about you to everyone who could hear. Then he kissed you so hard, even poor Orophin turned red." She sighed. "It was so romantic."

Talia smiled. It had been two weeks since Calion rescued her from Braduk. They'd spent a full day and night in their special place by the healing pool before coming home to *Osalai.* Their homecoming was bittersweet.

Ërestor, when he heard they were linked, accepted it, but Talia could see he wasn't happy about his son's new mate. She hoped when he held his grandson for the first time, his heart would mellow.

The burial ceremony for Amroth took place the day they returned. It had been her first official outing as Calion's mate, and she wasn't sure how the elven people would react to her.

Centuries of hate and distrust don't disappear overnight.

Castle folk wept as Calion and the royal guards carried Amroth's cloth-bound body slowly up the stairs to the funeral pyre. His jeweled sword lay on his chest, a golden coin on his forehead to give to the goddesses for entrance into Paradise.

But all eyes were on Talia when she too climbed the stairs and laid a wreath of willow branches and thyme on the body, symbolizing his bravery. Many were won over as she wept against her mate's chest for the brave elf who'd given his life for hers.

Calion kept his word. As the flames from Amroth's pyre filled the sky, he knighted each of his guards for their valor and bravery. The four new noblemen were speechless as Talia handed them deeds to their new properties close by the city.

Afterwards, the prince moved her immediately into his royal bedchamber. She was to sleep in his bed from that moment on, he decreed. He'd been too long without her, and his pleasure at her presence was there for everyone to see. He had all her things moved in, and soon was grumbling in amusement about all the feminine fripperies mixed up with his things.

In the days that followed, he made up for lost time, loving her as they went to bed at night and when they arose in the morning, as well as whenever he could sneak back down to their chamber during the day.

One of his greatest pleasures was lying spooned against her back as she slept, his hand massaging the tiny life inside her. Their love grew daily, and it was easy for Talia to give him what he wanted when he requested the formal linking ceremony.

Eámanë's chatter brought her back to the present as she moved behind Talia to tuck some errant hairs back in place. Talia's hair was piled artistically on top of her head with only a few tendrils of curls falling around her face. Tiny ivy leaves, signifying linking, and white rose buds for love, were placed in a crown around her head. During the ceremony, Calion would remove it and replace it with the tiara of a princess.

"Do you not agree?' Eámanë asked, meeting her eyes in the mirror.

Talia blushed. "Sorry, I wasn't paying attention."

Eámanë rolled her eyes at her new sister. "I said...you better get your gown on, or you will be late."

"I think she looks just fine as she is." Calion stood just

inside the doorway. His hot gaze rested upon his half naked mate. When Talia saw the look in his eyes, she blushed becomingly.

Eámanë squealed. "You cannot be in here, Calion." She ran over to him and started pushing him out the door. "I have been talking to your mate. In the human world it is bad luck to see the bride before the ceremony."

He frowned and dug his feet in. "What nonsense is this? I saw her this morning." He turned and looked at Talia and grumbled. "Everyone is keeping me away from her. First, the maids and now my own sister."

Talia giggled as Eámanë smacked her brother on the backside. Calion yelped and glared at her.

"Out," the princess said, trying to keep a straight face.

He shot Talia one desperate look before he cursed and walked out, slamming the door. Eámanë dusted her hands together, nodding in satisfaction. "Males are so childish. They always want what they cannot have."

"He has me already," Talia put in mildly.

The princess tossed her head. "Aye, many times if the stories I hear are correct, and only two days after you met." She clucked her tongue in pretended dismay as Talia blushed again.

Eámanë laughed and grinned at her friend. "Someday I hope to find someone that makes me feel the same way." She sighed, thinking about her own life. "I believe I have finally gotten Father to consider letting me visit your human world."

Talia almost dropped the brush she was using. "What?"

"In the old days, many were the elves who visited your world. It was like...a cultural exchange. I have read the parchments." She frowned. "For some reason they stopped doing it. But I am going to talk Father into it. Just you wait and see."

Talia nodded, not trusting her voice. Curious, lively Eámanë in her world?

"Come on now." Her friend clapped her hands. "Let us get you into your gown. I cannot wait to see it on you."

The princess walked to the bed and lifted the white gown. She helped Talia climb into it and then fastened the back for her. "There you go. Let me have a look at you." When Talia turned, Eámanë's eyes filled with tears.

The gown was exquisite. Soft, translucent white, it was sprinkled with green crystals that carried the sign of Talia's magick. Since her linking with Calion in the orcan wood, her gifting had increased enormously. Their shared magick was something they had barely begun to understand.

The bodice was V-necked and cut low, giving a generous glimpse of Talia's beautiful breasts. It had cap sleeves and a long draping skirt that hid Talia's slight pregnancy.

"He will not be able to take his eyes off of you," Eámanë breathed.

Talia smoothed the gown with trembling hands. Who was this woman in the mirror? Was it really her, or would she wake up in her dorm room bed weeping over a beautiful dream? Reaching for her arm, she pinched herself. The abrupt pain showed her once and for all, she wasn't dreaming.

"Do you have everything?" Eámanë began to pace again. "All the things we put together?"

"Yes, sister." Talia lifted the jeweled armband Calion had given her from her vanity table and slipped it up her forearm. "This belonged to your mother. She wore it on her linking day. It's my something old." She flicked at the shining crystals in her ears. "My something new, a linking gift from your brother." Reaching into the space between her breasts, she pulled out a tiny lace hanky Eámanë had loaned her. "My something borrowed, and this..." She hiked the skirt of her dress up and pointed to the sexy, sapphire garter high up on her thigh. "This is a garter...a human tradition. It is my something blue."

Eámanë's mouth dropped open as she looked at the tiny piece of blue silk. "Oh my. Calion is going to enjoy that!" They both giggled.

The princess glanced at the timepiece on Talia's vanity and gasped. "By the goddesses, I was so worried about you I am not going to have time to dress myself. I must go."

She turned to Talia and pressed her cheek to hers. "If I could have selected someone for my brother, she would be just like you. I am so glad you are here."

Talia's eyes misted. "If I could have picked one person to be my sister, I would have chosen you. You're the best friend I've ever had."

They hugged each other again, and then Eámanë ran off towards her own room. Talia turned back to the mirror and carefully wiped the tears away. She didn't want to go to Calion with red eyes, though it probably didn't matter to him. He'd seen her looking her worst and he still thought her beautiful.

She thought back to the last day at the waterfall. The time had been wonderful as they shared their hearts as well as their bodies. Talia had found Calion's love opened up her sensuality. She smiled secretively as she remembered his shock when she'd returned the favor and tasted him for the first time. He hadn't lasted but for a few minutes before he had rolled her over and plunged himself into her body.

"I hope that smile is for me."

Talia turned her head in shock as she heard Calion's voice coming from behind her. She watched, her mouth open in surprise as he climbed in her window, mumbling something about the maids having the door staked out.

He was dressed in full royal splendor, his regular clothes traded for spotless white breeches and a blue tunic jacket that carried the emblem of his house. His dark hair was pulled back from his face by two thin braids. He wore his sword on his hip, and it sang as he moved toward her.

He was the most handsome man she had ever seen. She almost hugged herself with the knowledge he belonged to her.

As Eámanë predicted, Calion was struck speechless by the vision that stood in front of him. He gazed at her, feeling all his love well up inside him. He wanted to lay her down on their bed and show her how much he loved her.

By the goddesses, how had he been so lucky as to have found her? He held out his hand, and without hesitation, she placed hers in it. Gently, he pulled her close to him.

"*Tia maer...* How do I even describe how you make me feel? I thank the goddesses every day for you. I cannot even imagine my life without you in it." Bending, he kissed her softly.

She sighed as his lips met hers. Every time it was fresh and new. Each time he touched her, she longed for more.

"Our destiny is to be together." She laughed and pressed her cheek to his. "I find myself in the difficult position of having to thank the orcs for kidnapping me, because they are the ones who led me to you."

"This prophecy has been fulfilled. The war has started, and—" he caressed her stomach, "—the heir is conceived."

"*She will be the first of three.* I wonder what that means."

"I do not know, but our part is done." He pulled back the sleeve on his jacket. "See, the scar is gone, as if it never existed."

She traced a finger over the prince's wrist, feeling him shiver at her touch. "It was to be a guide for you. Now you have found your way, so you don't need it anymore."

"So we will complete our destiny." Calion lowered his mouth to hers again. "We will raise our son and any other children we have, showing them it is love and not hate that rules this place. And whatever future our eldest has, we will stand with him, to protect and guide him."

"You are perfect, Calion." She placed a hand on his chest. "I gladly link with you a second time. You are my life."

Their eyes met, their lips came together. "I love you, *Mylari*," Calion breathed. "I will always love you."

Talia's eyes filled. "And I love you. Forever and always."

Together they made their way out to start their new life together. Soulmates found. Destiny fulfilled.

Faerie Word Glossary

In Alphabetical Order
(All in Elvish unless otherwise stated)

Ai eis si paelor, eil si paelor air ti—
I am a demon and the demon is me (a chant of grief)

Ai jhyli osu—I love you

ba-gronk—dung pit *Orcan*
(most commonly used as an insult)

baroli—jasmine

Calen'taur Elves—Elves of the Verdant Forest

Cylys—Honor

eidaer—apples

Eisi tia maelor oli. Ai cyro tyri sai tia case—
You are my special one. I hold you close to my heart.

Grundlug—the orcan stronghold *Orcan*

jhol—lion

jhyli—love

kydaer ol ei plyi—goddess on a donkey
(a common swear word)

kydaer pas air—goddess damn it
(a common swear word)

Malesia—Sanctuary

Malesia...Ai shael Malesia—Sanctuary...I beg Sanctuary
(a chant)

malyl—trout

Mylari—Soulmate

Mysyr—Forest of Misery

Osalai—Place of Perfection

paes—deer

pas os aer—damn your eyes
(a common swear word)

Roch'mellon—Horse friend
(Calion's steed)

sardai—taboo

shaeras—betrayer

shalia—brandy

shar—brat

sharas—bastard

shardyr—gum tree

Shia si kydaer—By the goddesses (a common vow)

shor—bitch

shyr—wolf

tadí—maple tree

taji ti ei baer—make me a net.

tar—cat

Tarol Festival—Mating Festival

thaelyrdor—love between friends

thasal—farmland

thastolor—love between those in a family

thes—fuck

tho'si—fire

thylaer—love between linked mates

Tia maer...—My sweet (an endearment)

tolí—mine

torear—mistress

tyri—mouse

vardor—rabbit

Varol thysi—The force of passion

vasodi—partridge

vol—pig

volai—orcan beast of burden

vyryl—poison

About the Author

For more information on CJ and her other work, visit her website at www.cjengland.com. And she loves to hear from her readers! Please write CJ at womanofthewind1@yahoo.com.

As a dark web of spells closes in, Magaith may be Sygtryg's only hope—and she his only destiny.

The King's Daughter

© 2008 MC Halliday

Magaith is resigned to fulfilling her father's command that she marry the King of Connacht. It is her duty as daughter of the King of Munster, even though she harbors a secret love for her knight protector, Sygtryg.

Sygtryg's honor will not allow him to betray his king, not even for the love of Magaith. His painful duty is to see her safely to the kingdom of Connacht, then neither see nor speak any more of her, forever. But as a web of black spells closes in around Magaith, she and Sygtryg join together to thwart the dark forces that would claim her life and gain dominion over all of Eire.

Ahead of her lies a destiny she could never have imagined, a journey in which she must follow ancient Druid pathways, encounter a sleeping dragon, and discover magical powers that are hers by right of blood.

As the journey grows ever more fraught with mortal pride, desire, jealousy, revenge and even her own terrible blunders, Magaith must risk everything, even Sygtryg's love, to fulfill her destiny and save Eire.

For if the evil wizard who covets her cannot have her, he will see her dead.

Enjoy the following excerpt from The King's Daughter...

The King of Connacht took pause at a bench and flung his cloak behind him before he sat down. His movements were quick and sure.

"Good wishes to the King of Munster," he called out. "Come near."

Bascogne left his daughter's side, took a place on the bench beside Borda and began talking in a low voice. As the King of Munster spoke, Borda looked at him and after a short while, lifted his head to look upon the small party from Cashel fortress.

When Magaith felt the warrior king's gaze upon her, heat burned at her cheeks and she willed her hands still at her sides.

Borda motioned to his first knight and still watching her, imparted words to the man. The knight came to Magaith.

"I am known as Mael, in service to Borda, King of Connacht." The knight bowed and then said, "The king desires to meet his betrothed."

She replied, "As the king wishes," while smoothing the folds of her tunic.

The knight, Mael, led the way to Borda and took position at the side of his king.

She was close to her new husband and could see his eyes were of the darkest blue, brightly gleaming.

Forthright, he stared back at her with a calm bearing and an inner strength that would stead him well in challenge.

When he arose from his seat, the King of Connacht offered a slight bow of his head. "Daughter to Bascogne." His voice was deep, strong. "It pleases me to meet you."

She fully lowered her head, a deed unknown to her. As daughter to a king, there had been no need to show reverence among her clan. How changed her life was and how further changed it would become. She lifted her head and saw the heavy draperies across the sleeping chamber. For a second time, a shiver took her body.

"You are cold." Borda turned to the knight next to him. "See the fire is lighted. And have the tables laden with mead and food. Mael, go now." He looked again upon her.

She forced herself to speak in her discomfort and fear. "I be obliged to you."

"It be my desire to care for you," the warrior king said and then added, "We shall talk of this at a later time. If you be willing."

"If it be your wish." Magaith felt the quickening beat of her heart.

Borda took a step toward her. "Moreover, I hope it be your wish."

He was so close, she could feel the strength of his limbs although they remained at his side. She searched his face, the brightness in his dark blue eyes revealed he was pleased in her. The curl of a smile formed upon his lips and she sensed his desire to give her surety. He seemed a fitting counterpart in wedlock and her fears lessened.

"Truth, it be my wish also," she said and fully lowered her head once more.

"You are a king's daughter and shall be a king's wife. Forever more, you shall bow to no man, not even this king."

Feeling his tenderness, she looked up to meet his gaze. As he smiled, he did seem a man of honor, worthy of the title, king. And he possessed a pleasing appearance, fit and strong, virile. She smiled from her heart, perhaps she could be content and bear him many precious sons.

And so, the wedding was arranged for the first day of the month of Duir, as wed vows were banned in the month of Uath. There were a few days for preparations to be made ready. Many hundred pounds of honey must be collected for cakes and mead, cows and sheep slaughtered for spit roasting, goats milked and cheeses made, oats and barley milled and baked into breads.

During this time, the betrothed pair engaged in walks and spoke of their future. Of herself, Magaith spoke freely to Borda as she found him a receptive, lively man with a ready smile and thoughtful attentions. He did not seem a warrior but then, she was not his enemy. Since the agreement for the wedlock, their clans had been united.

From dusk to dawn, Sygtryg was at her door but she would not look upon him. As she passed him on sentry, the tight lump in her chest almost burst with bitter anger. He possessed no affection for her and had slighted her love. She kept her words in check, for she was about to embrace a new life. She would aim to be happy in her husband and upcoming marriage.

Moreover, her father was pleased with her, telling her often of his affection and his pride. On occasion, he spoke mournfully of the time he was to depart after the wed vow. She was assured of his affection and her rightful duty for Munster.

Meanwhile, gaming parties took place with knights and noblemen collecting many wild fowl for the wedding feast. Clan artisans made drinking vessels and bowls of wood, and some platters of bronze for the noblemen's tables. Scores of cauldrons were set over fires to brew beer and prepare mead. Musicians, storytellers and balladeers from all over Eire gathered at Castlestrange to perform at the wedding feast.

In these days, Imagael stayed hidden in her cloak and sought out the malcontent known through her dreaming. She stopped at the homes of the villagers and listened to their tales and chatter. On the eve before the wedding day, she proceeded to the large wood shelter of Mael, first knight to Borda. And there she found him at supper with his wife, known as Gormfla.

Mael lifted a cup of mead and drank it down. As he set the goblet on the table, he said to his wife, "I did gain favor with our king as he looked upon me with my sword and shield against other men. I stand by Borda to protect him and go to battle for him. My life I give as my king does desire."

"He is a worthy king. You do well, my husband."

Mael poured mead into his cup and again, drank it down before setting it to the table. He spoke in a low voice. "I should not speak further."

"It is the wed vow to Bascogne's daughter that brings you to speak thusly."

He leaned toward his wife, whispering, "Borda takes Bascogne's daughter for his wife, in a pact of clan peace. This be not seemly for a warrior king."

Gormfla whispered back, "I know of what you speak, husband. There be no bravery in this pact. It is no longer warrior by which our king shall be known."

Shaking his head from side to side, Mael wailed, "What is to be done?"

"To remedy all, I know a way." Gormfla leaned in closer to her husband. "And this wed vow shall be ended."

"He is happy in his wife. How can this be done without loss of Borda's favor?"

Gormfla spoke softly. "I shall brew the berries of Yew, Hellebore and Devil's Bit. At the wedding table, you slip the potion into the maiden's cup."

"You be a pleasing wife to me, Gormfla." His face turned dark. "And if this plot be found out? We shall be sent to the otherworld by Borda's command."

"There will be much celebration with music and dancing, you shall know when to slip the potion without notice."

"And her passage to the otherworld will be swift?"

"Swift as an arrow that pierces the heart."

"Then it shall be so."

Imagael departed the house of Mael, making her way to her sleeping place in the copse where she left her herbs and roots in the linen bundle. She must make a remedy for the poison, lest her eye not be keen and the potion be sipped.

CPSIA information can be obtained at www.ICGtesting.com
Printed in the USA
LVOW042025141011

250627LV00001B/60/P